SOBER DOPE & SUNDAYS

NORDIKA NIGHT

SOBER DOPE & SUNDAYS

WEEKDAY WEIRDOS

NORDIKA NIGHT

Welcome to the **WEEKDAY WEIRDOS SERIES!**

A set of books all loosely based on days of the week—a couple per weekday! ALL MM romances.

They DO NOT need to be read in any particular order.

<u>**General theme:**</u> unique boys who have been through some shit and this is how they turned out.

<u>**What to expect:**</u> steamy weird romances within different tropes, odd love languages, humour, some depth of trauma or mental health, red flags, weekdays, quirks, and the type of love that heals despite being unconventional. Banter. Bullshit. Boys. A lot of eye rolls. They are standalone stories with no overlapping storyline! Though some characters show up in other books.

It is written in Canadian English.

CONTENT DESCRIPTION:

- While this book is about a recovering addict, it focuses more on the **positives of recovery** instead of the harder/more dire parts (to keep in theme with the Weekday Weirdos Series)
- triggering terms in reference to substance abuse: junkie, addict - while I don't like these terms, the substance abusers in this story are the only ones who refer to/use these terms
- one of the MCs lost his mom to an overdose during childhood
- Smut: there is smut, **but penetrative sex is not the focus**
- drug use, mentions of drugs by name, cravings, smoking
- Gage is neurodivergent, but that is not what makes him a weirdo!
- Substance abuse, sex addiction, kleptomania (not mentioned often), alcohol addiction

- If you have ever known addiction, you might understand that it is very consuming. It sort of steals the show and becomes the main focus … and I wanted that to be true to form in this book. While Alexei is one of my favourite characters, and he shines all on his own while going through a few life changes, he's a pretty content guy who has very healthy coping mechanisms, which means Gage's recovery does overshadow the story at times. I wanted it that way.
- Gage and Alexei both have rambly thoughts, and the writing indicates that
- The term weirdo is spoken with love, pride, and acceptance in these books.

NOTE: I know addiction and recovery look different for everyone. I understand there are variables, differing struggles, personalities, lifestyles, beliefs, and methods of recovery. Please do not criticize Gage's recovery or compare it to your own. It's written from a place deep in my heart and has very personal meaning to me :)

To those who battle addiction
To those who have loved ones who battle addiction
To those who have lost or been lost to addiction
To sober companions and support systems

gage

It's not that I don't want to pay for the coffee, honestly. I'm *trying* to pay for it. My phone is out, Apple Pay is on the screen, and the machine is telling me to go ahead and tap. But the twelve-dollar frappé with extra whip and toffee bits is already sweating in one hand while the other is stretching out, part way to paying for the highly overpriced milkshake with caffeine by the time the entire front window of the coffee shop implodes.

And while the entirety of the café is freaking out about explosions and shattering glass, and the odd person is even yelling something about a bomb attack in our small city, my mind is on the debit machine, thinking about a forced relapse. I'm not trying to steal the coffee, but there are bits of glass mixed in with my toffee bits, and the screen of the debit machine isn't really telling me what to do in this situation or if the payment went through, and if I take a sip, does that mean I'm going back to rehab?

Kleptomania is a bitch, and I've worked hard to kick her

—and all my other addictions—and now a broken window, a scared barista, a cursed Sunday, and a sweating frappuccino are the only things standing between me and my recovery.

The barista is on the other side of the counter, kneeling with her hands over her ears while people make a commotion to either leave the coffee shop or take on the hero role. I peer down at her, wondering if I should ask if my payment went through or if that's selfish. I mean, she's obviously scared, but I am, too. I don't want to relapse!

"Excuse me?" I call down to her. "Can I get a receipt?"

She looks at me, eyes full of tears, cheeks all red and splotchy, and that real kind of fear on her face.

"Shit. Sorry. Are you okay?" I set down the drink, knowing that if I don't take it, there's no way it can be considered stealing.

I climb over the counter just as something else comes barrelling into the café. I land on the barista, but she's clinging to me and screaming bloody murder in my ear, shaking like a jackhammer.

"Get down!" someone shouts.

We're already down, but I yank her down more. "There's a room in the back," she yells over the sound of the second window breaking and the patrons screaming.

I see the room she's pointing to, so I push her ahead of me and try to cover her body as we crawl towards it. It's a kitchen. Just a small one for making baked goods and the odd sandwich, nothing more complicated than that. When the door swings shut behind us, she yanks her purse from a hook. A million things fall out of it, but she's got her phone to her ear, calling 9-1-1 before I even settle enough to think of that.

I've never been good in a crisis. I've never been *sober* in a crisis. High me would have been quicker on his feet, but this slow version—a mix of doubt, fried brain cells, a completely lost way of life, and zero good traits—doesn't know how to handle a situation that requires me to focus on anyone but myself.

"Yes, I'd like to report a... something. The café on Simcoe Drive just... there's glass everywhere and things are coming in the windows!" In her haste, she accidentally puts the call on speaker, and I catch the tail end of whatever the operator is saying.

"—delivery truck with construction material. A strap snapped right in your location. It's not a bomb threat. First responders have already been dispatched and are on their way."

When she hangs up, she wipes her eyes and stands, letting out a long breath. "I'm sorry. That really scared me."

"All good." My hand is damp and clammy from the frappé I sacrificed. "Can I do anything?"

"I don't know. I'm going to go tell everyone that it's not a threat." With that, she leaves me on my ass in the small kitchen.

Despite my focus being on potentially stealing coffee during a possible attack, I'm proud. It goes to show that I've come a long way, put my health and well-being first, and recognize possible triggers and relapses.

It's been eight months and six days since I got out of

rehab for the seventh time, and I'm finally feeling really good about my sobriety.

... Right? I mean... who the fuck goes to rehab that many times? Something has to stick this time, I'm sure of it. Lucky number seven and all that.

Deciding I should probably get off my ass and either leave this place or help the barista, I press my hands to the floor to get up. But this woman's purse contents are everywhere, and before I even see what my hand has touched, I know what it is.

Don't look at it.

Don't acknowledge it.

Pretend it's a spider. We hate spiders.

But it's not a spider. It's a dime bag, and it's making the back of my throat burn with the need to taste the bitter powder. It's making my body shake and my head scramble. It's making me itch and scratch and itch some more, and I can't even rationalize that this isn't my favourite way to ingest drugs.

I'm a pill popper, but an addict is an addict, and I'll take whatever I can get.

Eight months and six days, Gage. No pills. No booze. No uppers or downers or inhibitors or muscle relaxants. No pain shots. No patches of fetty. No stealing. No conning. No swindling. No sex.

I let go of the bag and turn my head to the left as far as it will go, refusing to look at the baggie. I'm hot and cold all over, sweating and shivering at once. Maybe it's just a Fun Dip in a

4

very tiny package. Maybe it's leftover glitter from whatever glitter is used for. It's not coke. It's not brown powder. It's not ketamine or crushed painkillers. It's nothing but glitter that has no value and isn't worth stealing or snorting or licking.

I need to get out of here.

I'm sweating through my hoodie now, my knees shaking with temptation as I push to stand.

I didn't steal the drink. I didn't steal the drink. I didn't steal the drink.

By the time I'm standing, I'm pulling out my phone to call Kristen, my sponsor. Responsible. Yep. So responsible because I didn't steal the drink, and I didn't snort the glitter, and I'm calling my sponsor and walking to the door. Headed for escape. Removing myself from the situation. Just like I've been taught.

"Gage?" she answers. "Did you hear about what's going on downtown?"

"Yeah," I tell her, and my voice is strained, and Kristen is familiar with the strain of a junkie's voice.

"Where are you? I'm coming."

Consciously, I'm aware that I'm referring to myself as a junkie again. That's a big no-no in rehab, and here I am, tempted by a baggie of not-glitter, right back in the junkie mindset.

And I'm telling her where I am because I'm not entirely suicidal, but as I'm talking to her, I'm swiping my frappuccino off the counter, and that baggie of glitter is in my pocket, and the shouting and the sirens from the first responders aren't loud enough to drown out the voice in my head telling me that one time won't hurt.

One time isn't a relapse.

One time is *manageable*.

And really, I'll tell myself anything to justify stealing and snorting and chasing a high that never feels high enough.

"Maybe the eighth time is the charm," I tell Kristen outside the café. I walk down an alley and open the baggie. White powder. I drool for it. "Lucky number eight, right?"

"Gage, just hold on! Whatever you're about to do, it is not worth your sobriety. I promise you that. Just hold on. Talk to someone nearby. I'm coming."

But I've already snorted the powder and chased it with a sip of the twelve-dollar-but-free-to-me toffee frappé with glass bits and I'm soaring in the bitter aftertaste that has always promised the best of times. I lick my finger and stick it in the bag, rubbing some against my gums and letting the numbness wash over me. By the time I get halfway through the iced drink, I remember every fucking reason why I'm an addict. What a Sunday.

gage

1

12 MONTHS LATER

There's this look people give you when they're trying to be proud, but you've let them down so many times they don't really have any faith left. It's this tepid smile with reserved confidence and sympathy in their eyes that basically says, 'Well, let's see how long you make it' rather than 'I'm proud of how far you've come.'

I'm used to it, but it still fucking sucks.

"You look good, Gage," Paul says, wrapping me in a hug purely to hide his eyes from me. "Healthy. Good."

Yeah, that's what everyone says every time I get out of rehab, and trust me, I've been enough times to recognize patterns. Just that I look good and healthy—it's an automatic reply to a situation they don't understand, and I can't blame Paul for not knowing what else to say. I mean, how many times have we gone through this together? Two? Maybe this

7

is the third time. It says something about me and our relationship that I don't even know.

All I know is that it's Sunday. One year, almost to the day of *that* Sunday. The frappé and glitter Sunday.

"Thanks." I hug him back, feeling... nothing. There's no spark, no love, no gratitude. There isn't anything negative either. I'm just empty and numb, and maybe that's the status quo I need to get used to living in.

"Are you ready to go?" he asks, trying to take my bag from me.

But I'm a pretty shitty person because I haven't told him I'm not going with him. I could have called him, put him out of his misery, freed him from having to wait around for his loser boyfriend to get out of rehab. Again. But I didn't. Selfish, remember? I just wanted to look at him one more time before I set him free to the life he's dying to live, but I've held him back from.

"You look good, too," I tell him, not letting him have my bag.

"Thanks." He rubs the back of his neck.

See, Paul is a successful man in a respectful job, exuding a level of confidence that makes him prideful. He has no idea how to feel awkward. Unlike me, who just had to show all my vulnerabilities to a bunch of therapists, specialists, peers, and support workers for the past year. I *live* in awkward. I got used to the shame and lack of dignity, but Paul has never had to, so he doesn't know how to handle me. I'm the weak point in his life, and although he's tried hard not to make me feel like that, I do by default.

"Thanks for coming," I tell him. "It feels good to see you, and I'm glad I get to tell you this face to face."

His eyes widen, and he licks his lips. Again, Paul isn't used to being in the dark about anything. He prides himself on knowing everything there is to know and planning for all the possible outcomes he doesn't already know. So, blindsiding him with a breakup outside a rehabilitation facility he waited twelve months to pick me up from is about as low as I can go, but it has to be done.

"Gage?" he asks, hands in his pockets now.

Paul visited me twice over the past year, and we spoke on the phone once every two weeks or so. I talked to my mom every day, Kristen every few days, and my brothers once a week. I don't need Paul, and in my heart, I've already let him go. For me, not for him. But I'm going to make this about him because it'll make me feel better. Not to mention his ego.

"I'm moving back home. I can't keep putting your life on hold, and I'm sorry for how many times I have."

"Gage," he croaks, stepping back. "What?" There's more anger than sadness, but I think I expected that.

"It's what's best for both of us. It's good for my sobriety, and you won't have to explain me away with excuses and lies anymore." I reach out to grab his hand, but he pulls away. "I'm sorry. I should have told you sooner."

A flash of rage crosses his eyes, and I'm not sure I've ever seen it so intense before. "Sooner?" he scoffs at me. "Sooner? You should have fucking... given me a heads-up at least, Gage. Jesus."

I note the lack of actual hurt. I mean, he's butthurt because this took him off guard, but losing our relationship isn't what's cutting deep. It's the fact that he'll have to go home empty-handed and rework his plans. He'll take a few days to be weird about it, and then he'll realize how much weight is off his shoulders and how freedom tastes.

He can have alcohol in the house again, buy Tylenol at the drugstore in real-sized bottles instead of blister packs that get hidden or thrown away, and he can have a life that doesn't revolve around my needs and fuck ups. He can keep everything he owns out in the open without worrying about me stealing it, and he can fuck whoever he wants without asking if it's going to send them into a sex addiction spiral.

Because, yeah, that's me: Gage Loser Rossum, addicted to... everything.

"But your life is here," Paul says. "Your friends."

"What friends?" I laugh. "A junkie has no friends except his vices and the ones he's pushed away for trying to help. Honestly, I'm surprised you stayed with me this long." Even though Paul has a hero complex and saw me as his greatest project, I always kind of liked that he wanted to save me. Too bad it never worked. "This is better for you, Paul. You're better off without me."

Paul's eyes are sad, but mostly pissed off, and that's about all he'll give me. After a few awkward moments, he gives me another hug and tells me he loves me. I think he means it.

"I'm sorry I wasn't enough, Gage," he says. And I hate it

because he is enough. It's me who is the problem. "Thank you." *For setting him free.*

I sit on the curb after he's gone, not at all surprised that my mom is late. That woman would show up to a party in 2024, even though it was in 2023, and act like it was no big deal. So, while she's taking her sweet ass time coming to get me, I try to feel proud of myself because I've earned my own respect for once.

A whole year in rehab. Voluntarily. My choice to stay an unheard-of length of time. It's the longest I've ever stayed, and this is the strongest I've ever felt after walking out of those doors. Not many addicts go to rehab once, let alone eight times, and even though most stints were much shorter, this time I've got a pocketful of new tools, a bunch of new contacts, and even a sponsor lined up in my hometown. But all that shit can be deceiving. Who knows how I'll react when faced with anything that tempts me? My track record for willpower isn't strong, but my shame for going to rehab eight fucking times is at an all-time high.

Please, for the love of all that is holy, do not bring me here a ninth time.

Twelve months sober. Come on, Gage. We've got this.

A whole hour and a half later, my mom's run-down minivan squeals into the parking lot with an audible squeak in the front right tire and a clunk that doesn't sound right. When she stops right in front of me, the brakes screech and groan, and she reaches through the open window to open her door from the outside.

Ah, Mom. I smile.

"Gage!" she screams at me like I might not have noticed her pull up. "My baby!"

Her light brown hair looks more silver, especially around the temples, and her laugh lines are just as deep as ever. If anyone can laugh in life, it's my mom, and that's a goddamn monumental feat while having a substance-abusing son. She's shorter than me by a foot and a half, so when she rounds the front of the van, her short little legs pump out three steps to my one, and then I'm hugging her for the first time in months, and something feels right about it.

"Hey, Mom." I hold her tight, and even though she's still smiling against my chest, she's also laughing, crying, and hiccupping.

"You beautiful, beautiful man!" she says, giving me a cheap shot to the abs. "You might not have gotten my height and skin, but you're me otherwise."

I laugh against her hair. "Was that your way of calling yourself beautiful?"

"No. Maybe. Oh my god, I'm so happy to see you." She hugs me again, still laugh-crying.

Truthfully, I've been looking forward to seeing her for months. Visiting my mom used to fill me full of guilt and shame. I hated letting her down, and nothing gets by her—except time—so she always knew when I was high or jonesing. This time, I'm not using. I'm sober, clearheaded, and hopeful, and it's the first time I've hugged my mom in years while feeling this way.

"Thanks for coming to get me," I tell her, pulling back to look at her. "Even if you're two hours late."

She smacks my shoulder. "Blame the van."

"The van I've offered to upgrade for five years?"

She crinkles her nose at me, not wanting my money. Yeah, I'm one of those fortunate—or unfortunate, depending on how you look at it—addicts who have some money and a career despite rehab and perpetual drug use. Without that money, I wouldn't have been able to come here eight times. But if I was poor, I might not have gotten into so many drugs. Who knows? Hopefully, I won't have to spend another penny on this place.

"Blame the snacks then," she amends. "I had to stop at that cookie factory, and once I got in there, it was like a mismatched heaven. I got carried away."

I smile again as I open the back door. She used to take us to this cookie factory when we were kids. It took two hours to drive there, but it was fun. Whatever cookies got broken or didn't turn out right to be packaged and sold in stores got boxed up in bulk crates for the public to purchase wholesale. As soon as I throw my bag in the back, it bounces back at me.

"What have you done?" I ask, wedging my bag between the back of the front seat and a box of cookies. "There's... how many boxes did you buy?" Big boxes. Like, twenty-pound boxes of cookies. My god.

"We have a four-hour drive, Gage. I thought you might be hungry."

13

"For ten thousand cookies?" I laugh. "You know, sugar is an addiction, too."

Her face falls, and I immediately feel like shit.

"Shit, that was a terrible joke. I'm joking, Mom. Sorry. Thank you for ten thousand cookies." I smile at her.

Mom sighs, but she's still smiling at me. Not like that pathetic one Paul gave me, but one full of all the hope I'm currently feeling. "It's been a long time since you've lived with me. And this is the first time since you were a young teen that you've been with me while free and sober. Do you know how proud of you I am?" She bumps her knuckles to my abs again. "Do you know how proud of yourself you should be?"

I do know. I really do. But there's always that bit of self-doubt that creeps in. It's my kryptonite. That voice inside my head that sometimes speaks alongside the one that taunts me into getting high, having sex I shouldn't have, stealing something, or getting drunk, and it likes to remind me I've been an out-of-control addict for over twelve years and that I've failed sobriety eight times already. Being inside is totally different from being outside.

But right now, the stronger voice is the one coming from my heart, telling me I'm still fucking here. Still fucking trying. And that's gotta mean something, right? I have shit willpower, but at least I've got some heart.

"I know." I smile at the woman who loves me despite it all. "I am. Proud, I mean."

By the time we get home, I've eaten over thirty cookies in varying flavours, and my mom is spinning a riveting tale about her forging club. Yeah, my mom makes swords and shit. She's terrible at it, but she found a whole new friend group, and they go to the forge every Monday night to make weapons and gab and gossip. Pretty sure they all have a thing for the teacher, too, but she won't outright admit it.

"Well, this is it," she says, screeching the van to a halt in the driveway of a two-story house that has no memories and holds no nostalgia for me. My family moved out of the house we grew up in after I had my third overdose in it. This house is a little bigger, but a little older and more dire. I'm making a silent promise to myself right now not to overdose and ruin another home for them.

"It looks nice," I tell her, unbuckling my belt. "I promise I won't stay for long."

"Oh, shut it," she says, reaching through the window to open the door. Then she rolls the window up and turns the van off. Inside handle must be broken. I'll fix that. "You're welcome for as long as you want. Forever, even." She smiles.

Don't offer things you can't follow through on, I want to tell her but don't. If I fuck up again, I might get a grace period, but it won't last forever. The people who live in this house are far too important for me to risk being a mess around. Nerves slither around inside me like a disease, and the more they fester, the more my palms sweat, and my mind tells me there's a simple fix to settle them.

I clear my throat and stretch as I climb out of the van. The neighbourhood is old, which means there are mature trees, bigger yards, and older homes. It's all very middle-class and boring, but Mom says a few interesting families have moved in recently. Her definition of interesting differs from mine, so I asked what she meant, and she told me there's a Portuguese family next door. I'm like... *what?* I thought she was going to say something about ethnicities and big families being interesting, but instead, she went on and on about their cooking. She's a big fan, and now our family and the Portuguese neighbour family have cookouts all the time, apparently. Mom is very food motivated, and this family loves to cook for her. Win-win.

She also says there's a foster family up the road, an elderly couple that drive motorcycles, and the owners of a quaint little sex shop—her words—three doors down. At the very end of the dead-end street, there's a historical mansion that's seen better days, but the city won't allow anyone to tear it down, so now some single guy and his son live there or something. Mom's vague on the details, trying to stack boxes of broken and disfigured cookies in her arms while she chats my ear off.

"Anyway, I've almost convinced Marian to join us at the weaponry."

"Marian?" I ask, grabbing my bag and a bunch of boxes.

"The lady three doors down and across, Gage. She's in

16

her seventies and is more badass than anyone I've ever met, including you. Her hog is loud."

Her hog? My god. "I bet it is."

Mom balances boxes on her knee to get her keys out, dropping them twice before I set my boxes down and take over. The maple in the front yard is sprouting fresh buds, swaying in the wind, and when I push the front door open, it slams right back in my face.

"Cross breeze," Mom explains. "I left the back windows open."

We finally get inside, and I notice this cross breeze. There are big windows everywhere, blowing wind through the house. Papers litter the hardwood floors, blowing all around, and tufts of pet hair roll like tumbleweeds.

"Slash!" Mom yells, and I look at her weirdly. "What? I was in my *Guns N' Roses* days when I got him."

I am well aware of her dog being named after the rockstar, but, "I thought his name was Saul Hudson?"

"We got tired of calling his full name every time he got out of the backyard, so naturally, he gained the nickname. Also, we got some weird looks until we explained it was actually a dog we were yelling for."

Naturally.

Slash looks nothing like real-life Slash. He's a tiny blond chihuahua who has no chill for about three minutes a day, but otherwise, he's lazy in a way that comes with a lot of attitude and self-righteousness. I respect him for it. He doesn't even get up when Mom yells for him. He watches from his throne—literally; he has a little doggy throne—side-eying me as the newcomer. When he blinks at me, I feel like I'm being tested.

"Ignore him," Mom says. "He's snooty about being left home today."

We drop the cookies in the kitchen, go back for three more loads, and finally have them all in the house. No one else is home, so Mom shows me around the new place like it isn't anything special, but I can tell she's proud of it.

"You have two options. There's an attic room we renovated. There's even a cool little secret staircase that goes up there. I think Cole is secretly hoping you'll take that room, but there's also the bedroom in the basement. It's cooler down there, but that comes with spiders and the odd mouse. What do ya think?"

I laugh. "The attic sounds nice."

Even though it's a little pathetic that I'm twenty-seven, well off, and moving in with my family again after leaving home at seventeen because I didn't like their rules and judgement.

"Attic it is! I can't wait for you to try the tart things the neighbours make. Flaky, chewy pastry with this custard stuff inside. To. Die. For. Gage. I'm not even joking."

Hope I don't get addicted.

gage

The attic isn't bad, actually. The ceilings slant and I have to duck in some places, but it opens up in the middle of the massive room, and there's a giant picture window with a seat that overlooks the street. The cushion is the worst shade of olive green and has definitely seen better days, but it's comfy, inspiring, and bright. The old me would have hated the brightness, but maybe this is a new me. Maybe hope feels bright and I'm getting comfortable in it.

Or maybe I'm hyperfixated on hope right now, and when the obsession wears off like they all do, I'll drop right into despair. I blow that thought through my lips and try to move on.

I sold everything I owned. That might have been an impulsive, drug-fuelled idea from that café Sunday, but anything in my name got sold after I went to rehab and made enough for me to afford twelve more months there. The condo I lived in with Paul stayed with Paul. I mean, technically, my name is still on it, but I'll give him my half. He put up with me for years, including my year in rehab, so it's the least I can do.

I'm about to turn away from the window when a loud rumble draws my attention. Marian's hog really is loud, and she does look like a badass riding it. I kind of want one, but that might be another impulse buy and I'm trying to steer clear of those. I'll need a vehicle eventually, and a motorcycle probably isn't the most logical.

When I turn around, Slash is sitting in the doorway to the secret stairs as if he's telling me, 'These are actually my stairs, so watch your back,' or something along those lines. Like a king, he struts his shit right over to the window seat, sits back down on the floor, and looks at me. And Jesus, it's like I can read his mind or something because I immediately push an old box over so he has a stepping stool to hop up there. With a huff that might mean thanks, he climbs up, settles down, and keeps a vigil over the street while I sleep off the drive, the stress, the anxiety, and the weight of all this new hope. When I wake up, the calendar has turned another page.

It's Monday now, so my mom leaves in a few hours for her forging night. No one else will be home until later, and the addict in me is wondering if they've been asked to stay away so I can settle. The things people do to make sobriety easier. I appreciate it, but it comes with guilt; guilt leads to negative feelings, and negative feelings lead to bad decisions. At least in my case.

"I'm gonna go out," I tell my mom, hoping she'll invite

everyone back home while I'm gone. "Been a long time since I was here. Just kinda wanna walk around a bit and get a feel for it again before I hit up my meeting." Even though that's the worst fucking idea because I don't know if I'm strong enough yet.

Port Baylon, this town—which is more of a small city—is full of my original fuck ups. All the places I scored drugs, the stores I stole from and ruined my family's relationship with the owners, the high school I attended and almost flunked out of, and old buddies who never got out. I *did* get out, and I probably ended up worse than them, but it's still not wise for me to run into any of them.

"There are a few new shops uptown," Mom says. "And a new coffee place that makes the best scones." She drools. "Are you okay, hun?"

Forever, as long as I live, people will automatically ask me that anytime I don't act one hundred percent normal. My eyes shift; are you okay? I'm in a bad mood; are you okay? Something doesn't go according to plan; are you okay?

Are you going to use? That's what they really mean. I'll never escape that stigma or the worry it comes with.

"I'm good, Mom." I smile at her. "And you can tell everyone they can come home. I'm fine."

She winks at me, and with that, I'm out the door with a pack of cigarettes my therapist thinks are a gateway drug and a bottle of water with the cap still sealed. I flip my hat forward to block out the setting sun and walk down memory lane.

Memory lane hurts, and by the time I get downtown, I

just wait outside the building for the meeting to start. I'm an hour early, but I don't think I can handle walking around anymore, seeing the places that remind me of all the times I messed up. I wanted to come back here to get past this shit. To see it, accept it, know that I can handle my past, and learn to carry it into a future that's going to be different. I need to conquer this fucking town before I can face a new one.

THE MEETING IS the same here as it is anywhere. Someone wise and weathered runs it, a bunch of people talk about the worst days of their lives or how long they've been on the straight and narrow, and the rest of us listen, letting it all sink in. Mostly that we aren't alone, and that when we struggle and think we're all alone in it, we really aren't.

These meetings put things into perspective for me, and sometimes I feel like shit about that. I have made some major fuck ups, almost accidentally killed myself five times, tried to kill myself on purpose once, and lost more than I've ever gained. But listening to the stories from people who actually have injured someone, killed someone by accident, lost friends to drugs and suicides, and lost custody of their kids makes me feel... better. Like, yeah, I've got it bad, but other people have got it worse, and I need to remember that. Sometimes it's good for me to get a reality check.

This is an AA and NA meeting, so it doesn't help my

sex addiction, but my old sponsor has something lined up for that.

"Hi," Carla, the woman running this meeting, says to me with a kind but reserved smile. "Welcome to Port Baylon. Are you new here?"

Fuck, I hate this part. She'll respect my choice if I don't want to talk, but now everyone is staring at me but trying not to, and the least I can do is answer her question.

"Uh, new again. I grew up here. Just got back yesterday."

"Welcome," everyone says.

"Anything you wanna share? Or just a short introduction? No pressure," Carla says.

"Uh, okay. I'm Gage. I'm twenty-seven. I've been an addict since I was fifteen-ish, and as of yesterday morning, when I got out of rehab, I'm just over twelve months sober." Everyone nods their respect, and for some reason, I add, "It was my eighth time in rehab." I cross my fingers like it's a joke and I'm hoping it sticks this time, but it's not really a joke. I just don't know how to talk about it without seeming dire and pathetic.

"Congrats, Gage!" Carla says with a big smile. "Show us that chip!"

I pull the twelve-month chip from my pocket and flash it around. I really am proud of it, and to be honest, even though I've been to rehab eight times, this is only the second time I've received a one-year chip. "Thanks."

Not bad for a first meeting, and I don't feel too dumb about sharing that. As soon as it ends and everyone mingles,

I look at the door and debate bolting into the night just to breathe on my own again for a second.

"Hey, Gage?" A guy walks up to me in jeans and a work-style jacket. He's somewhere in his forties, pretty good looking, and well put together. "Nathan," he says, holding out his right hand. "Kristen called. I know her from the city when I lived there. She said you might need a sponsor, and I think she mentioned me."

I shake his hand, enjoy his grip, and nod. "Yeah. I'm, uh, looking for one."

"Wanna grab a coffee or something and talk it over? There's a good place up the street that has way better coffee than that." He nods at the carafe that someone is pouring black sludge out of and into a Styrofoam cup.

"Sure."

I follow him out and flick a cigarette from my pack as we walk. Nathan looks like your typical hot young dad, and I've met enough addicts over the years to not judge. Not every junkie looks like a scabby meth head, and not every alcoholic looks haggard and worn down. We all get hooked for different reasons, and no walk of life is safe from the pull of addiction.

The sun has set, so when we get to the front of the coffee place, it's lit up like a stage. Glass windows line the whole front, and every part of the counter and booths are visible from the street. It makes me uncomfortable, but I have to get out of the mentality of hiding. I step on my cigarette butt and kick it down a sewer like a disrespectful dick before following Nathan inside. The place isn't packed, but it's lively for nine at night.

He grabs a booth by the window, shoving his jacket along the bench before he slides in. I'm only wearing a hoodie and my hat, so I push the brim up, showing him my eyes to be upfront and honest. No point in lying to your sponsor.

"What do you want? It's on me," he says.

"Nah, I got it. As a thanks for meeting with me."

Nathan smiles. "Just a black coffee. I'll load it with sugar here," he says, laughing at the sugar packets he's already ripping open.

Luckily, nothing crashes through the window, and I actually pay for his black coffee and my latte, feeling weirdly proud of that everyday occurrence. Makes me feel normal, I guess.

"You ever had a sponsor before?"

"Kristen," I remind him. "But other than her, no. I've always been that one foot in, one foot out type. Thought I could do it on my own."

He smiles weakly, almost like he gets it. Maybe he does. "I've never been a sponsor before. This'll be my first time. You okay with that?"

I shrug, not really familiar with how any of this works. Kristen was my first and only experience, and she was basically a lifeline. I called when I wasn't feeling right, we went to meetings together, and we checked in with one another, morning and night.

"I'm fine with it."

"Can I ask one thing?" Nathan asks, and I nod. "You had a female sponsor..."

Not really a question, but I get where he's going with it. We're encouraged to have same-sex sponsors to not spark any sexual or romantic interests, especially because I'm also a sex addict. But that's a pretty old-school way of thinking and doesn't really help me much.

"I'm bi." I take a sip and choke on foam. "And a sex addict. And every kind of addict you can imagine."

Nathan raises both brows. "Not just substances, then?"

I blow out a long breath and lean back in the booth. "I'm a basket case. Wanna hear what you're getting into before you agree to sponsor me?"

"If you're comfortable sharing, yeah. Then I'll tell you about myself."

"Better get comfy." I laugh.

Here we go. The story of me and all my fuck ups. It's always hard to tell.

"Well, it started when I was fourteen. Actually, it started when I was six. I got diagnosed with ADHD."

He nods. "Dopamine deficiency and substance abuse."

"Yeah. Everything hits us differently. I started on Ritalin. I was fine, if not agitated and living through weird ups and downs straight from childhood. Switched to Adderall later. When I turned fourteen, I became that dare-devil type, you know? Freedom, high school, new friends and all that, on top of hormones and trying to prove myself. I became an adrenaline junkie first. Always searching for the next thrill. Stealing, setting little fires, committing small crimes just to see if I could get away with them. That sort of shit. I got into a lot of trouble, which gave me a bad reputation. So, by the time I got that bad rep, I literally didn't give a fuck about making it worse. I figured everyone already thought I was the worst, so let me prove them right."

"Issue with authority?" Nathan asks.

"I don't think so. Issue with myself. Nothing ever felt good, so I kept looking for what did." I shrug and take another drink, feeling okay so far. "Well, that bad rep also got me bad friends. I was fourteen, at a buddy's place, and his older brother was having a party. This friend triple dog dared me to do coke, and, well, ain't no self-respecting thrill seeker going to turn down a triple dog dare, so I fucking did it. And guess what?"

"It calmed you down," Nathan guesses.

"So fucking calm. It was an upper, a stimulant, I knew that, but as soon as it hit me, I'd never felt calmer."

"ADHD," Nathan says. "Neurodivergent. Uppers are basically muscle relaxants to you."

"Bingo. So, here I am, this fourteen-year-old idiot who finally found something to make me feel good and relaxed, and I had no concept of the future or consequences or anything because I was fucking invincible at that age, right?"

Oh, how wrong I was.

"So, no surprise, I wanted more. I didn't have a job to pay for it, but who cared, right? I got a buzz from stealing, so I did that, got as much coke as shady friends and dealers would sell me, paid for it with stolen things or money, and got hooked pretty fast. I hid it well for almost a year because it didn't tweak me out, so my parents and teachers never noticed."

"What about the comedown?" Nathan asks. "Coke and uppers have a shitty come down."

"Yeah. Moody and sick and insecure, so I did what any addict would do."

"You got more. And more turned into whatever you could score."

I nod, finishing my latte. "Yep. I was fifteen when I discovered the wonderful world of Dilaudids and Hydromorphone and Oxy. Vicodin, Percs, Morphine, and eventually Fetty."

"Jesus." Nathan motions for a refill and the barista smiles as she drops off a mug for me and leaves the pot. She must know Nathan, which means she maybe now knows I'm an addict. Shit. Good start. "So, pills became your thing?"

I fill my mug and add some cream and sugar. "Yeah, but the problem with pills is that you mix and match, and they all fuck you up in different ways. So, I was long past that calm phase I got from the coke, and I had fully embraced the adrenaline junkie phase. I got fucked up so I could use it as an excuse to do stupid shit. I fucked so hard and so often I wore my dick out, got a few STIs. Fortunately, they were the curable kind. Stole for no other reason than to get away with it, and made enemies out of anyone who tried to tell me what a mistake I was making. Sex turned into fighting, and once I got a thrill out of that, I picked fights with anyone who would take me on. Which was stupid because I'm not that big of a guy, and I got my ass handed to me more often than not. But I didn't give a shit because I was so drugged up I couldn't feel anything. Plus, when you're bloody and broken, people throw pills at you, and I obviously encouraged that."

Nathan leans back, mimicking my position. "Alcohol?"

"I mean, yeah. I drank. I started drinking in high school, and I didn't really like it with the coke, but I did it anyway. Mostly peer pressure and a desire to fit in. Everyone drank, so I figured I should, too. Even though those people weren't also on coke. But I'd always felt so different from everyone else, so I did whatever I could to feel the same as them. They drank, so I drank. I was stupid."

"Okay, so you mostly stuck to pills and coke in high school? When did everything change?"

"I OD'd when I was seventeen. Mixed a few too many pills, lost track of how many I took, and my mom found me in the bathroom, convulsing on the floor."

"Did she know?"

"She's not stupid. We'd fought about it a bunch of times, but on top of being an adrenaline junkie, I was a compulsive liar. I weaved stories so well that it was hard for people not to believe them. I learned to lie, and I was damn good at it, and people generally liked me because I faked being likeable, so they believed what I said, even with the bad reputation. Plus, I left home because I hated disappointing my mom. That was high school."

"And after?"

"After high school, I fucked up real bad. I OD'd again when I was eighteen. Snorted heroin. Mom found me again because I'd gone to her place for... comfort or something. She threw me in rehab. I stayed for three months, moved back home, promised her I was better as I walked out the door to score."

Nathan refills my mug. I hadn't even realized I'd finished the coffee.

"But I felt pretty shitty about it. So, when I OD'd the third time, Fetty, Mom sent me right back to rehab. Again, I stayed. Relapsed within the first month out. I got my first full year of sobriety when I was twenty-one to twenty-two. And you know what's fucked up about it?"

"What?"

"On the one-year anniversary, it felt like I'd hit a milestone, right? Like, okay, I proved I could make it. That's all I needed to know."

"You used that day?" Nathan asks.

"Yep. From twenty-two to now, it's been the same repetitive story. Hit my rock bottom, go to rehab, sometimes do alright, mostly struggle, relapse, get lost in life, hit another rock bottom."

"Vicious cycle. And you were alone for all of it?"

"No. I had a boyfriend for the past few years. I thought I'd be okay for the first time, you know? Like someone actually gave a shit about me, and that felt good. Better than the drugs and the sex and the stealing. Until I realized that he probably wouldn't love me if I wasn't an addict. He was just looking for someone to worship him, and I did for a bit. Until I started lying and cheating and being a secretive dick. More rehab. More relapses."

"And he never noticed?"

"He did. But he was a busy man. He didn't have the time to constantly take care of me, and he shouldn't have had to. By that point, he was too good of a person to throw me out because he couldn't have lived with the guilt of making me a homeless addict. Instead of loving him enough to set him free, I took advantage of him keeping our home safe for me to crash in. Anyway, this most recent time, I lost my fight with sobriety because a goddamn steel pipe broke through the glass window of a café I was in."

"What?" Nathan laughs.

"Yeah. And I had a coffee in my hand that I hadn't paid for, and I was having a moral dilemma about stealing it while the barista was hiding behind the counter and glass was flying everywhere. I snapped out of it when she looked terrified and helped her get to the back room until it was safe. It was her purse that fell when she grabbed it for her phone to call 9-1-1. She had a baggie of coke in there. I called Kristen, but I already had the coke in my hand, and... fuck. It was such a weak moment. I even stole the coffee on the way out."

"And now you're here?"

"Yep. Fresh out of a whole year in rehab. Recovering drug and alcohol addict, klepto, sex addict, and adrenaline addict." I hold up the mug. "And apparently addicted to coffee and cigarettes now."

"Well, let's keep it at that and only that." Nathan smiles. "So, what about now? How do you manage your ADHD?"

"Well, for the past year, the clinic handled my meds, so I got my one pill a day and nothing more."

"And now?"

I shrug. "My mom is gonna try to distribute it." And I really fucking hope I don't make a huge mistake and hurt her to get them.

"Would you feel more comfortable if I did that? Or even the pharmacy?"

"You'd do that?"

"We could try it," he says. "If you're comfortable with me being your sponsor."

"Yeah. Yeah, okay. I think... yeah." Something eases inside me, knowing I won't be tempted to manipulate my mom.

"You feeling good about it this time?"

"Good? No. Hopeful, kind of. More just... determined. I don't want this to be my life anymore. I'm twenty-seven and have nothing to show for it except wasted time and a bunch of ruined relationships with the people I love. I have a good job, but that's because of the ADHD. I obsessed over an online shop where I made digital products. I made them all, set up the shop, and it basically sustains itself. When I can, I update it and offer new things, but it's really the same ten things that sell over and over again." I shrug. "I'm determined, Nathan. That's how I'm feeling now."

"We can work with determined," he says. "Thanks for sharing all that."

I feel lighter. "Thanks for listening."

gage

3

I have a sponsor. An eight-years-sober sponsor. When we left the coffee shop, he drove me home, met my mom, took the Adderall from her, and exchanged numbers with me. I guess my morning routine will have to include meeting Nathan, which probably isn't a bad thing.

"I like him," Mom says, starting the kettle even though it's almost midnight.

I sit at the kitchen table with her, waiting for it to boil. "Do you know him? From around town?"

"Yeah. He's the mechanic who fixes the van all the time, and he lives in that falling-down mansion at the end of the road," she says. "I just pretended I didn't know him so you could ask me and I could be honest about it."

"So lie, tell the truth, and then be done with it?" I laugh. "So backwards."

Mom reaches for my hand, and I notice her nails are smudged black and her arm hair is all burnt off. Forge night, I guess. "Honey, you haven't lived here since you were seventeen. Talking and visiting is one thing, but it's been a long time since we shared a home. I am so happy you're here, but I'm also nervous. I'm gonna make some mistakes."

I shake my head at her, squeezing her hand. "My sobriety isn't your responsibility. You can't make mistakes. You're my mom, and I know you love me despite all the shit I've put you through, and that's the only thing I could have ever asked. It's more than I can ask. So stop worrying about making mistakes. This is on me."

"I know. But I'm always going to be in your corner." She smiles, showing me those laugh lines. "And we can drink tea in the middle of the night whenever you want because I love tea, and I'm always buzzing a bit after the forge."

"So only Monday nights," I joke. "Got it."

"All nights!" she shouts, and then covers her mouth. "Shit. Your brothers are sleeping."

I haven't seen the twins yet. They're seventeen, and I've missed a huge portion of their lives. We talk a lot, and I visit whenever I'm healthy enough, but I've been a terrible brother to them. And to be honest, I'm hella nervous about living with them. What if I do something that hurts them? What if I get fucked up and scare them? I don't want to make mistakes around them, and my only goal—other than my sobriety—is proving to them that I'm someone they can rely on.

There's a quick knock on the door, and I raise a brow at my mom. "Late-night booty call?"

She scoffs. "I'm making tea. I called your brother."

Then arms wrap around me from behind and happiness fills my body, and I stand to hug my other brother.

"Fuck, I missed you." Owen hugs me tight, and I swear my eyes get watery. He pulls back, cupping my cheeks, smiling right in my face. "You have no fucking idea how happy I am that you're here, man."

Owen is two years younger than me, which means he saw me at my worst in high school. It also means he's had to grow up with my bad reputation. He spent a lot of time hating and loving me at the same time, but he's been my rock over this past year in rehab. I've been through the amends phase of the twelve-step program with him too many times, and this time, we hashed that shit out when he came to visit me in rehab, and he made me promise I'd let it go once I got here. So, I hug him again and don't even try to hide the few tears that slip down my cheeks.

Before Mom can even boil the kettle, Cole and Nick—our parents had a thing for four-letter names—are awake, and it's a family reunion over tea in the middle of the night.

I love it.

NATHAN'S HANDS aren't what they should be for his age. While he opens my bottle of Adderall, they shake and tremble, making the pills rattle around something fierce.

"Sorry. Nerve damage," he says, finally shaking a pill free onto the reception desk of his mechanic shop. "Spent a lot of years as a heroin addict." He laughs like it's a joke, but it's just something addicts do. We downplay all our terrible decisions like it will somehow make our current selves feel better.

I dry swallow the pill—old habits die hard—and give him an understanding look. "Thanks. So, this is your place?"

The garage is small, only three bays, but they're all full. Two mechanics work in two of them, and one sits waiting for Nathan to get back to it. It's on the outskirts of downtown, and he seems to take a lot of pride in it.

"Yeah. When I was first getting sober, I had this old car from my dad to fix up. Guess I made it my hobby. I had two years of mechanic school under my belt, so I just needed to put in the hours and get the licence." He shrugs. "Here we are." He looks behind me and smiles at someone. "Hey."

I turn, seeing a young guy looking completely out of place. He's fucking with my head because I can't immediately read him. Dresses goth, but he's got platinum blond hair that's slightly tinted a pale blue, his septum is pierced, and his face is scowling. Bright and dark together, and moody about something, it would seem. He looks like that Lucky Blue model I creep on sometimes, but more rockstaresque. Edgy and tough, but a bit awkward and unreadable.

"Hi. Here." He sets a keyring on the desk and turns around to walk away.

"Hang on," Nathan calls after him. "Thought you might want to meet Gage."

The guy turns back around to face me, and I damn near wither under his assessing eye-fuck, and by the time he's done, his face still gives nothing away. He's shorter than me by a smidge, and our body types are mostly the same, but he's the one looking down on me, and for whatever reason, my skin prickles and I sweat. Jeez, he's moody and authoritative just standing there.

"Gage, this is Alexei. My son."

Oh. Jesus. That catches me off guard. "What? I thought you were like forty?" And this Alexei guy is definitely somewhere in his twenties.

"I was the downfall to his druggie teen years," Alexei says, full of attitude.

"That's not true," Nathan tells him like he's said it a hundred times. "I was sixteen when Alex was born. I'm forty-two. I thought it might be nice to... have someone." He motions between the two of us, but I think he's talking more about Alexei having someone than me.

"Hey. I'm Gage Rossum." I hold out my hand.

Alexei looks at it and eventually narrows his eyes before shaking it. His knuckles are tattooed with a bunch of symbols I don't recognize, and the very top of his hand says 'right' in bold font. When I take a peek at his left hand, it also says 'right.'

"Alexei Kopacek." His voice is bored, but deep.

Nathan's last name is Thompson, so I lift a brow. "His mother's last name." Nathan looks awkward around Alexei, so he shoves his hands in his pockets and asks, "Have you eaten today?"

"Oh my god, Dad," Alexei groans, covering his face. "Would you stop?" Alexei looks right at me through his fingers, nails painted light blue. "He's trying to make you ask me out to breakfast."

I don't hate the idea, and it might be nice to have a new friend who isn't tied to my old life here, so I laugh and say, "I could eat."

Nathan smiles, and it looks way more relieved than it should. "Great. Because I gotta get back to work. You'll call me if anything is... off, yeah?"

"Sure."

"And I'm reaching out to Kristen for whoever else she had in mind for you for... the other stuff." The sex addiction.

"Thanks." I face Alexei. "Ready?"

He doesn't answer, but he turns and walks out the door. Nathan gives me a smile that loosely translates to 'good luck,' and then I follow the blue-blond into the morning sun. Again, he throws me off because of his clothing choice— black sweatpants paired with a black hoodie with a black and white rainbow on the front, making him appear lazy and darkly casual. But his hair appears even more blue-hued in the sun, and his bare feet are in a pair of slides that show off his toenails, painted the same shade of blue as his hair and fingernails. Like... lazy punk? Is that a fashion choice?

The fast pace he walks doesn't match his lethargic attitude, and I honestly can't tell if he wants to be near me or not. My ADHD makes me an overthinker extraordinaire, and now I'm wondering if he's doing me a favour or if I'm doing him one. Maybe neither of us are, and we're just doing the favour for Nathan.

I barely pay attention to the sidewalk, forget to notice

anyone walking by us, and follow him straight inside a divey little diner I definitely remember from high school. Yeah, got fucked up in that back booth, and Cassie Greensby sucked my dick while rolling. Pretty sure I also got kicked out, found more drugs, and ended up getting arrested and spending the night in the drunk tank while my mom was called out of bed to come get me. She had the flu at the time, too.

Memories. Not so fun.

"Nope." Alexei startles me, turning right back around and leaving the diner.

"What?" I follow.

He doesn't answer. We walk down a few more blocks, me following his fast pace, and while my mind reels with what's going on, he pulls open another door and I almost smack into it.

"This place," he says. "Been here before?"

I look at the sign. *Breakfast Junkie.* "No. Seems fitting." I walk inside, barely catching Alexei's hint of a smile.

The place is small and cozy, lined with booths made of worn wood with tall backs for privacy. The middle of the restaurant doesn't have any tables for eating, but holds display cases for baked goods, takeaway meals, and home-made crafts.

Alexei picks a booth along the window, sliding into the bench seat all the way to the window wall. Before I even sit down, a waitress smiles as she drops off menus and asks if we want coffee. I say yes, and Alexei asks for hot water with lemon. Ew.

"So, breakfast isn't what you're a junkie for then?" he boldly asks. When I just stare at him, he lets out a slow breath. "Sorry. My dad is... he's never been a sponsor before, and I hate you a little bit for reminding him of all his darker days, and I'm just stressed and hating on you. That's all."

I push my hat up my forehead and rest my arms on the table. "That's all?"

"Please don't bring drugs around my dad."

Oh. I lean back, hiding my hands for some reason. He doesn't trust me around his dad. That's what this is about, and now that I understand that, I'm hating on myself a bit, too. No one ever trusts an addict.

"I won't."

"Except you just did." Alexei blinks at me. "I saw him handing you a pill. What was it? Oxy? Percs? Pain—"

"Adderall. It's doctor prescribed for ADHD, and he's offered to distribute it to me. Should I not leave that burden on him?"

"Oh," Alexei mutters. "No. Adderall is fine. He won't take that. He likes a downer instead of an upper."

"He's eight years sober," I remind him.

"Yes. And for seventeen years of my life, he wasn't."

"You hate him for that?"

"I worry about him for that."

I pull the brim of my hat back down, hiding in plain sight. "I won't fuck that up for him. For you." Feeling shitty isn't anything new to me, but right now it's hitting hard. I thought I was doing good by moving home, going to meetings, and getting a sponsor, but once again, me being selfish,

I didn't stop to think about how that might feel to my sponsor's kid. A kid who probably had to see his dad all fucked up for most of his life. "Do you want me to find someone else?"

Alexei huffs. "No. My dad is the best man for the job. I'm just being protective, and I suck at being protective, so while I've got the guts to do it, I'm going to try to threaten you a little. Don't worry. It won't last." His pale blue eyes meet mine, and I can see the bravery in them, but I can also see something like shyness.

"Be protective all you like, Alexei. I'm not—" I shut up when the server brings our drinks, giving us both a glass of ice water as well. She sets a bowl of creamers on the table, asks if I'd like a dairy-free option—hell no—and then leaves again when we realize we haven't even looked at the menu.

"You're not what?" Alexei asks, picking up his menu.

The truth will hold me accountable for keeping my declarations, but I say it anyway. "I'm not going back to rehab. I'm not messing up my sobriety anymore. I'm done. I can't do it again, so this is me being bound and determined to be better. I don't want to drag myself down, so I'll make sure I don't drag your dad down, too." The pressure is on now. I regret saying it as soon as I'm finished. With big words come big actions, and now I'm doubting my ability to follow my statements up with real-life choices. Fuck.

It hits especially hard when Alexei takes his sweet-ass time scrutinizing me, looking for lies, checking to see how committed I am to what I said. I hope he sees my desire to stick to that wishy-washy plan, and not the self-doubt currently eating me alive. I pause with a creamer above my mug, watching him watch me.

"Alright," he eventually says, and the rest of my cream drips into my coffee. "I'm still gonna hate on you for the rest of breakfast, if that's okay? I've already committed."

A laugh bursts out of me, and I pull my hat lower when the whole restaurant looks our way. "Fair enough. Maybe if I buy you breakfast as some sort of consolation, we can be friends after I pay the bill?"

"You paying the bill signifies a power imbalance that my neurotic mind won't tolerate. You pay for yours and I'll pay for mine, and then we can try to be friends after."

I nod to accept that. Maybe his mind is as busy as mine.

Alexei orders one poached egg, potatoes with no salt or spices, a side of fruit instead of meat, refuses the toast, and asks for more lemon water. When he gets his meal, he doesn't immediately dig in, as if he's taking account of everything before he consumes it. He doesn't use salt or pepper, refuses ketchup, and doesn't eat the yolk of his egg.

I just consumed a hungry man's special with all the meats, three eggs, toast, seasoned home fries, a pancake with way too much butter and syrup, and about four coffees. And I ate it all ten minutes faster than he ate his. And I haven't even had a sip of my water.

I take a sip. Alexei smiles, but he hides it in his hoodie.

alexei

4

We live on the same street, so we're walking in the same direction. I'm kicking stones and watching my feet, but I can feel Gage's dark brown eyes on me, and I haven't yet decided how I feel about him studying me.

"Did you grow up here?" he asks.

Small talk is bullshit, and more people would admit that if they weren't afraid of coming across as weird. I have no such reservations. I take pride in my weirdness.

"No. My dad moved us here when he got sober because he needed to get out of the city. What are you addicted to?"

Gage's steps stop, but I keep walking. He'll either catch up and accept my personality, or he won't be my friend.

"Drugs," he says, jogging to catch up, his sunset orange t-shirt coming into view. "Pills, mostly. Stealing. Alcohol. Anything that gives me a thrill. Porn. Sex."

I grip a stop sign and swing around it, stalling to let him catch up completely. We're on a back street now, and other than a few people out on their porches in the nice spring weather, we're alone for this conversation.

"Cigarettes," he adds, lighting one.

"Coffee," I add for him. "Sugar. Salt. Overindulging."

His eyes narrow on me, but it doesn't feel threatening. "Are you judging me?"

"Observing." I notice he hasn't once taken a phone from his pocket. "Not social media?"

"What?"

"Are you addicted to social media?"

"Oh. Uh, no. I guess that's maybe the one thing I'm not hooked on." He laughs a little pathetically. It's a nice, reserved sound, not dissimilar to how my dad laughs sometimes. "I don't have social media. Not a personal one, anyway." He takes a long drag and blows the smoke away from me.

"So, you're just twenty-eight..." I pause, waiting for him to confirm my guess at his age.

"Twenty-seven."

"Twenty-seven, living with your parents again after rehab?"

"Just my mom. My dad left. And yeah, I guess. And my two younger brothers. My other brother lives across town."

"Owen. I know him a little. We're the same age."

"Twenty-five?" he asks, and I nod. "And living with your dad?"

We're side by side now, our arms sometimes brushing between our bodies. We're almost the same height, but he has a bit of muscle on me. I like muscle, a lot, but not on myself; it doesn't suit me. The sidewalk is narrow and full of cracks with weeds growing through, so I keep my eyes down, watching my feet. "My dad is trying to get me out on my own, but I'm afraid to leave him. Not afraid, really, I just don't want to."

"Being a sober addict doesn't make him weak," Gage says.

I glance at him, noticing he pushed his black hat up a bit, showing me his eyes. "Do you believe that about yourself?"

He licks his lips and looks away, hauling on the smoke again. "Sometimes."

I fiddle with the sleeves of my hoodie while Gage finishes his cigarette. I keep my mouth shut when he litters the butt and slow my pace as we get to our street.

Gage is tall and lean, dressed in a basic pair of jeans and a hoodie. He's not giving off athletic vibes, but casual vibes instead. He either doesn't care about his appearance, or he threw on whatever he found first in order to get his medication from my dad. At least he didn't dress to impress his sponsor.

"Do... do you want a cookie?" he asks as we pass his house. I've met his mom and brothers before, mostly at their neighbours' for cookouts. "My mom got a bunch from that factory."

Sugar scares me, but one cookie might be okay. "Alright." My mind circles back to sex addiction because it's the only one I don't know much about. How does a sex addict recover? Abstinence? What if he wants children someday? Perhaps the methods of sobriety are different with sex addictions than drug and alcohol addictions.

I can think about that later. I follow him up the front steps, pause by the pillar of the cement front porch, and wait for him to get his keys out. His hands don't shake like my dad's, but he's nervous about something. Me, probably. I'm the stranger here, and I just hated on him during breakfast and then made him admit all his addictions to me. I'm not an easy friend to have, which is why the only one I have is deaf and chooses not to read my lips most of the time.

Gage gets the door open, inviting me in. As soon as I pass him, I get a whiff of tobacco, but stronger than that, he smells like the laundry detergent my mom used to use. Wow, childhood memory unlocked.

"I've never been in here," I say for no reason. Uncomfortable silences aren't usually uncomfortable to me, so maybe I'm talking just to ease Gage's nerves.

"Uh, me either, until the other day." He closes the door behind me. "I didn't grow up in this house."

"But you grew up in this town?" I've met Slash before, too, so I kneel to pet him while he side-eyes Gage.

"Yeah. I... I guess I ruined the last house with bad memories." He bends to pet the dog but decides halfway there not to. "Cookie?"

No, thanks. But I don't say that.

On their kitchen table, kitchen counters, sticking out of the pantry, and even on the floor, there are unlabelled cardboard boxes with clear plastic spilling out from the top of the open ones. Gage opens the one closest to us, and I peek inside to see broken and jagged bits of cookies with some sort of chocolate icing on them.

"It's a cookie factory," Gage explains. "Uh, they sell the broken ones. My mom goes overboard."

Wonder if he gets that from his mother or if it's a trait he learned all on his own. I pick a broken cookie from the box and watch him do the same. He's getting sketchy, his eyes shifting from place to place, and the way he keeps fucking with his hat makes me feel guilty. I'm not someone who puts many people at ease, so I take a deep breath, bite into the cookie, and walk around to the patio door at the back of the kitchen. The reflection of his bright shirt shows me his movements while my back is to him.

"This is a nice place. Do you like it here?"

"Wanna see my room?" He laughs. "That sounds weird because I'm twenty-seven, but I promise it's cool. It's in the attic. Secret staircase and everything."

This is awkward, and I love it. Gage has no idea how to have a friend, and I don't know if that's a normal thing for him or a since-sober thing. According to my dad, he only got out of rehab this week, and he spent a year there, so friendships in his old hometown probably feel strange to him.

I finish the cookie and follow him up the secret staircase, which is basically just a narrow set of stairs behind a door you'd think led to a closet, and Slash trots ahead of us. My eyes are level with Gage's ass, and the jeans he's wearing no longer seem so casual. I watch my feet instead.

The top opens up into one big room that has no sense being a bedroom. Anyone else would turn it into a games room, a storage room, or some sort of library. If it were mine, I'd turn it into one of those rooms from detective shows with a murder board and yarn on the wall, whiteboards everywhere, and coffee mug rings on every surface.

Slash jumps on a box and then makes himself comfortable in the window seat, and I gawk at everything in Gage's bedroom. I've never been in someone's bedroom in the daylight.

"Are there bats?" is my first question.

Gage grins. "I've only been here a few nights, so I don't know. And I spent most of last night at the kitchen table drinking tea."

"A good sleep schedule is important for someone trying to build a healthy routine." I peek at him, hoping he didn't hear me say that. "Nice view." I look out the picture window.

This house is taller than most on the street, so it gives a decent view of all the rooftops. I can even see the corner of our roof if I lean in far enough. Gage comes to stand beside me, and I smell that detergent and cigarette smoke again. I tug at the sleeves of my hoodie, unsure if I'm nervous or not, and when I look down, Slash is staring at us instead of out the window.

"I don't know how to have a friend," Gage admits, finally putting me at ease. I like it when other people feel awkward because it makes me feel less alone in my awkwardness. Quirks like company, I guess.

"Me either." I look at him. "We don't have to be friends. We can just be neighbours or something." I shrug. "Takes the pressure off. Pretty sure my dad was just pimping me out because he thinks I'm lonely."

"Are you?" Gage asks, sitting down on the window seat.

I sit on the other side, leaving Slash between us. "Kind of. Sometimes. Yes. Not all the time. I'm not friend material. I'm weird and proud of it."

Gage points at himself. "And you think I'm friend material? I've literally pushed away everyone good in my life because I'm selfish and a bit of a dick."

I can see that. "I'm just neurotic and, according to my dad, too intense." When Gage smiles at that, I blurt out something that has no business being said. "I'm gay."

"Okay." He laughs. "Neurotic, intense, and gay. Got it."

But I'm fishing. I want to know his sexuality, and now that I've brought it up, I can't outright ask him without it looking like I'm fishing. So, I do what my dad tells me not to do and keep rambling.

"I've never been in a relationship. I've never really even told anyone I'm gay because I don't have anyone to tell. Other than the few hook-ups I've had with strangers. I don't know why I'm telling you this. I'm also a Pisces and don't believe in astrology, but sometimes I look at horoscopes anyway. I have an app for that. It's next to Grindr on my phone, and even though I have a profile, I've never looked at the app outside of making the profile. My hook-ups didn't come from Grindr. They came from a gay bar in the city, and I'm still not sure why I'm telling you this, but also, this is just me. Want me to leave?" I stand.

Gage touches my sleeve and pulls me back down, our

hands landing on Slash's head. The tiny dog huffs, which forces me to take a breath.

"Neurotic, intense, gay, and rambly. I like it." Gage grins at me, and my whole body gets hot and I'm afraid my fingers are trembling, so I pull my hand away and clear my throat.

"And an oversharer," I add. "But secretive, too."

"Complex. Complicated," Gage amends. "I'm neurotic, too, but in an obsessive way. Clearly, I have an addictive personality. I'm intense, mostly because I don't have limit controls and just go all in on everything, which really helped my addiction along. I ramble a little when I'm nervous, but since being sober, I realize I'm more the shut up and listen type." He looks at me, grinning because he left out the sexuality part. "We have a lot in common."

"Like being gay?" I blurt.

Gage laughs, and again, I like the sound. It isn't as reserved as before. "No. Not like being gay."

Dammit. Probably for the best, though.

"I'm bi."

And a recovering addict. A sex addict. My dad's sponsee. My neighbour. My new friend. *And you look incredible in sunset orange.*

"And I had to delete all dating apps because the old me abused them." He cringes a bit. "Why haven't you looked at yours since you made the profile?" He rubs his hands over his thighs.

"Because I'm a hypocrite. I want to meet someone the old-fashioned way, even though I never go anywhere to meet people." Deciding a change of topic is probably best,

I ask, "Does it bother you when people ask if you're okay?"

"Yes and no. I know I've given them reasons to ask, so it's on me. But it fucking sucks knowing that I'll forever just be a junkie, you know? No matter how long I've been sober, people in my life will always be waiting for a relapse." Gage stands. "I need a smoke. Want me to walk you home?"

Is he asking because he wants to go outside and spend time with me, or is he asking because he's trying to get rid of me? If he needs a smoke, does that mean I'm agitating him and making him antsy? Does he not like me in his room? I should never have mentioned the gay thing.

He doesn't wait for an answer. We head downstairs, leaving Slash to the window seat, and Gage is already smoking by the time we get to the front porch. He spins his hat around to face backwards, thinks better of it, and turns it forward again. Pulled down low.

"What're you doing for the rest of the day?" he asks. "It's Friday. Do you work?"

"I have a gig on Fiverr. I work for myself." Because I don't want him to lead me, I start walking and hope he follows. "Do you know what Fiverr is?"

He follows. "Yeah, a site to offer services for hire. What kind of gig?"

"I build websites for small businesses. WordPress. Shopify. That sort of thing. Help them manage and upkeep their websites once they're running, and I do a little PR management."

"What's that?"

"Like I help people with the business side of a new product launch or an email campaign. Stuff like that. Book releases, new products, setting up an online store with new merch. Newsletter marketing." I shrug. "Mostly for indie artists, bloggers, and pop-up type places." I squint into the sun to avoid looking at him.

"That's cool. I run an online business, too. Well, I don't run it well. I hyper fixated on digital products when I was younger. I made a bunch of planners, spreadsheets, trackers, and page designs that are compatible with digital planners and apps like Excel, Sheets, Goodnotes, and Notion. It kind of runs itself, but I've really dropped the ball on it. I started it before digital stuff got so popular, so... I dunno, it was all good timing and luck. It's a lot harder these days."

"Sticker packs," I tell him. "You should sell digital sticker packs with digital planners. People eat that shit up. Is it an Etsy store?"

"I started on Etsy. It's from my website now. A website I haven't maintained in forever, so maybe I should look up your gig," he says, smirking. "Up for another client, or are you booked solid?"

I think I'd take him on even if I was booked solid. I'm steady, and that's how I like it, but I smile at him and nod. "I can help you out. No need to go through my gig."

When we get to my house, Gage stops on the sidewalk. "Wanna hang out again?"

"So this one is over?"

He rubs the back of his neck while his cigarette burns

down to the filter. "I, uh, need to find a meeting. Or something. Call your dad, maybe."

My face gets hot. "I'm sorry."

"Don't be. It's just who I am. Give me your number, though." He hands me his phone, so I put my number in and add a blue heart to my name. When he texts me, he sends the crossed swords emoji, and I tilt my head at him. "Sorry. That's because my mom is a metal... she makes swords, so I was joking with my brother... I didn't mean it as..." He looks at his feet, his cheeks flushed pink. "Nice meeting you, Alexei Kopacek. Text me." He backs away slowly, laughing as he goes. I watch him long enough to catch him looking back, and we both smile pathetically.

When I get inside the house, my mouth is smiling, my confidence is high, my head is buzzing, and my dick is hard.

Nice morning.

gage

5

First week and I'm already gearing up to lie to my sponsor. I don't even know why.

Like, 'Hey, your son told me he was gay, and I suddenly wanted to bend him over my window seat.' Or, 'No, I'm not jonesing for anything except your son's lips.'

Yeah, no. I can't tell him that. I don't even know if I want Alexei like that or if it's just a compulsive thought. That's the real bitch—I can't even trust my own thoughts anymore. I don't know if they're mine or if they belong to my addictions.

"Hey," Nathan says when I walk inside the bay door of his shop. "Woah. Everything okay? Are you okay? Alex?"

"Fine. Do you have a number I can call for that other person?"

He knows what other person I mean, and his face hardens at the timing of my question. Yeah, I just had breakfast with Alexei, showed him my room like we were thirteen, and then thought filthy, filthy things about him. So what?

"I called Kristen," he says, thankfully not calling me out on the timing of this. "She texted you the contact information, and apparently, she already booked you an appointment."

"Appointment?" I fuck with the pack of smokes in my pocket. "I thought it was another sponsor?"

"It's a therapist, actually. Someone who specializes in addictions that aren't... that you don't quit cold turkey."

Like sex. Jesus. I check my phone, seeing a voicemail, a text, and an email from Kristen, but I also see the blue heart beside Alexei's name, and I soften emotionally but harden below the belt simultaneously.

"Did my son do something?" Nathan asks. "I figured he'd be a good friend because of his neurosis."

"No, he didn't do anything. He's... I like him. I just need something right now." I pace, wishing I could smoke in his shop. "Any midday meetings around here?" Not likely in a city this small.

"No, but you can hand me that," Nathan says, pointing at a tool of some kind on the workbench next to me. I hand it to him, and then he snugs it up to something. "Hold it for me while I adjust this."

I'm not stupid. I know this is a distraction method, but I'm weak enough to accept it. Maybe strong enough? I don't even know anymore. Nathan works in silence, only giving me the odd command every now and then. After a while, the music in the shop settles me enough to start talking.

"It's weird being back here," I tell him, so he doesn't think this is all about Alexei. "This is where it all started, you know? Like I'm living in a town full of all my own ghosts, and everywhere I go and everywhere I look, I'm remembering shit I've done or mistakes I've made."

Nathan hands me a tool and I swap it out for the one he needs. "So, conquer them. They're the old you. You know better now."

"Do I?"

"You said you were determined, didn't you?"

Yeah, but my mind is focused on the dark parts of my past, not the bright parts of my future. I'm agitated and too alert, and a bump of coke would be so fucking perfect right now. But a bump of coke won't last, and I know that! So why the fuck do I want it so badly?

"Everywhere you go, you'll have demons, Gage. Hell, my entire heroin career took place in one city, yet I battle those demons everywhere I look. Bars, hotels, random houses, bathrooms in general, kid's parks, schools, everywhere. But you know what keeps me going?"

"Alexei," I guess.

"Yeah, but my need to prove to myself that I'm worthy of being his father. He's twenty-five, and it's far too late for that now, but I've been trying since he was seventeen. I missed a lot while I was high. Important things. Things I regret, and my new motto in life is that I don't want to live with regrets. You should find one."

"A motto?"

"Yeah."

"Lucky number eight," I say with some snark. "That's *my* motto." Weirdly, I feel better after admitting that.

Lucky number eight.

"What's for dinner?" Cole asks Mom as soon as he charges into the house with no grace.

"Uhm, cookies?" she says, glancing around to double-check that she didn't make anything else.

I hit up an early evening meeting with Nathan and just got home myself. Mom might be familiar with feeding two teen boys, but she's always been terrible at time management. Now there are three of us, and I'm not a teen, so I really should help out.

Just as I'm opening the fridge to check what I can make, a head pops up in the window above the kitchen sink. "Hello, neighbours! We have leftovers!" A lady with a thick accent stands there, her head barely reaching the window.

"Hi!" I gasp, laughing.

"I told you, Gage!" Mom says. *What'd she tell me?*

Mom starts speaking in a terrible attempt at Spanish, and I'm not sure I have the heart to tell her they speak Portuguese in Portugal. Either way, I'm introduced to Benedita, and despite being a twenty-seven-year-old loser who moved back home with his mom, I don't feel too weird about it.

Nick kicks my knees out from behind, and before I fully buckle over, I reach around and grab him by the neck.

"Gage!" he shouts, laughing. "I forgot how easy you are to fuck with."

I get him in a headlock, glancing at Cole to see if he's going to come rescue his twin. He's eating cookies straight from four boxes. "Easy? I'm winning."

He gut punches me and I let go. "Some people were asking about you at school today."

My stomach gets queasy. "Yeah?"

"Mr. Brenner. Remember him? English teacher," Nick asks through a full mouth.

I remember pissing him off and skipping his class. "He's still there?" Mom lets Benedita in the patio door, and I grab the dish of leftovers and put it in the oven.

"Yeah. He asked—" Whatever else Cole says is cut off by Marian's hog going down the street. His mouth is still moving, and I catch Alexei's name at the end.

"What? What about Alexei?"

"Oh, so you do know him?" Nick smirks.

"I met him today. His dad is my sponsor. Why?"

"Mr. Brenner said Alexei Kopacek is his nephew and something about being around our street and seeing you."

Oh, I don't really give a shit about that. I'm more curious about Alexei. Mom's still speaking bad languages with the neighbour, but she seems to be mixing in some Portuguese words now as Benedita gives her a vocab lesson at the kitchen table. I only know that because one of Paul's coworker's wives was Portuguese, and she would rant and ramble and be all loud and adorable in her language whenever her husband annoyed her. They were the only work couple Paul ever introduced me to, and I have no idea why that's just hitting me now. He always hid me.

"You guys got that?" I ask, nodding at the oven. "I'm gonna smoke."

Nick stays quiet, watching me, but Cole is the loud-mouth, so he asks the typical question. "You okay?"

They're seventeen and way too young to have to worry about me and my state of mind. So, I smile and smack Cole in the stomach. "Fine. Just a smoker."

I head out front for a cigarette, pulling my phone from my pocket as I go. Sitting on the front step, I triple-check my calendar app, making sure my appointment with that thera-pist is still in there for tomorrow. I'm not even sure what kind of therapist she is, but I trust Kristen, and she's the one who hooked me up with her.

> Gage: Hey

> Alexei <3: Hey

Why am I grinning at my phone like a tween? Jesus. I leave my cigarette between my lips to type.

> Gage: Did you hear Marian's hog go by?

> Alexei <3: Yes. And no one calls them hogs. This isn't the 80s.

> Gage: My mom does haha what're you doing?

Cole and Nick are bickering over something, and my mom is letting the neighbour yell at them, nodding along with hand gestures. While Alexei types, something falls off the van. A windshield wiper just slides down the hood, all cool and casual, and I seriously wonder how that thing is still running.

> Alexei <3: If you must know, I'm washing my whites.

> Gage: You have whites?

> Alexei <3: A few. Mostly wear them under my blacks.

I glance behind me, peering in the window. Everyone, including the neighbour, is sitting at the kitchen table eating dinner. It smells good, whatever it is, but I'm not really hungry anymore. Cigarettes are an appetite suppressant for me, and I should have eaten something before having one. But the scene through the window looks so wholesome and humble, and there's this fear inside me that I'm going to taint it as soon as I walk in there.

I'm not sure if that's me overthinking, the addict in me coming out, the ADHD surfacing, or if it's true, but whatever the reason, I feel it. I'm dark sometimes, and I never used to give a shit because there wasn't anyone in my life I cared about tainting. My brothers don't fall within that category, and my mom has already seen enough of my darkness. It fucking hurts to think of myself at the twins' age. By that time, I'd already been an addict for two or three years; my life was out of control, and I was out of control even more. My mom worried about me constantly, and I spent so much time giving her that grey hair she has now.

Maybe coming back here was a mistake.

Maybe I'm too damaged to live with Nick and Cole without dragging them down or scaring them.

Gage: Wanna go for a walk?

Alexei <3: Okay. Come get me.

"Mom! I'm going for a walk. I'm fine, I just need air."
"Kayyy, honey."

alexei

6

Dad isn't much of an eye-roller, but he rolls them at me now. Yes, I gave him a speech about my whites and which ones needed to be hung to dry and which ones were safe to go in the dryer. He wants to ask me why it matters—since I only wear whites under my blacks—but he refrains.

Instead, he asks, "Are you sure he seemed in a good place?"

"He just asked what I was doing and then asked me if I wanted to go for a walk," I say, shrugging into a new hoodie from my load of blacks. "I know how to handle mood swings and look for signs, Dad. I've had a lot of practice."

I'm a dick and we both know it. Yes, I'm proud of my dad for his sobriety and how well he's doing, but the kid in me will never forget all the times I administered Narcan, cleaned up his vomit, stopped an overdose, and called 9-1-1. I can't forget the nights I kept vigil over his spasming body, the terrible people he brought around, the sight of needles

SOBER DOPE & SUNDAYS

and rubber bands, and the multitude of lies and excuses I was too young to see through but did anyway. I don't even like spoons.

I'm twenty-five, never touched a drug, don't drink alcohol, and am very conscious of everything I consume, do, and get excited about. I'm as clean as a whistle, but I've lived the addict life because of the house I grew up in and the parents who pretended to raise me. I have a right to be salty about it, even if addiction is a disease and I thoroughly understand that. I'm nice when I can be and a dick when I can't. Sue me. I know it comes from a place of fear, of worry about a backslide and losing another parent, and at times, it gets to me. I already lost my mom; I don't know if I can survive the loss of my dad, too.

"Alright, well, let me know." Dad keeps his eyes on my laundry. "And try to have fun, Alex."

Fun. Something else I'm mindful of. Can't have too much of it, can I?

I whisper an 'I love you' that he doesn't hear and leave him in the laundry room. The house is so massive and outdated that my walk from the laundry to the front door takes three whole minutes and goes dark in some places where the lights don't reach. Dad's hobby turned into a mechanic shop, and he needed something more stimulating. Hence, the falling-down mansion. We're fixing it because it's supposed to be fun and fill us with pride.

We'll see. It's growing on me. A lot.

I pull open the restored front door, still not used to it being silent as it swings, and find Gage just about to knock. He smells like cigarettes, only this time, no detergent.

"Oh, hey," he says, sort of smiling and sort of looking awkward. "Hey."

"You said that already." I adjust my septum piercing and walk by him. "Where are we walking to?"

He pulls the door shut and shoves his hands in the pockets of his pants. Decides to take them out. Fucks with his hat a bit. "Uh, just around?"

The brim ends up high on his forehead, a mess of dark hair jutting out from underneath it. Sexy. But I can't think that, so I look at my feet and start walking down the darkening street. We're silent for a bit, wandering through the neighbourhood with no purpose or direction, and by the time we're a few blocks away, Gage lights a smoke and pushes his hat up even more.

"Are you scared of me?" he asks, surprising me.

"What do you mean?" I slow my steps, intrigued by the question.

"Because I'm who I am. Because you grew up with an addict, and now you're hanging out with one."

"Addicts don't scare me, Gage," I tell him honestly. "Addiction does. But I'm pretty hardened to it. And it's frowned upon to refer to an addict as an addict. You're a person with a substance use disorder." I learned that years ago when my dad never labelled himself as anything other than an addict, essentially taking his own identity away.

He goes quiet again, so I look at him with curiosity.

"I'm guessing my family feels the same way you do.

Hardened to it when they shouldn't have to be. Makes me feel like shit, I guess." He takes a drag, and I hate that I find it attractive. It's a thought that scares me because I'm conditioned to hate anything addictive, and now some guy comes along and makes smoking seem sexy. There's nothing sexy about smoking. It's a cause of cancer, a money pit, a stinky habit, and a way to worsen the health of a body that is most likely already unhealthy. Especially considering how much fried meat and potatoes he ate at breakfast.

"So, you feel guilty?"

"Damn right I do," he says. "The twins were pretty sheltered from me because they were so young when I lived there. But my mom had to live a life she never planned, and Owen had to suffer through my reputation because we're so close in age. I ruined their lives while ruining mine, and it just fucking sucks, you know?" He glances at me, pulling his hat down again. "And now I'm twenty-seven and barely have a relationship with the twins because they've always been hidden from me so I didn't taint them."

I don't have siblings, so I can't understand that, but I have lived a similar life to his family. I was the family member that never wanted that lifestyle but had it forced upon me anyway, and yeah, while I'm hardened to it, I'm not a robot, so it hurts sometimes. It left behind some fear, but I'm pretty skilled at coping these days. What I can understand is the guilt Gage feels. My dad feels it, too, and no matter how well he does and how hard he tries, it's always there. Gage will live with it forever, but I don't tell him that because there are plenty of other things to focus on. Better things.

"So, build the relationship now," I say as we turn a corner to a street we've already walked down. "That's what I'm doing with my dad. You're living at home again, so now's your chance to get to know them how you want to."

Gage doesn't say anything to that. He tosses his smoke and walks to a park, sitting on one of the swings, not swinging. I sit on the one next to him, facing the opposite direction.

"I came back here to conquer this town," he admits. "This is where everything bad started, and I want to be able to look at it, see it, remember it, and feel okay about it because I'm better now. Stronger. More determined."

"But?"

"But when we walked into that first diner, memories hit me, and I felt so fucking overwhelmed that I basically stopped breathing until you said nope and walked right back out." He looks at me, big brown eyes grateful, if not a little hesitant.

"I have a way of telling that sort of thing," I tell him, kicking my feet in the dirt. "I could tell you weren't comfortable, so I left."

"How?"

I shrug. "Not sure. Just know. You should go back there. When you're in a good mind space. Alone or with someone you trust, and just let it sink in. Just to prove to yourself that you can."

"Maybe we can go there to eat breakfast sometime," he says, eyes shifty and awkward.

I smirk. "Are you shy?"

"No."

"You sure?"

"I'm selfish, impulsive, short-tempered, and full of self-doubt, but I don't think I'm shy. You just make me feel weird things. I'm still getting used to it."

"What weird things?"

"Things I shouldn't feel, so I'm trying to be a good friend and talk about *literally* anything else."

"Tell me one."

He stares at me with an annoyed look masked by a smile. It doesn't bother me. "Okay, well, I can't figure you out. You're all gothy and covered in black and tattoos, but you have blue-ish hair and painted nails. You're quiet and moody, but you blurt things out that I don't expect. Like telling me you're gay and just straight up asking me what I'm addicted to. Not to mention your commitment to hating me during breakfast." He laughs. "You seem like a loner, but you don't seem lonely, if that makes sense. You're just hard to read, and I kind of like it. And I'm trying not to think about you being gay."

"Because you don't want to like me?"

"Because I shouldn't." That self-doubt creeps across his eyes. "Sex addict, remember?"

I did some research. Sex addictions aren't always handled with abstinence. Not that I'd ever encourage him to have sex when he isn't ready or doesn't trust himself, but a lot of recovering sex addicts learn better impulse control, healthier attachments to people, and more attentive reactions to arousal and sexual consent.

"Have you ever had sex sober?" I ask.

He hangs his head. "No. Drugs led to energy, and sex was a way to expel energy. Some drugs made me horny, so that made it all worse. I had a need that wasn't met, like an itch I couldn't scratch, and I turned to sex to satiate it even though it wasn't ever that good. Can't fuck in rehab, and while I was with my last boyfriend, we only ever had sex when he thought I was sober, but I really wasn't. When I was actually sober, I didn't want him. Or maybe I just didn't trust him. Or myself. I don't know. Basically, no. I've never been sober and had any sort of sex. Not even in high school." He cringes, already feeling ashamed about telling me all that. He could have just said no, but I like that he shared.

"I've never been drunk," I tell him.

"Ever?"

I shake my head. "Never tried weed. Don't drink. And walking with you is the closest I've ever been to cigarette smoke."

"Shit. I'm sorry. I won't smoke around you."

I smile at him, loving that he said that. "We're opposites, Gage. I have way too much control over my impulses, and you have none. We might be a good match. For friendship." I shrug. "My dad thinks I'd be an addict's best friend because I have an iron will."

"Aren't you worried I'll, I don't know, corrupt you or something?"

"Nope. You won't ever have that kind of control over me." And I've never been more sure of anything. "Because I value myself and never want the life my parents lived."

Maybe my life prepared me for this, maybe it didn't, but I became a master of control during my childhood, and as an adult, some might call me a control freak, but I take the title with pride. Fear is healthy when it makes us cautious, but I admit I tend to overdo it at times.

Gage groans, tilting his head back and gripping the chains of the swing. "Don't tell me things like that. I'm dumb enough to take it as a challenge."

"You want to control me?"

"I don't want to, but impulses and an adrenaline rush might make me try," he admits. "You always have to keep your guard up around me. Maybe we shouldn't be friends."

I want to agree with that because I don't think we should be friends. We should be boyfriends. But Gage doesn't seem ready and I've never had one before, and I just met the guy this morning, and oh my god.

No, Alexei! Bad impulse control!

But wait. I'm allowed to like people. Regular guys get crushes all the time, and it doesn't make them obsessive or compulsive or whatever. I'm allowed to have a crush on the new guy who can't read me.

"I have a therapy appointment on Monday," Gage says. "With someone who specializes in sex addictions."

"I have a dentist appointment on Monday," I say. "With someone who specializes in nervous patients."

Gage smiles at that. "Are you always factual and honest?"

"Yes."

"Do you lie?"

I think about it. "Not if I can help it."

Gage swings a bit, his feet scuffing the grooved dirt beneath him. "I lie. Or I did. I'm kind of a compulsive liar. Pretty good at it, too." He looks at me, not smiling or frowning. "I'm going to fuck up a lot. If we're going to be friends, you should know that."

"With your addictions?" Because I want no part of that. If he isn't here to give it his best shot and already has intentions of relapsing, I will walk away and never look back. I'll think about him, feel sorry for him, worry about him, and fret over him, but it won't be enough to draw me back.

"I hope not," he says sincerely. "I just mean, like, as a friend. A person. I make a lot of mistakes, and I'm still getting used to how that feels while... sober."

"Oh, well, yes. I expect that. No one is perfect." I nod. "I make mistakes, too. I don't often realize they're mistakes until someone tells me I didn't follow social protocol or I acted rudely because I was honest. So, you can expect mistakes from me as well."

"Are you neurodivergent? On the spectrum?" he asks while blushing.

"No. I was tested. I'm just weird." I shrug.

Gage looks up at the stars becoming visible in the clear, darkening sky. "A neurotic rambler and a neurodivergent recovering addict walk into friendship..."

I smile despite myself. *A friendship.*

gage

7

When my skin gets itchy, I know I'm about to get agitated. When I'm agitated, I'm impulsive. When I'm impulsive, my good decision-making capabilities get cut in half, and when I'm straddling that line between 'good for me' and 'bad for me,' I naturally gravitate towards whatever is most destructive. Because destruction brings big feelings, and big feelings create dopamine, and at the end of the day, dopamine chasing is what got me started with substance abuse in the first place.

I do drugs to feel. But then the feeling gets to be too much, too negative, and I turn to drugs to numb. And in the process of feeling and numbing, I'm constantly searching for that middle ground that is impossible to find because my equilibrium is so fucked up that I don't even recognize it anymore.

Sobriety fucking sucks because I feel all the things I numbed over the past twelve years and feel none of the feelings I chased with a pill. It's the opposite of what I searched for, and somehow, I have to learn to make it my new status quo.

"So, to simplify, you used sex as a dopamine hit, a rush of adrenaline, and then overindulged?" my new therapist asks.

"I guess." I shrug, sinking down on the bucket chair in her office. "I have no off switch. I use, fuck, steal, consume, whatever, until I either pass out or die. That's the only way I stop something once I've started."

"Because it feels good?" she asks.

"Because I *feel*. Period. Even if it feels bad." I glance at her, but she's not writing anything down. "Even when it stops feeling like anything, I keep going. It's just a motion, an action that my body is familiar with doing, so it does it. I don't know."

She nods, smiling. "And while you were in the rehabilitation facility, you worked with a sex addiction counsellor?" she asks.

"Yeah."

"So, you went through your abstinence period, found your triggers, recognized your compulsive thoughts, and were taught ways to manage and control them?"

"Uh, yeah. Six months of nothing, not even masturbation, and another six of nothing with masturbation. And it wasn't even that hard because... I dunno, I'm just not horny anymore."

"Good for you for committing, Gage."

"Thanks. I learned the whole three-second rule, disordered eating comparison thing."

"Recovering from sex addiction is much like recovering from an eating-related disorder, yes. We find new ways to be healthy about our choices. What is it exactly that you're worried about?" she asks, flipping through my file from rehab.

"Okay, so it's like this. I was a sex addict, like, no doubt about it. But only while I was on something. Sober me barely even touched my dick. I relate drugs and alcohol to porn, sex, masturbation, and once I start, I don't stop. So I guess what I'm worried about... can sober me become a sex addict too?" I look up at her, hopeful but weary. "Or can I be a regular guy, have sex and be intimate without the worry of overindulging because the drugs that made me overindulge are no longer there?"

"Substances are inhibitors, but your compulsion comes from you. That's not an insult. Just remember that. Keep it in the forefront of your mind. Remind yourself that you have the capacity to overindulge, and pair that with the natural inclination to hyperfixate because of your attention disorder."

I groan, feeling hopeless.

"Gage." She leans forward, smiling. "That's not to say you can't have a normal sex life. And there's a very good chance that you won't be compulsive towards sexual activity while sober. But as addicts, recovery is a process, and it just gives us that extra footing to stand on when we acknowledge our former behaviour and are aware of it as we move forward. That's all. We have tricks and tips and heaps of tools to use. Be proud of where you are, remember where

74

you've been, and take it all into the future with you. You're capable of so much, and if you really want to, you'll figure out what works for you. That's where I come in. I hand you the tools and the advice, you put them into action, and when we meet again, we talk about what worked and what didn't. That's how this goes. How do you feel about that?"

"So, I don't have to abstain forever? I'm not cold-turkey cut off?"

"No. You've already been cold-turkey cut off for a year, right?" She smiles. "You'll know when you're ready, and we'll work on making you very skilled at recognizing your triggers. Do you have someone you're thinking about social-izing sexually with? Because, while we don't typically recommend hook-up apps and one-night stands, we can offer tools for that as well."

I lean forward, elbows on my knees. "Not planning on random hook-ups. Trying to steer clear of that whole scene. And no, not really anyone in particular. Yet. No. Not at all. There's this guy..."

Natalie laughs. "Isn't there always?"

I grin. I like her.

"Okay, let's figure out a starting point then." She claps her hands together. "Bag of tools. Let's dig through it."

PEOPLE IN RECOVERY usually have a hobby. It keeps our minds engaged with something other than our former vices, provides a sense of accomplishment, and excites us enough to enjoy it while we're doing it or looking forward to doing it. Nathan has his mechanic shop, but he told me that once it became a job, it no longer felt like his hobby. Hence the fixer-upper mansion.

So, graphics and digital files are going to be my job again, which means I need something else.

I don't have the patience or interest to cook or bake. Running is boring as fuck. Sports have never been my thing. Other than partying or finding my next fix, I've never really had a hobby that sticks. My neuro-spicy mind makes me fixate hard and drop it fast.

"I'm just saying, hun," Mom speaks over her shoulder, hands turning red and wrinkly in the kitchen sink. "Making badass weapons is a pretty good hobby."

I grin and dry the dish she passes me. "Yeah, but I can't just do it whenever. I'll join your damn Monday night weaponry class, mostly so I can see why you and all your lady friends are so interested in the teacher, but I need something else. Something more accessible."

"He's tall, dark, and forges hot metals with his bare hands, honey. What more is there?" Mom says, handing me another dish before I'm done drying the last one. *His bare hands? Really?* I roll my eyes at her. "How about that guitar you used to play?"

"I'll just get frustrated that Nick is better."

Nick grins behind me, but I catch it in the window reflection. "Digital drawing? You're good at art shit," he suggests.

Yeah, but... again, it's too close to my job.

"Mowing lawns," Cole suggests.

"Yeah, you see, there's this part of my brain that can't ever see work as a hobby. It's an art, really. Benefits me super well in life." I toss the wet towel at him and grab a dry one. "And stop trying to pawn your lawn cutting job off on me."

"Come play volleyball with me on Tuesdays and Wednesdays," Owen says, walking in from putting new window wiper blades on Mom's van. "Yeah, yeah. You hate exercise and organized sports are akin to a dictatorship."

I wink at him. Horribly.

"Look who I found." Owen motions to Alexei behind him. "He was on his way over."

Alexei follows him inside, looking awkward and comfortable in it. "Fixing up old mansions is a great hobby. So I hear."

My heart gives a little *thwack* in my chest. It's not really an increase in speed or a flutter or anything, just an off beat that could mean I'm about to go into cardiac arrhythmia, or it could also just mean that Alexei is here and making my heart thwack.

"Yeah?" I ask him. "If you love it so much, why aren't you there now, painting old handles like I know you're supposed to be? You forget I'm tight with your dad."

Alexei's wearing baby blue with all his black today, and maybe that's why my heart is thwacking. He looks at the twins, nods at Owen for bringing him in, and then smiles at my mom. "I'm inviting you, if that wasn't obvious," he says to me. "Are you the type to miss the obvious?"

Yeah, while my heart is thwackin', I am. "I don't miss shit, Alexei. I just like making you point out the obvious. You get this patient but frustrated look on your face like you want to be accepting of my slow mind, but you're also unsure if you want to be friends with someone who misses the obvious." I dry the last dish and then yelp. "Ow! Mom!"

My ass stings from where she snapped a towel at me. "Stop taunting your friends. Alexei, how are you, hun? You want a cookie?"

"I just ate," Alexei says, and I wonder if that's true or if he's afraid of sugar like he is of fried food. "But thank you."

"Guess I'm going to paint old hinges and handles," I tell my fam. "Wanna come?"

"Volleyball," Owen lies. It's not Tuesday or Wednesday.

"Have lawns to cut," Cole says. It's almost dark.

"Better practice my guitar." Nick grins.

I look at Mom. "Don't look at me. I can barely feel my fingertips after last Monday's forge." She holds them up. They're wrinkly as shit from the dishwater. "But you have fun playing hobbies with your friends. Take some cookies." She sets a twenty-pound box in my arms and practically shoves me out the door. Then I stand on the sidewalk holding the heavy box for seven more minutes while she chats Alexei's ear off about custard tarts and some sort of bread.

"Your mom is very enthusiastic about custard," he says, joining me.

"And cookies. And forging class. And Marian's hog. She

78

goes all in." I shift the box in my arms. "Mostly because she's just a happy person and loves loving things."

"A good trait to have. Unfortunately, I don't have that one. Yet." He looks at me, taking his time, not at all rushing to sneak in a glance. No, this is a study, and he's being thorough.

"Well? Are you done staring?" I ask as we start walking.

"You look dubious."

I snort, already feeling better than I have since my therapy appointment. "What's so dubious about me? Is it the giant box of cookies I'm carrying even though I know you won't eat them because you have a weird thing about how much sugar you put into your body?"

"Sugar has no nutritional benefit in such a stripped form. I get my sugars from fruits and vegetables. But my dad will eat them. It's the look in your eyes. You look dubious because you're... annoyed or something."

My feet scuff along the sidewalk while his skip over cracks, avoiding stepping on any of them. "I need to find a routine, and since I haven't found a hobby yet, it's hard to form a routine. I'm... adjusting. Not dubious."

"Dubious," he accuses. "Restoring a home was never my idea of a good time, but... I don't know. It's nice."

"Nice?" I bark out a laugh. "Never heard someone describe home renos as nice."

We're walking slowly. Stalling. Being leisurely for a reason that's probably obvious but neither of us feel the need to announce. Nathan is in their house, and as soon as we enter, we won't be alone. I like being alone with Alexei and I still barely know him.

"Why didn't you have a boyfriend in high school?" I butt in before he can comment on my last comment. It's a comment battle, and I want to venture into his dating life because, apparently, I like breaking all my own rules. I said I wouldn't push myself on him, but here I am, pushing myself on him. Subtly. "If you like meeting people the old-fashioned way, high school is a pretty standard first love story."

Alexei slows his pace even more. We're three houses away from his, but I hope it takes us an hour. "Well, when I started high school at fourteen and then up until I was seventeen, I was that kid with a junkie dad. Not very appealing. Then when my dad went to rehab and started to turn his life around, I was that kid with a junkie dad who was trying to get sober. The only people I've ever been... intimate with don't know my dad, my history, or my past. And I don't date because I'm picky. I don't feel the need to tell my life story to just anyone, but if I'm going to be serious about someone, I'll want to tell them eventually. Like I said, I'm neurotic, so I have some explaining to do whenever I meet people. How they react to my initial personality is what really sets my standard for how picky I'll be."

"How'd I do?" I ask, shifting the box again. "What was your initial assessment of me?"

"It's different with you because you knew my dad before me."

"Don't act like you didn't assess me anyway."

He smirks. "I did."

"Go on."

"Well, I was pretty committed to hating you through breakfast, but even that was hard. You just... most people look at me like I'm weird and then don't know how to act around me. But you looked at me like I was weird but acted like it didn't throw you off. Which was disappointing because I was really setting myself up to be let down by you."

"Don't stop expecting that. I'll let you down eventually." I glance at him. "Not on purpose, but it'll happen. And I'm weird, too. It's funner being weird."

"You are weird, but you're not a let-down so far." He pulls his hood up over his head. "What'd your therapist say about sex?"

There's that thwack again. "Which part specifically?"

"Can you have it?"

"Alexei," I groan.

"I'm curious. I've never met someone with that kind of addiction. One that isn't quit altogether. I'm not asking because I want to have sex with you. I'm just an inquisitive person."

I stop and look at him.

"And okay, I kind of want to have sex with you."

"Jesus, Alexei! No. Bad idea. We're friends, remember? Platonic, neurotic, new friends who happen to be gay and bi and don't at all want to sleep with each other because it's a horrible idea, and your dad is my sponsor, and we're behaving and being good and doing the right thing so I don't ruin you and my progress all in one shot because I love it when you wear blue with your black and—"

"You do?"

I gulp air. "Which part?"

"Like it when I wear blue with my black?"

Black sweatpants and a black hoodie, but the front zipper of the hoodie is open to show a light blue t-shirt and the flatness of his hard chest. It makes his hair stand out and his pale blue eyes glow. Yeah, I like the fucking blue. "I believe I said I love it, not like it. And yeah, I do. Very much."

"I wear mascara sometimes," he blurts. "Very rarely."

I grin.

"My eyelashes are naturally light, and I like the way they look darker. If they aren't dark, I notice them in the mirror and can't stop looking at them because they aren't quite right. Sometimes it bothers me so much that I wear the mascara to put my mind at ease, really. That's the only reason."

"Is it?" I grin even wider.

"Yes." Eyes on me. "No." Eyes on the ground. "Maybe. What'd your therapist say?"

I start walking slowly again. "I have to feel ready. We're working on tools and tricks and recognition. For now, I'm practicing masturbating. Or even recognizing the urge to masturbate but being able to refrain from it."

"Oh, that's cool. Like a mental awareness thing. Recognize the arousal, understand where it's coming from, and realize it's not dire."

"You a therapist now, too?"

"Inquisitive," he repeats. "I ask a lot of questions."

"I know."

"I'll even ask the questions that have hard and very personal answers. If you don't develop some boundaries with me, I'll probably know more about you than your therapist."

The idea doesn't scare me. I don't know why. No one really knows me anymore, myself included. I'm in that 'getting to know myself' phase, and maybe it'll be nice to have someone else getting to know me, too.

"Okay, let's make a deal. For every intrusive question you ask me, I get to ask you one."

He squints, but it doesn't look like he's thinking too hard. "Alright. But you can also refuse to answer whatever you want. It will irk me, but I understand. I need to be told no sometimes."

My arms are burning because carrying a box of twenty-pound cookies up the street is apparently outside of my athletic abilities. "Maybe sometimes I'll just tell you things without you having to ask. You told me you were gay unprompted."

"I was fishing."

"I know."

He pulls his hood up higher. "Right. Painting fixtures and handles. We better do that if you don't want me to ask more sex questions." He hurries his steps through the front gate and up the sidewalk. "But I kind of want a status report about your restraint from masturbation."

I'm restraining the urge right now. "Of course you do."

gage

I have a daily arousal journal. Cool, eh? Here are my entries, and they're quite eye-opening.

Nothing.

Nothing.

Nothing.

Alexei wore blue.

Nothing.

Nothing.

Nothing.

Alexei asked me an intrusive question and then blushed about it.

Nothing.

Alexei smiled at me.

Alexei texted me and I saw the blue heart.

Nothing.

Alexei showed up at my front door and told me we were sanding drywall.

Alexei breathed.

It's eye-opening because the old me, the high me, would have gotten a stiff dick if my jeans rubbed just right, but the new me doesn't really get turned on by much. Other than Alexei doing totally non-sexual Alexei things. I even got tasked with watching one pornographic video. My dick didn't even get hard, and I shut it off three minutes in.

It begs the question: why the fuck was I so hooked on sex when nothing seems to turn me on?

Except Alexei breathing.

Am I broken? Am I too mind-numbingly sober to be aroused? Did all the drugs fuck up my sex drive? Because Alexei seems to be the only thing turning it on, and I'm not allowed to have him.

"It's because you're looking at sex through a new lens. Everything within you, right down to your chemistry and the way your brain's chemical reactions happen, is changing and developing. Your body went through a year of detox and healing while you were at rehab, and now it's learning to function in your old world again. You've never been aroused sober before. Or if you have, it was while you were young and hormonal and not having sex." Natalie smiles at me. "You aren't broken. You just aren't used to this state."

"How can a sex addict not have a sex drive?" I mean, this all seems like bullshit now. I can't even get sex addiction right.

"Just like some medications inhibit sexual arousal, sobriety can, too. But that's not the case with you." She flips my journal to show me my entries. "Alexei arouses you. Is he the guy?"

I nod and don't admit that he's my sponsor's kid, my only friend, and it would be detrimental to both if I actually slept with him.

"Do you know him, or is he a stranger?"

"I'm getting to know him."

"Okay." She closes the journal. "It's chemical again. Hormonal. Getting to know someone is exciting, and if you feel good around this person, it feels good all over. Feeling good can lead to arousal, but it's attraction that sparks true desire. What is it about him that turns you on?"

"Everything. Look at my lame entries."

"Alexei breathed," she reads, chuckling.

I don't want to admit to her that he's forbidden to me, which packs its own appeal. I don't want to be that guy. I don't want to use Alexei to get my rocks off, but I'm also selfish and impulsive, and when something is supposed to be off the table for me, I always want to put it back on the table. There are a hundred reasons why sleeping with Alexei is a bad idea, and only one good reason: because we both want to. But I still can't decide if I'd do it because it's thrilling or if I'd do it because I... actually thought it through and want to.

"Desires change and shift all the time. They're different from obsessions, so make sure you're noting that when you find yourself drawn to something or someone. The next time you find yourself aroused around this Alexei, I want you to assess your need for release. Are you just turned on but able to manage it? Are you wiggling on the spot, trying to get some friction going? Are you rushing off to a private room to handle it?"

She thinks I have dignity and class. I don't.

Or do I? Because I haven't done anything too shameful or embarrassing since I got home. Maybe sober me has some self-respect after all.

By the time I leave her office and meet Nathan for a meeting, I'm starving. He invites me back to their place for dinner, but I get this weird guilty conscience, like I need to ask Alexei's permission first.

> Gage: Your dad invited me to dinner with you guys. Yay or nay?

> Alexei <3: If you come with the understanding that the meal will not have fried meat, we're good.

"He say yes?" Nathan asks.

I hide my phone. "How'd you know I was asking?"

"Alex causes a certain look in the eye. You have it." He watches me and I watch him. I don't know what he's looking for, but I'm hoping he doesn't find it. I'm just trying to stand my ground and not buckle under the weight of being that guy who wants his sponsor's son. "So? Coming?"

> Gage: I hope there's cheese then.

I pocket my phone and climb into Nathan's truck. I don't want to give him the chance to start asking questions, so I blurt, "I think I'm gonna quilt."

"Quilt?"

"Yeah, as my hobby. Apparently, Marian with the hog is a quilter, and she's teaching a few of the neighbours, so I might sit in on a few of those so I can practice in my own time." Dextrous, finicky work might piss off my short fuse, but it's good for my mind to get caught up on all the tiny details. I can see myself getting lost in that.

"Quilting," Nathan muses. "Alright."

And I guess that's all there is to it because he doesn't say more, and he doesn't ask questions about Alexei. When we get to their broken but mending mansion, Alexei is standing in the kitchen—wearing blue with his black again—with paper bags and ingredients on the counter from one of those meal subscription boxes. The ones where the food comes portioned, and you still have to do all the work of cooking it. Lame.

"No cheese," is all he says to me.

After Mediterranean chicken bowls, Nathan is on the phone in some far-off part of the house, and Alexei is judging my sanding skills. We already stripped the paint, and now we're sanding the wood so we can restore it to its natural... wood. Whatever. Old house things.

"Am I doing it wrong?"

"I thought you were right-handed?"

"I am."

He looks at the sanding block in my left hand. "It bothers me when I get small details wrong."

"Well, excuse the fuck out of me." I switch it to my right hand. "Wouldn't want to bother you by holding the sander in the wrong hand. God, Alexei! Would you literally die if I told you I wasn't actually a smoker?"

"And go straight to heaven," he snips. "That'd be the best news of my life."

"You need a more exciting life." I do some sanding with my right, but despite being right-handed, it feels more natural in my left, so I switch back. "Tell me something exciting."

"Well, remember I said I had a dentist appointment with a dentist who specializes in nervous patients?"

I snort. "Yeah. Was it exciting?"

"After the appointment, I booked my next one, just like I always do, and just by mere coincidence, it brings me back to the city on the very same day I have another appointment with a doctor who specializes in genetic testing."

He looks at me.

I look at him.

When he doesn't add more, I ask, "Oh, is that it?"

"Yes."

I can't help but smile. "Riveting."

"Coincidences excite me."

"You know what excites me?" I ask, clapping my hands and erupting a cloud of woody dust.

"Adrenaline, chasing a high, thievery, anything that provides dopamine, and the thrill of getting away with something," he deadpans.

"It's like there are no hidden parts of me." I shake my head. "Guess this friendship has come full circle."

Alexei, who is sometimes blunt and sometimes shy,

doesn't miss a beat. "Natural progression would suggest a full-run friendship should morph into something more."

I don't know if it's what he says, the blush to his cheeks, or the confident look in his eyes while he's being coy, but there's one for the arousal journal.

Alexei got bashfully bold.

My eyes dip down to his lips. They're parted, but as soon as I look at them, they clamp together like they have to physically restrain more brazen words from leaving them. The blush creeps up his neck, standing out against his light blue shirt, and his hands fidget with the sandpaper. The paint on his nails is chipped from sanding, and his black sweatpants have white handprints on them from where he's wiped his hands.

Yeah, natural progression wants me to go there. I'm into him. Into not fully understanding him but liking the phase of learning his personality. I'm into the way he looks, harsh and subtle together, creative and reserved in one pale package. Tough but soft, lean and tall, cute but manly. I'm attracted to the way he knows what he wants despite never having had it before. I even like that he's a control freak. It makes us so different and provides a spark of interest because I want to understand how he can control so many things that should be outside his control.

But I also like that it's risky. That Nathan is somewhere in the house, ready and probably willing to catch us in the act. If I leaned forward and kissed Alexei, I'd do it until he moaned, drawing Nathan's attention just to get the dopamine hit of committing a crime. The guilt and shame would come later, far later than needed. I like the idea of pushing his boundaries and tainting him just a bit, forcing him to give up a fraction of his control. It's toxic, my need to ruin, and since Alexei is the only friend I've had sober since childhood, is the son of the man keeping me on track, and I really enjoy spending time with him, I can't do it. I can't act on the impulse to push his boundaries and bring him to my side of trouble.

"I have a knack for fortune telling," I say, sanding again because I can't look at him. "And the cards are telling me that if we go there, I'll hurt you. Ruin your life. Ruin your relationship with your dad, potentially putting his sobriety at risk and damning him to disappoint you all over again. Which, in turn, will lead to your complete heartbreak over having to watch your dad struggle again. All the while, you'll hate me, lose some of that control you have over yourself, and start eating fried meats or something."

Alexei hums. "And you? Where will you be in this hypothetical future?"

"Dead, strung out, or in rehab for the ninth time."

I hate this reality I'm building. Sadness overcomes me because I can never just have something nice without ruining it. But when Alexei touches me with his tattooed hand and I look at his face, he's smirking. "I told you I wanted an old-fashioned romance. Love leading to death is about as old-fashioned as it gets. Real Romeo and Juliet style. You're just attracting me more."

"You better be joking. That is an unhealthy thought, Alexei!" Because oh my god, I want him. All of him. I wanna hold his hand and touch his lips to see if they are as soft as they look. I want to feel his short blue-blond hair and rub my cheeks all over it while just holding him against my body. I wanna smack a kiss to his forehead.

"I never joke about true love," he says. "But I hear you."

"Do you? What is it you're hearing from all that?" I plant myself on my ass at the bottom of the staircase and level him with what I hope is a serious look.

He mirrors me. "That you don't trust yourself yet. You will. It takes time, and you need time to prove to yourself that you have what it takes to be selfless. You think you're greedy."

"I am greedy."

"Yes, but you're aware of it. You just turned me down for selfless reasons. You're protecting me and my dad."

"And myself."

"That's responsible. Not greedy."

"You aren't feeling all rejected and broken?"

He scoffs. "I'm not giving up. You think I haven't faced a million rejections in my life? I might look soft-hearted, but I'm hardened to a lot of things, Gage Rossum."

Under my breath, and hopefully out of earshot, I whisper, "Please don't harden to me too much."

alexei

My dad is afraid of me. Not because I'm particularly scary, but because I hold a level of control over his life. Because of what he and my mom put me through, I hold clout and status that most children don't. I became *their* parent figure at a young age, and because of it, our power dynamic shifted. Biologically, he's my dad. Fundamentally, we're just family. Father and son with no father and son roles. Simply put, he's afraid of letting me down, doesn't think he has any right to tell me what to do, and often tries to hide his pain from me because I've already experienced so much of it.

While there's a petty part of me that thinks, 'Yeah, you deserve this role,' there's an even bigger part of me that never wants him to hide from me just because he's protecting me. I want to protect each other. I want to be his haven and his rock, just like he is mine now.

"We can go again," I tell him over breakfast in our

ridiculously massive kitchen fit for a family of thirty-three instead of the two of us who barely cook.

"No. It's okay. I'm fine."

He's not fine. He gets weird this time of year. It's a built-up highlight reel of his teen years: meeting mom, having fun, doing drugs, having me. Then he loses a few years. They're scrubbed from his memory bank because his brain wasn't healthy enough to hold on to them during the worst parts of his drug use. But he remembers May 17th. A cursed day on two accounts.

My birthday.

Mom's death day.

Twelve years apart.

It's four days from now, and Dad's doing his usual agitated mess thing. So, since he won't admit he wants to go, I'll make it about me.

"I want to. It helps to visit her grave once a year." We go every single year, but he always makes a thing out of it beforehand. I take a bite of muesli and dairy-free yogurt, watching him. It honestly does help me to go. It reminds me that my slight fear of abandonment isn't for nothing, that she left us because of a disease, not by choice.

Relief falls into Dad's eyes, lifting them. He nods, knowing that I'm doing this for his benefit because I hold very little love and almost no fond memories of my mother. To her credit, she mostly sobered up enough during pregnancy that I wasn't born with a laundry list of health issues, but that postpartum depression hit hard on an unstable sixteen-year-old new mom, and it was straight to the needle after that. There wasn't a single time in my life when I knew my mom sober. Not even once.

So, I don't care about visiting her grave for myself. I don't get sad about her death anniversary, and I feel no guilt for still being excited about my birthday, even though it's usually boring. It's my day. The only one I get. But Dad cares, and I care about him. He cares because he was a teenage dad who didn't know how to care for a newborn, let alone a strung-out teen mom with untreated depression and mental health conditions. He didn't help her, couldn't help her, and barely kept me alive most of the time. So, we go visit her grave so he can put his guilt to rest until it creeps back up on the next May 17th.

"Okay," Dad says. "You should try these." He nods at the cardboard box of a hundred cookies. "They're actually pretty good."

"I had one. When Gage showed me his room."

There it is. That look. The one that got morphed because of our power imbalance. Dad wants to tell me not to date a newly recovering addict, but he won't tell me that because he has no say and knows it.

"We're friends."

"That's all?"

"That's all he wants." *For now*.

"I trust you, Alex. It's Gage who is... still a bit unstable. You shouldn't have to live through what I already put you through again."

"You make it sound like he's going to relapse." I finish my breakfast.

"I hope he's not, but there's always... just..." Awkwardness. It's so fun because I don't feel it, but everyone else does. I wait him out. "Do you like him like that?"

While I'm usually pretty careful with what I get attached to, I pinned myself to Gage immediately after my fake hatred wore off during breakfast. It's not because he's tall, dark, and handsome with a nice ass and gorgeous brown eyes. It's not because I've dreamed about what it would feel like to hold on to his hair while his mouth is wrapped around me. It's not because he interests me, makes me giddy, or makes me comfortable.

It's because he sees me and isn't trying to change me. He pokes fun at my quirks without actually having a problem with them. That's friendship. True friendship, even though it's new. But... boyfriend material. That comes from the way he makes me feel so comfortable under his attention that I'm uncomfortable in the comfort because I've never experienced it before. No one, not my parents, former friends, past crushes, colleagues, classmates, or distant family members, has ever sat in a room with me and been content in my judgmental silence. That's what attracts me to Gage.

And since I'm not the type to get embarrassed by my own thoughts, I'll mentally admit it. It's soulmate material. I feel it. Everyone, including my dad, will think I'm crazy because I barely know the guy, have hardly touched him, haven't seen his body or learned about his actual needs, but I sense it. Deep in my gut and throughout my whole metaphorical heart.

Gage Rossum is my soulmate. I just need to be patient until he figures it out.

Told you I'm an old-fashioned kind of romantic. Turns out I'm the werewolf and fae type of romantic. Soulmates exist, and I found mine.

"Yep," I answer Dad, grabbing my bowl to rinse.

"Does he know that?"

"What, like I'm subtle?" I snort.

Dad laughs softly. "You are the most sure of yourself person I know, Alex. But you're also the strongest. I don't want you to have to be strong for him all the time. Someone needs to be strong for you, too."

I look at Dad over my shoulder. That's one of the nicest things anyone has ever said to me, and it means a lot coming from him. "I know you don't always feel it, but you're a person. You know that, right?"

He quirks a brow.

"You see yourself as an addict. You see Gage as an addict. But you're both people." I dry my hands. "It's possible to fall for a person who happens to be an addict. It's only one part of who they are."

"And you have no fear about that one part of who he is?" he asks.

"Some," I admit. "My fear mostly stems from you. I can't lose you like we lost Mom."

Dad's eyes soften, and he stands. "You know, sometimes

I think you turned ninety-five when you were seven. How did you get so wise?"

"It's my old soul." I smile at him. "That was created for the single purpose of belonging to Gage's soul. And vice versa."

He smiles, eye-rolls, laughs, and nods all at once. "He's the one, eh?"

"Just need him to figure it out."

Dad grips my shoulder, feeling weird about it. He doesn't move his hand. "He seems smart."

He also seems like a compulsive liar, a self-doubter, a confused man, and a wayward soul. Fate plays tricks in funny ways.

"It's... you made this?" I ask Gage, looking at him over the top of his laptop.

He's leaning back on his bed, ankles crossed, tossing a bottle cap in the air over and over again. "Yeah. Originally, like five-ish years ago. Ran off Etsy before that, but I updated it at some point. Can't remember when."

Effortlessness frustrates me. Gage has a beautiful website, a thriving business, a loyal customer base, and judging by his online store's analytics, a ninety percent occurrence of recurring buyers. They buy the same products each month and year, even though he puts minimal work into updating them. And he charges too much, but people are still buying it. He's bringing in way more money than I thought he was, and he... barely does anything.

"I can see the steam building," Gage says, knocking his knee against my hip. "Let me have it."

I try to hold it back, but he gave me permission. "You are lazy. You set up an amazing business with products that people want, and then you fucked off and stopped caring. People with your mentality shouldn't be this successful. You should earn the success and work hard at it. Or at least work hard at setting it up and maintaining your frequently bought products. Bundles, a mailing list, loyalty programs, special offers, new products. All that. Yet you sit here and say you 'made some digital products, and now they sell themselves' while pulling in more money than the average salary of three people combined. And you aren't even proud of your success. I don't like you right now."

Gage tosses the bottle cap, and it goes high above his head. When he reaches to catch it, his shirt lifts and my attention sinks to his abs. How does a drug addict have abs? He hates sports! He barely walks faster than a distracted toddler! God, he's infuriating. His skin tone is tanned, he has the sexiest little pleasure trail I've ever seen, and fuck him for having a V!

I glare at him. "I hate you."

He catches the cap and sits up. We're facing each other, chests close, hips side by side. He licks his lips, and I'm a fool for bracing for a kiss—hoping for one—because it doesn't happen. "I do care about it. Now, anyway. I know it's all been pure luck up to this point. Which is why I want you to help me fix the site. I'm hiring you."

"Well, I charge a lot for website maintenance when the website belongs to an asshole."

He chuckles, showing me his teeth. Nice teeth. Again, how does a smoker have such nice teeth? They should be yellow and stained, but they're pretty white and mostly straight. "I have to pay an asshole premium?"

"Double asshole premium. One count for your lack of effort, and one count for your physical appearance, which also took no effort. Oh, and there's a douchebag tax for just being a general douche."

"Fees are getting pretty high."

"You can afford it." I point to the annual income numbers on his website stats.

"You're worth everything I have to give, Alexei."

I'm swooning. And mad about it. He's not supposed to say such sweet things after telling me he won't be with me because he will actively ruin my life. And he makes it worse when he turns the laptop, tucks his head in close to mine, and clicks right into his business bank account like he's not private about banking information.

There are big numbers on the screen, showing his account balance, but all I'm thinking about is how he's radiating warmth that is travelling straight to my dick, and he smells like cigarettes, and I hate him for it because cigarettes have suddenly become an aphrodisiac and that's just absurd!

The laptop tilts.

Because. Of. My. Boner.

I'm a little mortified, to be honest, but I own it. When Gage looks, notices, and then meets my eyes with a sexy grin, I say, "Coincidences are exciting, and compliments are a turn-on. Sue me."

He leans in. Grinning. Casual. Tempting. I'm gone for it, hoping he does something about it while knowing how bad of an idea it is. My morals are getting all skewed, and that should be a red flag. I've lost my damn mind!

"I have so many compliments to give," he says, voice rough and perfectly abrasive. "Fuck, Alexei, I have so many compli—" He pulls back. I'm almost drooling and he looks scared. "Shit. I'm sorry. I should not be flirting with you."

Yes. Yes, you should. "You will. Eventually." I look right into his deep brown eyes, trying to subliminally inform him that he's my soulmate.

"Don't let me hurt you, Alexei."

"Give me more credit, Gage."

"Alexei."

"Gage."

His tongue swipes his lower lip and mine mimics the motion. We're six inches apart, both breathing like we share his bad lungs, resisting a temptation we both want to give in to but are too afraid to submit to. I don't want to push him, and he doesn't want to ruin me. We need to learn to trust each other first.

Luckily, I'm awesome at pretending I'm patient.

"There's also a non-flirting fee. Once you start giving in, I'll bring it down in ten percent increments."

"You're so expensive not to flirt with," he says.

"I know. So, to be financially smart, you should consider starting." I'm still sporting a woody, but it's manageable enough to ignore. I rip my eyes away from his with great effort, clear my throat, and say, "Okay, your home page could use a little work to showcase the newest products."

"The ones I haven't made yet?"

"Yes, those ones. So, you do that. I'll do this."

I'm not easily distracted, but focusing is hard when I know what kind of abdominals sit under that sunset orange t-shirt.

gage

10

'm trying to be chill, but I'm failing at it.

For starters, focusing on a task when someone specifically told me to focus on it is pretty much a no-go. ADHD doesn't like being told what to do, so I'm fucking around with a design that has nothing to do with my business just to make it look like I'm working on something.

Secondly, I'm mentally cataloguing all my feelings and thoughts. Natalie told me to be aware the next time Alexei turned me on, so I'm being aware. I'm hiding a hard dick by keeping the crotch of my jeans stretched wide. But I'm not rubbing. I'm not pursuing. I'm not jacking off in front of him or running to the bathroom to blow a load. I'm just fucking dandy in my aroused state. Not rushed. Not agitated. It feels good to be turned on after so long of... nothing. I almost don't want to come because I want the feeling to stick around.

I'm starting to second-guess my status as a sex addict. I got that slapped on my file for good reason, but the reasons

SOBER DOPE & SUNDAYS

have changed. Or I have. High me is a sex addict. Sober me is still trying to figure it out.

"Gage?" Alexei calls, pausing his clicking from the end of my bed.

"Yeah?"

"I can see your screen's reflection on the surface of the lamp."

I look beside me. There's a really shiny metal lamp with a flat-ass surface, like Mom thought it was cool, but not cool enough to put in a public part of the house, so it ended up here. It's glowing white with the background of my almost blank ProCreate screen.

"Stickers," I lie. "You told me to work on sticker packs."

"That one says, 'fried meats are our friends.'" His blue eyes blink at me, and fuck me, now my concealable boner is turning into an unconcealable one. Blink some more, Alexei. It's fucking adorable.

"New line I'm working on." I smirk at him. "Wanna buy one?"

"I would never condone something so sinister."

I'm printing ten of them and sticking them all over his things. Decided.

"I suck at focusing. It's just the way my head works. I'll get a random bout of inspiration, matched with high motivation and energy, fixate on it, and make a buttload of things all at once. Then I'll crash and burn and never look at them again because my executive function won't function anymore." I shrug. "Still want me to flirt with you?"

"This isn't flirting?"

I love this. I love the feeling of being cozy in my bedroom at my mom's house, not feeling at all uncomfortable about having a friend over in my room like I'm a teenager again. I've been living in a 'home to meetings to Alexei's house' bubble for the past few weeks, and sooner or later, I'm going to have to start facing my past.

"I think building this friendship with you is making me confident," I tell him.

"Tell me more about how I make you feel good." He leans against the wall. I'm at the head of the bed and he's somewhere near the end, our legs and feet skimming in the middle. I'm flirting but trying not to. I'm being subtle about it, but Alexei is smart and ridiculously observant. He knows. Wonder if he'll take ten percent off my non-flirting tax?

"I was scared to come back here. I wanted to be around my family and face the town, but... honestly, it terrifies me. And then I found you. My first sober friend, and you're difficult as fuck, but you've made everything so... simple. Being around you feels good. Like I've established some sort of stasis, and now I'm ready to get rocked a bit by facing my past."

Alexei tilts the screen down, eyes connecting to mine without making it weird. "So, you're saying I'm basically like a silky but sturdy foundation?"

"That. Yes. I love when you read my mind. What am I thinking now?"

"About meat."

"Which meat?" I ask.

"Is this you not flirting?"

I laugh. "I was thinking about fried meats, just so we're clear. I'm going to get you to eat a sausage someday."

"You're making this worse." He groans.

To save the moment and protect us from more unwanted boners, I ask, "Wanna help me face my past?"

He mouths the word yes without saying it. "What's that entail?"

"We could start by going to that diner you walked out of."

"Alright. But now this feels transactional, so I'm going to ask you for a favour, too."

"Fair."

"Let's cancel our former deal about asking intrusive questions and focus on this new deal. I bought a car three months ago."

"Your dad is a mechanic. Please do not ask me to fix it, or you won't think I'm as cool as I'm pretending to be." I beg him with my eyes.

"I want you to teach me how to drive it. Confidently."

Oh. "You don't have your licence?"

"I do. And insurance. And Triple A. But right when I bought it, I witnessed a terrible accident, and now I get nervous driving in the city. I'm fine in town. Fine on the smaller roads. A bit nervous on the highway. But very nervous when there's traffic and... lights and pedestrians and impatient drivers and big trucks and garbage trucks and people who drive with their dogs in the car and—"

"Those heathens who eat burritos while driving, right?"

"Yes! The goddamn audacity. No responsibility. There

are children on the road!" He's heated, and holy shit, it's cute. He huffs. "Do we have a deal?"

I nod, liking this. "One driving lesson for every part of my past we face. Shake on it?"

He looks at my proffered hand. "Is there fine print?"

"You can back out whenever you want. This deal has no limit and no deadline. And some things I can face myself. Or try to. My past is not your responsibility, but you're a strong friend to have around while doing it."

He takes a whole minute to think about it before nodding. "Okay." He takes my hand.

Thwack!

There goes my heart again.

He squeezes, but not too tight, and my fingers roam, sweeping across his skin. He has a few callouses from mansion renos, and his nail polish is still a bit chipped, but I watch as his fingers move between mine, the symbols on his knuckles confusing me nicely. We aren't shaking anymore. We're fiddling.

I fucking love fiddling.

"This is better than my fidget spinners," I say.

"You can play with—" His eyes meet mine. "Not flirting."

"Definitely not."

"Would never."

God, I never had all these heart-thwacking sparkly moments with Paul. Or anyone. Alexei makes me feel alight. Humming with currents of electricity. Lit up like a fucking heart monitor. Loud and beeping and obvious as fuck.

Haven't even thought about a cigarette in hours.

Bad, Gage. Do not replace one addiction with an Alexei addiction.

MARIAN KNOWS WHAT'S UP. Quilting night comes with tea, tea biscuits, a fruit platter with awesome cream cheese and marshmallow dip, and a bowl of raisins. Never been a raisins guy, but something about the quilting vibe has me plucking them out of the bowl.

"Now, Marian, why can't I get this stitch right?" I show her my tile—which is apparently what all the individual parts of the quilt are called. "I think I'm swooping when I should be looping."

She studies it. I don't know her age, but if I had to guess, I'd put her somewhere in her seventies. She's wearing copper-coloured pleather pants and a cardigan, and it doesn't get any cooler than that. Her reading glasses are the drugstore kind, but they're cat-eye and dangle on a beaded chain around her neck while she squints at my work without them.

"Ah, you've got a double loop and swoop issue. Don't worry. We can smooth it all out when we move to the sewing machines."

I'm just hand-sewing frilly things on a tile. After that, we sew all the tiles together. Cool beans. And to keep up with my hobby, Marian has already set me up with a to-go box of five thousand other square patches and frilly things to sew on before the next quilting night. The other ladies are working the sewing machines, but I have to learn the basics first.

"Gotcha. So more of a swoop and loop?"

"More of a swoop and loop." She shows me.

I pop a raisin into my mouth. "Okay, I've got it." She doesn't leave until I show her I do, in fact, got it.

"So, sweetheart, what's this buzz I hear about you and the Kopacek boy?" Pearl asks.

"He's cute, right?" I gossip, throwing more raisins into my mouth.

"I'm making this quilt for him," Nancy says. She holds it up. Baby blue and black.

"So him." I wish I had thought of that. "No deal. We're friends. He's kinda like my first real friend ever. Well, since I was a kid. Trust me, ladies, you *did not* want to know me in my teen years."

"We've heard the stories," Marian says.

My heart sinks as shame washes over me, but then Pearl pipes up.

"Like that one about how he saved the Millers' cat from the roof of the church." She chuckles.

"Or the one about how he bought all the *KitKat* bars in the whole town because his mother had a craving with the twins."

"How about that one about him staying up all night just to be at the library as soon as it opened so he could be the first one to get the new Stephen King book for his grandfather?"

"Or when he put on a whole ceremony to celebrate the twins graduating kindergarten." Marian shrieks out a laugh. "And bought Owen his first box of condoms!"

They all laugh and talk around me like I'm not even here. Meanwhile, I'm just having a mental breakdown because... people know good stories about me? Here? Some of those are even from my bad teen years. I'm on the verge of tears, wondering why the hell these lovely ladies are so nice when I've literally put my mom through hell and back, and they're supposed to be her friends.

It's all weighing on me very heavily because... I'm more than just a junkie. I have a past that isn't all about drugs and sex and crimes. I'm known for funny and kind things as well as bad things, and I never fucking realized that until this very moment.

I'm more than an addict.

Holy shit.

"Oh, hun," Pearl says. "Have some more tea."

"Yes, please." I try not to cry into my quilt tiles, shoving biscuits, raisins, and fruit dip in my mouth to swallow down the relieved sobs.

alexei

11

I'm not a huge fan of feeling conflicted about things.

I make plans and execute them. I stick to what I'm interested in, know where I stand, and have an iron will about pretty much everything. Life taught me to prepare, fear made me a bit anal retentive about it, and my neurotic mind just appreciates organization and planning.

But now my interests are conflicted. It's the middle of a Wednesday, and usually I'm focused and productive, knocking out client demands and completing my online jobs. But on this particular Wednesday, I'm thinking about tile grout. More specifically, which colour of grout would look best in the upstairs, west side, third bedroom bathroom. It's one of four bathrooms on the second floor, and I love it in there. Dad's letting me have free rein.

And it's confusing. Because I'm not the kind of guy who thinks about tile grout on a Wednesday afternoon. Maybe a Sunday, but definitely not a Wednesday.

Alexei <3: Want to go to the city with me after our dinner date? I need grout.

Gage: Shh. I'm working.

Gage: Do you know Morse code? Look out your window.

I do. And see nothing but the couple who own the sex shop chatting with the parents of the happy foster home.

Gage: I'm flashlight signalling you.

Alexei: It's daylight...

Gage: You're no fun. Yes, I'll go to the city with you after our dinner/friend date ;) I need to score some needles.

Gage: For sewing.

Gage: That's addict humour. Was it funny?

Alexei <3: No.

Gage: Pick me up at 18:30 in your fancy car. Xoxoxox

He'll hug and kiss me in text form, but I've not experienced it body to body yet.

I set my phone down, try not to think about grout, and focus on work. But again, my mind is elsewhere. It's on Gage and his flashlight signals. Does he really know Morse code, and if so, what message was he sending?

Why do I hate my job today? Am I distracted because it's almost May 17th?

Why am I maybe realizing that I don't love my job as much as I tell myself I do? Am I seriously so set in my ways that I can't even admit when something I used to enjoy isn't as enjoyable anymore?

I blow out a slow breath and get back to work. Gage and grout can wait.

GAGE ONCE MENTIONED that I dress a little gothy, but the goth vibe isn't why I wear black. I wear black because it's easy to be deceptive in.

Black hides sweat, spills, and intent. So, because it can be both classy and bummy, Gage won't know that I dressed up in my best dark look just to impress him. He doesn't have to know the intent behind my outfit because I know it, and that's enough for me.

Black pants with a black button-up might come across as effort, but the black zip-up hoodie I layer on top gives it a casual mood. I *feel* classy; Gage will *see* casual. It's the perfect illusion. I feel masculine and confident and awkward and it's great.

I wasn't expecting the nerves, though. It's just dinner at a diner that holds a part of his past, and he was very insistent that I knew it was a friend date, but in my head, it's a real date. And it's the first one I've ever had. I'm nervous about that.

More than that, I'm nervous about being seen in town with Gage. Not because of his past or who he is, but because of who I am. While I'm not usually one to worry about what other people think of me, I'm worrying about what they're going to think of Gage for being on a non-date date with me. I'm the weird guy around town. He's the former cool guy. What sort of pairing do we make? I'm cool with being weird, but is Gage cool with me being weirdly cool?

We aren't wine and cheese or peanut butter and banana. We're more like the egg white and the yolk: we belong in the same shell but are made up of completely different compositions. He's the yolk.

Because this is a date in my head, I walk to his front door and knock. One of the twins opens the door, and Slash stands behind him, staring me up and down to assess my worthiness.

"Hey," Nick says. "What're your intentions with my brother?"

I know he's being witty, but I answer anyway. "To convince him that this is a real date without actually stating so."

Nick laughs. "Good luck. He's trying pretty hard to pretend like he isn't into you."

"I know."

"Gage! Alexei is here!" To me, he adds, "Wanna come in?"

Just as I step through the door, Gage practically trips down the stairs, shirt half on, abs and chest on display, jeans slung low on his hips with the button still undone. Hair messy from a shower, dark and damp. He hasn't shaved, and I like the stubble that lines his jaw almost as much as I like his abs. And his chest. Which is tattooed with mechanical looking things, real steam-punk style. That surprises me.

"You're staring," he says to me, grinning.

"I'm wondering how an anti-athlete gets definition like that. Doesn't work for me."

"Genetics." He shrugs. "Too bad Nick got all the wrong genes."

Nick punches Gage and steals his shirt before he can get it all the way on, buying me a few more minutes of shirtless staring. Nick smiles at me like we're in cahoots before running away with it.

"Mind if I wear this?" Gage asks, smiling wide, showing me his naked torso.

"Not even a little."

Because I'm not nervous or worried about what anyone will think anymore. I'm not daydreaming about tile grout or Morse code. I'm looking at a body I want to be all over, seeing the man of my fate bare before me, impressive and sexy. I'm too busy being attracted to a body I desire, matching the imperfect perfection of it to Gage's personality, wondering how I'm going to be patient enough to let him realize we're soulmates all on his own.

And maybe, in the back of my mind, I'm thinking about

sex addiction recovery and how I can support him in that while wanting him as badly as I do.

"You look good, Alexei," he says, drawing my attention from his chest tats to his face. "Really good."

"Friend-like?"

"Mm, so companionable, yes. Totally innocent and entirely platonic thoughts are running through my head right now."

"Same." I link my fingers behind my back. "Feel free to show me your cool attic bedroom again."

Gage laughs. "Careful, Alexei. Hang on a sec."

While he runs off to fetch his shirt, I face the front door and adjust myself. It's going to be one of those nights where my dick goes up and down and annoys the living hell out of me. His companionable thoughts need to take a turn soon.

When we get to the diner, Gage acts fairly normal. He's not locked up and tense like the first time we walked in here, but he's not happy-go-lucky either. He's attentive and reserved, and when we pick a booth near the back, he flops onto the bench and stares straight at the circular booth to our left.

Across from him, I keep my hands on my lap and try not to look disgusted by the smell of all the greasy food. This is not my typical establishment. In all honesty, I'm not a fan of restaurant eating. I prefer to prepare my meals at home, even if they come from a meal subscription box.

Gage orders Pepsi to my water and a burger with fries to my chicken salad with lemon wedges. When the food comes, he scarfs and I chew.

"Right there, in that booth, I got a handie under the table while I was rolling way too hard to even really notice. Maybe it was a blowjob. I can't even remember."

I look at the circular booth. So unsanitary.

"I spent a lot of time in this diner in high school. I'd be mostly drunk when I got here, high on something by the time I left, and probably paid for less than half of the meals I ate here. I had like three different friend groups at that time. One was artsy, and I liked being around them because they were inspiring, but when my buzz wore off, I always reverted to the other two groups. The one that just drank and partied like normal teens, and then the other one... the one that kept encouraging my habits."

"You blame your friend group?" I ask, picking at my salad.

"Nah." He wipes his lips with the back of his wrist and swigs some Pepsi. "But I kept hanging around them because they didn't judge me for the shit I did. When you wanna get high, it's always more fun to be around other people who wanna get high. Makes you feel less shitty about yourself. Like, everyone else is doing it, so I'm not so bad."

He looks at the plastic cup, almost empty.

"First time I've eaten here without spiking my drink." He smiles, but it's a reserved one that means he thinks himself pathetic. "Tastes better this way. You don't drink pop?"

"I've had ginger ale for an upset stomach."

"You have no vices?" he asks, appalled.

"Not really. I just cope."

"What about pleasure? Like... do you ever have an ice cream cone just because you're craving one?"

"I don't really crave sweets. If you must know, my food choice for guilty pleasures is popcorn. And yes, I put butter and salt on it. I also enjoy a shrimp cocktail every now and then."

Gage laughs, looking beautiful and bright. "You're so wild, Alexei. You never indulge?"

"Not really."

"Ever heard of moderation?" he asks.

"How has moderation worked out for you in the past?"

"Touché." He sighs.

"That wasn't an insult. I'm just aware. Addictive instincts can run in families, and since I had two drug-addicted parents, I try to avoid whatever I can. I'm not afraid of bad food, and I don't judge others for eating it. Well, except you because you're already pretty unhealthy. But the benefits I would get from consuming an unhealthy diet aren't worth the mental health implications they'd cause me. I don't love a burger enough to eat one often. Milkshakes make me feel way too full, so I just get water. I don't feel like I'm missing out on the 'guilty pleasures' you speak of. I feel more like I'm avoiding a bloated and bogged down feeling. I prefer my way. You prefer yours. That's okay."

Gage sets down the last bite of his burger and stares at the single fry left on his plate. "I do feel pretty bloated and bogged down. But I wouldn't have stopped because I finish things. I don't think about the feeling afterward. I just eat."

"I know. How's it feel to be here?"

He looks around again, taking the whole place in. The grimy but well-loved counter, all the pies and desserts behind the glass case, the little window that shows a peek into the kitchen, and the other patrons dining. He spares another glance at the circular booth before looking right at me, eye contact and everything.

"Like... like maybe I'm over that phase of life." He's reluctant to admit it because he doesn't want to give himself false hope, but that impresses me because it means he's determined yet realistic. He's self-aware, and what is sexier than being self-aware? "Like maybe the eighth time really is the charm."

I've wanted to ask this since I found out he's been to rehab that many times. "What kind of person goes to rehab eight times? That's not... very common. One time, maybe two or three, before the person decides it's not for them and they try another method."

"Or overdose," he adds. Pushing his last bite and last fry away, he leans back and fiddles with his cup on the table. "Because I think I'm a bad addict. I'm pretty fucking awesome at coming up with excuses to use, reasoning with myself that it's just one more time, how bad can it be, right? But deep down, I'm scared. Always have been. Despite how many times I've almost died because of myself, I don't really want to."

I nod, encouraging him to go on. He's so fascinating. The reasons behind actions are my favourite part of a person.

"So, Mom threw rehab at me that first time. I went, and

even though I already had one foot out the door and didn't take it too seriously, it gave me a safety blanket. Like, okay, I'm a fucking mess, but this is always an option. It's here, waiting for me, ready to keep me alive when I can't do it myself. So whenever I went to rehab, I guess it was when I was feeling like... if I stayed away, I'd die."

My chest cinches. "So, to protect yourself from yourself?"

"Yeah. That." He nods. "It's stupid, and I failed at it so many times, but... I'm still here. So those eight torturous detoxes and states of withdrawal were worth it. This is the longest I've been sober since I was fourteen."

"And the longest time you spent in rehab? A whole year, right? Is that common?" I ask.

"No. Not common. I guess the rehab portion was only a few months, but I stayed at the facility for a year by choice. Almost like a wellness retreat," he says, laughing a bit. "But not that calm wellness you see in movies. It was hell, but it made me stronger, especially with the sex portion, and I dunno. I'm glad I stayed a year. I needed to hit that milestone while there this time."

"Feel good about it?"

"Yes and no. Proud but pressured. I hate measuring things in lengths of time. Makes me feel like there's an expiration date on it, so it gives me this urge to ruin the timeline so I can stop feeling so much pressure."

I remember my dad saying something like that, too. Back when I didn't believe a word out of his mouth and always assumed he'd fail. Now that Gage has expressed the feeling of pressure it brings, and I'm in a state of mind to listen and understand, I realize that *I* was the pressure my dad didn't need. I assumed his failure. I brought up lengths of time. I doubted every minor-to-me but monumental-to-him accomplishment and undermined it with a doubtful thought that he'd never hit the next one.

"You should talk to my dad about that," I tell Gage. "I think he felt something similar, and he started measuring progress in projects instead. *If I can complete this project, it's a win.* But he'd already have his next project aligned by the time the current one ended, so it felt like he was hitting milestones without the 'now what?' feeling attached at the end of them."

Gage's eyes are still on mine when he smiles, looking down at where my hands are hidden beneath the table. "Thank you. But fuck, I'm sick of everything being about me and my recovery. Tell me something about you."

I inhale, and on the exhale, decide to tell him about my lack of focus. "I think I'm starting to lose interest in my job. I don't know. I'm a pretty easy person to please, and it's not like I have a lot of issues I need to work through. Bit of an irrational fear that my dad is just gonna die like my mom did, even though I know he's healthy now. But it's my control freak personality that's messing me up a bit lately. Like, I don't enjoy my job, but I've told myself I need to, so I'm struggling to accept that I am going against my own rules." Whoa, there it is.

"You can still be in control even when your interests and passions change. That's allowed, you know?"

"I'm trying to accept that, yes." I nod.

"I wanna hold your hand right now, Alexei."

Do it. Please fucking do it.

It's a biological response to a mental reaction, but I'm thankful I wore black because my body flushes and I break out in a light sweat. Not many things have the ability to make me sweat, but Gage is disrupting all the firm lines I thought I knew about myself. I'm tongue-tied, too, which is new for me.

"So, let's get out of here before I do it," he adds, deflating the moment, but not enough to cool me down. He makes it worse when he adds, "I'm paying. You can shut up about your power imbalances."

Further proof that this is a real date. I knocked on his door, picked him up, sat across from him as we shared a meal, and now he's paying. He's slow to pick up on the cues that we're starting a relationship, so I inform him. "This is very date-like behaviour, Gage."

"Mhm." He grins, hiding it from me. "Or I'm just a nice guy taking my web designer out for a meal because I'm trying to get you to drop the non-flirting tax."

"I won't be fooled by bribery, so I'll pay for my own." I reach for my wallet.

Gage. Touches. My. Wrist.

Skin to skin. Fingers wrapped around my knobby wrist bones. Fires are burning and black clothing is essential, and despite how cliché it is, sparks are floating around everywhere, threatening to combust this whole diner and the grease in the air. Because Gage is touching me, and I'm more certain than ever that he's my soulmate.

He's looking at me, and his lips are moving with spoken words, but I'm not hearing anything he's saying about me not paying and him actually flirting because he's still touching me. Gage already had a relapse in a coffee shop when the window exploded, and I don't want him in further distress when this diner blows up from our tension, so I look down at where he's touching me, trying to rationalize it.

It's just his hand on mine. His skin against mine. He's touched my hand before. People touch all the time and nothing happens, so I don't know why I'm making such a big deal out of it while standing here with a completely stoic face. But my world is turning and my axis is tilting, and every fundamental part of me is changing.

Because I understand addiction now.

All my years of trying to get to the bottom of chasing a high and getting caught in a loop of ups and downs are making sense. I'd chase this feeling forever. The feeling that brings my blood to life and opens new parts of my brain. An effervescent moment of clairvoyance like I'm not actually supposed to have this super ability to feel things this ferociously. Everything before this touch felt good. Everything after it will pale in comparison. I'll try to find it again forever.

Gage finishes saying whatever he was saying, offering a smile before he drops my wrist. I look down again, wondering if I can see the tether that stretches between him and I. Because the intensity of the moment has faded, but

I'm still tingling. Warmth battles coldness, and I'm in the middle. My sweat is the condensation, the result of a tick in time, signalling my transfer from 'before' to 'after' Gage Rossum touched me on a date.

"Alexei?" Gage's voice comes back online through my muffled hearing. "I asked if you wanted anything for the road? A dessert?"

Maybe the new me is someone who gets dessert now. "Chocolate," I mumble, completely dazed and unsure why I say it. Do I want chocolate?

I don't know what he ends up getting, but I'm following him and a bakery paper bag out the front door into the evening hues.

"Rossum! Rossum, is that you?"

Our moment—or maybe just my moment—shatters when Gage stiffens.

12

gage

Feeling panic in a sober state isn't something I've experienced in a long time. High me would have faced this guy from my past, shot the shit with him, recognized the fact that he was about to string me along on a trip I'd go on willingly, and have a good night followed by a terrible morning. But the new me is unsure where I stand.

I can't judge this guy. Because *I am* this guy. I've been this guy for over twelve years.

I can't be high and mighty around him because that was the worst way for someone to act around me when I was struggling on my wayward path. Paul, my ex, did that a lot.

But now I'm stone-cold sober with a full gut and sparkly hope about a future that's fun and enjoyable, maybe with a neurotic gay rambler at my side, and I don't know where 'past me' meets 'future me' and combines with 'present me.'

And Alexei is here, and despite how deeply he understands addiction and has lived through the agony of it, I'm trying to impress him regardless of how adamant I was about not flirting. I'm flirting! And now my past is flirting dangerously with me.

"Hey, man," I say.

Hey, man? Jesus. I don't want to be around this guy anymore, but at the same time, he's the whole reason I came back to town. He's a part of that friend group I just told Alexei about, the one that liked to get high. He looks high right now, and I hate that there's an itch inside me, petty and jealous about it. I forgot what it looked like. Almost forgot what it felt like. It looks horrible but feels awesome, and fuck... I'm craving it a bit.

"You back?" Brian asks, looking from me to Alexei, barely sparing him a glance. "I heard you were back, but you never came around." He smacks my arm playfully.

I don't know how to act.

"Yeah, back," I say, unsure if I want to shift closer to Alexei to use him as a safety net or turn my back on him altogether so he doesn't see the cravings in my eyes. "Uh, just got out of rehab not too long ago." There. It's out there. I'm sober.

Please don't offer me anything.

Please do.

"Oh, good for you, man." He doesn't mean it. It's something other still-using users say to show a little recognition, but in the back of his mind, he's already planning what he'll give me when I predictably go crawling to wherever he's about to invite me. His celebratory drug. "Stop by my place sometime. Me and Becky are living in my dad's old place."

There it is. The invitation I need to refuse but don't know how to.

Brian and Becky are a pretty solid couple, considering their lifestyle. Becky is actually smart as a whip, but drugs have dulled her, and Brian is skilled with his hands when they don't shake. They bond well because they get high together well. I've never had that. Never wanted it.

But Alexei...

Instead of answering Brian's invitation, I step beside Alexei and bump him with my shoulder. "This is Alexei. Not sure if you know each other."

"Yeah, hey," Brian says dismissively. Because Alexei is standing in the way of Brian having one more drug buddy.

Alexei nods but says nothing. My hand lands on his lower back, out of sight, and I think I'm shaking. Or trembling. Or maybe I'm entirely still, and I just feel wobbly inside.

"Stop by!" Brian says, backing away. "Awesome to have ya back, Rossum!"

And then he's gone, and I'm staring, numb but oversensitive, unsure where to go or how to take a single step off this cracked sidewalk. Then Alexei shifts from foot to foot, reminding me that my hand is on his back.

Oh. That's nice. That feels better. I look at him, not sure if I'm about to say something or just settle myself with the sight of him. The blue of his eyes perfectly matches the hue of his hair in this lighting, and my god, pale blue is my forever favourite colour now. Icy yet calm. So Alexei.

"Still want to get grout?" I ask him, trying to break out of the moment.

"Yeah," he answers, but he's pressing his phone to my ear and it's ringing. I place my hand on top of his, holding it there just so I can touch him.

"Hey, Alex," Nathan answers.

Oh.

"Alex?"

"I think I need help," I say. Admit. Confess.

I\'s one in the morning, and after he got back from getting grout on his own, Alexei went to bed at ten because 'a good sleep routine is essential to optimal health,' but I'm drinking my fourth coffee at the kitchen table with Nathan. And loving that Alexei still went to get grout without me. He won't allow me to let him down, and that... helps me feel like less of a loser.

"You're avoiding," Nathan says. "You know avoidance isn't a good method."

I know that! And he's not talking about Brian and Becky and stopping by for celebratory drugs. He's talking about home. I won't go there.

"I don't want them to see me like this." I spin my mug, reading the quote on the ceramic. *Apparently, Rock Bottom has a basement.* I don't know if this is Nathan's funny way of talking about his hard times or if it's Alexei's warped sense of humour and lack of filter about literally everything, but it makes me feel better to read it.

"They're your family, Gage. They know you, and they're here to support you."

"My mom, maybe. But the twins shouldn't have to worry about me. None of them should have to worry about me. Like fuck, all I did was run into a guy on the street, and it rendered me so useless I couldn't even give Alexei his driving lesson in the city!" My mug tilts, spilling tepid coffee on the dark countertop.

"He asked you for that?" Nathan asks, surprised. "Nevermind. This is about you. I know you want to shield your brothers, but they aren't stupid. They want to know you. Even the rough bits."

I know he's right, but I don't feel ready to see them yet. Mom knows where I am. She knows I'm safe and alive and not dead on a bathroom floor somewhere, so at least I can give myself a point for that. Even if it was Nathan's idea to call and let her know.

"I know. I just need a minute or something. Can I sleep in one of your sixteen spare bedrooms?"

He laughs. "Anytime, yeah. But first, take a minute to be proud. You got triggered. You called."

Alexei called. Would I if he hadn't? Or would I have gone to the city with him because I felt obligated to, ruined his night, and fucked up his grout and his driving even more? If I'd been alone when I ran into Brian, would I have followed him home and taken whatever he offered? Hypotheticals aren't my friend, so I try not to overthink it.

"Am I ever going to get to a point where seeing random people on the street doesn't send me into a tailspin?" I ask.

"You will. Takes time, and to be honest, you're just starting to face it all. It's gonna hurt. It's gonna rattle you. But you're strong, and you have a good family at your back."

But I've always had a good family at my back. I fucked up most of my life with a good family at my back. But maybe Nathan is right; I am stronger now. I think. I have some hope and a lot of determination. But...

"I got jealous of his high," I admit. "I saw his eyes and recognized the way he was acting, and it brought me right back to feeling that way, and I wanted it. Really bad."

"Go stare at the bathroom floor, the toilet, the sink, and try to remember what the downside of it feels like. We like to remember the high of the high, but we block out the low of the low in order to justify it. It's normal. When I first got sober, I looked through photo albums of Alex. I didn't take those photos. His mom didn't take them. They were from a neighbour who babysat him. They were my low point because I missed every single one of those memories. Someone else got to witness them. What'd you miss when you were puking your guts up?"

What'd I miss? The high. So I kept on chasing it.

But life-wise? My brothers. I missed most of their lives because they're so much younger than me and I spent most of their lifetime being a mess. I think they blame me for Dad leaving, even though they won't say it. A teen junkie, another teen doing well, and twin kids isn't easy, and he left because of it. But so did I...

"You're right. I left them just like my dad did." I stand. "I missed Nick and Cole. And Owen. I'm gonna go creep on them."

"You're going home?" Nathan asks.

Yeah, to spy on my brothers while they sleep so I can drink in parts of their lives I've never experienced before. Creepy? Yeah. But I'm gonna roll with it. "Yeah, but first, I'm gonna go take a pee in the upstairs bathroom. The one right inside Alexei's room..."

Nathan pins me with a hard look. "Hurt him, I'll end you."

"I'm trying to be platonic."

"How's that working?"

Not awesome. Harder than I thought. "I know I'm not worthy of him..."

"You are. But he's everything to me, and I'll protect him from anyone. You. Other men. Life. Everything."

"I know."

"And don't let him push you. You're still a sex addict in recovery, Gage."

"No sex," I say, meaning it. I've got a ways to go in understanding my impulses and lack of impulses when it comes to sex.

He stares for another minute before turning off the kitchen light. He nods at the stairs to give me permission to see Alexei and adds, "Lock the front door on your way out."

"Thank you. For... just thanks."

It's hard to sneak around in an old mansion. Every step creaks, and all the floorboards in the hallway groan, but I make it to his door. I know for a fact the hinges squeal, so I'm happy to find it open. I thought he'd be the type to sleep straight on his back with an eye mask or something, but he's all sprawled out, blankets tangled everywhere, one foot hanging off the edge of the bed.

Fucking adorable.

Bare chest. Bare feet. Blankets blocking everything else.

Fucking sexy.

"Are your thoughts still platonic?" he asks, making me jump.

"Fuck, Alexei! I thought you were asleep."

"I was. I have a weird ability to go straight from deep sleep to wide awake in an instant." He pulls his leg back, tucking it under the blankets. "Instinct from the days I watched over my parents, I guess. Why are you standing over me like a creepy ghost?"

"I thought I was throwing out more of a guardian angel vibe?" I sit on the edge of his bed.

Alexei blinks at me through the dimness of the room. His glossy eyes reflect the moonlight glinting off the mirror of his dresser. "What're you doing in here?"

"I can't have sex with you," I blurt, but he doesn't look shocked. "Yet. I want to."

"You want to?" He lifts a brow.

"Yes. I really want to. But... it was a date, okay? I took you to the diner and paid because it was a date, and I don't want to pretend that it wasn't because I want to date you even though you can do a million times better than me and

I'm the last person you should be dating. Remember all that stuff I said about ruining your life?"

"Vividly."

"Well, I don't want to do that, but I tend to have a shady track record, so... I might. By accident. So, before you go and plant me in the boyfriend box, you should slap a bunch of caution tape all over me and set warning alarms or something."

"You think I haven't done that?" He sits up, facing me with his back against the headboard. The blankets pool at his hips, and... *motherfucker.*

Alexei's smooth, naked torso glows in the moonlight is going into the arousal journal.

"Have you?"

"Do you know me at all?" He huffs. "I am suspicious by nature. I have trust issues. In my world, you are guilty until proven innocent. I have categorized your red flags and made subcategories under them, filed them with sticky tabs about warning signs and all your tells. I have you annotated in my mind, Gage. Give me more credit than that. You know I'm neurotic."

I laugh. "Good. Because neurotic is exactly what I need in a future boyfriend."

"Not so distant future." Alexei's eyes meet mine. "Are you going to kiss me now?"

Fuck, I want to. "No, but you told me to let you know how I make out with being aware of my arousal, right? I'm turned on, Alexei. You turn me on. And since I'm allowed to jerk off now, maybe I'll go home and do that while thinking about you. I'll show you the entry in my journal tomorrow."

He wets his lips and bunches the blanket around his lap. "You better be a detailed writer."

"I am." I grin at him, and when I lean in, listening to his breath stop, I exhale against his cheek before planting a soft kiss there. "Goodnight, Alexei."

"Goodnight, Gage."

Okay, full-on raging boner by the time I make it to the front door, locking it behind me like Nathan told me to. New plan: jerk off over memories of Alexei, write a journal essay, *and then* go appreciate the lives of my brothers while they sleep.

alexei

13

"H ello?" I answer my phone.

"Don't answer. I'm hanging up and calling again."

"Why?"

"Because. I'm going to leave you a voicemail," Gage says. "Hurry and hang up so I can call again."

"Why not just tell me whatever you want to say?"

"Because. I'm chickening out of saying it straight to your ear. I need to talk to a machine. Hang up. I miss you, but hang up."

I hang up, and when Gage's name flashes across the screen, it kills me a little not to answer it. Because I'm counting seconds and staring at my phone like a loser, three whole minutes go by before a voicemail notification pops up. Before I can listen to it, Gage calls again.

"Am I allowed to answer this time?"

"Delete that."

"No."

"Alexei! I should have asked if you're the type to be filthy-romanced via voice or in the written form. I forget how to date. I'm doing it all wrong."

"You left me a filthy romantic message?" I ask, already flushing with anticipation.

"Yeah, I read you my journal entry. But now I'm wondering if I should have just given you the journal. So? How do you wanna be wooed? Vocal or written?"

"And you're too chicken to read it to me in person?"

Gage groans, but fuck me, it's a sexy sound. "Yes, I'm too afraid I'll actually try to... I'm not at the filthy, sexy romance portion of my recovery yet. It can't be in person. Not until I talk to my... yeah, just... listen to it, okay? And then call me back."

There's that sexy self-awareness again. "Okay."

"Okay," he says, breathless.

"Okay," I repeat.

Dead silence on the line. We're both holding our breath. I don't know why I'm not hanging up.

"Okay," he says again. "Three. Two. Two. Two."

"One." I smile as I end the call.

Dad's not home, and I should be working, but instead, I take my phone to my room, close the door, and hesitate. Because the natural progression of a relationship isn't supposed to go this way. We're supposed to flirt, touch a little, tease and taunt, kiss for the first time and set our worlds on fire. I'm not supposed to hear the gritty details of his arousal journal before I've even kissed him, but then again, maybe dating Gage Rossum is different from dating anyone else. Yes, because he's a recovering sex addict, but also just because... he's Gage Rossum. And I'm Alexei Kopacek, a proud weird guy. Neither of us is traditionally normal, so it makes me smile shyly to know that our relationship isn't normal. Normal is boring. What even is normal?

I pick up my phone. Unlock it. Click the phone icon and toggle over to the voicemail part. Hover my thumb over the button. Stalling. Anticipating. Building.

Gage's name flashes across the screen instead, calling me again.

"Forget something?" I answer.

"Have you listened yet?" He's breathless. Frantic.

"No."

"Don't. I have a better idea. I'm coming over." He hangs up.

Oh no. *Oh yes?*

"I LIKE THE GROUT," Gage says, forcing me into my favourite bathroom. "The dark tones will look good with the dark tiles."

"Did you seriously come over here to talk to me about grout while there's a filthy romantic arousal journal entry sitting in my voicemail inbox?"

Gage steers me from behind, closing the bathroom door behind us. "No, but if you do this grout work without me, we're gonna have our first real fight. Did you bring the speaker?"

I hold up the portable Bluetooth speaker he demanded I bring. Gage looks at it, nods, runs his hands through his dark hair, and blows out a breath.

"I have an idea."

I love ideas. And I love how much effort it's taking him to pretend to be chill about it. His sweatpants are rumpled and his t-shirt is on inside out, but that just adds a certain allure to the vibrant picture he's painting.

"Go on."

"I wanna listen to it together. While watching each other," he says, looking nervous.

"No."

"What? Why?" He sags.

"Because you just told me we can't do it in person because you're not at the filthy—"

"Yeah, I know. But I have a plan for that part." He nods to the walk-in glass shower. "I'm putting a barrier between us. I just want to watch you, Alexei. I want you to watch me. To see me." He steps forward, so close to me I can smell that same laundry detergent and the subtle hint of cigarettes. "Because I tried so hard not to flirt, and now I'm flirting while being horrible at it, and I want you to know... fuck, I want you to know what you do to me." He swallows, and my peripheral vision watches his throat roll while my eyes stay on his. "Because I'm so fucking into you, Alexei, but I'm trying to be responsible about it. Because you're..."

Important. He wants to tell me I'm important, and it

means everything to me. Not because he thinks it, but because he *knows* it. I *am* important, but so is his recovery.

"Dating me is going to be hard," he says instead. "And I won't blame you if you change your mind. You deserve—"

"Don't presume to know what I deserve," I say, backing up until my ass hits the vanity. I sit on it, feet dangling. "Come here."

Gage steps between my legs, hands dutifully balled into responsible fists at his sides. His eyes are wide, almost scared, but there's an excitement in them that empowers me. He's a thrill-seeker, but he's not seeking a thrill right now. His vulnerability is seeking validation. I love it.

"How many people have you had sex with?" I ask, the inside of my knees brushing against his hips.

"A lot. Too many."

"How many have you kissed?"

His eyebrows furrow, and he tilts his head. "Uh... not that many."

"So, sex was more freely given than kissing was?" I ask, already knowing the answer.

"Yeah, I guess. Kissing is more... personal. More intimate. And when I'm drunk and high and horny as hell, I'm chasing an orgasm, not intimacy."

For the first real time, I touch him. I wrap my fingers around his wrists and gently work his fists free. When his hands relax, I twine our fingers together slowly, exploring him. Gage's eyes drop, watching our hands, exploring with me. I let him watch, taking my time, living in that spark of vibrancy that started when he touched me at the diner. It's more subtle now, and it's because the mood is more tender, more raw. When his eyes meet mine again, I set his hands flat on my thighs.

"We can chase orgasms if you want, and only when you're ready," I say. "But it's the intimacy I'm after. You can get me off with voicemails and arousal journals. You can touch me and tease me and make me watch you. You can confer with your therapist and make sure you're on track and that I'm helping you in a healthy way."

I reach up and wrap my fingers around the back of his neck, pulling his face down to mine. Our noses touch and our foreheads brush, and Gage's breath hitches in his throat while mine just breathes through the moment. He wets his lips and I lick mine, and then I turn and lean in, my lips brushing his cheek.

Against his ear, I whisper, "And when chasing an orgasm isn't enough for you anymore, I want you to kiss me. We're going backwards, Gage. Make me come first and kiss me after. But when you do, when you give in and kiss me, you better be ready for the level of intimacy I'm after."

Gage's exhale comes out as a groan. He leans his temple against the side of my head, locked in restraint but taking in my words. His hands travel up my thighs, caressing and squeezing until he gets to my hips.

When he turns his head, his lips against my cheek, he says, "I'm fucking dying to kiss you now."

He almost does it—tries to do it—but I press two fingers to his lips to stop him. He kisses them anyway, pressed up against my lips, eyes closed and chest panting.

"Press play," he demands.

With his forehead still against mine, I press play. The sound of his voice comes from the speaker, filling the bathroom with the husky yet jittery timbre that proves he was as nervous as he was excited when he left the voicemail.

"Entry number eighteen. Alexei's smooth, naked chest glows in the moonlight."

"Get in the shower," I tell him, my dick already getting excited just from his first words. I'm a master of discipline and the gatekeeper to my self-control, but Gage tempts my willpower.

"I will. Give me a minute," he says, while the recording says, "Fucking hell. To see him in bed, asleep and cute, was the first thing that turned me on. Then he moved, and the blankets dropped down to his hips. Fuck me, his body is... I want to wrap myself around him and feel him everywhere. He's all hard and tattooed and manly, and...fuck. My cock was so hard when I kissed his cheek, and to hear the way he held his breath made it fucking leak."

"Gage," I warn, speaking against his cheek. I pause the voicemail.

"I won't touch you," he promises. And then his hands are moving up my thighs and his fingers are popping open my fly, contradicting his words. His eyes meet mine and his lip gets tugged between his teeth, and goddammit, the backs of his knuckles graze my hard cock. "Will you touch yourself?" he asks, moving my hand to rest on my dick.

I'm not shy, but I'm not fearless, either. I'm scared, but excited about it. Sex has only ever been a transactional thing for me. Meet someone, hook-up, have a good time, go home. I've never performed or been watched. I've never jacked off in front of someone. I've never been the centre of attention or at the mercy of someone else's demands. But Gage, whether he knows it yet or not, is my soulmate, and despite how intimidated I am, I'm even more frantic to have this experience.

I nod, wiggling my fingers under where he holds them. "Will you? Can you?"

He pushes his forehead to mine, groans, and then pushes off me. Backing away until he's in the shower with the glass door closed, he rubs the crotch of his pants, showing me how affected he is.

"Fuck yeah, I can," he says. He sits on the stone bench in the shower, legs spread, hand rubbing. I mimic him, feeling the outline of my cock through the material of my pants. "Press play."

My blue eyes on his brown ones, hands on our own dicks, I press play and lean back against the mirror. While Gage's recording sets the scene, describing all the ways he felt when he saw me in bed, admitting to himself that he wanted me, and recalling the mess of my hair and the way the moonlight reflected off my glossy eyes, I rub myself through my pants and feel my body warm, a slow build of heat that matches the flush tinting Gage's cheeks.

"I wanted to pin him to his bed and force him to look me in the eye while I fed him my cock. Ah, fuck. His lips would stretch around me, and he'd whimper and drool and silently beg for more."

Through the recording, I can hear the desperation in his tone. In front of me, I can see the pure lust in his eyes and the way he's imagining it again now. Picturing me sprawled out beneath him, his ass on my chest and his cock down my throat. I grip my dick hard and Gage notices. Before he can dare me to, I reach inside my pants and boxer-briefs, unsure if I want to keep myself hidden from him to taunt him or if taunting a sex addict is a bad idea.

Gage beats me to it. His sweats are pulled down, and right there, in his firm grip, is his hard cock. He strokes, the tip already glistening, his touch careful but experienced.

"And when his begging could no longer stay silent, he'd take charge. Push me off him. And demand what he wants."

He knows me. He knows I'm not a pushover.

I pull my cock free and let him watch me stroke it. His eyes glaze while my neck heats, and when his voice continues to fill the bathroom with the perfect imagery, reality makes it even better.

Our hands work in synchronization. Our chests heave with the same laboured breaths. Our hips gyrate, phantom fucking through six feet of space and a glass wall.

"And when I came, it was because I imagined Alexei looking down at me, taking exactly what he wanted. Me. Because no one has ever wanted me like Alexei wants me. And I can't wait for us to fuck."

My eyes flutter and my orgasm builds. Gage's lips are slick with spit, and when his hand drops all the way down to the base, a pulse of cum spurts from the tip of his cock, landing on his abs.

"Fuck, I want you, Alexei," he says here and now.

My hand follows the path his took. Circling the tip, I slide all the way down to the base, and my orgasm hits like a slow-building storm. The tremors start first, the shaking comes next, and the toe-curling mingles with it all. I force my eyes open to watch him come, coating my own stomach in a release I couldn't have stopped if I tried.

"I want you so fucking bad, Alexei," the recording says.

"Oh, fuck," I moan, choking out an exhale while my mind goes calm and my body tenses everywhere.

"You're goddamn gorgeous," Gage says. "My god."

I'd tell him he was too, if I knew how to speak. I'm all jumbled up and stupid-calm, but boneless and shivering. I slump against the mirror and watch Gage's abs glisten with his cum, drooling to lick him clean. Those abs...

"Tell me what you're thinking," he prompts, still breathing hard.

What I'm thinking? My thoughts are background music. They're there, but I can't catch them. They're running a million miles a minute but aren't in a rush to get anywhere. I can't slow them. I can't stop them. I can't even remind them to make themselves clear and obvious. They're just in there, alive and thriving, but I'm not actively thinking about any of them.

So, I blurt, "I know we're doing everything backwards, but I'm trying not to fall in love with you so soon."

Instead of being spooked, Gage laughs. "Don't try too hard." He smirks.

gage

14

I'm sewing frilly things on quilting tiles when Mom walks in the front door. I promised her I'd go to the forge with her, but I was too tired and wanted to hit a meeting then quilt instead. She smells like fire, has black smudges all over her arms and face, and drops her purse and all its contents right on the kitchen floor.

It brings me back to the coffee place and that barista's purse. It feels like so long ago, but the memory is so vivid and terrifying. Great. Just fucking great. I'm triggered by dropped bags!

"Are those mine?" Mom asks, stuffing everything back into her bag.

I tilt my head and look at her from above the reading glasses I borrowed from the counter. "Yes. Do they look good on me?"

"You could make a straightjacket look cute, hun," Mom says. "Did you eat?" She sorts through my finished sewing jobs. "What are these?"

"Well, they're supposed to be butterflies, but sometimes I fuck up the wings a bit, so they're more like... just fucked up butterflies." I study all the frilly things I've sewed on. "I'm not double looping when I should be swooping anymore, though, so that's progress. How was black-smithing?"

"I'm making a Katana. Gonna be awesome." She sits down at the table with me. "How're you doing, babe? Things going well? You look well."

I take off her glasses and get up to start the kettle. Tea time with Mom at night is one of my new favourite things. Especially while I'm trying not to hyperfocus on Alexei and accidentally turn him into a new addiction. Moderation. I'm trying that whole thing. Taking note of my feelings and my desires, treating him like a human being I'm falling for instead of a substance I can abuse.

But watching him come is playing on a loop in my mind, and I hope it never stops.

"I ran into Brian on the street. It was... well, it was shit. I felt so stupid and weak. I almost wanted to go with him. Actually, no. I didn't want to go with him, but I got kind of jealous of his high." I look my mom in the eyes. "Sorry I'm like this."

"That's why you stayed at Nathan's so late?"

I nod. "Yeah. Just... I don't know how to act, Mom. Like... I don't want Nick and Cole to see me like that. They shouldn't have to worry about me."

"And you shouldn't have to hide from them," she says. "Boys! Tea!"

"What're you doing?" I hiss at her, smacking her arm so suddenly her chapstick goes flying. "Shit. Sorry." I laugh.

"No more hiding, Gage. We're family. Family supports family, no matter what we're going through." She's got her phone pressed to her ear. "Owen? Oh, sorry, Marian. Thought I dialled Owen. Yes. Yes. Gage is working on his tiles."

"Hi, Marian!" I yell.

When Mom finally gets Owen on the phone to invite him over for inappropriately timed tea, the twins shuffle into the kitchen, bickering about whether a taco is a sandwich or not.

It isn't.

Is it?

Shit.

"Okay, let's all yell at Gage about hiding from us," Mom says when we're all sipping Oolong and complaining that it isn't as good as Earl Grey. "He's trying to protect us from his hard times, but we don't want him to do that, do we?"

And then I get attacked with love and all that bullshit, and by the time the clock strikes midnight, I'm a crying, venting mess of a loser who doesn't feel so loser-y anymore because my family fucking loves me. And to make me feel even less loser-y, I find out that all of them are going through shit.

Owen has no idea why he can't keep a relationship, and even started going to therapy because he thinks it might have something to do with Dad walking out on all of us.

Suddenly. Without a word. And then I made it worse by doing the same thing. Shit.

Cole says he feels blank. Like has never had a crush. Doesn't find anyone attractive. Doesn't wanna have sex. I told him that's okay, and Mom, that fucking genius woman, made him comfortable enough to admit he's trying to decide if he's maybe aro or ace. Or both.

Nick, on the other hand, has the biggest crush on the absolute wrong person. Owen's best friend. Owen laughed his ass off at that, but Nick didn't seem deterred.

And Mom? Despite how busy she keeps herself and how many friends she has, she feels lonely sometimes. And I hate that for her because she's the best person I know, and I never want her to feel lonely. So late-night tea is a must.

All in all, I'm so glad I moved home. I need this. I think my family needs it, too.

Alexei is glancing around obsessively. He's checking every mirror, gripping the steering wheel too tight, and pressing hard on the brake and the gas.

"There are people everywhere, Gage!" he yells at me. "And cars. And bikes. Oh, don't get me started on the bikes!"

I smile at the traffic. "I know, but you're in your lane, doing fine, in control. Honestly, if you're timid and hesitant, it gives those bikers the chance to think it's their right of way. You gotta take it, and they'll back off."

"Don't bikers have the right of way?" he asks.

"Yeah, at crossings and shit, but they aren't allowed to zip through lanes like that. It's your lane. Own it, baby!"

He looks over at me. "No, you did not."

I laugh. Hard. "Call you baby?"

"Yes. That."

"I was just in the moment. I meant it more like an Arnold Schwarzenegger kind of baby. Like *hasta la vista, baby*."

"It better have been that," Alexei snips, driving so much more confidently now that he's not over-focusing on the traffic.

"Not a fan of pet names?" I ask, honestly just wanting to get to know him.

"I am, but I selfishly want my pet name to be unique. Like something only for me. You know how many 'babys' there are in the world? I don't want to be one of them."

I kind of love that. "Oh, I'll come up with something real special for you. I'll know it when I stumble across it. But I also love Alexei. I don't know any other Alexeis."

"My mom used to call me Alyosha. I never knew why, but I looked it up years later. It's Russian, but she wasn't Russian, so I have no idea why she called me that. And weirdly, just because I don't understand it, it makes it special. Dad doesn't know either, so I guess it's one of those mysteries I'll never find the answer to." He shrugs. "You're the only Gage I know, too. Although, I know a Gabe. How's your sex journal?"

God, he switches gears in a single breath. Always

keeping me on my toes. "It's an arousal journal, but maybe soon it'll turn into a sex journal. Guess we're about to find out how I'm doing. Turn here."

Alexei puts the blinker on and makes the right turn. He follows the map's commands to the office building my therapist works out of and expertly parks the car, backing into the space because he feels more at ease when the car is ready to go. It's also a safe car. Nothing flashy. Has all the latest safety features and a middle-aged parent would probably drive it.

"You drive just fine. I know you're uncomfortable in the city, but I think it just takes practice and getting used to it again."

"We aren't skimming over your sex journal comment," he says, turning the engine off. "Are you sure you want me to go in with you?"

"No pressure if you don't want to, but yeah. I think it'll help us both. Don't you?" I ask.

"Am I allowed to talk? Ask questions?"

I grin at him, taking his hand and joining our fingers together. "Ask anything you want. I'm not hiding, and she knows she's allowed to tell you anything. This is me being a responsible, reformed man."

"I'm telling her about the shower show," he says. "I want her take."

And for some reason, all I can think about is kissing him. He said I needed to be prepared for the level of intimacy it'd bring, but fuck me, all I want is intimacy with him. And not just the sexual kind. I want to hold him and snuggle him. I want to laugh with him and sleep next to him. I want to get so caught up in a make-out session with him that we forget to eat and my lips hurt after. I want to differentiate him from a fixation, love on him without obsessing over him, and learn new ways to make him smile every single day.

I'm just staring at him, being totally weird and creepy about it, having an epiphany while he stares back, completely at ease with the intense and unnatural eye contact. Alexei isn't someone who buckles under scrutiny, and I kind of love that he has no idea who he is while knowing exactly who he thinks he is. He's set in his ways, firm on so many things, confident about not being too confident, and totally in charge of himself. He said no to me. When I told him to press play while I was still physically touching him, he said no until I explained it. I don't want to look at him as someone who is going to be good for my sobriety, but at the same time... he's good for my sobriety.

"Will you hate me if I relapse?" I ask.

"Hate? No. Hurt? Yes." He tilts his head, eyes on me, hair glinting in the afternoon sun. "Why?"

"What if I accidentally start pressuring you to eat fried meat? What if I offer you so many cookies that you get a sweet tooth and change completely? What if you get second-hand smoke from all my cigarettes and, I don't know, get lung cancer or something? Then I'll have to get cancer just so I can be sick with you."

"Gage," he says, placing a hand on mine. His eyes are unshakeable, but his neck and cheeks still flush from the contact. "You won't. Wanna know why? Two reasons, really. One, I'm not fucking around when I say you'll never have that kind of control over me. My heart, my mood, my infatuation, and my sex drive, yes, but not my lifestyle. I am too firm in a lot of my beliefs to ever let you influence them, and I have the history to treat them as important. But secondly, because you barely smoke near me anymore. When we're walking, you step away. You haven't smoked in my car. You respect me. So, when we get cancer, it'll be of our own making. You'll get throat cancer from your cigarettes, and I'll get bone cancer because I don't drink enough milk. We'll fade away together, but not because of each other."

Is it possible to love someone without fully knowing them? "Are you making casual jokes about cancer?"

"I never joke about cancer. I'm being serious. Our lifestyles and our genetics determine our future, and you smoke while I avoid the calcium in dairy. They are unrelated to each other, but the end result could still turn up cancer. Anything could turn up cancer. You respect me and worry about these things, so I trust you," he says. "It's you who doesn't trust yourself. So, let's go learn how to do that." He nods at the building. "Everything in life has risks, Gage. Just gotta find the ones worth taking."

I'm thinking about kissing him again. A soft, gentle, long and drawn-out slow kiss that gets my heart pumping but not my dick hardening. That's what I want with him. As we climb out of the car, I take his hand, joining our fingers together while we walk.

He unlinks them. "I prefer this kind of hand-holding."

He just holds my hand, palm to palm, no linking. "More of a natural fit, don't you think?"

So fucking natural. I smile at him. "You know, there are plenty of other foods to get calcium from."

"Don't educate me on nutrition, Gage. I'll win."

There's no waiting room breather when we walk into Natalie's office. She brings us right into her room, introduces herself to Alexei, and he introduces himself as 'the guy' I referred to, then we both sit back and watch him pull a tiny notebook and pen from his pocket, readying it on his thigh.

"You brought notes?" I ask, grinning at him.

"I brought notes, and I am going to take more notes," he confirms. "How do we start?"

So, Natalie asks me how I'm doing and if I've been struggling with anything, and Alexei listens intently while I tell her I'm confused because I'm horny but not compulsive about it. We're back on the 'sobriety can affect sex drive' topic, Alexei is jotting notes, and then she adds that my rationalization skills are improving with my recovery, and it's a great step in my progress. I'm still on the fence about it because I don't understand how I can be a sex addict if I'm not addicted to sex. Nothing makes sense, and when I tell her that, she tells me that addictions, especially non-substance ones, don't always make sense.

When Natalie looks at Alexei, nodding to his list and giving him the green light to go for it, he clears his throat, straightens his back, and clicks the pen. "We had a sexy encounter. Shall I explain it?"

"Gage should," she says, looking at me. "I want to hear your take."

Alexei smiles at me. So, I go for it. "Well, I've been keeping the arousal journal, right? And the other night, he got me all worked up, and I told him I'd show him the entry. I said it to him instead. In a voicemail. But before he could listen to it, I went to his place, put us in the bathroom, touched him a little, and then we listened to it together with the glass shower door as a barrier."

"While masturbating," Alexei adds helpfully.

"To absolute completion," I add, winking.

"That's fun. And respectful. Can I ask why you put the barrier between you?" Natalie asks.

"Because I don't understand anything!" I kind of yell at her. "I'm so confused about this diagnosis. Old me fucked until I dropped, but new me barely gets a stiffy unless it's over him, and even then, none of it feels out of control or anything, so it's like I'm just waiting for it to spring up on me and turn me into a sex monster." I huff, feeling better about letting that out. "Am I an impulsive sex addict or not? I don't get it."

Alexei nods beside me. "Yes, that. That is also my question, and how we can be responsible about it when I don't really understand what he needs."

"Mindfulness," Natalie says easily. "When someone recovering from disordered eating makes meal choices, they do it with mindfulness. The same way someone recovering from compulsive sex acts approaches sexual activity again. Usually, there are steps involved, exercises, journalling, and

practice phases, but since I'm seeing you after a year of abstinence, and you're already in your journalling and practice
phase, I think it's okay to move into actual activity. If you
feel ready, Gage, you're ready. All you can do to prepare is
be aware, trust your partner, and trust yourself. Do you?"

"I trust Alexei," I say.

"And I trust myself," Alexei says. "But I'm also just a
person. I get urges. What if I get carried away?"

"That's not your responsibility," I tell him. "It's mine."

"It's both of yours. Awareness. That's the key. You're
allowed to get carried away. It's sex. It's supposed to feel
good. We want it to feel good! You're allowed to enjoy it and
get swept up in it. It's the addictive, compulsive mindset
we're watching for. Honestly, Alexei, you don't seem like
someone who's intimidated by conversation, am I right?"

"Not even a little," he says, and I laugh, remembering
when he bluntly asked me what I'm addicted to.

"So, have the sex when you're ready. Take slow steps.
Start with something less invasive if you want. And then
talk about it. Check in with each other. Create a channel of
openness. It's not like you're hiding your situation from him,
Gage, and that is a huge factor in taking ownership of something. It makes it possible for you to communicate about it."

She's right. I'm being honest about everything. Alexei
knows my darker past, and he isn't afraid of it. Plus, he's a
fucking gremlin with willpower, and I trust him so much
more because of it. I... "I feel ready."

Because maybe this kind of addiction was fuelled by my
others, and now that I'm healing, progressing, I have what it

takes to have a normal sex life with an icy blue-haired guy who makes every part of me come alive so much more than drugs ever did.

"I'M THINKING about having sex with your son!" I blurt, immediately sinking behind the hoist of Nathan's shop. "Don't kill me!"

I'm a hypocrite and a liar because I literally just told him the other night that there would be no sex, but now Natalie is encouraging me to enter the practice phase of my treatment, and Alexei is letting me lead by being responsible for the both of us, and I'm just a sober asshole with urges that feel manageable instead of out of control, so... yeah. I want to try things. I want to make Alexei feel good. I want to connect with him in a new way. I want to experience him sexually and then sit up, half naked in the blankets of our beds, scribbling our thoughts into my journal. It's not just the sex I'm looking forward to. It's the whole experience. The build-up, the act, the silliness that will come after, when we jot-point down all the important bits and then get serious about the awareness parts. I feel comfortable enough to do that with him. I'm *excited* about doing that with him. And I think I know Alexei well enough to know he's excited about the after parts as much as the sex itself.

Nathan has a big, ominous metal tool in his hand, and maybe I should have waited to blurt that until we were away from all the mechanical weapons. He lifts a brow, saying nothing.

So, naturally, I over-explain.

"It's just, he's amazing, right? And I'm learning to be better and look at life differently, and basically just start over. And here he comes, all angry at me when you forced us to have breakfast together, which, by the way, makes this whole thing your fault, and now I'm dreaming of things I've never dreamt of before. Because I used to want a partner who would be my caretaker so I could just get fucked up and have a safe place to go, but now I want... like, I wanna be his caretaker. I wanna make him happy and smiley and all that shit, and since he's so strong-willed and a bit snippy, if I'm being honest, I feel like he's the perfect person to be around me without me rubbing off on him. But now I'm making it sound like he's just good for me and I'm not good for him, and I guess what I'm trying to say is that I want to be good for him. I will be. Because I care about him more than I've ever... and you know? Like... he's Alexei." I should have just led with that part. He's Alexei. There's no better explanation.

"Jesus," Nathan groans. "Pass me that and stop hiding."

I pass him the part from the trolly, backing up a step in case he gets any ideas about smacking me. "He's Alexei," I repeat.

"I'm aware," Nathan says. "Which means he knows what he wants. No one is going to deter him until he changes his mind about it."

"You saying he's going to change his mind about me?"

Nathan huffs. "Not unless you hurt or mistreat him. He won't tolerate that, which makes him..."

"Alexei," I fill in. "And I'm being very self-aware about how I'm treating him."

"I know you are," Nathan admits. "He's... happy. All I want for him is happiness, and if you help that, I can't really complain. But..."

Oh, anxiety! *The but!* I gear up to listen to all the ways I'm bad for his son. About how I'm a junkie who has fucked up rehab seven times, stole a frappé and snorted a baggy of not-glitter just because it was there, ruined the lives of everyone around me because I'm a selfish asshole who gets easily hooked on destructive behaviour. My heart is sinking already.

"But your happiness is just as important. So is your recovery. Alexei can be... stress-inducing, so you better be mindful of that is all I'm saying."

Oh. My eyes burn and my chest tightens, and I don't know what to say because nobody's really ever told me I'm important before. Outside of my family, I'm just... that guy who got messed up and stayed messed up. To Brian, I was a fun party friend. To my teachers, I was a letdown and someone they worried about. To Paul, I was someone who needed to be hidden.

That boy is troubled.

He's such a bad influence.

His poor mother.

Did you hear what he did?

I'm Gage Rossum, the disappointment.

Until now...

"And as much as I hate adding this part, and we're not talking about it again, it better be more than just sex with my son," Nathan adds while I'm still suffocating on kindness. "He likes you."

"I like him too," I whisper to the hoist. "I like him so much."

Nathan sighs. "His birthday is tomorrow. In case you didn't know."

alexei

15

D ad couldn't sleep, and I'm a light sleeper, so he woke me up with all his pacing, and now we're standing on growing grass with hot paper cups in our hands while the sun comes up.

"Do you miss her?" I ask Dad.

"I don't know. Not really. I just miss... I regret that her life ended so early." He stares at Mom's tiny headstone, small stickers peeling everywhere. I put one there when she first passed away, and I guess it sort of became a thing to stick a weird sticker on her stone every year. Most of them are faded or disintegrated, but the outlines are etched into the stone. "We wouldn't be together if she was still alive."

"How do you know?"

"Because we weren't good for each other. We did one awesome thing together—you. Otherwise, we were bad for each other in all ways possible." He looks at me. Looks away. "It's important to know that. To know when two people are good together or not, despite the fun they have together."

My fingers drum on the paper of my cup, still burning hot from green tea. "Is this your way of giving me dating advice without actually giving me dating advice?"

"Yes."

I nod, smiling at Mom's grave. God, I love it when he's a dad. "Noted." I pull a sticker from my pocket and show the holographic side to Dad. "This one work?"

"Fried meats are our friends?" He squints at it. "Fuck it. Sure." He's smiling now, and I like that Gage's ridiculous sticker is playing a part in our morning. He stuck one to my steering wheel when we left his therapist's office, and when I looked at my bed later that night, there was one stuck to the headboard, too.

I wipe the dirt and dust off the stone, place the sticker there, and stand back up. It's right next to a sticker from two years ago that says 'vegan for the animals' and I enjoy the hypocrisy of that.

"I'm gonna go walk over there and not eavesdrop," I tell Dad. "But don't fuck up like last year."

"Fuck up how?" he asks.

"You forgot to get out all your guilt, and that shit clung around for a few more months. So take your time and get it all out so we can leave here being happy." I lean against him in my best attempt at a familial hug and then leave him to it.

We're going to pick up the light fixtures we dropped off at a restoration shop a few months ago. They're finally ready, and I can't wait to put them up. I don't know how it happened, but my level of pride in this mansion we're keeping from falling down is soaring at an all-time high.

When I look back at Dad, he's talking to a headstone, knelt low so nothing can intercept his words. Pressing his finger down to make sure the sticker stays put. I take a deep breath, knowing I have a weird level of attachment to my dad. I mean, he almost died so many times while I was growing up, and my mom really did die, so I don't think it's too crazy for me to cling to him. I love my dad, always have, even when I hated him as a kid, and now I finally get to have him as... him. Our relationship has done a lot of mending over the past few years, and now that Gage is around, giving me another perspective on addiction and addicts, it's mending even more. I smile when Dad looks back at me to make sure I haven't wandered too far.

Nice Sunday so far.

"Am I allowed now?" Dad asks on our way to the restoration shop.

"Fine."

"Happy Birthday, Alex," he says, permitted now that our dire business is out of the way. "Twenty-six and falling for your soulmate." He laughs, unable to help himself from mocking me. Although, I'm pretty sure I'm being lovingly mocked because he believes in *my* belief that Gage is my soulmate.

"Thank you. I always knew twenty-six would be my

year." Feels like a lucky number, even though it holds no significance to me. It's just a feeling.

"I just..." Dad pauses to squint and gather his thoughts. "Uhm, well, Gage's recovery seems to be a very large portion of your 'getting to know each other' phase, and I just don't want you to feel neglected. You're allowed to talk about yourself, too. To focus on yourself."

"I do." I smile. "And I don't mind that he takes the cake. He deserves it, and I like helping him feel hopeful. I'm a pretty content person if you don't count the fact that I'm losing interest in my job and have no plans to ever move away from you." I shrug. "Not every person has some big traumatic thing to get over. My trauma has to do with you, not Gage, and you and I are working on it, are we not?"

"Of course we are," Dad says. "And I love you for giving me another chance."

I'll give him as many chances as he needs. He's my dad, and I'll love him no matter what. "I do miss Mom sometimes," I admit to him. "And I worry about you dying an unhealthy amount. So don't... do that. Okay?"

"Okay." He laughs. "I won't."

"Deal."

"Wanna talk about your job?" he asks.

So, I do. The whole drive to the restoration shop. Basically that I'm just confused about why I'm losing interest in it, but that I'm not too worried about it yet. Soon.

When we get to the shop, the guy who worked on our fixtures is busy, so I snoop around and get... interested. What are all these things? These tools? These trinkets and antique bits of history that are being fixed up and mended to continue thriving in the modern world? There's junk everywhere, and normally, I'd look at it like it really is junk, but for the first time, I'm seeing a past, craftsmanship, appreciating the hard work and methods of creation that went into building and making these *things*. I'm appreciating the dedication and the love of the person who spent so much time restoring them.

And when the man finally comes out to show us our restored fixtures, I chat his ear off for a whole hour without Dad complaining. Because... I'm intrigued. *With old things.* With mending and repairing and restoring old things and making them new again.

> Alexei <3 : how do I know when I'm fixating on something? I like old things. Is that a bad sign?

> Alexei <3 : Like, I like old things so much that I'm debating trying to fix old things into new things. Is that a fixation? Should I be worried? Gage?

> Alexei <3: I'm aware of the double entendre. I know I'm fixing my old relationship with my dad into a new one, and maybe that's why I suddenly love old things becoming new???? Thots?

> Alexei <3: Thoiughts *

> Alexei <3" Shit. Thoughts**

Alexei <3 : Okay, I may have done a thing. I bought some tools. Like, tools I have no idea how to use, but the man at the shop said they were a good starting point, and then he just… gifted me some things. Said not enough people cared about the past and told me to stop by anytime I wanted. I'm not even nervous to drive here.

Alexei <3 : Gage? Answer me so I know you're not in a fried meat coma somewhere.

Gage: I have no idea what you're rambling about, but please keep going.

So, I do. I tell him about everything I see in the man's shop. I send him thirty-seven pictures of old shit, and then three more pictures because thirty-seven didn't seem like enough. Gage replies to every single photo like he cares about old shit as much as I suddenly do. I send him my thoughts in voice notes when typing is too much, and I repeat the man's advice, and then I'm sending him more photos of the new tools I'm buying, and oh my god. Why do I suddenly love old things and take such pride in our battered mansion?

When we get home and I'm carrying bags of tools and a shrimp cocktail through the front door, I smile at the house I didn't want to move into. This house is just a part of me now, and… how the fuck am I gonna move out of it when I eventually get the courage to leave Dad on his own?

I put my blood, sweat, tears, and so much time and manual labour into this place. So much so that I am attached to it now. Even though it looks like a crumbling mess from the outside, it's full of stories with my dad, near kisses with Gage, and happier moments in general. I love things with character, and over the past few years we've been living here, we've given it character of our own. I've basically become a carpenter, and now I'm gonna be a 'restorer of old things' on top of that.

I set everything down on the kitchen island, listening to Dad close the front door behind him.

"Get dressed," Dad says, setting the rest of my new tools on the floor by the stairs.

"For what?"

He pulls out his phone and squints at the screen. "Uh, blue with your black? Whatever that means."

A heatwave works through me, starting in my chest and radiating all the way to the tips of my toes. "Gage?"

"Yes, Gage. Get moving." Dad nods upstairs.

I start to rush but slow my pace so I appear to have a bit of chill in front of my dad. On the inside, I'm a sweaty, agitated, neurotic mess of excitement and nerves because I don't know what this means or what it is. Blue with my black? But how?! Dressy? Casual? Where are we going and what are we doing and does he know it's my birthday? Is this a date?

When I get to my room, I rip open my closet door and just stare at all the blacks. My whites are folded in a drawer, and my blues are sparse but growing in number. Oh god. Which blue?! What blacks?!

> Alexei <3 : I don't like vague instructions. Be more clear.

> Gage: Shut up and wear something or I'll spend the whole night having to resist your nakedness. Don't worry, we'll take it off later. ;) 1 hour, Alexei.

That heatwave picks up lava and I burn alive. But by the time I've settled on some blues with my blacks, I feel like a new man. A phoenix from the ashes of my own making.

"Are you wearing a fedora?" I ask Gage, even though it's obvious he's definitely wearing a fedora. A black one with a blue ribbon he terribly sewed on. It's not even straight.

"Yes." He wrings his hands together on my front porch.

"With an orange hoodie?"

"It's my favourite colour. And sweatpants," he confirms. "My nice ones. I put on real shoes, though."

He did. Slip-ons. Black and baby blue checkered, and I'm wondering if he already owned them or if he bought them for the occasion. He looks unbalanced. A little bit classy, a lot sassy, all paired up nicely with a strong under-tone of 'I tried, but not too hard.' And my god, it's charmingly sexy, especially because his tanned skin looks even more tanned in that shade of sunset orange. The fedora suits him so much better than his normal hat, and I can't even tell why. Maybe because no one wears fedoras around here, so it makes him as unique as he actually is.

I'm standing here gawking at him, not rushing to take him all in. I consume him piece by piece while he stands there and lets me, making me comfortable in my slow perusal. Because Gage is a beautiful man with an unhealthy inside that sometimes shines through but mostly stays hidden. He's mentioned being a little dark-minded before, but when I look at him, I don't see darkness. I see nerves and insecurity. I see a man determined to be better without actually knowing what better looks like. I see his sexy self-awareness and how hard he's trying to make me feel special, not because he has to try, but because he knows I'm special and wants to ensure *I* know that *he* knows.

"Goddamn, Alexei," he says on a rushed exhale. "You look fucking awesome."

I tried—but not too hard—as well, and I feel like I look fucking awesome. I'm wearing real pants, but they're casual linen ones that are one step up from sweats, a blue hoodie, the only one I own, and a black scarf to balance it out. It's May 17th and I don't need a scarf, but I felt fashionable.

"Platonically awesome?" I ask.

He hums low in his throat. "No." Gage steps forward. Just one step. "Sexy awesome. Cute and handsome and fucking birthday boy awesome." He reaches forward, grabbing my left hand that says 'right' on the top. "Happy birthday, Alexei." His thumb swipes all the symbols on my knuckles, but his eyes stay on mine.

I'm burning up again. "I should have found something fire retardant to wear."

He smirks, but his eyes shift down to our hands like he can feel the heat, too. "Just say thank you."

"For what?"

"I wished you a happy birthday. The proper social protocol would be to show some gratitude."

"Why do I have to be grateful for something you said on your own?" I ask, flipping his hand in mine, tracing my finger over the lifeline on his palm. "Social protocol is weird."

Gage snorts. "Never conform, Alexei." He squeezes my hand. "Ready to go? I planned a thing."

I hate things. I love things. I don't want to be the centre of attention. I want to be the centre of Gage's attention. I want to stand here and stare at each other in awkward silence forever, but I also want to know what thing he planned. When I look past him, there's no car on the street or in the driveway, and he's not carrying anything, so... even more intrigued.

"Ready." I step outside and close the front door.

Gage links his arm through mine, but when I start walking down the steps, he turns me right back around and opens the front door.

"Where are we going?"

"Did you know that your gigantic ass house has three

separate doors that lead into the basement from outside?" he asks.

"I'm familiar with the gigantic ass house I live in, yes."

He grins, leading me towards the basement stairs. "Well, with your dad's permission, I've been slinking in and out of here all day. Real 'forbidden lover, *Romeo and Juliet* style' slinking, too."

While that surprises me, I'm hooked on one word. "Lover?"

"Yep." He doesn't flinch or balk at the word. He opens the door to the stairs, clicks on a flashlight from his pocket, and takes my hand to lead me down.

"Do you have a murder room down here?" I ask once we get to the damp bottom.

This house is ancient, and over the years, many weird families have lived here. The basement is an accumulation of all the shit they never took with them, and now that I'm someone who likes old things, I'm looking at it like a cave of treasure rather than an accumulation of junk. Mixed in with the cobwebs and exposed pipes are... things that can become new again. A rush of adrenaline hits me straight in the chest, making me excited about what I can do with this stuff.

"Sort of," Gage admits. "But I'm hoping it might be your new murder room. More like a doctor's lab." He stops before a closed door that leads to a cluttered and completely dark workshop I never go into because the lights don't work. "Since your rambling texts today, I... I changed from my original plan and did a thing."

That adrenaline buzz inside me is amplifying. "What thing?"

"Wanna see?"

I do, but now seems like a good time to stall by abiding by social protocols. "Thank you."

"For?"

"For wishing me a happy birthday."

Gage smiles, and then he tugs me to his chest. We've never hugged, but when he wraps his arms around me and holds me tight against him like he's wanted to do this for as long as he's lived, I sink against him and circle my arms around his lower back. Cigarettes. Laundry detergent. The same kind my mom used to use. Gage and the warmth he radiates. God, it's the best hug of my life. My eyes close and I take the moment in with all the gratitude he told me to have on the porch.

I'm just a little shorter than him, so he rests his cheek against my temple, plays with the hair on the back of my head, and exhales so slowly that it feels like his demons are leaving him to lurk among their new home in my basement.

"Alexei?"

"Shh. Don't ruin my moment."

I feel his cheek pull into a smile. He stays silent for long moments, letting me have *my* moment. Living in it with me because it's his moment, too.

"Yeah?" I finally ask.

"Will you be my slow-moving boyfriend that I haven't even kissed and barely know?"

God, he just makes the moment better. He's starting to

believe in soulmates. "Being my slow-moving boyfriend comes with opinions and a bit of attitude," I tell him, still hugging him in the dank basement.

"Like what?"

"Like I'll probably scoff at your food choices and get snippy about your lack of regard for your health."

He nods, like he expected it. "I know."

"And I'm kind of needy. I like compliments and a lot of reassurance, but don't lay it on too thick or I'll assume it's all fake."

"I know." He hugs me tighter.

"And you still won't have any control over my lifestyle, but I'll try to control yours. It's hypocritical, but I'm a hypocritical kind of guy."

He's smiling again. "I know."

There's more, but maybe that's enough of a start. "Okay. I'll be your slow-moving boyfriend."

alexei

16

The wooden door swings open on unapologetically obnoxious hinges. It's loud and squeaky, screaming at us to announce permission to enter the old room.

And when I get a peek inside, my knees wobble, my heart ticks up in speed, and a lot of warm and tingly pressure fills my head. My eyes burn. I'm gripping the sleeve of Gage's hoodie for... I don't know, balance or something, and my shaky legs are taking slow single steps into the room. I'm blinking at all the lights set up, glowing warm and romantic in the cavernous stone room.

Gage trembles next to me. "I've never done a grand romantic gesture before," he starts while I look at everything. "But I wanted to... and you seem like the kind of guy who enjoys setting up his own space, so I mostly just cleared it out and cleaned it up and brought your new things down so you could... do it yourself. I'll help. If you want help. Or you can be independent as fuck about it and I'll just cheer you on from the door. I don't know, Alexei. I just know that after all your messages today, and then talking to your dad about how excited you were, you might... like this space." He pauses, breath shaking. "I know I monopolize so much attention with my recovery, and I want you to know you're just as important. Fucking fuck, did I presume too much with this room?"

"Shut up, Gage." I drop his sleeve and walk into the room. "God, you suck at the slow part of slow-moving boyfriend. This is... monumentally fast, considering I just decided to get obsessed with old things today." I look at him. "I like your hustle."

He smiles shyly. "Yeah?"

So much yeah. There are workbenches and shelves made of wood and stone and metal. There are lanterns all over the place, lighting up the parts of the room that used to have spider webs and bats. All my new tools are set out on one of the benches, waiting for me to find them homes in my new workshop for my new hobby. The stone floor is swept and washed, the old stools from the storage room are sitting in front of the workbench, and there's a new pegboard lining the wall, waiting for me to fill it with things.

"What's this?" I touch a book on the bench.

"Oh, I, uh, got that. For you. Today."

Okay, so his nervousness is just as sexy as his self-awareness. "From where?"

"I faced another part of my past. I went to my high school," he admits. "I, uh, asked the old shop teacher if he had any books on antique restoration, and he gave me that.

And... and I apologized for being a fuckup in his class and stealing so many tools. And then I picked the twins up and took them for a drive down memory lane where I told them stories I was ashamed of."

"And you did all that around making this room in the past eight hours?"

"I hyperfixate on things and go hard. Yes." He steps inside. "And up there, in that blank space, I... started making something else. It's not done yet." He points to a spot above an arched walkway, the perfect place for a sign. "Here." He hands me his phone.

On his screen is the start of a logo. Or a sign. It says 'Alexei's Old Things,' with one of those 'new' kind of stickers used by storefront marketing whenever a new product comes in, placed at an angle atop the word 'old.'

"Obviously we can change the words and you can call it whatever you want, but I thought it'd be fun to have your own little shop. I'm... I'm gonna burn it into wood and hang it there. If you like it. I ordered a soldering tool and need to practice first."

I love it. I love it so much that I'm tongue-tied again. I love it more than I've ever loved anything, and I don't know if that's because I finally have a boyfriend who is my soulmate, or if it's because Gage is encouraging a hobby I haven't even started yet, or if it's because he does such nice things while being completely nervous and unsure about them. Maybe it's because he worked together with my dad to accomplish it.

I'm not typically someone who shows emotion in the

form of tears, but Gage blurs as I stare at him. His phone screen locks in my hand, and I'm still staring at him, wetness dripping down my cheeks without me doing anything about it.

"Oh, Alexei," he says, pulling me in for another hug. "Are you okay?"

I lean against him, happy and nostalgic and feeling all the things deeply. "Other than my dad, no one really does nice things for me. I don't really have anyone close in my life. This is... you just... damn you for making me unable to blurt my neurotic rambly things!"

He chuckles, pulling back to look at me. His thumbs don't even try to swipe my tears, and I like that he's comfortable with them. "I wanna do all the nice things for you," he says, and then he changes the mood entirely when he adds, "and all the dirty things." He bites his lip.

My tears dry up and my breath hitches. "You flip moods on a dime."

"You flip conversation topics on a dime," he retorts. "Okay, so you like it?"

"I more than like it."

"Good! Hang tight. I... just wait here!" He runs away, skipping through the basement and up the stairs. I hear him mutter things to my dad, and I hear my dad ask if I like the workshop. It only makes me smile more because they're in cahoots.

I already feel completely buzzed about this room. I know my interest in old things is brand new, but maybe it's been building ever since Dad and I moved into this house and started fixing it up. I've never felt pride in something like I feel for this house.

When Gage signals his return by tripping down the stairs and swearing a whole bunch of times, I smile to myself and sit on the stool, looking around my new space. Despite how damp and shadowed it is, it's awfully homey. I'm comfortable here, locked away in a basement to experiment with my newfound interests without prying eyes.

I think I love Gage for doing this. I love my dad for helping him.

Gage's fedora is skewed when he comes back carrying a real old-fashioned picnic basket and a bottle of... wine?

"It's kombucha," he says right away. "Healthy. No alcohol. Junkie safe. Alexei approved."

His dark brown eyes are still shy, but there's pride in them. He's proud of what he's done for me and of himself for finding a way to celebrate a birthday that doesn't include a party. I don't like that he refers to himself as a junkie, but I've come to learn that a lot of substance abusers do that. Maybe it's an awareness thing, or maybe awareness hurts and it's their way of hating on themselves just a bit.

"I love kombucha," I tell him, hand on the book he got me from the high school.

"I figured." He laughs. "Wait until you see what other healthy shit I got. Not a fried meat in sight." He sets the basket down on the workbench. "I know you already had lunch with your dad, so I went the snack route, because who can complain about snacks, right?"

My shrimp cocktail is a birthday tradition. The only

time of year I let myself eat it, because even though shrimp isn't the most unhealthy food there is, I like it so much that I'd overindulge. It's sitting on the top of the basket when he opens it. Along with cut-up veggies and hummus, a tray of strategically arranged grainy crackers and dips, a bunch of things that look like he just grabbed them from the vegan section of the grocery store thinking they were healthy, and a single cupcake in a plastic container.

Gage sets it all on the workbench, dragging another stool over to sit with me. "Wanna eat snacks and put tools away?" he asks, straightening his fedora.

When I smile, all my breath comes out of my nose. I nod. "Yes, please."

So, we do. Gage puts on film scores because his mind can't tune out lyrics and have a conversation simultaneously, and I'm dandy with that because I love film scores. When I start naming them and all the composers and movies they come from, I fall a little harder for Gage when he knows the ones I don't. Soulmates!

We peck at snacks and find new homes for tools, and when Gage finds another lantern on a shelf, we take it out into the basement and start finding things I can work on. Make new. Fix up. Learn how to restore. And I realize I'm rambling, talking his ear off about what the man at the shop told me, probably over-explaining something Gage doesn't give a shit about, but he never complains. He talks back, asks me more questions, and offers ideas.

How is he so imperfect and perfect together?

Somehow, hours pass. Like, a lot of hours. My dad came

down to check on us, indulging in a few snacks before saying he was going to bed and taking the leftover shrimp with him. And now it's two in the morning, and I had no idea because there are no windows down here, and time doesn't exist when Gage is around.

"Is your mom worrying about you?" I ask once I realize the time.

"No. She knows where I am." He smiles at me. "Did you have a good birthday?"

"I believe in monogamy," I blurt instead. "Since you asked me to be your slow-moving boyfriend, you should know that." I'm fishing again. Gage knows it.

He grins. "Yeah? Meaning you're mine and only mine?"

"More like *you're* mine and only mine. I'm going to need you to tell me your stance on monogamy or I'll fret about it forever."

Gage stands between my long legs. I'm on a stool and he's upright, putting him a bit above me, but I enjoy being under his watchful eyes. "Monogamy is such a societal standard," he teases. "So not you."

"It's one hundred percent me when it comes to you."

"Just me?" he asks, hands moving up my thighs.

I've never had a boyfriend or been in a relationship before, so I nod because it's not a lie. Just him. He's the only one I've wanted to be monogamous with. "Yes."

"My monogamous, neurotic, slow-moving boyfriend. I like it. I believe in monogamy, too." His hands are moving higher again, and his lips are brushing my cheek without kissing. "We haven't even discovered if we're compatible in

SOBER DOPE & SUNDAYS

bed yet. Maybe we're both bottoms. Both tops." He dips his face beneath my black scarf and plants a light kiss on my pulse point.

Oh. My. God.

I'm tilting my head towards him instead of away. I want to expose my whole neck to him, but I also want to feel his dark hair against my cheek. "Maybe. Or maybe we're both sides. Both vers. Both nervous."

"Are you nervous, Alexei?" His voice is a scratchy whisper, and shit, it's making my dick hard. When his hands travel higher at the same time as his tongue hits my neck, I shiver all over.

"No. Are you?" I'm lying. I'm so fucking nervous it isn't even funny. But I'm excited, too. Turned on. Extremely aroused and lost in Gage's build-up.

"A little," he admits, planting one more kiss on my neck. He pulls back to look me in the eye. "Do you trust me to do sexy things?"

I trust him, his therapist, and us together, so I nod. But... what sexy things?! What are we about to do when we've never even kissed? I want him to kiss me, and I'm dying to kiss him, but refraining is essential until he understands what it means to kiss me. I want intimacy, and until he knows he wants it too, we'll skirt around it, tease and taunt it, build it up until it's impossible not to kiss any longer.

Luckily, I am a master of restraint.

"I don't want to come," Gage whispers against my cheek. "I don't want any of this to be focused on my orgasm. But I want to make you come." His hand rubs the hard outline in my pants and my breath shudders out of me. "Can I?"

His hair tickles my temple and his caressing hand turns me into a pliable substance, ready to be manipulated and morphed into whatever he wants to turn me into. I'm clay, and this is a pottery class.

"Yeah," I whisper.

And when I think he's going to reach into my pants or drop to his knees, he puts his face right against mine instead. Foreheads together, hair mingling, breaths joining. His hand rubs and his lips tease, touching mine without kissing. And I realize that this is awareness and restraint for him. He's taunting a kiss, not to tease me, but to tease himself. To learn what it means to be intimate with me, like trying before buying. And now I'm the one testing my restraint because I want to kiss him. The same way my hips are slightly lifting against his hand, I want to lean forward, press my mouth to his, and feel his tongue against mine. And that's the mind-fuck. That's Gage Rossum. That's why he's my soulmate. Because he can rub my cock with enthusiasm but drive me wild with a non-kiss.

His fingers pull my waistband away, dipping into my pants to brush my cock lightly. "You have no fucking idea how badly I want to kiss you right now," he says, voice abrasive and barely restrained. "But I don't want you to doubt me. So when I do, when I finally kiss you, it won't be because of sex or temptation. It'll be because you know I can handle your intimacy. That you trust me to handle it."

I'm so fucking gone for this guy it's ridiculous. "You—"

My words get cut off by a choke of surprise and delight when his fingers wrap around the length of me and his thumb swipes over the tip. The cool basement air hits my bare skin next. I tilt my forehead against his, watching his hand slide up and down the length of me languidly. I'm not even embarrassed by the swell of precum that flushes my tip and makes me shiny. I like the way I look in his hand. I like the way his hand looks wrapped around me. A fit that complements as much as contrasts. Perfect.

"Might get hot in that scarf," is what Gage whispers against my ear before sinking to his knees and not even hesitating for a second to run his tongue up the underside of my dick, tonguing the V under the head.

The unstable stool rattles and I grip the edges of it.

He tugs my pants to just below my ass, and I'm delusional or unaware because I don't even feel the cool metal of the stool against my bare skin. He's making me sweat, and I'm already hot in the scarf, but on principle, I leave it on and let him burn me alive. I'm watching him with eager eyes, and I don't really know if that's socially acceptable behaviour during a blowjob, but I can't stop, and Gage doesn't seem put off by it. He looks at me, too. His eyes, deep and brown and sexy, are on mine, and when he grins slyly, I sink down the stool.

His lips wrap around me. I tremble. He lowers his mouth down the length of my cock. I pant. He pulls up and runs the tip of his tongue over the slit and circles it around the flushed head. I moan. Out loud.

It spurs Gage on and makes me aware of sounds. And

now I'm getting my dick sucked to Ramin Djawadi's epic score from *Game of Thrones* about a Lannister always paying his debts. The melancholic mood of the song doesn't fit the sexy atmosphere, but I don't think I'd change a thing about this moment because it's all being written into my history as the first perfect hands-on sexual experience with my soulmate.

The stool is still shaking, and I know it's from me. My legs are trembling and my hands are quaking. The whole vibe of this experience is explosive, and I love it.

When I slip down the stool a little more, my toes *just* hitting the floor, Gage steadies me with his hands on my hips. His smirk comes back before he lets his open lips run over the tip of my cock and down the side length. When he gets to the base, he buries his whole face against my balls, sucking them lightly into his mouth.

"Shrimp," I blurt. "Fried meats. Old things becoming new again. Spiders. Web design." My face is red and my scarf is killing me.

Gage laughs, making my balls pop out of his mouth. "You can try to avoid coming all you want, Alexei. The end result will still be the same."

"I fucking know that," I snip at him. "I'm trying to drag it out. At least until the song changes." I don't know if I should check in with him or not, but I don't because I don't want him to think it's what I'm thinking about. "Jesus," I groan when he sucks me back down.

The stool shakes so hard that Gage pulls me off of it.

Still on his knees, he steers me to the side of it and presses my lower back to the workbench. "Grip," he demands.

My hands hold the workbench, my tattooed knuckles turning white under pressure. I don't feel any steadier on my feet, but it doesn't matter because Gage is keeping me upright while threatening to bring me to my knees.

He sucks. He licks. He fucking looks up at me. He shows me desire in his eyes and comfort in his movements. He keeps a hand on the front of my hip to steady me, but the other wraps around the base of my cock, stroking in time with his mouth.

"Gage," I call, unsure if I want him to hear the complete arousal in my voice or the utter desperation I'm trying to hold back.

He pulls his mouth away, fingers circling the head of my cock and gently pulsing. "I want it, Alexei. Give it to me."

The song changes, giving me permission to come. Now Alexandre Desplat and the London Symphony Orchestra are aiding Gage in bringing me to liberation with melodies from *The Imitation Game,* and holy fuck. I'm gonna lose it.

I watch Gage. I watch him use his hands and mouth in perfect synchronization. I watch him keep his hands on me, preventing them from touching himself. I watch his sweatpants grow strained and his fedora fall to the floor, passing his sunset hoodie in a blur of orange and black. And I feel. I feel the constriction of his throat when he gags and the eagerness with which he consumes me. And I last the whole song, because as soon as *The Hunger Games'* whistle fills the room, I'm done for.

"Ah, fuck," I pant out in choppy breaths. "Fuck. Gage."

He pulls back slightly, my cock throbbing inside his mouth. The orgasm hits hard enough to make my eyes close, my fingers tighten on the bench, and my knees lock. When I look down at him, he's looking up at me, drinking me down and enjoying it as if it were his own orgasm. My stomach clenches with the last spurt, and then I'm exhaling so hard I tremble even more.

"Oh my god," I wheeze.

And then I just... fall. Straight down onto my ass. Gage tries to catch me, but my dick popping out of his mouth and my *Bambi* legs completely failing brings me down hard. He grabs me enough to pull me against him, my shoulder leaning against his chest.

"I'm useless right now," I tell him, catching my breath. "I'm... you're..."

"Yeah," he agrees, kissing my hair and sinking down to his ass. I see him lick his lips, but I'm too afraid to look at them in case I kiss them. "Happy birthday, Alexei."

It's not my birthday anymore, and social protocol wants me to tell him that. Instead, I follow the former rules and thank him. His dick twitches under my forearm on his lap.

"Can... can I?" I ask.

"You can, but not right now. I... it seems stupid, but I want to prove to myself that I can refrain."

"It's not stupid," I tell him, getting the energy to sit up and look at him. My dick's just flopping outta my pants, not at all looking cute, so I tuck it back in and meet his eyes. "Uh, wow."

"Speechless?" He laughs. "Wow is right."

I smile wide because I can't help it. "You know, I have a bed upstairs."

"Shit, really?" he teases.

"Do you wanna sleep in it with me?"

Gage smiles, and my heart grows four sizes. "I'm not the best sleeper. But if you can handle that, I'd love to sleep in it with you."

I snort. "I just ran three marathons, so I'm gonna be dead to the world in five minutes. Take me there."

gage

s it weird that I didn't want to borrow a toothbrush because I didn't want to scrub Alexei's taste from my mouth? Yeah. Yeah, that's probably weird. Nothing sexy about stale cum, but... everything about Alexei is sexy. Even the way he sleeps.

He made me cuddle him. I mean, I was going to anyway, but he practically forced me to. Then he changed his mind. My arms were wrapped around him from behind, my still-hard dick nestled against his ass without any compulsive urges. After a whole two and a half minutes, he said nope, made me turn over, and snuggled up to me from behind.

Guess I'm the little spoon. Kind of love it because his long body fits perfectly behind mine, and his blue-blond hair felt nice against my neck.

I slept alright, considering it was a new bed, a new house, and a new body next to mine, but as soon as the sun poked out from the horizon, I was wide awake and a bit jittery.

So now I'm slinking through the creaky mansion, wondering if I can make coffee or root through cabinets to see where Nathan keeps my meds. Or should I go home? Maybe I can have breakfast with Alexei if he wakes up before I need to leave for my therapy appointment with Natalie. It's a video appointment this time, but I want to be alone and in my attic room for it.

"Here," Nathan says, scaring the shit out of me. I'm just standing at the bottom of the stairs in sweats, a t-shirt, and bare feet, unsure which direction to turn or where to walk next. He hands me an empty coffee mug.

"What's this?"

"It's a rule that everyone gets their own mug here. Alex is specific about mugs."

It's a black mug with an alien face on it, the words 'welcome intruder' written beneath in spacy letters. I lift a brow at Nathan. "This your way of offering me a coffee and calling me an intruder at the same time?"

"Yes. I'll get your pill."

So, I sit at the island in the giant kitchen and dry-swallow my medication, and when my intruder cup is full of sweet and creamy coffee, I look at Nathan because he looks like he wants to say something.

"How're you feeling?" he asks.

Proud. Exhausted about being proud. A little skeptical of myself for taking pride in not coming like it's some sort of weird accomplishment.

"A little like I'm waiting for the other shoe to drop," I say instead. I sip coffee and try to own the feeling.

"How so?"

I shrug. "I don't know. Like I've mostly been doing okay, but I don't want to get caught up thinking it's going to be easy. I've barely faced my past. I'm just waiting for it to all come crashing down."

Nathan nods, glancing at the stairs. "That's normal. But don't let it consume you. You're still allowed to be happy with your progress. Recovery is... it's hard. Don't diminish how far you've come. One day at a time. Hell, one minute at a time."

"But what am I going to do when things get tough? When I run into Brian again? When I get depressed and don't know how to handle it? When I have a fight with Alexei and think my world is ending?"

"Call me," he says plainly. "I don't care what time it is or what I'm doing. That's what I'm here for. Your sobriety is just as important to me as it is to you."

Something eases inside my mind. It's the same feeling I used to get knowing that rehab was an option. Nathan is my safe space, and I'm allowed to go to him when I don't know if I can cope or keep myself alive. "Thank you."

"And if you don't think we're a good match anymore because you're, uh, dating my son?" he states it like a question and moves on, "Then I'll help find you someone new. I'm on your side here, Gage."

"Okay," I say, sipping. "But... no thanks. I don't want someone new. Not unless things get weird, and I'm hoping they don't get weird. I like that it's you. That you're you... to me. I like weird."

He doesn't comment on that, but I think he gets what I'm saying. "I don't want details, but... feeling okay after last night?" he asks.

I look at my steaming coffee and blush. Smiling. Remembering the way Alexei blurted random words to stave off his orgasm, the way he felt trembling under my touch, and the complete lack of control he had over his legs once his orgasm ebbed.

"Yeah, good. Proud of something stupid."

"Do I wanna know?" he asks. "You can tell me anyway. Spare the details."

"I did things for him..."

"Spare. The. Details."

"And not for myself," I quickly add. "And it didn't feel impossible to resist. Like I have some actual control over my... urges. Like I can handle them. And even when he asked if... yeah, sparing the details, I said no. And he listened. And it felt good. Almost better than actually... yeah."

He breathes in through his nose, and when he exhales, steam from his coffee comes my way. "That's definitely something to be proud of. And the rest? Any cravings?"

I'd kill for a fucking upper right now. I'm so tired and drained. "Uh, almost constantly. Like it's there in the back of my mind, not demanding I take something, but reminding me that it feels good. I hope the whisper doesn't start yelling at me."

"Even if it does, you're strong enough to ignore it. Keep quilting. Do something else that takes your mind off it."

Yeah, the sewing isn't really cutting it. It's fine because I don't hate it, and I like quilting nights at Marian's house, but I need something a bit more consuming. A bit more stimulating. A bit more enjoyable.

"Have you tied things up in the city? With your old place? What happened there?"

I snort into my mug. "Well, I stole a frappé and snorted a baggy of coke, and then, since I'd already fucked up and called my sponsor, I went on a bit of a bender for the whole day. Got high off my ass to *really* give myself a reason to go to rehab for the eighth time, sold almost everything I owned in a drug haze that got finalized during my detox days later. But yeah, I just... left. I still own a place there, but I guess I should tie that up. Get my name off it. End that chapter."

"Feel up to it?" Nathan asks, getting up for a refill.

"Soon," I say, letting him pour me more coffee. "I'm gonna smoke. I'll be right back... if I can stay?" My voice wobbles and Nathan notices, so he throws me one of his jackets and joins me on the front porch.

What is wrong with me? I had an awesome night, feel proud of myself for how I handled it, got to sleep in the same bed as my new slow-moving boyfriend, and now I'm broken about it or something. Like I got a taste of the good life and have no idea if I can keep it. I know my track record. I know myself. I'm that shadow that clouds sunshine and the toxin that spoils freshness. I'm a bad omen in a smiling package, and I don't even know if my smile is real or if it's forced.

I'm happy! My smile should be real. But emotions are overwhelming, whether they're positive or negative, and I'm crumbling a little. Suffocating under the weight of every-thing that feels good and dying under the pressure to keep it good.

Nicotine fills my lungs and my hands shake. Nathan says nothing, but he sits next to me on the front step, watching the street wake up with the sun. A part of me wants to sprint home and hide in my attic like a vampire, sucking up loneliness instead of blood. I'm feeling guilty about my thoughts. I'm assuming the worst just because I'm living in the crash after the high of last night. I'm afraid to let too much happiness creep up on me... because what if I get used to it and then it disappears?

When I exhale smoke, my breath wavers and a choked sob sneaks out. I close my eyes, trying to lock it down, keep it inside, and not taint the sunrise with the eclipse of my feelings.

"The first time Alex invited me to spend time with him, I was so excited and overwhelmed about it that I said no," Nathan says, and now I'm leaking from my eyes but not fully crying. "I'd been wanting it for so long. I spent so much time trying to earn his trust and make him believe in me, but he never took the bait. He was so skeptical of me. He kept me at arm's length because he didn't want to get hurt by me again."

That's probably how my family feels. I blink, and more tears drip, so I smoke harder.

"And when he finally trusted me enough, believed in me enough, to actually invite me to simply watch a movie with him, I suddenly didn't trust myself. It was a Leonardo

DiCaprio movie, that one about him walking through dreams, and Alex loves Leo. Loved him. He's changed his mind now, but at the time, he was a big fan. And all I could think about was ruining a celebrity for him. What if I messed up, made a mistake, said the wrong thing, or was in a bad mood and ruined Leonardo for him? It was a damn movie, and the pressure of what it meant turned me into a pathetic coward. So, I said no. And guess what?"

I up-nod to ask what.

"He didn't invite me to do anything with him again for a year after that. I let him down just by refusing something I'd wanted for so long." Nathan looks at me. "You're doing that now."

"Doing what?"

"Crumbling under the weight of wanting things without thinking you deserve them. You do, you know. Deserve them. You know that, right?"

I stamp my smoke and light another. "What have I ever done to deserve anything? Anything other than come-uppance?"

The front door is open, and I forgot that it's silent now, but Alexei is standing there in all black with his pale blue hair messy. He's glaring at us, poised but pissed.

"You went to rehab eight times. You got better. You earned sobriety chips and moved back home with your family. You care about your brothers and want to make life better for your mom. You sew and spend time with older ladies. You make my dad feel proud of you. You make me happy despite how hard that is. You're a good person with a past that just so happens to have some substance abuse in it, but that's not your whole fucking personality, Gage. If you won't see yourself as a person, I will." He levels me with a very stern and cute expression. "Hi, you're Gage Rossum, former substance abuser and current slow-moving boyfriend. And you're going to give yourself some damn credit. Yeah? What about comeuppance for all that?" He widens his eyes at me, and I'm awestruck and alive, and then... and then he slams the door on us and shouts, "That's not the mug he was supposed to get!"

I'm still staring at the wooden door, my smoke burning down between my fingers and my coffee cooling while my mind rearranges itself to take in everything Alexei just said.

Then Nathan snorts. "What he said."

Slowly, I look at him.

"Slow-moving boyfriend?" he asks.

"It's a thing we're trying." I wave him off. "Am I more than an addict?"

"Fuckin' right you are," Nathan says. "I get that speech from him all the time. It's like some default setting where we refer to ourselves as addicts and only addicts because we're preparing everyone to be let down by us. Alex will never see you that way."

"But he saw you that way."

"He was a child. He saw me *only* as a junkie for seventeen years of his life. I was his dad biologically, but I wasn't a dad. Alex only ever saw me as an addict he had to take care of and the man who brought danger to the house, and because of that, he was very skeptical of me. He's never known you high. The situation is different, and he's learned a lot because of what we put him through. Let him remind you that you're a person. It's okay to accept it." He smiles at me. "I gotta get to work, but wanna hit a meeting tonight?"

"Yes, please." I hand him my mug when he stands. "What mug was I supposed to get?"

Nathan just shakes his head and leaves me on the front porch to finish my cigarette.

"I DON'T THINK it's the best idea, Gage," Natalie says during our video appointment.

"Why not?" I slump against my headboard and jostle my laptop around.

"Because that's not the purpose of it."

I told her that I was about to write in my arousal journal, recapping in great detail everything I felt and experienced with Alexei last night. While she's very proud of me for how last night went, she's now stern about the journal.

"It's not meant to be a toy in a sex act. It isn't there to build temptation and arousal. It's perfectly acceptable for you to share it with him, but not as part of a game. It's meant to be a tool. A coping method. A practice in mindfulness and self-awareness. Make sure you're using it as such."

Oh. Yeah. I guess that makes sense. "But you never said anything the first time we told you about it."

"Because it was healthy at the time. It got you over the

hurdle of *wanting* and into *practicing*, but now it needs to remain a tool for your awareness. Find other ways to entice one another from now on." She smiles at me. "Now, tell me about last night and how you're feeling today."

I inhale hard. "Get ready. It's the full spectrum of feelings."

And by the time I'm done recapping the high of last night and the low of this morning, I'm drained. But Natalie makes me feel better about it because recovery is draining. Especially in the beginning. And it's okay to be tired and confused and doubtful as long as there is still pride and hope there. And there is. I'm full of pride, and even though I'm sinking beneath my blankets to take a nap instead of working, I'm remembering Alexei from this morning.

If you won't see yourself as a person, I will.

He's right. Maybe it's time I actually start seeing myself as a person instead of just an addict. Mom's friends and the neighbour ladies know good stories about me. Alexei thinks I'm a person. My brothers see me as a brother. My mom sees me as a son.

I'm a person.

gage

18

A person with sudden anxiety!

About reconnecting with friends from high school. Ones from that artsy group that felt good to be around, but I inevitably ditched when I needed to chase a high. We're sitting in a restaurant that serves ten-cent wings and half-priced pints, and I'm getting the wings spicy, and the server is asking me if I'd like anything to drink.

And anxiety!

Because, yes. Yes, I would like something to drink. It doesn't even matter that alcohol was never my method of destruction because I want some now. Half-priced pints sound splendid and sudsy and delicious.

But I'm a person. Not just an addict. And everyone is staring at me while I have an internal debate about ordering a drink, and the server is being awkward, like he knows I'm stalling but can't fathom why. I'm a person, but I'm *also* an addict, and unless you are *also* a person who is *also* an

198

addict, it might not make sense to stall on something as simple as a drink order.

Just say water.

Say Pepsi.

Say you'd like a glass of chocolate milk.

Order a goddamn Oreo milkshake, Gage.

I say nothing, and the server tells me he'll give me another minute to decide. But then Ruby, this edgy chick a year older than me, pipes up for me and takes the pressure off.

"He'll have Coke."

"Pepsi," I mutter in absolute relief.

"Pepsi," Ruby repeats. "So will I. And a water with no ice. Thanks."

She's squeezing my sweaty hand under the table and giving me a look full of love or something, and I breathe a little easier. "Thank you."

She winks and doesn't make a thing of it. I try not to make a thing of all the half-priced pints that show up on the table four minutes later. They're sweating as much as my hands are, so I eat spicy wings and order more spicy wings, and when those are gone, I order honey garlic ones because there's a craving inside me that wings are going to have to fill.

"So, how's it feel to be back, Gage?"

And like magic, that's exactly when my brother Owen shows up. He's late because his shift ran late, and I'm so happy to see him.

"I love living with Mom again," I say, scooting my chair

closer to my brother when he sits down. "And being near Owen."

Owen looks at my many empty plates that haven't been cleared and the three empty Pepsi cups that only have melting ice in the bottom. He smiles, which makes me smile.

I'm a person.

Owen isn't an artsy guy, but he gets along with everyone, so we chat and laugh and actually have a good time with this group of friends I pushed away ten years ago. Just like that, I'm mending bridges and forging new relationships, making old things new again, just like Alexei will do in his workshop. I text my mom.

> Gage: I hope your forging class is good. I'm doing some forging of my own.

Then I text Alexei.

> Gage: Was it supposed to be the blue mug with the moustache on it? Are you trying to get me to grow a moustache?

Mom doesn't text me back. She'll probably find the text three weeks from now and think I'm talking about something else entirely, but Alexei answers.

> Alexei <3 : I hung your fedora on my bedpost. And I'm wearing your black and blue checkered slip-ons.

I have no idea what that has to do with mugs and moustaches, but I smile at my phone and send him a picture of all my empty dishes. Then I send the 'fried meats are our friends' design and an orange heart emoji.

He rolls his emoji eyes at me.

Then the anxiety gets better because I'm surrounded by pints and cocktails, and I'm no longer hungry for one.

I'm a person.

Owen has to stop me from stealing a bottle of BBQ sauce, though, so there's that. I haven't stolen anything in over a year—haven't even had the urge to.

The next day, I get really motivated. I update almost all of my digital designs, create some new layouts for planners with so many more hyperlinks, and when that doesn't feel like enough, I start on sticker packs. Somehow, I end up with twelve different sticker themes for twelve different planner designs, and I'm smiling at everything except Slash. Because he's sitting in my window seat, grumping at me about my productivity while he's been a lazy asshole all day.

"Boys! Dinner!" Mom shouts, and holy fuck. A whole day has passed and I've barely left my room.

Maybe I'll start making t-shirt designs. Maybe I love digital art again. Maybe I'm going to start digitally drawing again.

I'm a person. I'm an artist.

I'm clambering down the stairs, ready to compliment Mom on her dinner-making abilities, when I realize the back door is open and we're going to the neighbours' for dinner. And when I trip Cole, body check Nick, and win the non-existent race into Benedita's backyard, I pause and stop smiling. Because there's *the* friend. The wife of Paul's co-worker.

The only one I ever met, and she's shocked to see me but still smiling. And Mom says these are the neighbour's third cousins on her aunt's side, and wow. What a small world.

"Hi," I squeak. Memories are coming back, hazy ones from times I pretended to be sober, reminding me that she told me she has family in my hometown. We bonded over it. And then I forgot it because drugs were more important.

"Hey, Gage," she says, beaming at me. "You look amazing! How are you?"

"I'm... good. Really good, actually," I say and mean it for the first time. "You look different." I obnoxiously point to the very round belly she's sporting. "Are you just fat? Or happy to see a baby soon?" That was so insensitive and I have no idea why I said it.

"Just fat," she jokes. "And eager to see a baby in less than a month."

"Congrats!"

"Hello?" Alexei's voice drifts to the yard from my kitchen.

"Alexei!" I shout, but then I'm speedwalking back home to grab him. "Hi." I grin at him, taking his hand that says right. It really is the right one.

He has hearts in his eyes, but there's skepticism, too. "Dubious again?"

"A little," I admit. "Remember I said I had an ex? Well, someone I knew through him is in my neighbour's backyard, and I'm being weird and making fat jokes. Please stop me."

He watches me. Hard.

"And I made sticker packs and planners all day, and I

need you to help me with sales and bundles. Am I still paying the non-flirting tax?"

"I'm the neurotic rambler in this equation," he says. "What's happening?"

"I'm nervous," I admit. "Will you come to dinner with me? There are probably fried meats, but I don't know."

I want to kiss him.

"Okay."

"That easy? I would have asked a lot of questions and assumed your family wouldn't want me there."

"Should I assume those things? I can ask a lot of questions if you want me to."

"Nope. Just come with me. You look sexy today." I link our fingers, and he corrects the hold, palms together without our fingers linked. Right. I smile. "I like these pants."

"You can call them jeans," Alexei says.

"Well, I didn't want to draw attention to the fact they're jeans, in case you weren't aware. Never seen you wear jeans before."

"I'm aware."

"You told me you wear mascara sometimes, but I've never seen you wear it."

"You pay that close of attention to my eyelashes?" he asks.

"Yes." To all of him. Every bit. I notice everything about him every time I see him. If his hair stands up in a different direction. If it's been recently re-dyed or is a bit more faded. His septum piercing switching from a silver humbug to a

black metal one. I like the black metal one. A lot. His pale
blue eyes and the state of his nail polish.

We're still holding hands when we walk into the backyard. I haven't really told my family I'm dating Alexei, but
no one blinks at it. Not even Sonya, who only ever knew me
as Paul's hidden boyfriend. She smiles. I smile. The family
smiles. Introductions to Alexei are made, and then we're
eating a Portuguese chicken dish that Alexei really likes, and
he even has a slice of the orange honey almond cake for
dessert. And the neighbour loves him, so she's trying to
force-feed him more and sell him on another serving of
chicken, but my boy has an iron will.

And since my neighbours are very neighbourly, Marian,
Pearl, and Nancy come by for a slice, and we chat about
quilts. The sex shop owners stop by, and a whole other cake
is pulled out of thin air. Then Nathan comes, and all the
ladies love him, and Mom says he should come meet their
forging teacher. Suddenly, there are kids and foster parents
and neighbours I've never met but who have heard about
me. Good things about me. Wow.

Everything is so happy and normal again. So I leave,
disappearing to my own front porch for a cigarette. Once
again, I find myself wondering if everyone is accommodating
me. Are they avoiding alcohol because I'm there? Would
there be an awesome Portuguese drink to pair with the
awesome Portuguese meal?

I know people do it to be kind and courteous, but I can't
help but feel guilty about it. I make people change. I require
accommodations. I don't know if I actually have a justifi-

able reason to require these resources, and it makes me feel like shit. And it's not something easy like a fucking fidget spinner. It's the whole vibe of the night. It's forcing people to stay sober until I leave, which inadvertently makes me feel unwelcome even though they're doing it to be welcoming.

Fuck. My. Mind.

"I don't feel overly enthused about moustaches." Alexei swings around the porch pillar, making me breathe a little easier. "Sonya wanted to say goodbye before you left." She follows him, waddling with her gigantic belly sticking out.

I smile at her but pat the step next to me to invite Alexei over.

"I don't wish to die of second-hand smoke, Gage. I'll be back." He grins at me before heading back to the neighbours' yard.

I offer Sonya a hand and help her get situated with a cushion under her ass. "We have chairs," I inform her.

She looks at them on the porch. "I'm settled here now. No getting me up." Her knee bumps mine. "I like him."

"Who?"

"Alexei. He's so weird and rude about it, but bashfully polite at the same time. Sexy, too. Way better looking than your last boyfriend."

I laugh, putting my smoke out because... pregnant lady. "Yeah, he's a bit of a mindfuck, but he's adorable about it. I can't believe we're having dinner together. Like our lives were sort of connected, but now that the connection is broken, you're still here. It's strange."

She smiles at the street and the maple on the front lawn. "Gage, I wanna say I'm sorry."

"No," I butt in.

"Let me say it!" She laughs. "Because I knew, okay? I knew what you were struggling through. I saw it, and instead of offering you any sort of hand to hold on to or a person to confide in, I just let it happen."

"My sobriety nor my drug use is your thing to say sorry for. You had no responsibility to me, so stop with your sorrys."

"I don't mean that part," she says, taking me right off guard. "I mean Paul."

"Paul?" I look at her.

"He used you, Gage."

"What? No. I used him. I manipulated him into giving me a safe place to live. Someone to take care of me."

She shifts her body around until she's facing me. "He used you, too. He told stories about your drug dependency at work. I don't work there, but Henrique would come home and tell me about it. He pulled pity from people and made himself seem like this stand-up guy for taking you in. He used you to build himself up as a hero."

Oh. I don't really know how that feels. "Well, it's no worse than what I did to him."

"It is, though." She takes my hand. "Because he... I know you didn't see it or even care because you were caught deep in addiction, but he..."

"Sonya, I'm stronger now. You can tell me."

"He wouldn't be such a hero if you were sober, you

know what I'm saying? He... kept you that way. Even when you went to rehab, he already anticipated you relapsing, and I never liked the way he looked when he talked about it. I think he... encouraged you. Offered you alcoholic drinks when you weren't aware you were drinking. Left pills out on purpose. Not in large doses, but enough to give you a buzz and keep you looking for more."

I'm already shaking my head at her story despite how badly it hurts. "No. I'm the junkie. I took the pills on my own. I looked for them and found his hiding spots. It had nothing to do with him."

She smiles weakly, and maybe... maybe I'm on the cusp of believing her. Because Paul really did have a lot of single pills around that I couldn't explain. I thought they were for his sore back or his migraines, but now that I'm thinking back on it, I don't remember seeing him take them. But why? Why would he waste that kind of money on me? Especially when we fought so much and the comedown from the high was horrible for him?

"Wanna know something about Paul that you might not have noticed?" Sonya asks when I say nothing. "He needs to be needed. It's his affliction. He needed you to need him."

I look at her, trying to decide why she's telling me this now.

"You know how I know, apart from witnessing it?"

"How?"

"He's already got someone else. He moved a guy in a few weeks ago. This guy is in a lot of financial trouble, and Paul is about to become his hero." She squeezes my hand.

"So yes, your sobriety is on you, but I don't want you to think you were the only one hurting yourself back then. He enabled you."

But *I* picked him. My poor decision-making skills led me to Paul, and to be honest, I was in a similar situation to this new guy when he found me. I had money, but I had no home and no safe place to go. I met Paul at a bar, and we had a few drinks together and went back to his place to hook up. God, it was literally a week after that I moved in with him. Fuck, I'm such a loser. A few months after that, I forked up a lot of money to buy us a better place and didn't care about the money because Paul took care of me.

"Why tell me now and not back then?" I ask.

"Because I was a little scared of you," she admits. "You were happy-go-lucky most of the time, but... you weren't always. And you lied a lot. I saw you cheat on him a few times, caught you sneaking people out of your place when we came to visit." I cringe. "But mostly because I didn't know how you would react, and we barely knew each other. I was scared."

My eyes burn. "I'm sorry for scaring you."

"Oh, baby," she says, laughing. "That's in the past. And now that I know you a bit better, I love who you are. My auntie and uncle love you, and I'm glad you're neighbours. Means we get to see each other more often." She pats my cheek. "I like you sober. And you look amazing. And you deserve Alexei. He's so great."

She's gotta be ten years older than me, but for the first time, I think I've made a friend who actually knew me while

I was a fuck-up. "Thank you. For, uh, not being scared of me anymore. For seeing me now."

I haul her to her feet, hug her around her belly, and watch her walk away.

"I know you're there."

"How?" Alexei asks from beside the porch.

"I sense your soul." I grin at him.

"You believe in soulmates?" he asks, sitting next to me now that I'm not smoking.

"Maybe. Never really thought about it before." I trace the lines of his knuckle tattoos, wanting to ask what they are but enjoying the mystery of them. "How much did you hear?"

"I pretty much eavesdropped on all of it," he says. "Sorry, but also, this is who I am."

I like people who are unapologetically themselves, and Alexei has that in spades. "Wanna see all my new stickers?"

alexei

19

We've been talking about Paul, but I can tell Gage doesn't know what to say about him. And I'm not ready to push him on it, so now my legs are over his thighs, and he's rubbing my feet, and the blankets of his attic bed are all bunched around us.

It's so nice.

"I feel like we never talk about you," he says to me. "Like I require too much focus and it leaves you quiet about yourself. Tell me all your problems, Alexei."

"Not everyone has to have big problems that need fixing," I state. "I don't have any."

"None?"

I shrug. "Just a bit of an attachment to my dad that probably isn't healthy."

"How come?" Gage massages my calves to encourage me. "What sort of attachment?"

"Just like, the kind that means I wanna be near him, and I sometimes worry about him dying like my mom did. It's a fear I have, but I'm getting better at managing it. It helps to be closer with him now so that I know what's going on."

"I think that's fair. It's not unhealthy, it just means that you love your dad and want him to stay in your life." Gage smiles, and I settle a little, knowing that he understands. "Do I cause you that kind of fear? I know I'm not your dad and we don't have a lifelong history like you do with him, but I was an addict, so... do you worry about me leaving you or letting you down?"

I'm shaking my head to say no, but I stop to think about it. "No. Not yet anyway. It's different with you because I haven't been broken by you. The relationship is different, you know? If you hurt me, we break up and move on, but if my dad does... he's still my dad. The expectations are different. Does that make sense?"

Gage nods and smiles at me. "It does. You can talk to me about it, you know. Anything. Anytime."

"Okay, I have questions about other things then. Funner things." I look at him for permission, and when he laughs and nods, I ask, "Did you come out? Back in high school?"

"Yeah, I guess. It was never a big thing with my family. They just knew. And Nick is gay, too."

"Too? I thought you were bi."

"Right, yeah. I am." He laughs. "Only been with guys in the last while. You're gay-gay?"

"Yeah."

"And you knew it all along? Like you were a straight-away-gay?"

"What's a straight-away-gay?"

He rubs my foot. "Like you knew right from the beginning you were into guys. Didn't go through that trial period with girls."

"Oh, no trial period, no. Knew it was guys pretty early on. So I had crushes but never really dated anyone. But when I was fourteen, I walked in on a girl naked in the showers."

"What?" He laughs, eyes alight, smile bright.

"I went to this nerdy camp, okay? It was for gaming and cool dorky shit." I blush. "My neighbour signed me up, and I have no idea who paid for it, but I went there one time when my dad went to rehab. And we stayed in these cabin things, but the bathrooms were in another building. So I walked in to brush my teeth, and some girl was in there just... naked. It was the male bathroom, but... anyway, I have no idea why she was in there, but she just stood there, and I stood there, and it was so awkward. But... nothing. I looked. She was so pretty, and her body was nice, but... no attraction to it in a sexual way, so maybe that was my trial night. I looked and didn't get the tingles."

"And fourteen is a pretty tingly age," Gage says, smirking.

"It is," I agree. "How'd you know you were interested in both?"

"I think *all* is a better word. So maybe I'm pan. I don't know. I lost my virginity to a girl. It was good. I didn't have an obsessive compulsion at that age, so I slept around a bit, and it was fun, even though I was either high or partially drunk during. It wasn't until a few years later that I hooked up with a guy for the first time. I mean, yeah, I knew I was into guys, but I'd never actually slept with one. I knew my way around a vagina at that point, you know?"

"No, Gage. I don't know. I'm not very familiar with vaginas."

He laughs. "Right, well, they're pretty awesome. Anyway, I knew my way around a vagina, but not really a dick. So it was a fumbly experience, but then it got worse. I bottomed. And I had no idea what bottoming entailed at the time, so it hurt really bad despite the cocktail of drugs I was on, and I hated it. So yeah, didn't go there again for a long time. Then I hooked up with someone who was pretty gender fluid and actually knew what they were doing, and I guess they taught me that bottoming can be way better."

I smile at that. "Yeah?"

"Yeah."

"You telling me you're a bottom?" I ask.

"This might sound weird, but I kind of like the feeling of not knowing that about each other yet. Like, we might be incompatible, but I feel like we'll find a way to make it work. Right now, it's just fun getting to know you slowly. Does that bother you?"

I shake my head and love this conversation. I also know that we'll be compatible. I just know. "Tell me more about your depth of vagina knowledge. I've always wondered."

Gage chuckles and gives me a female anatomy lesson I absolutely don't need, but it's the way he talks about women and people in general that makes me feel at ease with him.

I've hung around some pretty set-in-their-vagina-hating-ways guys, and Gage is a nice breather.

When Gage asks me if I want to stay over and then offers to walk me home in the morning to get his meds anyway, I barely even panic. I'm not someone who is comfortable outside my own bed, but something about this one and the attic and the conversation we've just had in here makes me comfortable enough to stay. Gage even texts my dad for me to let him know I'm staying. Such maturity.

Gage gives me a toothbrush, and then he doesn't leave the bathroom. Cole and Nick are laughing at things in the kitchen. Gage's mom, Jenny, is chatting animatedly on the phone with Marian, and I'm sharing a bathroom and spitting into the same sink as Gage. I've never lived in a busy house before.

"You get used to it," Gage says, rinsing his mouth. "The noise."

I kind of like it, to be honest. But maybe only on occasion.

And I like the matching pyjamas we're wearing, too. Both decked out in orange and black plaid, white t-shirts from Gage's drawer, we laugh our way into bed.

"Do you have a side?" I ask.

"Yeah, usually right in the middle." He settles himself there, pulling my back against his chest. A minute later, his boner pokes me in the ass. "Shit. Maybe I'm better at being the little spoon. Switch."

So we roll over, and I snake my arm around his middle. A minute later, my boner is poking him in the ass.

"Maybe we should sleep on our backs. Or face each other." He rolls over until we're face to face. The room is dark, but the streetlights come in the picture window. "Why blue?" he asks. "I love the blue."

"It's just my favourite colour," I say, our knees knocking and our hands playing together in between our bodies.

"Is it?"

"No," I sigh. "I mean, it is now, but... my dad got me a light blue hoodie. I have no idea why he got it for me because I only ever wore black."

"Go on." Gage smiles, hands all over me.

"And I was moody at the time. It was right around his first year sober. So, seven-ish years ago. I still didn't trust him, and when he gave me the blue hoodie, I wanted to throw it in his face that he didn't know me at all. Wouldn't even take the time to get to know his own son. So, like I do, I went overboard. I painted my nails light blue, dyed my hair, wore the hoodie everywhere just to shove it in his face. Like, hey, look how fucking different I look. Notice me now?"

"And he did."

"He did," I admit. "He commented on the blue and said it made me look nice. Happier. And for my birthday the next year, he got me a black hoodie. Maybe just to prove that he knew me. I dunno, but I came to like the blue. It's just a rinse for my hair, so whenever I walk out of the bathroom after just having redone it, it's this petty little inside joke with my dad that makes us both smile."

Gage laughs, and our bodies inch closer together. His pillow is uncomfortable as shit, but to be honest, I don't feel very uncomfortable. "And the septum piercing? So fucking sexy, but what made you get it?"

"I have a friend, you know."

"Do you?" He laughs. "Tell me more."

"He has an older brother who is in a band, and basically, I just got it because he has one and I thought it was cool." I shrug. "For how deep I try to be, sometimes I'm pretty shallow."

"Hey, wanting to be like the cool guy in the band is like a rite of passage. And the symbols?" He brings my left hand up, kissing my tattooed knuckles and the word 'right' on the top.

"They're actually quite impressive, I must admit. They're a code. Each symbol represents an equation that correlates to a letter. Like I said, I went to a nerdy camp, and one summer we made encryptions and things. So, my equations and codes are only known to me, so I'm the only one who knows what it says." I flip my hand. "And the right is which direction to read it. Instead of straight across my knuckles, you start with the left hand and read from the right, and then go to the right hand and read from the right. Do you think I'm cooler now?"

"So fucking cool," Gage agrees, pressing his body against mine. "I think nerdy intelligence is sexy."

"I can tell." My hips press against his, but the mood is still simmering, gentle. I like that he doesn't ask me to tell him what it says. "Why the mechanical things on your chest?"

"Because I mixed uppers with downers and blended it

with MDMA and came out of a tattoo shop with them." He frowns. "I'm not deep either. Just stupid and compulsive."

"At least your stupidity and compulsiveness resulted in nice art. Better than the Chinese symbol for cat or something."

Despite the conversation, we're wrapped around each other and our cocks are grazing. Gage's knee slips between my legs and mine hooks over his hip, and now we're just firmly rubbing like it's no big deal. But it's a huge deal, and my face is hot!

"Is this okay?" I ask him, trying not to breathe too hard.

His forehead nods against mine. "Yeah, it's okay. I'm okay. I'm *really* okay."

"Can I touch you?"

Against my jaw, he breathes, "Yes."

I reach between our bodies, shoving my pants down just enough to free my cock. When I do the same for Gage, he lifts a bit to make it easier for me. His ragged moan as soon as my hand lands on his dick is so strained, so I tilt his chin up by nudging him with my head.

"Still okay?"

"Y-yeah. I wanna feel everything. Every part of you. Go slow, Alexei."

I don't even know what I have planned, but I move slowly. I explore the way his hard cock feels in my hand, warm and solid and with a bit of its own mind. I take it slow while I learn the way he trembles and the sound his throat makes when he tries to hold back a groan. I'm goddamn glacially slow when I shift my hips forward and wrap my fingers around the both of us, sweating in my plaid pyjamas.

"You have no idea how good this feels," Gage speaks into my neck, voice even more abrasive than usual.

"I do, actually. I'm feeling it, too."

"It's been over a year since I felt another body next to mine." He reaches down to skim his hand over my hip. It ends up on my ass, and he pulls me forward, rocking us together. Slowly. "Skin to skin. You feel amazing."

So that we really can be skin-to-skin, I line us up and then let go. Our cocks rub together, hips grinding, his hand trying to control the pace and keep it slow. I know sex and penetration are the ultimate goal for most people, and I enjoy it myself, but this... this slow rub and dry hump is fucking everything. It's fresh and terrifying because it's a brand new experience for both of us. It's a sexy way for our bodies to learn to work together. It's attraction and an undeniable pull, a build-up that isn't rushed or forced.

And holy shit, it's hot as hell. It's better than sex. It's... more intimate.

His hand leaves my ass and weaves into my hair, our bodies creating friction all on their own. "Don't let me kiss you," he rasps. "Not while I'm horny. Not yet."

Then he yanks my hair and forces my face up, nose to nose with him. Our lips brush, craving a kiss that isn't allowed because he respects my take on kissing. I want it so badly, but I want his meaning behind it even more.

"I'm gonna come from this," he admits. "Fuck, Alexei."

So I breathe against his lips, close my eyes, picturing what it will feel like to kiss him, and move my hand down to his ass. I squeeze it, rocking him forward. The heads of our cocks slip and slide together, spreading precum everywhere. Our arms on the bottom are haphazardly numbing in the middle somewhere, but it doesn't matter because everything else feels so good, so right.

"I want to feel it," I tell him, so into this that my body won't stop moving. "I want to see you and feel you when you come."

"Come with me so I don't get selfish." He pulls our mouths together. Groans. Backs off and pants against my slick lips. "Where the fuck did you come from, Alexei?" he asks, but I'm pretty sure it's rhetorical.

In my head, I'm telling him I'm his soulmate.

Slickness coats our cocks and stomachs, and the blanket is way too warm, but neither of us moves it. When Gage grinds his hips, I moan against the corner of his mouth, grinding right back. His knee is still between my legs, and he hikes it up, pressing it all the way up to my ass, making us crush together perfectly. We both moan, and then Gage is biting my lower lip, and I'm shaking all over again, and...

"Gage."

He chokes, tightening his hold on the back of my head. "Mmmm," he moans. "Fuck, Alexei. Fuck!"

A burst of yellow blinds me from behind my eyelids, and Gage's long, drawn-out moan is the hottest thing I've ever heard. But when I feel his cock twitch against mine, and he presses us together so hard that our sticky abs rub together, I lose all sense of colours and blindness because this is bliss. My cock throbs, my cum joining his, a mingling of moans and panting breaths and shaking bodies, all meshed together in an attic bed. Gage dips his head, lips landing on my neck to suck the skin beneath my jaw. I breathe in his hair, the smell of cigarettes and detergent and sex.

We stay together, entwined and tangled, until my heartbeat isn't threatening a heart attack and his lungs are settling down from the workout. My head on his, his face in my neck, arms wrapped and numb.

"Are you okay?" I check in. "Happy? Content?"

I feel him smile against my neck. "So happy." He pulls back, looking at me with those big brown eyes and a lazy grin. "You're something else, you know that?"

"Something else like what?"

"Just magic or something. This is magic. Us."

Because we're soulmates. "I know." I smirk at him.

When we separate, everything is a mess, and we laugh a little while cleaning up, changing into clean clothes and leaving the sheets because they aren't bad. I'm yawning, sedated and relaxed, but Gage pulls out his journal, and I get a second wind.

"Ready for this part, or want me to do it on my own?"

I prop myself up and just stare at him. His therapist says we aren't allowed to use the journal as a prop to entice one another, but she more than encourages us to write in it together after the fun is over. "So ready for this part. This might be my favourite part." Like I said, actions and the reasons behind them intrigue me. I can't wait to sex journal with Gage.

He shakes his hand out. "My whole-ass arm is numb."

gage

I've been in a bit of a rut. A mood rut. I don't know how to feel about the whole Paul thing. Part of me wants to be pissed off and mad at him for it, but then that part fights with the part of me that knows I did shitty things to him, too. I lied compulsively. I fucking cheated on him. Often. I stole from him, abused his kindness, and used him as nothing more than a guy who'd put his fingers under my nose to make sure I was still breathing.

So, do I really have the right to be angry?

But what kind of low-life fucking prick strategically places pills and drinks around the house to entice his addict boyfriend, who was too greedy and stupid to notice? I mean, I expect it from another substance abuser, but not Paul. But then Alexei said a thing. He said that power is like a substance, and Paul abused that. And... it helped. It helped enough that I was able to put it out of my mind for a bit.

But now my mood is still confused.

I'm happy, strong, proud, and falling for a neurotic rambler, so that gives me all the good feels. But I'm also doubtful, scared of failure, and worried about tainting everyone, so that locks me in the bad feels. Pair that all with the ups and downs of neurodivergence and a full day spent in ADHD paralysis, and it's a clusterfuck of an emotions party in my head.

So I leave the house, shouting at Mom and the twins that I'm hitting up a meeting. Nathan and my old sponsor Kristen both say that when you're feeling any sort of way, find a meeting. So, I'm taking their advice and sitting in a chair, listening to the same group of people and a few new faces talk about their lives. And it's good. Uplifting. Temporarily helps my mood.

After, I walk out the church doors with a smoke between my lips and a lighter that refuses to light.

One lights up in front of me, and I lean into it before I even look to see who offered it. My blood chills. Or gets thin. Or burns or something.

"Hey," I say to Brian. "What're you doing here?" *Why are you here? Did you follow me? What the fuck is going on?*

"Lost my truck keys," he says, nodding to it parked way up the street. "So, walkin' home. You headed that way?"

Yes, I am headed that way because he has to pass my street to get to his house, and I still don't have a vehicle and... shit. "Yep."

We're walking, and I offer him a smoke, and he's kind of quiet, but I can tell he's on something. I'm terrified. Not because he's a user, but because he's got something I want. He's feeling something I want to feel. He's controlling his mood with a substance that could help control mine. And I'm thinking about it. But kind of rationally. Like I'm weighing the pros and the cons, trying to remind myself that it'll help in the moment and make it worse after the moment is over.

Then I'm picturing the sadness in my mom's eyes when she sees mine glossed and bloodshot, the subtle worry from the twins, and the disappointment from Owen. I'm thinking about quilting night at Marian's and how I'm supposed to bring a snack this week, so I've been planning my grocery trips to make something special.

I'm thinking about Alexei and how he said he wouldn't hate me if I relapsed, but that it'd hurt him. I don't want to hurt him. Ever. But I'm destructive. I hurt things.

But I don't want to, and maybe that's enough of a change in me not to ask Brian what he's on and then pretend like I'm not drooling over it.

"So," he starts, jarring me from my freeway of thoughts. They're all just zipping around up there with no traffic lights or speed limits. I clench, preparing for the worst, readying my excuse to either accept his offer or turn it down. "What's rehab like?"

Oh. My feet stop moving and I'm staring at him, and I think he feels weird about it, so I pick up my pace again and try not to show how mind-blown I am.

"Yeah, it's, uh, tough, man. It's so hard, but it's... I've got a lot of experience," I say, chuckling because, once again, I'm

224

prepping to poke fun at myself and my addiction. Like, wow, nothing is more funny than addiction, right? So lame. "I've been eight times."

He finishes his cigarette and has no shame about asking me for another. I hand him one. "Eight? Shit, that's nuts, man. It, uh, worked? This time?"

I'm nodding like it's true. Like I'm saying yes. "So far. I feel good. I don't ever wanna be hooked on that shit again. Feels good to have control. Uh, of myself."

He's asking me about rehab. Why? Does he maybe want to try it? I'd fucking pay for him. I'd pay for him to go eight times if that's what it takes.

"Yeah," he says, slowing down a bit. "Think maybe I, uh... might need to give that a go."

"Yeah, man," I'm saying, smiling. "It's tough, but it's worth it." But that's not what he wants to hear. That's a sales pitch that all family members make, trying to convince you that something you don't understand will be worth it in the end. We don't rationalize that while we're trying to stay cozy with our vice of choice. So, I add, "Honestly, Brian, it fucking sucks to detox and go through withdrawal, but once that shit is out of you, it's like you fucking meet yourself for the first time. Like, I'm twenty-seven and just getting to know myself now. And it's the first time in twelve years that nothing but cigarettes have controlled me. Pretty damn surreal, to be honest."

"You got a number or something for a place?" he asks, not looking hopeful but not looking defeated either.

So I give him the number for the place I just spent a

whole year at. I don't tell him I stayed a year because that's the longest commitment you can make, and it's terrifying your first time. Did I need a full year after a frappé and a day-long bender? Probably not. But probably yes. Because it made me take it seriously. I hit my one-year mark while in there instead of out here in the real world, where drugs and pills are more readily available. It got me over a hurdle and helped me jump into my new life. I walked out of rehab on that one-year day, and... wow, I haven't looked back since.

I open my mouth to tell him it's expensive and that I can help. I close my mouth. He's not ready. If I tell him I have money, he'll come for it for a different reason. He needs to be ready first.

"How's Becky?" I ask when the conversation drops after that.

Tough guys don't cry. Not tough guys like Brian. But he blinks away some tears, takes another cigarette from me, and then says, "She's pregnant. And I'm scared."

That took balls, and I'm so proud of him.

THERE IS an awful grating sound coming from the basement, but I'm not allowed to go down there and look. Alexei kicked us both out of his workshop for prying, and now Nathan and I are cooking the meal subscription box while Alexei tinkers with his old things.

I'm so happy.

Am I allowed to be this happy?

"I think I'm gonna get in touch with a lawyer," I tell Nathan, chopping veggies for the stir-fry. "About the house I co-own in the city."

Because now I'm afraid of Paul. I was going to give him the house, but everything Sonya said has been plaguing my mind, and I'm unsure about confronting him. Maybe it's better to go through a real estate lawyer, sell the place, pay off the rest of the mortgage, and split the rest right down the middle. He can't be mad about that, can he? Especially since he already has someone new living in a house I partially own and pay for.

"Want some backup?" he asks. "I can come along. Help out."

"Yeah, maybe. I'll let you know when I have something concrete." I glance at him. His back is to me, but he seems at ease. Not like he wants to kill me for dating his son. Not like he's disappointed in me for being a welcome intruder in their home. Not like he's judging me as not being good enough for Alexei. "Do you date?"

He looks at me over his shoulder. Then he looks towards the basement stairs. When Alexei starts making a bunch of noise by grinding something, he says, "No. Sort of. Not really." A deep breath. "It's new."

I grin at him. "Alexei doesn't know?"

"I'm afraid he's going to tell me I'm not stable enough for dating."

I snort. "Who is? It's fucking mind-bending, the emotions people go through while dating. Recovered addict

227

or not, it's tough shit made worth it by all the good feels."
When he smiles but doesn't say anything, I ask, "Do you
believe in soulmates?"

He spins to face me. "Did Alex tell you?"

"Tell me what?"

"Nothing. And I don't know. Not really." He shrugs.
"Some people do. So... yeah, some people do." He turns back
around.

So, Alexei then? Does Alexei think I'm his soulmate?
Oh, shit. Or does he think I'm not his soulmate, so this thing
has an expiration date? Fuck.

"These are chopped. Can I go creep on him?" I drop the
knife and don't wait for an answer. I keep my socks light on
the stairs and only step on the creaky ones when Alexei is
using some sort of tool. Then I lurk.

Because goddamn. For a guy who mostly wears sweatpants and hoodies, it's almost jarring to see him in a pair of
work-style pants, a thick, rough leather apron slung over his
neck and draping down to his mid-thighs. It's worn brown,
so much warmer than his blacks and icy blues, and he makes
it beautiful. Alexei can make any colour beautiful.

Then I panic a bit when he picks up a blowtorch and
has no idea that it's now spewing fuel while he tries to get it
started.

"Woah." I place my hand on his and turn the knob off.
Alexei jumps, swearing at me. "I know this place is made of
stone, but Jesus, Alexei. There is wood in here!"

"I know what I'm doing," he insists. "I thought I kicked
you out?"

"I kicked myself back in. What're you working on?" I peer over his shoulder.

He starts to hide his project from me, then thinks better of it. "Light switches," he says. "Or more like the covers that go over the light switches. I found them on that shelf out there, and they're all rusty and corroded, so... I'm fixing them. Grinding the rust off. Yep."

Yep. I smirk. "They're gonna look perfect in this house. How many are there?"

"Like twenty. Maybe eighteen if I can't get these two restored." He points at two pretty badly corroded ones.

"They'll look amazing in the sitting room, don't you think?" I meet his icy blue eyes, falling for him a bit more every single day.

"Yes, Gage. I do think. That's exactly where I... how did you know?"

I tug on the front of his apron and bring him against my front. "Maybe our souls know how to read each other."

His eyes widen, and shock mixes with his melting. God, he really does think we're soulmates, and that just makes me fall for him even more. "You think? I mean, natural progression of slow-moving boyfriends would be straight into—"

"Casually moving boyfriends? Fast-moving boyfriends?" I smirk. When I tell him we're soulmates, it'll be when I kiss him. When he knows with absolute certainty that I'm committed, trust myself, and am acting on nothing but my feelings for him. I want to kiss him now, but first I need to squash a few self-doubts and this constant buzz of negativity that tells me I don't deserve him.

He's leaning against me but won't wrap his arms around me, but I think that's just his bold defiance. He wants to hug me, but he's going to make me do it first. He turns his face, nuzzling against my neck, and switches conversational gears once again. "Do I grate?"

"Grate?"

"Yeah, like on your nerves. Am I stress-inducing? Am I bad for sobriety?"

I push him back and palm his cheeks. "One hundred percent no. You're amazing for sobriety, for more than sobriety. Why would you ask that?"

"I did some ADHD research," he says. "And basically just discovered that the way your mind works is super complicated. And since I'm also a complicated person, I just wondered if we're two complicated guys in a slow-moving relationship that only has room for one complicated guy. Like, do I make your already busy mind even busier, and that's gonna be bad for you?"

"Here's the flip side to that, Alexei. Because flip sides are important." I move my hands down to the sides of his neck. "Boring people don't stimulate me. Boredom leads to bad decisions. Bad decisions will land me in rehab for the ninth time. So, be complicated because it keeps my mind engaged. Be you because I fucking lo—need you to be you because you're crazy perfection just like this. Just as you. I don't want less than your best."

He stares at me. I stare at him. It's comfortably awkward. Then he exhales through his nose. "I guess my

SOBER DOPE & SUNDAYS

dad introducing us is like meeting the *really* old-fashioned way. It fits my romantic dreams."

Another switch flipped fast. I laugh. "See? I'm making your dreams come true, and you're far exceeding mine with your complications. Be you. Be us. I love us."

He smiles so wide that he gets embarrassed about it and hides it in my neck.

alexei

21

My light switch covers are done, and I don't know what else to do. I could go to bed, but Dad isn't home from his meeting with Gage yet, and... I kinda wanna wait up for them.

> Dad: We're just finishing up and chatting. He says he's going home because his mom is at a girl's night, so he wants to be there for the twins. You can go meet him there if you want. I'm good.

It's after ten since their meeting started late, but that's exactly what I'm going to do. I shut off the lights to my workshop, double-check that the blowtorch is completely turned off, and head upstairs for a change of clothes.

> Alexei: Okay, going there now. Let me know if you need anything.

The walk to Gage's house takes four minutes, but the

night air is warm enough to make my hoodie a bit much. Still, I wear it because I feel more comfortable in it. When I knock on the door, there's a crash, a few bangs, and a lot of whispered yelling, but no one comes to answer it. I knock again.

"Heyyy," Cole says, swinging open the door.

My back straightens and all my instincts kick in. "Hey."

"I thought Gage was at your place tonight? Isn't he staying over?" Cole asks, glancing behind him. "I thought... he's not coming home, is he?"

Not now. Because I won't let him. "Are you okay?"

"Yes."

I tilt my head at him. "Is Nick okay?"

"Yes."

His eyes aren't focused and his pupils aren't the right size. There are still crashes happening inside the house, and Nick is laughing and swearing at something from the kitchen.

"What is it?" I ask. "What'd you take?"

Cole shifts his weight from foot to foot, his eyes moving too fast, his fingers all pulling at one another. "Nothing."

I look behind me to make sure Gage and my dad aren't coming down the street, and then I push my way inside. Cole yells at me, but it doesn't really have any heat behind it, so I walk into the kitchen to make sure Nick is fine.

They're both high. Coke, by the looks of the powder Nick is trying to swipe off the table into a small little bag.

"We thought he'd be out all night!" Cole says. "We didn't think he'd... don't let him come here, Alexei."

"How could you?" I ask them both. "When you know what he's been through and what he's still going through?"

"We're allowed to experiment!" Nick shouts.

Sure. They are. But I'm surprised they want to after watching their older brother struggle for so long. "But here? In the house he moved into to try to make his life better? During his recovery? Could you disrespect him any more?"

They both look ashamed, but the drugs buzzing through their systems make them cocky. I try to remind myself that they're young and dumb and allowed to make mistakes. They're allowed to be stupid, and it's not their fault their brother is a recovering addict.

"He's not home. Mom isn't home. No one was supposed to know. We're being safe by doing it at home, and we're being respectful by waiting until we're alone."

"Are you?"

"It's not our fault he's an addict!" Cole snaps, repeating my thoughts. "Doesn't mean we are."

No, it's not their fault, but... "Means you have higher chances of becoming one," I tell him, calm on the outside and panicking on the inside. "Are you both okay? It's not... you're not having any trouble with it? Feeling alright?"

"We're great," Nick says, a slow and disgusting laugh following his words. "So fucking great."

I look at the bag still in his grip. "You better get that out of the house. Take his sobriety seriously. Respect him."

"Yeah. We will. Just make sure he doesn't come home."

I watch them for another few seconds. I mean, they're definitely high, but they don't seem to be in any danger of taking too much or having a bad reaction. I want to hold out my hand and demand they give me the rest of the coke, but I don't. It'll cause a fight I don't have time for because Gage will be home any minute. I know, for an absolute fact, that this will kill Gage. It will hurt him so deeply, test his sobriety, and break his healing heart.

I hear a car door slam, so I rush outside. My dad is driving home and Gage is walking up the front steps. I close the door behind me and watch his lazy smile make him gorgeous when he sees me.

"Hey, complicated," he says, teasing me with a kiss to my cheek. "I was just thinking about you, and here you are. Our souls really can read each other."

I don't want to lie to him. He asked me once if I ever lied, and I told him I didn't if I could help it, but I can't help it tonight. I need to lie to him. I need to keep a secret from him. Because he's not going to like what he hears, and I'd rather tell him tomorrow when the twins are sober and the little baggy is long hidden somewhere Gage can't find it.

My heart hurts because I love the new pet name he finally gave me, but I'm too emotionally distraught to appreciate it.

"Wanna go for a walk with me?" I ask, pressing my hand to his chest to push him away from the house. "I need it."

He frowns at me. "What's wrong? You okay?"

"Yeah, I just need to walk. With you. Let's go."

He's nodding, spinning from the door, taking my hand to lead me down the steps. We're almost free, almost clear of this tragic mess.

Then something crashes inside. My stomach sinks when Gage looks.

"What's that? I should check on them first." He turns around, but I block him, standing between him and the front door. "Alexei."

"Please, let's go. They're fine. I just talked to them." I'm begging but trying to be casual about it. I can't let him panic like I'm panicking. "Please, Gage."

More crashing. Something shatters. Stupid laughter follows.

I block Gage and my heart completely cracks in half when he looks at me like he hates me. "Move."

"No."

"Alexei," he growls, hand on my chest. "Get out of my way."

"No. You shouldn't go in there." I meet his angry brown eyes. "Please, trust me."

That's the wrong thing to say, though. Because now Gage is worried. He's envisioning terrible things happening to his brothers, and he has no idea what he's about to walk in on, but he's protective and needs to know. I see it in his eyes. I see the devotion to care for them and the need to make sure they're alright. At this moment, I hate them. I hate Cole and I hate Nick and I hate drugs and I hate Gage for being noble and good.

Because being good is about to emotionally ruin him. Test him. Put him in a position he's avoided because he's determined to be sober, just like he said.

"Get the fuck out of my way, Alexei," he snaps at me, all

anger and rage now. "If you won't move, I'll make you move."

"Please don't."

He does. Of course he does. Because he's Gage Rossum, the man mending his relationship with the brothers he barely got to know growing up.

He shoves me so hard my back hits the door, and it stuns me. Stuns me so much that I start to slide down, but then I'm falling backwards, landing on my ass while Gage steps over me and through the open door.

"Gage! Please!" I yell, trying to scramble to my feet.

But it's too late.

I'm scared. I'm scared enough to call my dad and put him in this situation he should avoid. And I feel selfish for doing it. His sobriety matters just as much, but maybe I'm realizing I trust him. I trust his devotion to me and his eight-year streak. He's strong enough. I don't give him enough credit.

For the first time in my life, I need him to be strong for me.

"Alex?" he answers.

"Dad..."

"I'm coming."

gage

22

There's a recognition of the situation that shouldn't feel comfortable to me. Deep down, under the extreme hurt and the intense worry, it's there, calling to me, reminding me we're old friends and have a sordid history.

It's obvious. I know what they're on. I see it in the way they jitter and smile, the glaze to their eyes, and the guilt on their faces. I see it in the smashed bowl on the floor and the shifty looks they share through wrong-sized pupils, trying to come up with a story to explain this situation away. Been there. Done that.

But then I see the baggie.

It's a promise.

The promise of a fun night with my brothers, bonding in a way we never have before. I'll never get to take them for a drink or go to a party with them like most older siblings do, but I can have this one night. There's still enough left in the bag for me to join them in their high.

We could laugh and feel no pain. We could have so much energy that we feel invincible. We could chat without expectations and buzz with a vibrancy that's been dead since I returned home.

Because the drug-addicted part of my mind isn't reminding me that coke is a downer for me. It's promising liveliness and fun. It's not recalling the comedown and the dope-sick feeling that comes when it wears off. It's telling me the trip will be worth the fall. It's not being responsible enough to put the facts in order. The fact that they're seventeen and experimenting with a drug that could ruin them, and doing it very irresponsibly. That they brought drugs into a house with a recovering addict. That it should hurt me because it's not my house and they shouldn't have to conform for me. But this is our mom's house! How fucking dare they disrespect her like this? No, it's just fun and happiness and energy. It's a way to calm my ADHD.

And I want it so fucking badly.

I'm shaking. Maybe in excitement. Maybe in restraint. I'm staring at the baggie and drooling at the thought of the taste. I'm picturing myself snorting the coke and numbing my mouth, bitterness dripping down the back of my throat.

"Gage," one of them says. I don't know who because I can't look away from the bag. "We're sorry."

I don't need them to be sorry. I need them to toss me that baggie and chill the fuck out.

My phone is vibrating in my hoodie pocket, and a faraway part of me is remembering there's a number on there I should call in a situation like this. But can I? I treated

Alexei like a piece of shit after he asked me to trust him, and now I don't know if I have the right to call that number. I hurt his son. I disrespected my slow-moving boyfriend.

But I've already fucked up, right? Might as well fuck up a little more. I take a step.

"Gage?"

Alexei. I can't look at him because his voice is shaking, and it sounds like he's crying, and I don't want to look at him crying because I know I'm the cause of it. I never meant to hurt him.

The coke will wash that guilt away.

Cole tries to grab the baggie, but I growl at him. "Don't. Fucking. Touch it."

He snaps his hand away, his back bumping into Nick's chest. "Just go outside, Gage. Please," he says, his voice also shaking. "Please. We'll clean up and make sure—"

But the bag is in my hand. I grip it so tight, almost wishing it'll disappear in my fist. It's enough to get high, but it's not enough to keep the high going for as long as I'd like it to. I shouldn't do it. It's not enough.

But Brian might have more. I could snort this and then take him up on his invitation to stop by. He hasn't gone to rehab yet. He probably won't. Not if I have anything to say about it because he's my enabler, and drugs are lonely. I need my druggie friend and the pills he provides! He's perfect for the role. Becky is, too. Pregnant or not, she'll get high with me.

I open my fist. People are calling my name, but I don't hear them because the coke is calling it louder.

I don't even know why I want it. It's not even that fun. But... it's the courage I crave. The invincibility and to use it as an excuse. Nothing can hurt me while I'm high because that's the whole point. The chasing and the numbing and the cycle of chasing and numbing. Feelings don't matter when you can numb them.

And there are so many feelings lately. Happy ones that I don't deserve. Doubtful ones that will haunt me forever. In-love ones that feel guilty because I'm not a good soulmate for Alexei.

I can turn them off with this bag of numbness.

We get what we deserve, right? And this is what I deserve. A life of ups and downs because I can't self-regulate. A lonely path with no true friends and no real connections to anything but the cycle of chasing and numbing. No love. No friendships. No family. I'll scare them all away and chase them to the edges of their sanity until they give up on me completely. That's what I deserve. For them to give up on me. I'm not worth their worry. Their love.

I'm Gage Loser Rossum. Addicted to... everything.

I open the bag.

"Gage."

And I'm turning at the sound of his voice. Not because it's particularly different from anyone else's, but because my stupid, slow brain has somehow linked him in the contacts of my mind as a safety net. He's my rehab. The thing that will keep me alive when I can't do it myself. He's standing there, right next to Alexei, looking at me with no understandable expression on his face.

Nathan. My sponsor. The man I'm trying to impress because I love his son. The holder of my medication and the lifeline I need.

"It's your choice, but don't let it trick you," he says, nodding to the bag clutched in my hand. "I'm here. We're all here. Alexei is here."

My eyes are starting to water, but my anger is still here. I don't even know where it came from because I shouldn't feel angry. I should feel embarrassed for how weak I am, and then I should ingest this coke and forget about it. Instead, my eyes are shifting to the icy blue ones that are watering on Alexei's beautiful face.

He's not sobbing. He's not angry. He's not judging me or yelling at me or hating me. He's scared because I'm scaring him. And that... shit. That loosens my hold on the bag. Not enough to drop it, but to think about it.

Will you hate me if I relapse?

"Hate? No. Hurt? Yes." Alexei's voice shakes but his chin lifts.

And it takes a fucking minute. Like a monumentally long minute that is pathetic and feeble, but I drop the bag. I don't look at it. I can't look down and see it on the floor. I hold Alexei's eyes and start to shake all over.

"Go," Nathan says.

So, I go. I abandon my brothers like a selfish dick. I escape. I run like a fucking loser out the front door, and I don't stop running until I'm at the falling-down mansion that has become a second home to me when I didn't intend to make it a home. And I want a cigarette. I want a hundred cigarettes. I need something to fill me up with more than emptiness and pain and longing for a life of freedom that I'll never have. Ever. Never again. I lost it when I was fourteen, and I'll never get it back again.

Alexei doesn't come. But Nathan does. And he brings cigarettes and water and says coffee is coming. And I'm smoking and trying to slow myself down, thinking without being able to catch a clear thought.

"My brothers," I croak. "Someone needs to make sure they're alright."

"Alexei is," Nathan says.

Then, a pack of smokes later, Mom is here, having left her girls' night. She's holding coffee mugs, mine that says 'welcome intruder', and Nathan's black one with 'world's okayest dad' on it, and now my mom has one, too. It says 'come at me, bro', and it has a sword on it, and I love it so much that I start laugh-crying, falling against her while she holds me.

Then I break.

The old me breaks away from the new me, and it hinders as much as it heals, and the whole fucking process hurts like hell.

I can't breathe.

Mom says she loves me.

gage

I'm experiencing the comedown without having gotten high. Holy fuck am I crashing. Hard. It takes me a whole forty-eight hours to even get the energy to leave my bed. And even then, I only go to the bathroom and half-ass my way through a shower. The toothbrush Alexei used is sitting there, and I'm weird because I put it in my mouth and start to cry.

On the third day, I miss Alexei so much that I shuffle my way down the street to knock on his door. But Nathan tells me he doesn't want to see me right now, so my heart breaks all over again. I go for too many coffees with Nathan, and then the two of us eat a whole box of factory cookies on my front porch while Nick and Cole are at school.

That night, I don't sleep a wink because stress and insomnia are a mad combination. So I drink tea in my window seat with Mom and Owen until two in the morning.

> Alexei <3: I finished the light switch covers and now I'm working on a grate cover for the fireplace. No blowtorch this time.

I smile at the message and type out sixty-six replies. I never send one.

On day four, I'm hungry for something other than cookies and I go to a meeting with Nathan. When I walk in the front door at home, Nick and Cole tense up in the kitchen. I cry. They cry. Mom makes tea. They're sorry, and I'm sorry that they had to witness me like that, and there's so much tea and cream cheese sandwiches. It's not mended, but it's not broken anymore either.

Then a few days go by, and I get a lot of messages from Alexei.

> Alexei <3: Another coincidence happened today, and you know how much I enjoy coincidences.

> Gage: Are you going to tell me what it was?

> Alexei <3: Coincidentally, no.

Time passes for me in increments of Alexei's rambles.

> Alexei <3: I got stumped with the fireplace grate, so I had to go to the city and visit the shop, and OMG Gage I drove confidently because a good song came on that made me think of you.

> Alexei <3: I don't remember what song it was.

> Alexei <3: I think I know what it means to fixate on something now. I'm taking a break. No more workshopping until I finish my actual work. How's my sign coming?

And because he reminded me of it, I open my iPad and start working on it. Another whole day goes by, and I somehow have three thousand versions of Alexei's workshop sign. I ask for his email, and when he gives it to me, I send all three thousand to him. Exaggeration, but it feels like that many.

I go to quilting night and finally get to use the sewing machines. Pearl is almost done with her quilt for Alexei, and I love that she made the thread baby blue on the black parts and black on the baby blue parts. My frilly butterflies are kind of shitty, but it still feels satisfying when I sew them all together. And eat raisins. Nancy and Marian compliment my snack. I baked a phyllo pastry stuffed with spinach and feta cheese. It took me three hours to roll it up right, and it looks horrendous, but I guess it tastes alright. Next time, I'll make some sort of dip for it because it's a little dry.

At the meeting a few nights later, I actually share something.

"I don't know how to feel proud," I say. "Because I didn't inhale that bag of coke, but I treated everyone I love like shit at the same time. It's overpowering my pride."

Carla, the woman who runs the meetings, tells me it's okay to feel conflicted. That we make mistakes, but that doesn't mean our wins aren't wins. I'll do better next time, she says.

On our way out, Nathan shoves his hands in his pockets and asks, "Everyone you love?"

And yeah, he knows I love his son now, but I can't really talk about it because Alexei still doesn't want to see me. I wonder if I still have a mug there.

Today, it's been ten days since that horrible night, and I'm back in the city I spent so many years in. It took me and Owen almost four hours to drive here, and even though Mom and Nathan don't think this is the best time for me to be confronting my past, I'm doing it anyway. Because Owen is with me.

"Think he'll show?" Owen asks as we wait in a breakfast restaurant. We left before sunrise, but Paul agreed to meet us at 10 a.m. It's already 10:15, and it's not like him to be late. Or it *wasn't* like him to be late.

I have a folder of documents from a lawyer Kristen put me in touch with. Pages with signature lines that state we're splitting everything financially down the middle. The house, mostly. He can keep everything else, but if he wants to get rid of it, I'll split the cost of throwing it out. I need to end this chapter.

When Paul walks in forty minutes late, I offer him a small smile. His falls off his face when he notices my brother with me, but he sits down opposite us anyway.

"You look good. Healthy." Same thing he said when I got out of rehab. "Tired, though."

It's on the tip of my tongue to ask him if he purposefully kept me an addict. Not that it would ever all be his fault, but it hurts me to know he hindered any progress I'd made. In the end, I just say, "Thanks."

And so we move on. I show him the documents, and he gets a little mad about them, but at the end of breakfast, he's signed the one that says he'll buy me out. He wants to keep the place, pay the difference, and cut all ties with me. I'm fine with it. We agree to get the house appraised, come up with the amount he owes me, and be done. The rest will go through the lawyers.

He stands, looking down at me like I'm weak for needing my brother here. "Wish you the best, Gage. Honestly."

His *honestly* means nothing to me anymore. I stand to level the power imbalance. "Thanks. Wishing you the best, too. Honestly."

I order two more refills of my coffee before I get the balls to leave the breakfast place. Looking at my brother and feeling a little better about things, I ask, "Wanna go get another coffee and I can show you where I relapsed because of a frappé and a busted window?"

He laughs, but he's nodding, telling me to lead the way.

248

Alexei <3: Wanna go for a walk?

THIS IS IT. It's been almost two weeks since I pushed Alexei against my front door and barrelled over him like he meant nothing. Tonight is the night he can face me. Break me. Break *up* with me. As much as I want to text back and tell him no, to delay the inevitable and live in the illusion that we're going to be fine for a bit longer, therapy and recovery are teaching me not to bottle my feelings.

Gage: Meet you halfway.

There's no witty banter or headlocks when I pass the twins, but maybe—hopefully—we'll get there again when the sting of that night stops stinging. Mom has books about swords and knives open on the table because she's about to pick her next project, but she smiles at me when I walk down the stairs.

"Meeting?" she asks.

"Walk. With Alexei." I swallow my nerves.

"Okay, honey. Say hi for me." It's like she's not even worried. Not even aware that this is the night my first and only good relationship ends. Though, to be fair, I pretty much wrote the ending of us almost two weeks ago when I didn't trust him when he asked me to.

God, why didn't I just trust him like he asked me to?

I shake a cigarette free from my pack, promising I'll only smoke it until I meet Alexei halfway, but he's already here. Standing on the sidewalk by the street, no blues with his blacks tonight. It's the first time I'm seeing him since then, and holy fuck, he's gotten more... *more*. He's gothier, moodier, hotter, and brighter all at once, and the combination is breathtaking. So much so that the cigarette slips between my fingers and settles in the dewy grass somewhere.

His pale blue eyes are curious like they usually are, but I can't tell if the hesitation in them is made up in my mind or real.

"Hi."

He smiles. "Hi. Ready?" He starts walking and I follow, shoving my pack of smokes back into my pocket.

We walk for three whole blocks before I get up the nerve to look at him. I can't read him, though. We walk another block while I practice my speech in my head. I chicken out of it on the next block. It feels so good to be around him again, but I don't want to get too comfortable here since it's ending. I drink it in, breathe it through my nose and close my eyes to cherish it.

And then I stop delaying the inevitable. "I'm sorry, Alexei. I'll still make your sign if you want it. I kind of want to make it still. But I hope we can remain friends when the hurt of what I've done wears off."

He stops, and since he's kind of in front of me, I run right into his back. He doesn't budge forward, so when he spins around, we're almost nose to nose. "What're you talking about?"

I take a step back. "Uh, well, I know you were just giving me time to get myself settled a bit more, but you don't have to drag it out any longer. I can handle it. It... I hate myself for losing you, but you're allowed to break up with me even though I'm in recovery. You don't have to walk on eggshells."

His nose crinkles and his eyes squint. "I'm not walking on eggshells. I'm walking on my own two feet, just like I always told you I would. And guess what? So are you. You didn't lean on me or use me as a guilt trip. You handled a shitty situation and finally learned that you have people to rely on."

"I... yeah. What?" My turn to squint at him. "But I hurt you. I didn't trust you or listen to you."

"Most people just say sorry for that. Social protocol and all that nonsense." He waves his painted nails in the space between us. "So go for it. Apologize. I'm listening."

"I'm sorry," I blurt. "I'm so fucking sorry, Alexei. I can't believe I did that to you, and I know it's no excuse, but I warned you I'm a bit destructive, and... I'm sorry I got destructive." I meet his eyes. "I never want to destroy you. Or hurt you. Or treat you like that. And I understand why you want to break up."

He snorts. "If you think I want to break up, you *do not* understand the concept of soulmates. Don't worry. You'll get it eventually." He grabs my wrist, pulling my hand from my pocket. "Just because we fight, need space, treat each other poorly, or disagree on something doesn't mean we're breaking up, Gage. We're going to fight. It happens in all relationships. Good ones and bad ones, and since I happen to think we're one of the good ones, a bit of fighting is tolerable. Unless we turn into one of those bad relationships, we're okay to fight and not break up. You understand that, right?"

No. No, I don't understand that because I shoved him. Hurt him both emotionally and physically. I made him cry because of my own stupidity. And now I'm tearing up, staring at him in dumbstruck awe because I honestly thought this was it. This was our break-up moment.

"I'm not going to leave you just because I give you space," Alexei says. "And you need to stop fearing that we're going to break up every time something happens."

"But you didn't want to see me for two weeks," I say, my throat hitching.

"Oh, I *really* wanted to see you. Like, more than anything. I annoyed the shit out of Dad by talking about you all the time, and now the name Gage is banned after dinner. And since I didn't send you all the texts I wrote, I took screenshots of them all so I can show you them later." He smiles.

I still don't know if I'm dying or living.

"I gave you space so you could process, Gage. So that you can come back to me as my boyfriend instead of as a guilt-laden dick. And later on, in the future, I'll be right by your side when you go through tough times like that, but this time, because it's still so new and it's one of the hardest things you've faced since getting home, you needed to know that you had what it took. That you could handle it. Without me. So that if the unspeakable ever does happen and our soulmateship comes to an end, you already have the proof that you can handle things without me. I did it for us. For you. For the survival of us."

I'm so snotty, and my eyes are crying so hard. A choked sob leaves my lips, and my knees scream in pain when I land right on them against the hard sidewalk. Alexei falls with me, pulling me against him, hugging me in the middle of Lindon Street, three streets over from ours, in front of house number 759.

Alexei proved a point to me. A point I never knew I needed. That I can handle things on my own. That we're getting into a relationship as *people*, not as an addict and the son of an addict. Those things are there, but above them, we're two guys falling in love because of our personalities and the way they mesh together. He proved to me that he won't let me ruin him, that he can handle things without me too, and that he *honestly* has my best interests at heart while making sure he's taking care of himself, too. More than anything, that puts me at ease because it means he really won't let me taint him. No matter how toxic I am, Alexei is stronger. The only way I'll lose him is by turning our good relationship into a bad one.

"Soulmateship?" I choke out the word, knowing there are a thousand things I should thank him for instead.

"Yeah, just accept it, Gage. And call me complicated again."

It's sort of gross when I laugh because a snot bubble comes out. He cringes at it, pushing me back with a smile on his face. "Thank you. For doing all that. For... for still wanting to be with me even though I made a huge mistake."

I wipe my eyes and nose and then hold his hand in my snotty one. "And I'm sorry, Alexei."

"You boys okay?" the owner of 759 Lindon Street asks from her porch.

"All good! We're just having a moment," Alexei tells her with a small smile. "You okay?"

I nod, more okay than I thought I'd be. "Can our first kiss come with snot and a lot of drool?"

"That's what sleeves are for," he says. While I'm wiping my nose with my sleeves and trying to get my act together, he asks, "Are you sure you're ready for the intimacy it'll bring?"

I'm nodding before he's done asking, but I take a deep breath to ensure he knows I'm taking it seriously. "I've been ready since that first night in your bedroom, Alexei. I know what it means to you, and I want you to know that it means the same to me. That it's not just chasing orgasms and having fun. It's a relationship, built together because... you made me believe in soulmates. I just wanted you to believe in me, too."

"I do," he says.

It's slow and appreciative, not cautious, but respectful of the milestone when I lean forward and kiss him. I swear I feel his lip-print stamp onto my heart.

Our lips connect, breaths mingling, gentling the already hesitant kiss. Not hesitant because we're worried about it, but hesitant because it's been so built up to that it requires a slow appreciation.

"Wow," he whispers.

Wow is right. Our mouths meld together, moving seamlessly. But when our tongues get involved, our synchronization goes out the window because we're both trying to deepen an already deep kiss. He pants against my mouth, and I can't breathe through my nose, so I suck in his breaths like they're keeping me alive. My hands come up, one on the side of his neck and the other at the back of his head, holding him against me because I will never get enough of him. I don't want to let him go.

My knees stop aching from falling to them, and my world rights itself. His tongue slides against mine, perfectly ungraceful enough to make me moan. The sound makes him shiver, his teeth sinking into my bottom lip to slow us down. Because it's not just a kiss with lips and teeth and tongue. It's one of those ones that makes your whole body tingle, and I already know my dick is hard from it, but when Alexei groans out a raspy sound that tickles my nuts, I know he's feeling it too.

"Fuck, you can kiss, complicated."

"I've been dying to show you my kissing skills forever," he whispers against my mouth. "You in this soulmateship with me, Gage?"

First night I'm hearing the term, but fuck it. I've always been impulsive, and this is one impulsive commitment I've been slowly committing to since the breakfast he hated me through.

"All in. All my cards are on the table. Because I trust you around me, and I trust me around you, and I'm going to do better not to make mistakes, and I love the way we are together... and I'm falling—"

"Jesus!" He pulls back so fast and slaps both hands over my mouth, glancing around all sketchy-like. "You *cannot* say that yet. I haven't had the proper time to digest this kiss yet, so give me time to appreciate one milestone before you spring another one on me. Especially not under a full moon. My god, Gage."

I laugh really hard because he's so ridiculous. "Okay, you tell me when I'm allowed to tell you, and we'll go from there." I peck him one more time. "Are you wearing my shoes?" I ask as he shifts around. The blue and black checkered ones.

"Yes. We share clothes in this soulmateship since we're basically the same size."

I love that. "Wanna get off the sidewalk and stop putting on a show for all the peeping neighbours?"

He blinks, looking around at all the curtains shoved to the side. "Yes. I actually want to show you something."

I stare at his eyes, his septum piercing, his wet lips, just... admiring the fuck out of him because he's fucking awesome. I think he really is my soulmate, and it gives me a silent strength, like something inside me solidifies and becomes more defiant. I think it's because I want a life with him, and the determination I had that morning I left rehab is fortified now, stronger because I'm even more determined now that I know how incredible my future is going to be.

It's hope. Real, live, breathing hope. I'm not scared of it anymore.

alexei

There are seven coffee mugs on the island, and Gage is studying all of them with bloodshot eyes from crying. He's adamant that the *'welcome intruder'* mug was the one he was meant to get from my dad, so I guess I'll give him that. He can use it when he has coffee with my dad, but I have another one in mind for him. And I need him to pick it out of a lineup.

This is a test, and I will smack him if he fails. I mean, it's pretty obvious.

"Well, I know it's not this one because you said you aren't fond of moustaches." He pushes the blue one back. "But I kind of like this one."

It's purple and has a buff-as-fuck unicorn with a big dick on it. Dad won't drink out of it, and it tends to get shoved to the back of the cabinet.

"You have a nice dick, but it isn't buff unicorn nice, Gage. Try again."

He grins shyly. He fiddles with all the mugs. Hesitates

257

on the one that has my name and a heart on it, and then his eyes catch on the winner. Then he looks past it, and I scowl.

Laughing, doing it just to rile me, he picks up the mug meant for him. "I know my soulmate is out there some-where... pushing a pull door." He holds it up to his face. "Does it suit me?"

"Turn it around."

He spins it to read the other side. "I think you are lacking in vitamin me." He barks out a cute laugh. "Fucking right I am. Gonna give me my dose?" He tugs on the front of my hoodie, lips barely grazing mine. What a tease. "Can I design you a mug?"

Oh my god, I thought he'd never ask. "You better."

Still right up against my lips, he asks, "So, I'm sensing a theme. Kind of like what the person means to the person who gives them the mug? You obviously gave your dad the 'okayest dad' one, and someone gave my mom the sword one, so is that how it works?"

I have a 'world's greatest shitty dad' one I'm gonna swap my dad's out for soon. He really is an awesome dad now, so I want him to get an upgrade. I've been holding him at arm's length for too long, and it's about time he realizes just how much I love and respect him. "Yeah, that's the general gist of it. What am I to you?"

"Everything," he breathes the word against my lips, and then he's kissing me and I'm losing track of time, and holy shit, I have a soulmate.

His soulmate mug sits on the counter next to us, but his hands are around my back, sliding up my shirt, pressing his scratchy palms against the smoothness of my lower back. When his grip falls to my ass and he gives me a hard squeeze, I pant out a rambling bit of nonsense.

"Ohmygodwhencanwefuck."

"Is your dad home?" he asks, picking me up to sit my ass on the countertop. His mouth never leaves mine. Even if he isn't kissing me, he's breathing against me, biting my lips, licking me everywhere that counts.

"Work," I mutter. "A work thing." I weave my fingers into his hair and tug, slamming his mouth against mine even harder. "With the guys. Work."

"Wanna say work one more time?" he teases. His breathing starts to increase rapidly, and the sound is almost better than a moan.

"Oh, fuck off," I groan. "But seriously? When can we fuck? How are you feeling? What's the status of your therapy and your... stuff? Be honest. There is no wrong answer. I don't even care if we never fuck. I just want you in any way we can be together." I tug on his hair to pull his head back, and when I see the lust in his brown eyes and the swollen lips he's still trying to place on mine, I almost melt. My hoodie is too much! "Don't lie to me."

"The sex part?" he asks, hands all over my hips and thighs.

"All of it. But yeah, that."

He grins. "The sex part is... weirdly easy. It feels normal. Like, I really want you... like really fucking badly, but... it's manageable. I don't feel like a madman. Well, I do because you kind of make me unhinged, but it's not that compulsive kind of behaviour from before. It's just straight-up lust. I wanna fuck so bad."

Mmm, likewise. "And the rest?"

Gage licks his lips and takes a deep breath. "A lot of shame lately. Shame that I acted that way that night. Frustration that it's still something I crave when it's put in front of me, even after all this time. I'm grateful to you because you were there and called your dad. It's a mixed bag of feelings, but it hasn't driven me to want to use again. Not since that night. I mean, it's..."

"It's what?"

"It's like... high me craved high dope. Does that make sense? Sober me doesn't really crave anything in particular except the high. When I was high, I wanted something that'd make me higher. But sober, I crave anything that'll switch off the negative. So, my therapist says that once we're sober and more rational, we need to learn to get our 'highs', so to speak, from healthier sources. Dopamine chasing, endorphins and exercise, positive feelings, that sort of thing."

That makes sense. I like the comparison. "Okay, so you're saying you're craving something, but you're leaning more towards a healthy thing?"

"High me had high dope. Drunk me had drunk dope. Now I need to find my sober dope." He smiles so wide and then it falls into something shy. He buries his face in my neck, hugging me to him. "You're my sober dope, Alexei. My feel-good drug. And instead of you being a substance or a thing I can overindulge in or abuse, you're the best kind of dope because you tell me when to stop."

Sober dope. I've never been anyone's feel-good drug before. I wrap my arms around his neck, lean my head against his, and just breathe with him.

"So, what I'm hearing is that I'm your feel-good drug, you're good with the sex part, and we can fuck?"

"That's exactly what I'm saying," he says, lips pressing to my neck. "But first, I wanna fucking worship you, Alexei. I missed you so much, and I'm so grateful for you." He pulls back, hands on the sides of my neck. "And isn't that what soulmates do?"

I'm a gooey mess inside, but I cover it with a scoff and an eye roll. "Fine. Worship me if you must."

"Oh, I must."

A CLAWFOOT TUB, a towel heater, and a cold stone floor are apparently the sexiest things to ever exist. Bathrooms must be our thing.

Because my ass is sitting on the edge of the tub, a hot towel is wrapped around my waist, and my feet are resting on the cold floor, all while I'm learning that nipples are *incredible.*

Gage's tongue is incredible.

His mouth is fucking sinful.

"Jesus, Alexei. Hold on to something." Gage moves my hands from his hair to the edge of the tub I'm falling into. "Breathe."

I can't breathe! Or maybe I'm breathing too much. Gage's lips suction around my nipple and I tremble all over, shivering and breaking out in goosebumps because I can feel it all the way down to my bones. When he flicks his tongue over my erect nipple, I groan so loud that it echoes around the bathroom.

His hair tickles my chin when he moves to the other side, and at the first lick, I'm breaking all the rules and grabbing his head again. Effortlessly, Gage slides me down to the floor, a heated towel now laid out.

"You're a safety hazard," he says, getting me onto my back.

"You're the safety hazard. You're putting me in danger." But I'm already pulling his head back down to my chest.

"Never thought you'd like this so much," he teases, tongue running over my nipple like it's the easiest thing he's ever done.

"I only like it a little bit," I insist. I insist so hard that I shove my chest against his face and moan like a glutton when he gives me what I want. And then teeth are involved, and I'm about to lose my mind. He tugs and nips, soothing it all with broad licks before firming his tongue and driving me insane again.

I'm on the precipice of coming, and all he's done is play my nipples with his skilled mouth. "Gage," I groan, wanting more but unable to handle it unless I want this to end early. *What the fuck, nipples?!*

"Shh," he whispers. He blows cool air against my wet skin and my hips buck off the floor. "I'm still worshipping."

He worships his way between my pecs and down my stomach, kissing my hip bones and my thighs. Spreading my legs, he nips my inner thighs and licks a wide path down to the inside of my knee. He comes back up, nose grazing my hard dick all the way from the base to the tip.

I convulse embarrassingly hard. "God."

"No, you're the god. I'm just your measly little subject. Your slave." He blows more air on my cock, and I choke on nothing. "Fuck, you are perfect like this. So goddamn needy, but defiant about it."

I *am* needy, but I don't want to admit how needy I am because I'm trying to have a little chill. "I'm totally calm. You could quit anytime and I'd be just fine."

Gage starts to sit up, testing me. I bring him right back down, force him to straddle my hips, and bend him over until his lips are on mine and my hips can rut up against his.

"I'm needy," I admit against his neck, desperate enough to suck a mark there because he's mine! My soulmate. My slow-moving boyfriend. My Gage. "And I want you so bad. Am I being too much?"

"Never too much," he rasps. "Flip over."

He flips me over before I get the chance to, and a small part of me wants to feel insecure about my bare ass on display for him, but a bigger part of me is confident he'll love it. Gage repeats the slow worship down my spine, biting the dimples in my lower back.

"Mm," he hums, low and throaty, when he gets to my ass. He smacks it lightly. "Still so much we don't know about each other," he says while his fingers trail down my crack and test my reaction to being touched there. He dips them between my cheeks and I give him a hint. I lift my hips, freeing my cock from being trapped between my body and the floor, giving him permission to touch more. Go deeper. Ass play is always fair game.

His fingers tickle my balls, rolling them between my thighs. Then his mouth is on me, leaving gentle bite marks across my ass cheeks. He's straddling my calves so I can't open my legs anymore, but that doesn't stop him from burying his face against my skin and spreading my cheeks apart. When his tongue hits my hole, I cry out something so strangled that it can't even be considered a moan.

I turn into a boneless body, slumping back down to the floor. My cock gets wedged between my abs and the towel, but Gage tugs me back up, lifting my hips just slightly off the floor. He isn't shy to explore, his tongue dipping inside me and his fingers digging hard into my hips.

"Hands beside your head," he commands, and holy gods, yes. *Get bossy with me because I can't wait to get bossy with you.*

I press my palms to the towel on either side of my head, staring at the claw feet on the tub, chest on the towel, hips slightly lifted. When Gage spreads me open and tongue-fucks my ass again, he gives me one more command.

"Hands-free, Alexei. I wanna see you hump that towel. I'll help." And he does help. He buries his tongue in my ass as if he's fucking me, my cock brushing against the soft towel with every thrust of his tongue. His hands grip my hips, rocking me against the floor.

"More," I beg.

Spit hits my crack, dripping down to my hole. With his tongue still on me, he adds a single finger, slowly easing me open. When I'm basically easing back to fuck his finger and tongue, he relaxes his hold on my hip and starts to make me sweat.

Because Gage knows exactly where the prostate is, and he goes straight for it.

"Ah, fuck," I gasp into the towel. My cock rubs perfectly, the fabric smooth and caressing. "Don't make me come this early."

"I'm gonna make you come twice, Alexei." Gage's voice does *not* settle me down. It's scratchy and low, and holy hell, I can feel the tone of it resonate in the pit of my chest. "Don't make this complicated, complicated," he teases.

His finger twirls and my eyes roll back. My hips move on their own, humping the towel like I'm chasing an orgasm so hard I can't stop myself from grinding. Then his tongue is back, and it's a trifecta of perfection. His finger. His mouth. The towel.

I bite the fabric into my mouth, focusing on all three at once. He fingers my prostate and sucks my balls into his mouth at the same time as my stomach perfectly rubs my cock against the towel.

I moan his name with the white cotton between my teeth, damn near delusional and happy to be. "Gage... I'm... *fuck.*"

Light sparks my vision and my ears go underwater. My

ass clamps down on his fingers and my abs slick with cum, making the friction even better.

"Fuck yeah, Alexei. Holy shit, you are hot right now."

I'm a moaning, writhing mess of sensation, and it won't end because Gage is still finger-fucking me, rolling my balls and driving me mad. My eyes close and I can't breathe, and I don't care about breathing because coming is so much more important.

I gasp. "Ahhhhhhh." It won't end, and I'm shaking and spasming until Gage pulls his finger out and abruptly flips me over. My lower back hits the wet spot on the towel, cum still leaking from my dick. I swallow hard and look at Gage, his eyes so goddamn dark they're half demonic. "Oh, fuck…"

"Take a breath," he says, straddling me. "Right now."

I inhale hard, and then it whooshes out of me when he wraps his fingers around my cock. I'm protesting, telling him it's too much, but he's reminding me to breathe and bending forward to kiss me so I can't.

He just holds my dick without jacking it, but fuck, it feels good. I bite his lip and clack my teeth against his, desperate for something but not even sure what. I can't stop moving, wiggling, shifting around to chase a thing I don't recognize.

"Look at me," he demands.

I meet his eyes and whimper. He's checking for something, and even though I don't know what it is, he finds it because he grins and I start begging for something.

"I got you," he promises.

Hand still on my cock, he dips his head down to my

neck, kissing my throat hard. But when his mouth ends up on my nipple again, I shriek and buck my hips against his boner. I'm so sensitive, almost too sensitive, but the way he works my nipples brings a slowness to the moment that has my hips rolling gently. Before I even know I'm doing it, I'm fucking his fists and holding him against my chest and moaning in his ear.

I'm there. Again. Shaking all over, toes curling, breath catching. How is this happening?

"Fuuu... ck." I white out. Come. Combust. Go deaf for a second and blind for more seconds. My body is erupting everywhere, and I can't stop shaking and moaning his name and fucking his hand. The orgasm is explosive, even if there isn't as much cum, and I have no idea how I'm still fucking coming. I've never gotten off twice in a row, especially not this close together, and I don't know where one orgasm starts and the other ends, but Gage is letting me lead while also forcing me to live in this euphoria.

"Alexei," he whispers my name, lifting up to look at me. When I see the way he regards me, absolutely worships and admires me, my lungs rattle and I shake out my first real breath. "My god, you are incredible."

But I'm still needy. So needy! Needy for him, and I get it now. He isn't ready to have penetrative sex tonight, so this is his way of bringing me absolute pleasure in a whole new form, and I'm desperate to do the same to him. Unfortunately, he's turned me into a weak-muscled mess of incoordination, so I can't do much more than slide down the towel.

"What're you... Alexei, you don't have to," he warns.

But I'm already shifting down, pulling his ass up, lifting my head so I can suck him off from below. "I know I don't have to," I wrap my hands around him. "I fucking *need* to. Say yes?"

He must see the desperation in my eyes because his lips pop open in awe as he says yes, and then they fall open even more when I suck him into my mouth. He's hot and hard and leaking like crazy, and the taste of his precum damn near threatens a third orgasm out of me. I can't swallow him deep at this angle, so I suction my lips around the head of his cock and suck hard and slow.

"Oh, fuck," he moans, watching me.

I flatten my tongue and slide it across the slit, lapping up every dribble he gives me. I tongue the V on the underside and pop him back inside.

"I won't last long like this, Alexei... fucking fuck, you are so sexy." I suck harder, once, twice, and Gage tenses all over. He hardens more in my mouth, the tip swelling, and I'm so goddamn needy for his cum that I lift up a bit, opening wide. "Fuck. Fuck. Fuuuuck." I pump him gently with my fingers circled under the head, and he spurts hard and fast against my tongue.

I look him straight in the eye, angling his cock so it all goes into my mouth. His eyes don't flutter and his gaze never leaves mine, but a million pleasurable expressions grace his face, and I fall for him even more. When his eyes harden at the sight of all his cum on my tongue, he moves so fast I barely have time to adjust.

His mouth lands on mine, and a cum-filled kiss makes a

fucking mess of our faces, dripping down my cheeks and neck. When it slows, Gage already has the towel that was wrapped around my hips earlier, wiping my face before wiping his own.

"Fuck me, complicated. You are... goddamn." He crushes me with his body, but I don't care. I can't even move right now.

"We're sleeping here," I state. "Right on this stone floor. I can't move. Hope you brought your journal."

Gage laughs against my shoulder. "I'll piggyback you to bed." He props up on his elbows. His smile is slow and content. "Hey, soulmate."

"Oh my god, stop! My dick needs to get soft at some point!" But I'm pulling him down for another laughing kiss because my eyes are watering and I've never been happier.

gage

25

Alexei isn't a bottom. I don't think. I tried to get a feel for it last night on the bathroom floor, and while he loves something small in his ass and against his prostate, I don't think he's a full-time bottom. How did I come to this conclusion?

I have no idea. A vibe. A sixth sense. I don't usually trust my sixth sense, so I could be completely wrong, but my gut tells me he's more of a top. At least vers.

Either way, I don't care what he prefers. Last night was hot as fuck and I'm... just wowed by him.

Nathan points at all the coffee mugs on the island counter. "Got the soulmate cup, did you?"

"Yep!" I beam at him and then cover my mouth because Alexei is still sleeping. He was so tired after our bathroom shenanigans, but then he got a weird bout of energy while we were journalling, and it took him forever to fall asleep. He was angry about it. Blamed me. Said journalling gets his blood pumping and his energy buzzing. My fault. "But from you, I only accept coffee in this one." I spin the alien mug and smile at him.

He looks relieved. "He takes soulmates very seriously."

"Don't worry. So do I." I sit down and accept my medication from him. "Want me to find another sponsor? Does it weird you out that I'm sleeping with your—"

"Ah!" he cuts in. "No, it doesn't. Yes, it does to talk about it. I'm more than happy to be your sponsor, but if you want a new one, I understand. We can figure it out as we go. Feeling okay about everything?"

I tell him about Paul and the city. About how things are still a bit strained with the twins but getting better. About the absolute relief that Alexei wasn't breaking up with me, and then about the amazing night we had together. I spared the sexy details, but I admitted that I love him and that I got in trouble for almost saying it under a full moon.

"And now?" Nathan asks. "What comes next?"

Isn't that the question of my life? "And now... now I try to find a routine. A balance and a life that makes me happy. I gotta start living in this new world I'm trying to stay in, so... meetings and you. Natalie and sex therapy. Hobbies and getting back to my job. Maybe buying a car again and, I don't know, dating Alexei. I'm trying to keep it simple while also letting myself be hopeful for a manageable life. A happy one."

One where I love a neurotic rambler but love myself, too. Because it's been a long-ass time since I loved myself.

Nathan slides my alien mug across the island and sits

down with me. "Why are you already wearing shoes? You sleep in those things?"

I look down at my slip-ons. Black and blue checkered. The ones I got for my date with Alexei because he somehow makes black and blue something more than colours. I stole them back from him. "It's an ADHD thing. Shoes on means productivity. Shoes off means... ADHD paralysis and the inability to get anything done." I shrug. "Learned lots of tricks over the years." Elbows on the counter, I study Nathan. "After eight years, you still go to meetings this frequently? I'm just trying to understand what I'm in for."

"Yes and no," he says. "For the past few years, I've maybe gone once every few months. Mostly because I'm friends with Carla and it makes her feel better to see me show up sometimes. But when Kristen called about you, I figured a meeting was a good place to bump into you, and now I go for you."

I frown.

"It's no burden, I promise. It's good to touch base with your sobriety, even if you think you're doing well and don't need it anymore. Maybe someday you'll be a sponsor and you'll get it."

I huff into my mug. "I'm a long way from that."

"You're over a year sober, Gage."

"Yeah, but that first year was spent in a facility that helped me stay sober. I'm only a few months sober in the real world and I've already almost fucked up more than once. Does it get easier?"

He nods. "It does. When life starts getting great, and

you have all these things you never knew you could have, the pull of the high isn't as tempting because you're already high on the happiness of what you have. So, life being good is step one to recovery. Gotta enjoy it so you aren't trying to numb it."

Must be triply as hard for people who don't come from or have good lives. That's a reality check I need. I have good things in my life that some recovering people don't.

I know addictions happen because of a whole slew of reasons, but numbing and covering feelings were my reasons. It started with ADHD and that calm feeling, and then it became an adrenaline chase, but throughout it all, I just needed to shut my real self off so that high me could shine. I think I've always disliked myself, and now that I'm thinking about it, I have no idea why. But I self-loathed enough to mask myself in drugs and completely cover my real personality. I think I need more therapy.

"I think you're right about routine, though," he says. "You work for yourself, which means you cram a bunch of work into a few hours and then do nothing. You need set hours or something. Or events. Schedules. Something to break up your day into compartments that feel more manageable than all this open space."

I've been thinking that exact same thing over the past two weeks, so shyly, and with so much hesitation it's ridiculous, I put my phone on the counter, pull up the ad, and spin it so he can look. I'm so embarrassed about it that I get up for a refill even though my coffee is three-quarters full. I haven't even shown Alexei yet.

"You applied at the coffeehouse? As what, a barista?"

I get defensive for no reason. "I love coffee, Nathan! Why shouldn't I make it? Don't judge me because it's minimum wage and I'm that big of a loser."

"My god," he scoffs at me. "You always this touchy?"

"Yes."

"It's a good idea. I like it. And Alex won't go there because he doesn't like their tea, so it gives you a bit of separation from him, too." He flicks my phone back to me. "It's a good idea."

I ramble. "It's only four-hour shifts three days a week, but it might be nice, you know? Like, I love coffee, so being around it might be rewarding, but it also might make me sick of it, and that's nice to balance my coffee addiction out, even though that method does not apply to drugs. Anyway, the people who work there aren't people I knew from before, so it's like a good way to meet new people without the 'hey, you're that junkie guy who almost died a bunch of times, right?' type conversations. And it... that place reminds me of you." Because that's where I told him my story after the very first meeting.

He snorts. "That's a good thing?"

"Yeah. Because you saved me. I was determined, but I was also unsure. I have no idea where I would have walked after that meeting if you didn't ambush me for a coffee." I grin at him. "So, thanks for taking me there."

"Yeah, yeah," he says dismissively, unfamiliar with gratitude. Alexei never really gave it to him, so I will. "What're you doing today?"

Topic change. Got it. "I have a therapy appointment with Natalie this afternoon, but until then, I'm debating slinking around in the room that's supposed to be a library, but you filled it full of tools because you disrespect books. I want to clean off those built-in shelves and see what we can do with them. I'm picturing a rolling ladder."

His brow quirks. "You're designing my house now?"

Shit. Forgot I don't have that right. "Um... can I put in a rolling ladder?"

He smiles, and it's different from his usual smile. He's happy about something, but I'm not sure what. "Clean it out and we'll see what we can do."

After kissing Alexei awake and bringing him herbal tea in bed, I start my walk home feeling like a new man. A soulmate. A person.

The sun is up and the birds are happy, and I can't stop smiling because everything is getting better. I'm getting better. I'm looking forward to the day instead of dreading it, trusting myself instead of doubting myself, and more hopeful than I am daunted, so that has to mean something. It has to be a good feeling I can live in for at least a little while.

"What the heck, Frankie?!" I stop at the For Sale sign on the front lawn of the sex shop owners. "You're moving?" I gawk at her just as her husband comes down the porch steps with a million things in his arms.

"Just across town," she says, slamming the trunk and accidentally making her husband try to open it again with his arms full. "Bit of a last-minute decision, but when that house on Robin came up, we fell in love."

"Oh, okay, so you'll still come for Portuguese cookout nights?"

"Damn right. Your mom got me hooked on those custard tarts, and Benedita won't tolerate no-shows. She'll come drag us over if we don't come on our own." Frankie smiles at me. "You look happy, sweetie."

People notice those things? She can tell? Have I looked unhappy up until now? "Yeah, I think I am happy." I hook my thumb back toward the falling-down mansion. "Icy blue hair, snippy attitude, bit of an awkward duck. Ringing any bells? Has something to do with him."

Her smile is gorgeous and her husband's matches it. I barely know these people, and I slunk home as a junkie to live with my mom, and they know it, but they still like me. I'm a person. "Well, you two are adorable. Stop by the shop sometime. We've got a great friends and family discount." She winks.

And since I'm feeling this incredible high of being content and happy, I skip the rest of the way home, grab the keys to the van and Slash under my arm, and look at my mom.

"Working today?"

"Off, hun. What's up?"

"Wanna face some of our past together and put it behind us?"

She smiles, grabs a box of a hundred cookies, and races me out the door.

THE BACK HATCH of the van is open, propped up with a hockey stick, and our asses are weighing down the back end. Our feet swing, and the box of cookies is open between us. Slash is snoozing in the front seat, the captain of our ship.

My childhood home sits a hundred feet away, and I hope the new owners aren't home because we are creeping on it hard.

"What's it like?" I ask Mom. "To be the parent of an addict?" I munch.

"It's terrifying," she says. "And there are phases to it."

"Tell me."

"Well, at first, it's just disappointment and anger. A lot of worry. When you find out your kid is doing drugs, it's such a letdown. Like you tried so hard to raise them right and give them a good life, but they still turned to drugs. But that's before you even know they're addicted. At this point, you just think they're experimenting, so you still hold onto some hope."

"I'm sorry."

She smacks me and grabs another cookie, staring at our old house. "And then it's worse worry. Worry about everything. Where you are, what you're doing, who you're spending time with, if you're dead somewhere. But also worry that I didn't do a good enough job. That I was a lousy parent and didn't give you what you needed to survive."

"You did," I promise her. "Always. Everything I ever needed. I'm the fuckup, not you."

She smiles hesitantly. "Every time I heard sirens, I'd worry. Every time you didn't come home and I had no idea where you were, I worried. I sat up, watching out the front window so many times, waiting to see if you were still alive enough to stumble home. And as much as it was so disappointing to get a call from another parent or a store owner about what you'd done, it was a relief, too. Because I'd get to go pick you up from the police station and know you were alive."

Fucking hell, that's bleak. I'm such a shit person.

"And then the fighting started. I tried to control you, make you better, get you cleaned up, but you didn't want that, and I wasn't the right person for the job. And it takes a long time to realize that I'm a mother, not a counsellor, and I can't force myself to be the right person for that job. So we fought, and the fighting was so exhausting, but not near as exhausting as the worry. And I was stuck in this weird place because I knew that if I pushed you to get better, you'd leave home. So I didn't want to push too hard, but I also didn't trust you around the boys. They were so young, and you were reckless and dangerous."

Oh god. My eyes water, so I eat another cookie to aid in swallowing my guilt.

"And then it happened. You flew off the handle, hated me for trying to help you, and left."

"I never hated you. I promise. I was just so messed up

that I didn't want you to control me, but mostly, I just felt so ashamed and didn't want you to see me like that."

"I know, hun." She smiles at me. "And even when you were gone, I worried. And I drank up every little detail I could get from people. Someone saw you in the city. Someone heard you were back to visit a friend. You texted Owen and the twins, called them on their birthdays, kept in touch with them, and I lived for those little bits of information. Loved it even more when you called me."

I look at my hands, hating myself. I cut my mom out for three years. I saw her on very rare occasions, but I didn't talk to her much, and that's on me. Not her.

"I'm sorry, Mom."

"At least you came home once since you moved out," she says, trying to laugh it off.

But it's not funny because it was a horrible night. I knew I was beyond fucked up, but I managed to get home somehow. Don't even know how. But I went to my mom's house and overdosed in her bathroom. Again. The bathroom in this house we're both staring at. After rehab that time, I moved to the city for good and met Paul.

"Paul called me, or he was open to me calling him," Mom says. "He gave me updates, even though I never really liked him. Something off about that one."

"Yeah," I snort. Didn't see it at the time, but I see it now.

"And then you were okay for a bit. Still using, still struggling, but you started visiting and coming home and getting to know your brothers again. And it hurt so bad to see you like that, but it felt so good to have you around. Then I got conflicted again. Because the twins were getting older and I was afraid you'd try to... I don't know, encourage them. I know better now, Gage. I know you wouldn't have."

I'm breaking apart at the recap from my mom's perspective, but I need to hear it. I need to hear how I made the people who love me the most feel. Healing hurts, and that's what I'm trying to do.

"Then we moved into the new house as a fresh start, and about that time, I was also in contact with your sponsor," Mom says.

"Kristen?"

She nods. "Yeah, you put me down as your emergency contact, and she called me one night when you were staying at her place, trying to get away from Paul."

Holy shit. I completely forgot about that. Paul had been trying to get me to go to some club with his work friends, and I was mostly sober at the time, sort of, and I ran to Kristen's house and spent a few days there.

"So we kept in contact. You called a lot at that point, and our relationship was mending, but I knew you were still lying to me, so I talked to Kristen to get the real information. She didn't shield me from it. Then you stole a coffee, got better, and I've never been happier to have you home. I love having you here, like this, happy but hurting, healing and recovering and doing so well." She squeezes my hand.

"I'm so sorry for what I put you through, Mom. Holy fuck, I'm sorry. Like... I put you through hell for so long."

She laughs. "Oh, I think hell will be a cakewalk

compared to what you put me through," she jokes. "But now I know it's all been worth it for these moments right here."

alexei

I took Gage to the restoration shop, and now I'm vibrating with excitement and rambling about making old things new again, and he's saying that my driving is amazing and not at all timid anymore, and we're having two conversations at the same time, and I love it. Everything about it. That he can keep multiple conversations running effortlessly. That we're together. That he's interested in my newfound love for old things. That he's smiling and healthy-ish and happy-ish. That he's mine and he believes in soul-mates now.

"Gage?" I say, pausing all running conversations. My hands sit loosely on the steering wheel, and my back is comfortable because my car has excellent lumbar support and heated seats.

"Alexei?" He looks at me with a genuine smile on his face. Because I think he's happy to be around me, and he's still feeling the good vibes from his interview at the coffee shop this morning.

"I think now is a good time to talk about our living situation," I tell him.

He snorts. "Oh? I'm not allowed to tell you how I feel about you yet, but we can talk about living together?"

"That's a ways away. You need to live with your family for a bit longer. I'm more interested in the town. Are you staying in Port Baylon? Do you have plans to go back to the city? Are you leaving? Because I can't leave my dad. Actually, I can, but I don't want to, but I don't want you to leave either. But I understand if you want to get out of the town you came back to face. Even though it will break me. But... what's up with your plans? Tell me so I can stop overthinking it all."

He's fiddling with a pack of cigarettes, but he won't light one in my car. He looks out the front window at the big city surrounding us. "Why do you wanna stay near your dad?" he asks instead of answering me.

"Because I lived through a lot of shitty years with him, and now I get the good years. I want to be here for them."

He smiles at the windshield. "That's how I feel about being near my family. They lived through a lot of shitty years with me, and now I get to have the good years. I want to stay. I like living in town again." He slides his hand over, massaging my thigh. "I mean, it seems like a great town to have our soulmateship in, doesn't it?"

"Indeed," I agree, so fucking happy it isn't even funny. I try so hard to hide my smile that my facial expression must be weird because Gage laughs at me. "What?" I bark.

"So conflicted, complicated," he teases. "You're allowed to look happy."

"I'm trying to appear cool and collected. I told you that I'm very aware of how I react to things, and this is me trying to pretend I still have some control over how you make me feel." I glance at him. "Is it working?"

"Not even a little bit." He squeezes my thigh, hand running a bit too high. "You're not a bottom, are you?"

The question takes me off guard and my hand slips down the steering wheel. "What? What makes you say that?" I turn onto the road that leads out of the city, the traffic finally ebbing.

"Just a hunch," he says. "Gonna answer me?"

"I thought you liked the mystery of not knowing?"

"I do." He nods. "But after all these appointments with Natalie and getting a real hang for my journal and how I feel when I'm turned on, I'm ready to fucking fuck."

"Fucking fuck," I repeat, breathless.

"And maybe it'll be hot to just go into it with no idea what's going to happen. Whose cock will go where. Like a total 'acting on instinct' experience."

"Like a test to see how well we can read each other?" I ask. Because I love tests, and I like to think I can read Gage really well. I already know what positions we'll take.

"Yeah, sure. To test our instincts about each other." He rubs my leg. "And no matter which way it goes, I just fucking want you, Alexei. I don't even care if we don't fuck right away. I wanna touch you and have you. Taste you and be with you. God, that night in the bathroom?" He groans low in his throat and adjusts himself. "So hot."

It was hot, and I apparently *love* nipple play. "So, you don't even care if we have sex?"

"We've had sex. Just not penetrative sex. And yes, I do care, and I want it really bad, but... this slow getting-to-know-each-other phase has been amazing. I've never had it with anyone before and it feels special. Is that lame?"

"No, it's goddamn romantic. Penetration is just one... thing. There's no rush."

He smiles, leaning over to plant a kiss on my jaw. "Thank you for going slow with me, Alexei."

Slow is my jam, even though I basically fell for him when I had a hard time hating him through breakfast. Guess I'm more of an instant-lust but long-drawn-out romance type. I'm glad we've been going slow. I'm glad I've been invited to some of his therapy appointments. I'm glad I got to hear about the causes of sexual addictions and where some of them stem from.

Natalie mentioned that a whopping eighty percent of sex-addicted people are also survivors of sexual abuse, and my eyes had snapped to Gage at that point. I mean, I didn't expect him to tell me, but he did. He said no. He said nothing like that had happened to him that he is aware of, but he can't even remember all the times he's had sex.

So Natalie said he fell into a different category. The one that means he had a lot of sex to cope with depression, negative feelings, and shame. That he had a lot of sex in order to feel something through his haze. Something good, but even just something at all. That it was fuelled and mostly propelled by drug use, especially drugs that increased his sex drive, and that he should be proud of how far he has come. He's not compulsive anymore. He's not covering all his feelings with drugs and sex. He's managing, coping, and processing years of numbness, and he's doing amazing at it. And we know what behaviour to watch for if he ever regresses. He's mindful, and respectful, and taking himself seriously.

So, because of all that, I also love that we've been going slow. Slow is safe, but it's also sexy. And I know that when Gage feels one hundred percent ready, we'll get there. I will wait forever and enjoy every moment leading up to it.

To simplify Gage is impossible, but he's given me a newfound respect for how minds work.

Gage has a neurodivergent mind, so he spent a lot of his childhood and early teen years feeling out of sorts and over-whelmed. Doing cocaine calmed him down, and he self-medicated to repeat that feeling. Self-medicating turned into drug abuse, and by the time he was addicted, he had no idea how to process himself or his feelings, which led to chasing good feelings through sex and continually numbing bad feelings through drugs. He got caught in a cycle that never had a happy point, so he kept searching and failing. I can't even fathom how hard that must have been for him.

My favourite thing he says now is that he feels settled. Whenever he says it, oh my god, I swoon. Because I'm so happy for him. It must be such an incredible feeling to feel settled when his whole life has been unsettled.

As an added bonus, being with Gage has given me a whole new understanding of my dad. He was an addict for a different reason than Gage, but the outcome of addiction was the same. I resented him from such a young age that I didn't fully understand his struggles, and now that I'm looking at it from a new vantage point, our father-son relationship has done a lot of mending. I'm going to give him the new mug soon.

"Any other parts of your past you wanna face today?" I ask him when we're getting close to Port Baylon. As much as I wanna head home and get to work on old things, I'm content to wait and spend more time with Gage.

"Actually, remember that guy we ran into outside the diner?"

"Yeah."

"Wanna pop over to his place with me?" he asks, looking at me, hand still on my thigh. "He roundabout expressed an interest in getting sober, and his wife, Becky, is pregnant. She's also a drug user and a heavy drinker. So... I dunno. Maybe we could just check in on them?"

The overprotective part of me wants to keep Gage away from situations that might be hard for him, but the boyfriend in me wants to support him and his progress. Gage is strong. He can handle it. And he's smart enough to ask me to go with him so he has a buffer. I know Brian didn't like me when he met me outside the diner, but maybe he won't care now that he has at least a small spark of interest in getting some support.

"Sure. Just us? My dad will probably come if we call him."

Gage squeezes my thigh. "Let's tell him we're going, just so he knows. Then he can kinda be on standby if we need some help."

There's that sexy self-awareness again. So goddamn swoony.

AFTER KNOCKING on the door for a solid fifteen minutes, Brian finally pulls it open. He squints at the daylight, shields his eyes, and shakes from head to toe. There are purple circles around his sunken eyes, and I swear he's lost half his weight since the last time I saw him, which isn't much to begin with. The amount of sweat coating him sends me right back to my childhood and my dad's sweaty, spasming body on the bathroom floor. He stinks. The house stinks, wafting to us through the open front door.

"Oh, uh, we aren't really... we're sick."

I'm about to yell at him for trying to attempt this level of detox all on his own, but I clamp my lips and squeeze Gage's hand instead.

"You need help," Gage says, taking charge. "You can't do this alone. You need medical assistance, Brian." He pushes his way inside, dragging me with him.

"I can't afford help!" Brian shouts, but his voice is weak

and strained. And it's a poor excuse because there's always money for drugs but never for therapy.

Don't judge, Alexei.

"I can," Gage tells him. "Where's Becky?"

"Please, don't go in there. She doesn't want to be seen like that. Not by you."

"I've been like that eight times, Brian," Gage says, trying to reason with him. "She's pregnant, man. She needs help."

"I'm helping her."

"You're in no state to help her. You need help, too."

Brian holds onto the back of the couch for balance, looking like he's going to sway right over. He looks at me, trying to remember where he's seen me before. When he notices Gage holding my hand, I brace for a few opinionated comments, but they never come.

"You can check on her. You seem... like you know what you're doing," Brian says to me.

I'm flattered because I do know what I'm doing, but I'm not comfortable leaving Gage alone yet. "Are there drugs in this house?"

"Uh, not in the house, no."

I look at Gage. He smiles at me. "I'm feeling good, Alexei. Leave the door open and I'll make sure you can see me."

I trust him. I drop his hand and walk over to where Brian is pointing. I wedge the door open to a bedroom off the living room and cringe at the smell. Sweat, vomit, more sweat, just general musk and dirtiness, and unwashed sheets.

"Becky?" I call.

She cries from the other side of the bed. With one more glance at Gage, I leave the door open and walk around to where she's curled into the fetal position on the floor. The curtains are closed, but they aren't blackout ones, so there's still enough light to see her clearly.

And holy hell, does it ever bring more flashbacks of my mom and dad when I was a kid.

"Hi, Becky. I'm Alexei." I've never even met her before. I've seen her around town, but we don't know each other at all. "I'm here with Gage. Tell me what you need." I crouch down next to her, and when I reach out to brush her stringy hair off her face, she latches onto my wrist so hard I wince.

"Coke," she says. "Meth. Anything. Just... something to make this stop!"

She's wet her pants, and if the stain on her butt is anything to go by, she's shit herself a bit, too. She's in full-on withdrawal, and nothing about what she's going through right now will be pleasant. Sickness, sweats, chills, a gnawing clench in every part of her body, mental stress, physical weakness, hallucinations, and a desire to just die... all while she's pregnant. Absolutely horrific for her.

"How long since you last used?" I ask, taking her other hand and trying to get her into a sitting position. She slouches, crumpled in half from pain, but she manages.

She's sobbing, an emotional wreck, but I'm already proud of her. "Don't know. Days," she chatters. "Don't make me go to a hospital. They'll take the baby." Her bloodshot eyes meet mine. "Please. Help me."

I'm going to help her, but not with coke or meth. "I will."
I sit down next to her. "Gage? Can I call my dad?"

Brian says no, but Gage says yes. Eventually, he talks
Brian into allowing it. I press my phone to my ear and listen
to it ring, knowing my dad will come because he's reliable.
Holy shit, he's so fucking reliable.

"Alex?" he answers.

"Still have that number for the home-visit doctor?"
I ask.

"Yeah. What's happening? Are you okay? Gage?"

"Two of Gage's friends are going through some terrible
detoxes, and they need help. One of them is pregnant and
afraid to go to the hospital."

Dad doesn't say anything for a while, but I can hear him
breathing. Becky is breathing louder, still crying next to me,
latching onto my wrist like I'm single-handedly keeping her
alive. I'm not. She's doing that all on her own, and I know it
doesn't feel like it for her yet, but that's already something
incredible to be proud of.

"Found it," Dad says. "I'll call him now and come over.
See when he can come. Uh, he's not cheap."

"We'll figure it out," I say. Because I already know Gage
is going to pay for this. This is his chance to help someone
like he's been helped, and he isn't going to pass it up. There's
no point in reminding him that there's a good chance Becky
and Brian might relapse because Gage will find it worth-
while anyway. He relapsed eight times and never gave up on
himself, so he's not going to give up on them either. Not
until they tell him to.

"Help is coming," I tell Becky. "Someone who will make this a bit easier for you. It's still going to be hard, though."

She looks at me, rubbing small circles on her crunched-up belly. "I know," is all she says.

I look at Gage through the open door. Instead of looking tempted or unsure, he looks at me with confidence. This is a reality check for him. He never again wants to look like Becky and Brian do right now. Because this has been him, and he's stronger for it.

God, I love him.

gage

Four months.

Four months of being out of rehab, living in the real world, falling in speedy love with my complicated boyfriend, and finding out that soulmates exist. No relapses, a few weak moments, a lot of self-pride, and even a little self-love.

Only one missed Sunday with Alexei.

No drugs. No booze. Haven't considered stealing anything since the BBQ sauce on wing night. Well, unless you count the coffee beans from work because, my god, I wanted a bag to take home so badly, but I forgot my wallet. Almost took them anyway. Didn't in the end. No sex. Still.

But... I'm ready. I think.

I'm learning that I have obsessive-compulsive tendencies, but I am way better at rationalizing and managing them while sober. Like... a million times better because it's barely even been an issue for me. Still, there's a part of my mind that wants to be hesitant because it's been easy. Easy isn't...

comfortable. I don't want 'easy' to fool me into thinking I'm ready when I'm really not.

It's Sunday. Exactly four months since my 'got-out-of-rehab' Sunday, and everyone knows it, but no one is mentioning it. Because I'm weird like that. I don't know if I want the recognition. What if it puts pressure on me and alters my state of mind? I'm still a bit susceptible to that, so for now, we're all going to celebrate without actually celebrating. Skirt around it without ever mentioning it.

Except Alexei.

"Happy four months," he says, picking me up from the coffee shop after my shift.

"Alexei! You aren't supposed to talk about it."

"About what?" He barely spares me a glance, taking the tea I offer him. He likes it now. Says I make it better than anyone else, even though it's literally just putting hot water in a cup with a tea bag.

"My four months sober since I got out."

He snorts. Adds a scoff. "Please. I'm talking about us. If you wanna get technical, it's three months and twenty-nine days, but whatever. Four months since I started courting you into our soulmateship."

Oh. Well, shit. That makes me smile. "Courting me? Right from day one?" I grab his hand and link our fingers.

He corrects the hold, unlinking our fingers. "Yes, Gage. I was my normal weird self and you accepted it at breakfast, and it was all over from there. Knew you were mine." He glances at me like I'm dumb for not knowing. "Had a real hard talk with Fate that night in bed. Like, why the fuck would she throw my soulmate at me in the form of a dubious smoker? So random and against my wishes, but there you were."

"There I was," I agree, smiling as we walk home. God, he always makes my mood better, even while he's being a condescending prick. "Any regrets?"

"One," he says, sipping. He burns his tongue and glares at me for it.

"What one?" I ask.

"I should have played hard to get a little longer."

"You played hard to get?"

Another side-eye comes my way, our hands swinging between our bodies. "I tried. The pull was too strong."

I stop him in the middle of the sidewalk by tugging on his hand. Grabbing his jaw between my thumb and fingers, I press our lips together, kissing him to remind him I know exactly what level of intimacy comes with it.

"It's not a full moon," I whisper.

"Pick a more romantic place."

"Our street isn't romantic?" Because I want to tell him I love him so badly. The words are champing at the bit to come out, but Alexei has expectations, and I want to meet them all. Four months is a ridiculously fast time to fall for someone, but like he just said, the pull is too strong. When you know, you know.

"I can hear Marian starting her hog," Alexei says against my mouth, pressing his lips to mine for another kiss.

The sun is almost down, but the night is warm and comfortable. I'm not currently worrying about anything.

Brian and Becky are doing well-ish after their visit from the doctor, my relationship with the twins is getting back on track, Owen and my mom are both great, and Alexei completely took my mind off my *other* four-month anniversary. On top of that, I started a new sewing project with Marian and the ladies, and I can't wait to give it to Alexei when it's done.

"Marian's hog is like the soundtrack to our romance, no?" I ask, pulling back to look him in his pale blue eyes. "I associate motorcycles with the start of our relationship."

He narrows his eyes at me.

"Soulmateship. Sorry." I smirk.

Alexei leans into me, forehead against mine. He just breathes for a second, and I close my eyes to enjoy it.

There are moments in my new life that feel slow. The old me was fast-paced and in a rush to get nowhere. I missed so much and forgot all the tiny details. But now that I've learned to appreciate the slowness of everything, especially my relationship with Alexei and the family bonding tea nights in the kitchen, I love the way it feels to be able to drink in a moment and appreciate it at the same time.

We're standing in the middle of the sidewalk at the beginning of our street, people are around, cars are driving by, the night sky is coming fast, and the streetlights are turning on. But we're stuck in our moment, appreciating it, drinking it in, having it despite the rest of the world moving all around us.

"Thanks for being mine, Gage," Alexei says softly. "Thanks for making me yours."

SOBER DOPE & SUNDAYS

Fuck, he's precious. I wrap my arms around him, rest my temple against his, and don't even care when he just leaves his hands hanging, one holding the tea. He leans against me and continues to breathe.

"Thank Fate. It was her doing."

"Love her."

"Me too, Alexei. Me too."

ALEXEI ISN'T afraid of being naked, and he's even less afraid of the way I admire him slowly.

Laid out on his dark grey sheets, legs spread, eyes on mine, and his smooth skin glowing from the moonlight coming in the window, I peer down at him with nothing but lust, love, and complete adoration. After all the shit I've done in my life, no part of me believes I deserve him.

Not only is he absolutely beautiful, he's quirky perfection and eager brilliance. He's understanding and compassionate while also hardened and tough when he shouldn't have to be. He's intriguing because he's so different, and he's funny because of his quick wit. He's my perfect person, and if I had to pick him out of a lineup, blindfolded and deaf, I'd always gravitate to him because our souls really are connected.

On top of that, his body is stunning. He's tall and lean, tattooed and softly masculine. I love that his stomach has abs but they aren't overly defined, the way the veins in his arms stand out, and the blend of harsh grungy vibes meets artistic curiosity in the way he moves and dresses.

"What're you thinking?" he asks, hands casually beside his head on the pillow while he looks up at me. He's in no rush to cross another barrier, and I love that he's the kind of person to enjoy the lead-up to something as much as the actual something.

"That I can't believe you're mine," I tell him, settling all my weight on top of him. He wraps his legs around my waist and pushes his fingers into my hair. "That after all this time and all the bullshit I've put myself through, here you are, right when I needed to find you."

"Hmm," he muses, fingers tickling my scalp. "Honestly, I thought you'd be more of a dirty-talker than the mushy type."

"You gotta get through the mushy parts to get to the filth." I laugh, smiling against his neck. "I bet my dirty-talking game is better than yours."

"It's Sunday," he says randomly. "The Lord's day."

"You believe in a lord?" I rock on top of him, our hardening cocks brushing lightly.

"No, but I always extra-behave on a Sunday, just in case I'm wrong. You never know, and no one has the answers, Gage." He tugs on my hair and brings my mouth to his. He doesn't kiss me, but he grins against my lips, forcing me to close my eyes and enjoy it. "Wanna tempt our ruin?"

"Temptation is what got me into this mess in the first place," I tell him, smiling too. "But fuck yes. Since I'm such a good boy these days, and you're always a good boy, we should push our luck. Just a bit."

"Just a bit?" He grinds against me, lifting his ass off the bed enough to make me groan. "Just the tip?"

I bite his lip and capture his mouth with mine. Alexei moans against my tongue, sucking it into his mouth hard enough to have my cock pulsing precum. "Fuck no. Not just the tip. The whole thing."

"Whose whole thing?" he teases as we grind together.

"Guess we'll find out. Our instinct game starts now, and apparently, we're pairing it with filthy talk and tempting God."

"Good luck," Alexei says.

Then he bucks me off and flips me onto my back, stronger than I thought he was. I gasp, and then my legs are being forced back, knees by my ribs, and Alexei is smirking at me as he leans between them. He gyrates his hips and I'm a goddamn slut for it, panting and grinding back.

"Oh yes," he teases, "such a good boy." He pairs it with a wicked grin and an eye roll.

He kisses my neck, sucking a mark into my skin that has my eyes rolling back. When his tongue runs over my nipple, I whine for more, but he doesn't give it to me. He keeps moving south, licking and sucking his way to my leaking cock, and when he looks up at me with playful eyes, he runs his tongue from base to tip and makes me tremble all over.

My legs push out of his hold, dropping to the bed with him in between. But Alexei doesn't let me move. He takes me into his mouth and turns me needy. My hips buck, chasing the back of his throat, and my sweet Alexei doesn't even gag. He languidly sucks me down and lets me control the pace, grinning at me from around my shaft.

"Had no idea you'd be so playful," I pant at him. "Loving this side of you."

"Playful is cautious. I'm making sure to read you first." He smacks his lips and licks them, hand holding my dick straight upright. "Am I winning?"

He is, but I don't mind. Still, I'm competitive, so I need to even the playing field, and I know exactly what to tell him to startle him enough to flip the script. "I made you your own mug, Alexei. I designed it and used a machine to press it to the mug. Planned to give it to you tomorrow for our four months."

He falters, gawking at me with heart-eyes. Romance doesn't mix naturally with his filthy playfulness, and I've got him right where I want him.

I grin, sitting and picking him up until he's straddling my lap.

"You play dirty with your romance," he complains, grinding down on me with our cocks trapped between our stomachs. "Are you wondering if I'll like this position? If I wanna ride your cock?"

Yes, actually, I am. "Do you?"

"Cheater."

Alexei doesn't let me take control for long. He pushes on my chest, forcing me to lie back, and then he's crawling up to my face, knees on either side of my head, and I'm lifting to suck his balls into my mouth. Hooking my hands over his thighs from below, I hold him exactly where I want him, driving him just as crazy as I'm driving myself. Because I'm so turned on right now, but no part of me wants to rush to the finish line. I'm not blinded by desire or lost in the chase. I'm enjoying every goddamn step of the way there and hoping he is, too.

I'm not being selfish.

"Fuck," Alexei moans when I pull him down and run my tongue over his hole. His thighs shake in my grip, and he swears again. But that's all he'll let me have. He climbs right over my head and stands at the edge of the bed, naked and brazen. "On your knees, soulmate." He grins, eyes on fire.

I scramble to my knees, pointing my ass right at him. He uses his knee to spread mine apart, making me sink down a little lower, and then he pushes on my mid-back, making me fall to my elbows.

"Time to test a theory," he says. Then he licks me, and I instinctively press my ass back against his tongue. "Oh, yeah. You like that, don't you? Knew you'd be greedy."

"I've told you I'm greedy from the start." I'm panting, and I can't even try to hide it because I'm a ten-year-long smoker and my shitty lungs are obvious. But then I choke on a groan when Alexei's hands spread me wide open, and his warm, wide tongue runs a straight path down my crack and over my hole. "Mmm."

My head hangs between my arms as Alexei works me over. And once again, I'm just wowed by him. He knows what he wants and goes for it, and even though we're new to this and still getting to know one another, he's bold in his experiments. And he's nailing it. Because when I look between my body and the bed, seeing my flushed and swollen cock jutting out proudly, it's leaking a line of precum all the way down to the grey sheets.

"Alexei," I moan, wanting more but also wanting him closer to me. "Come here." I spin to reach for him, but he shoves me back down. "Alexei," I complain.

"Shh." He swats my ass playfully. "You know how long I've wanted to perform for you, Gage? Let me have the spotlight."

I twist out of his hold and settle on my back, holding my own knees up. "Fine. Perform, but let me fucking look at you while you do it."

He's not grinning anymore, but there's pride and defiance in his eyes as he sinks to his knees at the side of the bed. In minutes, I'm so wound up I'm squeezing my dick in an effort not to come. Alexei's mouth is pure magic. No other explanation, because the way he rims me, sucks me, nips at my flesh and teases every sensitive part of me is the best damn illusion I've ever witnessed. And he looks like the sexiest magician while doing it.

But then he adds a finger.

And... oh my *god*. "Fucking hell, Alexei. Have mercy. It's been over a year since I—oh, holy fuck." I barely stay flat when he squeezes two fingers inside me and his thumb outside me, essentially pinching my prostate between his grip and massaging it perfectly. "You're the devil," I pant. "No point in being extra-good on Sundays with that kind of hellish skill."

Am I lucid? I glance around the room, trying to get my bearings for just a second to make sure this is actually real. To slow myself down, to take it in, remember it, appreciate it for the epic first time we're about to have.

"I knew you'd beg," he says, still working those fingers. "Just didn't think it'd be for me to stop." He smirks at me, finger fucking my ass like a goddamn expert.

"Over a year, Alexei. Over a year. My tolerance to last is... you make it nothing!"

With another grin, he stands. He nods at the bed, basically commanding me to move up it without words, and fuck me, I do it. Because Alexei might be bold yet bashful outside the bedroom, but in here, he's in charge, and he knows it.

Grabbing lube from the bedside table, he settles between my legs, squirts some onto his fingers, and then bends over me, kissing me so hard I see stars behind my closed eyelids.

"How's my instinct, Gage?" he asks, dragging my lower lip between his teeth. His fingertips tease my hole, not breaching again, but making me wiggle hard enough to try and force them to. "Hmm, pretty good, I'd say."

We've been playing this guessing game for months, and there's no sense in dragging it out any longer. I want to fuck. Right now. "Fuck me, Alexei. No more waiting. Your instincts are—"

Two fingers push inside me and his mouth captures the moan that leaves my lips. "Pay attention," Alexei says, removing his fingers. "To me. To you. To everything."

When he leans back, I watch with focused interest as

he puts a condom on. The whole picture is intriguing. From the way his hand rolls the material down his length to the way his stomach muscles bunch in the background, and up to his icy eyes and the way they watch me instead of his hands. His gaze shifts to the lube, so I grab it and take the chance to lube him up. I'm already lubed and ready for him, but I use the excess on my cock, eyes watching Alexei.

"Are you paying attention, Gage?"

Rapt fucking attention. I couldn't focus harder if I tried.

When the head of his cock presses against my hole, I blink, making sure my eyes are lubricated enough to stay open the entire time he pushes inside me. With my legs spread and Alexei between them, I hold my breath as he breaches my body and causes a beautiful pain I haven't felt in so long. But when his hand slides up my chest, caressing and tickling, I inhale and remember to exhale.

"God," Alexei moans, eyes closing for a second to appreciate this monumental step we're taking. I don't know if it'd be monumental to anyone else, but to me, it is. Because I'm a sex addict in recovery. Because he's my soulmate. Because this is our first time. Because we've been building and building to this, and maybe, just fucking maybe, I feel like I've earned it instead of expected it.

His eyes open, meeting mine, and he pushes in deeper. I groan, but not in pain. In sensation, because fucking hell, Alexei has consumed every part of me since the moment I met him, and to feel him consume my body too? It's everything.

"Still paying attention?" he asks, his voice taking on a sexy, abrasive edge.

I nod, breathing through the stretch.

"What do you notice?" he asks, hips thrusting ever so slightly.

I notice my hands are balled into tight fists, so I relax them. I notice my neck muscles are strained, so I open my jaw and remind my body to soften. I'm clenching around him, so I bear down, immediately making it easier to take him.

"There you go," Alexei says, smiling softly. "Talk to me."

"I'm emotional," I admit. Sex has never been an emotional thing for me. It's been about orgasm chasing, like I told him before. This is different. It's hot and sexy, and it's barely begun, but it's also loving and deep just because it's with him. It's powerful because I trust myself. "And proud."

"Of what?"

"Of getting here. Of recovery. Of learning my body and trusting it." I reach forward, hands on his hips. "Of earning this with you." *Thank you for being patient with me, Alexei.*

"You should be proud," he says, bending forward to kiss my neck. "You feel good, Gage."

I wrap my legs around him, digging my heels into his ass until he's all the way inside me and we're both moaning through it.

"Holy fuck, complicated." I grit the words, not even meaning to use his nickname. My fingers dig into his skin, and he watches me like he's waiting for permission to move. I exhale slowly, letting go of my tension, my fear of a relapse, and my self-doubts. I've got this. I'm in control. Natalie said I'm allowed to get swept up and enjoy it, and that's exactly what I plan to do. Because I finally have Alexei inside me, and I've wanted this since the day he bluntly asked me what I'm addicted to. I look into his eyes, a grin tilting my lips. "No point in even trying to be good on this Sunday, Alexei. I can't believe we're finally…"

Alexei bites his lip. He pulls out and pushes back inside of me, stealing my breath and my sanity in one slow thrust. When he does it again, I push back, trying to take him as deep as I can. It feels good. So good. His eyes are on mine, and I'm trying to keep mine on his, but I look away.

Shit. I look away…

Alexei stops moving. He gently touches my chin, giving me time to look at him again. When I meet his eyes, he does that thing where he takes his time studying me, and for the first time, I panic a little at what he'll find. Because my mind is busy… He's inside me; we're having sex, the first sex after recovering from a sex addiction, and my mind is… on it. Thinking about it. I'm letting worry consume me, worry I don't even understand because it wasn't there a second ago. I start to sweat, afraid of what's happening to me or why it's happening now when I've literally just begged him to fuck me.

Oh my god. What is wrong with me?

He pulls out, sinking down to kiss me instead. I kiss him back, but a thousand apologies are already on my lips. Because I've ruined it. I've ruined our first time. I'm embarrassed, full of shame, weirded out by my own thoughts. I have been craving this for four months. I've wanted Alexei this way for so long that I can hardly resist him. Literally seconds ago, I writhed beneath him, eager and overexcited about getting his dick inside me. It felt good. It felt really good. But my fucking head!

"Alexei, I'm so—"

"Don't you dare apologize," he whispers against my lips. "We made a deal to trust our instincts and see how well we could read each other, right?" He pulls back to look at me, and I nod when he smiles. "Well, we're doing that. It's not the right time for sex." His smile is so sexy, so confident and sure, and it makes my head pound with pride. I picked an asshole in Paul, but I picked a fucking winner in Alexei. "Look at how well we read each other, Gage." He smirks.

"But I want this," I insist. "I don't know why my head is caught up."

"Because it's a big step," he says. "Because you respect yourself. You respect us." He dips to kiss me again, and when he adds his tongue, my hands snake around his neck to keep him here. "Stop feeling guilty. Try to set it aside and listen to what your body wants. What does it want, Gage?"

"You."

He reaches between our bodies to take the condom off, and then he slides his cock against mine. I've softened a little, but I'm already hardening again. He rubs against me, and my legs wrap around his hips, my heels digging into his ass to bring him down against me again.

"You can have me," he whispers. "Just like this. Mm."

"You're not... upset?"

"I'm proud. And more turned on because you're admitting to yourself what you feel."

Alexei isn't making this weird, so I'm going to try not to be the one who does. I take a deep breath and listen to my body. Everything we've done together up until this point has been hot, and I've never gotten in my head about it. Now that penetration is off the table for tonight, I relax into the way our bodies meld together, the feel of his hard cock against mine, and the way his hands hold me with nothing but love and acceptance.

I'm comfortable with Alexei. I want him. I need him. And I don't feel stupid. My guilt vanishes, my embarrassment changes into arousal, and I give myself permission to still be horny even after screwing up the sex.

"Alexei," I say, pushing him up so I can reach down to grip us in my fist. He moans as I rub us together. "Thank you."

The way our bodies move together settles my mind, and the gentleness of the moment isn't void of lust. It's still there, and the build-up to a new type of orgasm is subtle yet sexy. It's comfortable because Alexei read me. He followed his instincts, gave me permission to feel mine, and didn't let either of those things ruin our moment.

When we come, it's through a kiss that doesn't end for hours. And when we journal about the experience, only one small part of it is about my hesitation. The takeaway lesson is that I'm just not fully ready yet. I need to trust myself a little more.

I love him for understanding. I love myself for picking such an incredible partner.

alexei

28

'm all spaced out and blissed out and smiling into my morning bran cereal when my dad comes downstairs with a cringe expression on his handsome face. He wasn't home when we tried sex for the first time, but I can't promise we were quiet during the night when Gage woke me up with a slow handjob, and I rewarded him with my mouth on his cock. He might have even heard the chat we had about his hesitation and inability to trust himself yet. God, I loved that chat! As soon as I sensed a bit of fear from him, I knew it was time to stop, to let him process, to have the talk about it because we're great at talking.

That chat turned into a chat about condoms. I used one, but Gage bashfully wrote in his journal that he has a clear bill of health and had been tested, and then he wrote the word 'condom' with a question mark beside it. I crossed it out, telling him through the journal that I trust him not to use one if we try again. And now I'm daydreaming about being inside him bare. Eventually. Someday. Not today. We decided fantasizing about all of it is perfectly healthy, even if we don't plan to do any of it yet. I'm so proud of him! So proud of how last night went.

So, to distract my dad from commenting on it, I nod to the wrapped box on the island.

"For me?" he asks, and I nod. "Where's Gage?"

"Coffee shop. Had to work."

Dad grunts. "Did he get his meds?"

"I gave them to him, yeah. Open it."

Dad looks uncertain, but he unties the ribbon and opens the box. Pulling out his new mug, he tries really hard not to let his emotions show, but I'm a goddamn detective and see them all anyway. I was going to give him the one that said, *'world's best shitty dad,'* but you know what? He's not the world's best shitty dad. He's not a shitty dad at all anymore, and it's about time I tell him that.

He clears his throat, wanting to read what it says but unable to. Instead, he turns it towards me, and I smile at the inscription. *'Dad. Superpower: fucking being there.'*

"Are we gonna get awkward?" I ask him. "Because I don't normally feel awkward in typically awkward scenarios," I remind him.

"Thank you," Dad says, voice hoarse. "This is... I don't even... thank you, Alex."

I smile at him and get up to rinse my bowl out. "You've proven time and time again that you're always there for me. Thanks. For coming so far and working so hard, and never giving up. It's not unnoticed." I lean against my dad, not hugging him with my arms but with my body. He's awkward, so he hugs me back and does a weird back-pat thing, but it only makes me smile more. "And thanks for everything you did with Brian and Becky."

He nods, clearing his throat again. "Gage, uh, left something for you, too. In my goddamn bedroom because he has no concept of boundaries. Just texted me with instructions and said it was on my dresser." He grabs a tin can and a small box. The tin can says, *'Soulmate Blend.'* Inside are tea bags that smell like ginger, fennel, and lemon. Mmm. On each tea bag is a string with a sticker on the end, every single one different.

My turn to choke! I slam the canister shut. "They say nice words!"

"What?" Dad asks, taking it from me and peeking. "Icy blue. Neurotic. Rambler. Blue with black. Secret codes. Instincts, with a winky face. Morse Code. No flirting tax. Attic bedrooms. Blunt blushing." Dad looks up at me after reading a few. "What do they mean?"

They're all the reasons Gage loves me. "They mean he really is my soulmate. I told you."

Dad laughs, passing me the can again. "Open that one."

"Did he chicken out of giving me these while he was here? It's not like him to not want to watch my reaction." I pull the box towards me.

"He just said to give them to you and to make sure you get romantically weird about them." Dad shrugs. "Said you might need the privacy to feel your feelings." He shrugs again.

Gage is so romantic. Dad watches over my shoulder as I open the box, finding the mug Gage designed for me.

'One hit is all it takes...'

"What?" Dad asks. "Some sort of drug humour? I don't get it."

I do. Because when I flip the mug over, I know exactly what kind of drug he's referring to, and one hit is all it takes...

"Sober dope," I tell my dad. "It means I make him feel good. That I'm his happy drug."

Dad grumbles about not liking addict humour, and while I'd usually agree with him, this is different. This is Gage's way of saying that he's learned to be happier and healthier, and I'm a part of his journey. It's his way of saying he doesn't miss the high of his vices and has learned to enjoy the feeling of being sober and alive and with me. He had his high dope, his drunk dope, and now he's declaring that he's reached a level of comfort with his sober dope. *Me.*

"I love him," I tell my dad. "Just so you know."

Dad looks at me, and the smile on his face is the most gorgeous thing. He's happy for me. "I'm glad you're finally letting someone get to know how amazing you are, Alex. I'm happy for you. And proud. And here, if you need anything."

"I know. That's why I upgraded your mug."

Back to awkwardness because Dad doesn't know how to accept praise. I don't care, though. I'm hugging a mug and sniffing soulmate tea, feeling so giddy and in love, drinking in this moment with my dad here.

I LIKE to think of myself as a pretty stand-up guy. I do my taxes and abide by most rules. People generally like me because I'm superficial enough not to scare them off with my weird ways and lack of social protocol. I give people the benefit of the doubt, don't cause unnecessary drama, and hardly ever offend anyone on purpose.

Right now, I'm a slinky, sneaky, narrow-eyed spy, and I don't even care. Because that's him! Paul. Gage's ex-boyfriend who allegedly—maybe—wanted to keep my soulmate an addict just to feel important. I don't like him one bit. I don't like that he looks so much more buff than me, and I definitely don't appreciate the way he dresses so smart. Like, what's a guy need all those colours and buttons for? Who's he trying to impress? It better not be Gage.

"Nope," I tell Gage. "I'm putting my foot down. Denying you access. Demanding that you aren't allowed to go in there." I slurp a matcha tea frappé through a wide straw. "I don't trust all that tan! Who wears tan with yellow? He's obviously a serial killer."

Gage laughs from the passenger seat of my car, dressed in jeans and a sweater to show that smartly dressed twat that he doesn't give any fucks about fancy pants. "It's a legal meeting. I have to go, but I kind of like it when you put your foot down. Do that more often. Especially while I'm naked."

I turn my rapt attention on my boyfriend, narrowing my eyes at him. "You think I'm joking?"

"Oh, I know you're not," he says, trying to hide his smirk. "That's your angry, serious face."

"Yes, it is. So let it rule you."

"One form. A banker and a lawyer. Then I'm done with him forever." He takes my wet hand, slick with condensation from my cup. "Will you feel better if I take a dig at his outfit? I can make a real snarky comment about tan and yellow."

"Please do." Because blues with my blacks is what Gage is supposed to love. Not khaki and sunshine.

"I will," he promises, laughing. "I'd invite you in, but it's supposed to be a closed meeting."

"Gage Rossum," I say, turning in the seat to face him, "after this one and only time, there are no more closed doors in our soulmateship. If you need privacy, you tell me you're going to be private, okay? I'll give it to you if you tell me you need it, but I don't want any secrets. I want openness. Vast, wide-open, glaringly obvious and sometimes intrusive openness. I should have mentioned that before you kissed me, because that's what I expect with our level of intimacy."

He's not put off. He simply smiles, his brown eyes looking straight into mine. "We'll take all the fucking doors off our house, complicated. Promise."

Our house.

As Gage gets out to go settle his shit with the ex in tan and yellow, I sit in my car for an hour trying to envision our house with no doors. Where will we live? Eventually. Because I'm not totally crazy to want to live with him so soon, but since he's basically my fated mate, it'll happen sooner or later, and now I'm trying to picture the kind of house we'll live in.

The stupid, falling-down mansion is all I can picture. How will I ever leave my workshop in the scary basement that doesn't scare me so much anymore now that I've discovered it's basically a troll's den of antique treasure?

As I'm snacking on crispy seaweed, a voice memo from Gage comes through. I play it through the car speakers.

"Sorry. I need my sunglasses because of all the yellow."

I grin, loving my sneaky boyfriend who never breaks a promise.

But, okay, let's be serious for a quick sec. Because my website gig is starting to feel like a chore, and I don't know what it means! Do I hate it?! Am I just distracted by making old things new? Am I a cave dweller who feels more comfortable in my basement lair? Why do I suddenly want to start a side business of restoring things? Like, I'm barely green at it, so it's not like I'm qualified. But I must admit my fireplace grate turned out clutch, and now I'm working on an old set of matching light fixtures that have me all hot and bothered.

Dad thinks I should scale down my website business, not take any new clients, but keep working for the ones I have until I can get a foothold in the restoration business. And while I'm not usually an impulsive kind of guy, a Gage-influenced part of me wants to quit cold turkey and go all in on restoration.

I won't. Simply because Gage would do it.

I'll do it better. I'll ease in. Get my feet wet. Ease out of websites. Smart. I'm so much smarter than Gage regarding impulse control, though he's been pretty top-shelf at it lately, too. So proud of him.

Looking at the office building's front door, I see them fly open and Gage runs out. Literally runs, kind of with a skip, beaming a massive smile at me. My windows are up, but he's yelling something excitedly. When he grabs the door handle, he must miss, because he falls forward and faceplants against the passenger window. So clumsy.

"Did you hear it? Get it? My sunglasses comment?" He climbs in, ungracefully settling onto the seat. "It's done. Over. I'm $250k richer! HA! It's almost what I paid for the place years ago, but the appraisal says this is what he owes me, and here it is!" He waves around a folder of papers that I can't see, but I'm smiling anyway because he's taken on the neurotic rambler role today. Just more upbeat about it than I usually am. "Alexei!" Papers go flying when he irresponsibly tosses the folder into the backseat so he can smack my cheeks between his palms. "It's over. Just us now."

His smile is wide, showing his teeth that should be nicotine-stained but aren't. Coffee-stained, too. Gah, he gets away with everything. "You look so handsome like this," I tell him. "Happy and excited and clumsy. Do it more."

"Yes, sir," he says right before leaning in to smile-kiss my lips. "Hey, complicated?" he asks.

I get warm everywhere. "Yeah?"

"Thanks for everything. All of it. Being my weird friend and then my slow-moving boyfriend. Now my soulmate. Just, thanks, for meeting me."

It was fate, but I nod against his forehead and press my lips to his. "You're welcome."

"Take me home, Alexei. My sex journal is lacking entries. We gotta experiment and get to the bottom of my trust issues with myself."

Oh my god. I pull back, open my door, and walk around to his side. When I rip the door open, he looks at me with a 'wtf' face. "You can't just drop that on me and expect me to drive. I'm not that coordinated. Switch."

When Gage smiles and stands up, he speaks against my lips. "I love that I'm such a distraction."

"It's the journalling. Not you," I lie.

29

gage

After a lengthy video appointment with Natalie about our first attempt at sex, I feel better about how it all went down. Especially because she made me admit that if Alexei hadn't stopped and switched gears, I would have let it continue, even if I felt uncomfortable the whole time. She says it's the sign of a great partner, and that it should make me feel very comfortable to express myself from now on. If Alexei can take me seriously, I should be able to take myself seriously, too. Progress isn't linear, and I need to remember that. It's okay! I'm okay. We're okay. So, I'm moving on to work on the library.

I don't know why I want to bring the former glory of this library back to life. I'm not even a book guy, but this room and all its shelves and windows have been calling to me since I first got the full tour of the mansion. The *Beast* gives *Belle* a library, and maybe I'm feeling a little beasty, and Alexei is a little beauty, and it'll make me feel more loveable if I bring this place back to life. Alexei will tell me I don't need to build a library to be loveable, so I'll just do it with my own secret intentions.

I smile at the cleared and dusted shelves, hands on my hips, to admire the effort it took to clean this room out. When I look around, I see parts of me. Like, I don't even live here and have barely done anything to the space, but I see myself in the shelves and the gleaming windows. I see myself sitting in here, getting work done on my iPad, inspired by the room it will become, with a rolling ladder and everything.

"Told you," Alexei says, making me jump when he walks in like a ghost.

I place my hand on my thwacking heart. "God, complicated! I was perving on this room in peace. I didn't know you were perving on me." I smile at him, and I love how his septum piercing scrunches when he smiles back. "What'd you tell me?"

"That fixing up old mansions is a good hobby. You're getting invested. I can tell." He looks around, judging my cleaning job. "Okay, hear me out. What if I restored that ancient old coffee table tucked away in the basement? It'd look awesome here with a nice rug and some reading chairs. Tell me I'm right."

He is right. About all of it. About the coffee table and chairs and about me getting invested in the house. I'm going to have to get a little less invested in it because it's not mine and it's going to hurt to leave this place someday. "I'll help you dig it out tonight." I grab his hand, palms together without our fingers linked. "Tomorrow is Sunday," I remind him.

"Our day," he says, looking at me with his warm, icy blue eyes. "Are you being dubious again?"

One year, four months, and one week sober. Yes, I'm dubious because that's a big fucking deal! I think I'm in a mental state to celebrate it now, but I kind of like his idea to measure progress in projects instead of time. So, this library will be a good project to measure by, but mostly, Sundays are a good goal. Every time I make it to a Sunday, our day, I get to celebrate the day we allotted just for each other.

"Only a little dubious because I want to do something special for you."

"Yes," he says, not needing to hear more detail. "Do that. Because I'm special."

I laugh. "Eat fried meats special?"

"Too special for that."

I want to tell him I love him. I checked, and it's not a full moon, so the lunar calendar says it's allowed. Now I need to pick a more romantic place because Alexei told me the street isn't romantic enough. And although I know we'll be tempting our ruin on the former Lord's Day with all sorts of sexiness as we build to my comfort levels, I don't want to blurt it while he's turning me needy with arousal. No. My love confession has to come at the most perfect moment, just like our first kiss—one befitting a pair of soulmates who finally found each other.

When he blinks at me to draw attention to his eyes, I pretend not to notice he's wearing the mascara he's blatantly trying to make obvious. "You look nice today," I tell him instead.

"I know. What about me looks nice?"

"Hmm." I sweep my eyes over his body. "The blues with your blacks, for sure."

"That all?" he asks, flattered and pissed off at once.

"Your hair looks sexy. I love it when you redo it. So, do you have to bleach it and then add the tint?"

"Yes," he snips. "What else?"

I lick his septum piercing. "This is my favourite one. The black one."

Alexei narrows his eyes at me, caught between enjoying the compliments and being frustrated that I haven't mentioned his lashes. "I'm very detail-oriented, Gage. I thought you were, too. I'm so let down right now." He purses his lips and presses them to mine, angrily non-kissing me before he spins to leave the library.

"Hey, complicated?"

He stops but doesn't turn around.

"Fucking love the mascara. Love you without it, too."

He won't look at me, but I know he's glaring at the wall. And blushing. And trying not to smile. "Go work on your sticker packs, Gage. And don't bother me in my workshop."

"Oh? So you get to do your hobby but I'm not allowed to? I have to work?"

"Yes."

Hypocrite. I almost shout that I love him as he walks

322

out, but I bite the words back and return to planning my big love confession. A more romantic setting, eh? Hmmm...

MIDNIGHT TEA COMES with awkwardness and feelings tonight. Earl Grey because it's our favourite, and ain't nobody wanna be grumpy about Oolong when we're trying to have a hard conversation.

"We're sorry," Nick says for the tenth time. "If we'd known you were going to come home that night..."

I shake my head at him, my eyes wet. "If I wasn't who I am, you wouldn't be feeling so guilty right now. It's on me."

"No, the heck it isn't, hun," Mom butts in, coming to sit at the table with the sixth teapot because we go through this shit like it's holy water. "Drugs are not allowed in my house. You all know that. So, respect it." She looks at the four of us sternly, even though she doesn't have the best stern face. It's more... suspiciously troubled. "That's not to say I want you out there experimenting with drugs in an unsafe place, but please, boys. Haven't we lived through this enough?"

My heart sinks, but I know she has every right to say that. "I'm sorry."

"Let's stop being sorry!" Mom shouts, tilting her tea enough to spill it. "Let's just do better."

Cole is usually the loudmouth, but he's barely said anything tonight. He's apologized, but mostly, he's drinking tea in silence and listening to everything we're saying. "Cole? You okay?"

"No," he admits, looking at the wooden grain of the kitchen table. "Because I get it."

"Get what?" Owen asks.

"Addiction. I get why you'd wanna chase that feeling."

Fucking... fuck. I respect that he gets it, but I'm worried that he *gets* it. I hope it scared him into avoiding drugs, but if he's anything like me, the fear won't register over the complete desire to feel that again.

"I never really got it before," Cole goes on. "Why you'd throw your whole life away for nothing but a high. Because half the time when I saw you, it didn't look fun, so it never made sense to me."

"It's not fun. Not after the initial fun phase," I admit. "After that, you just get stuck in a loop of never being able to replicate that feeling. It's bullshit, Cole. Don't be like me. Honestly, it's a life of feeling sick and panicked and sweaty and out of control. It's not fun, and it's damn near impossible to kick the habit."

"But you did," Owen says. "And it was hell for you."

I nod because it certainly is hell. Not just the detoxes, but all of it. The incessant need to get more, the fear and panic of getting caught, the worry that I wouldn't be able to find what I needed, and the guilt and shame of being such a letdown.

"What're you thinking, honey?" Mom asks Cole. "Safe space."

Nick nudges Cole with his shoulder to be supportive,

and Cole clears his throat. "I wanna be like you," he tells me, looking right at me. "This you. Not the druggie you. Help me."

I reach across the table and take his hand. "Always. Trust me, man, I get the hype of experimenting. And for most people, they can do just that. Experiment and never have anything bad come from it. But some of us just aren't cut out for that, and I wish I knew that beforehand. I still would have done it because I didn't grow up watching it ruin someone's life, but you did. So I'm here to remind you how fucking pathetic I've been."

"Not pathetic," Mom says. "Just off track. We're all here. For each other."

When the eighth teapot comes around and someone is always peeing, we're laughing about it and talking about hobbies and other ways to feel good. We're talking about therapy and quilting and the forge.

"Okay, it's settled." Mom stands, holding her bladder. "We're doing a family forging night. I'm signing you all up."

"Sign Alexei up, too." I smile.

Climbing up to my attic room, I don't even try to sleep because I know I'll have to pee again soon. Instead, I run my hands over the perfect piece of wood. The one I'm going to burn Alexei's workshop sign on. I've practiced on other pieces of wood, but this one is the winner, and I'm nervous about making the first mark on it. I have a very romantic plan for this particular piece of wood, and I'm grinning about it in the privacy of my room. I've also been quilting something for Alexei, and I know he's going to love it simply because I made it.

I've had some big realizations over the past few months. Like what it means to be a person, how strong I actually am, and how happiness is happier when it's something I can appreciate with a clear mind. I've learned other ways to balance my ADHD, that it's not pathetic to go to meetings with Nathan, even if I'm just using them as a social event some nights, and that friendships come in all shapes and sizes. I love the ladies from quilting night, and Benedita, my Portuguese neighbour who is so much more than Portuguese, is going to teach me to make those custard tarts so I can surprise Mom. Since being home, I've realized that she and her husband are more of a support network for my mom. They give her a sense of community and familial love, helping out with the twins, keeping an eye on them while Mom is at work, and sharing yard tasks that are sometimes too much for my mom. They're family, and I'm learning that I not only have an awesome immediate family, but an incredible extended one, too.

I have things to look forward to and live for. I have a fucking soulmate! Like, how cool is that? The old me would have never taken the time to get to know Alexei, and that's such a shame because his personality is so epic. Druggie me would have been confused by him, not had the patience to learn or tolerate his judgements, and pushed him aside as someone not worth the effort of my one-track mind. Getting to know him has been one of the biggest perks of my sobriety. Because he's not boring, and he's not like anyone else, and it feels like such a monumental gift to actually know him.

God, I'm so in love.

I'm gonna ask Natalie if that's an impulsive choice, but... I don't think it is. It feels real and right. Like it's not a choice, just a fact.

Alexei is my person.

gage

30

I'm sweating! Ridiculously. Swallowing words and acting like a shy boy. I feel weird about it, but not as weird as I would if I were doing it alone. Alexei is acting the same.

"What's wrong with you?" he whispers at me with a hiss. "Stop acting so immature."

"You're doing the same thing!" I nudge him, trying to hide my flushed cheeks from Dave.

"No, I'm not!" Alexei glares at me, but his cheeks are just as flushed.

I'd like to say we're blushing because these forge fires are so blistering and the room is hellishly hot because of them, but no. It's all Dave. Dave, the forging instructor I teased my mom for having a crush on. Dave, the rugged and tattooed middle-aged man who makes weapons for a living. Dave, who has the darkest and most perfect rough stubble along his demonically chiselled jaw.

"I mean, who looks like that?" Alexei scoffs. "I can see

his abs through his shirt. Why isn't he wearing a protective apron?"

"I'm glad he isn't," I mutter, but Alexei hears it and gives me another smack. "What?! You're gawking, too."

"Not on purpose. He's just all... there. Manly and... there." He swallows. "God, Gage. Get your shit together."

"I will when you do." I watch my melting metals that are somehow going to turn into a cool hunting knife with Dave's help. Oh, maybe I can feign ignorance to get a little extra attention.

"Excuse me, Dave?" Alexei calls. "Am I doing this right?"

Alexei bats his lashes—his mascara-coated lashes—at Dave. I'm about to smack him, but then Dave smiles. *Smiles!* Like one of those bad-boy smiles that make the ladies wet and the men hard. One of those panty-dropping ones that makes me wanna kneel and tell him to do whatever he wants to me. Oh my god. He's coming right for us, muscular arms all tanned and sweaty, tinted a bit black from the soot that's coming from who knows where?!

"It looks perfect, Alex," Dave says, leaning over his shoulder. And I'm jealous. Not a malicious jealousy, just jealous that Alexei gets to be that close to Dave. "Keep going. It's almost melted, and then we can start moulding and shaping it."

Alexei's lashes are still batting, and I'm pretty sure he leans his sweaty back against Dave's sweaty chest. Gah!

"Dave?" I attempt to bat my own lashes, but a drop of

sweat gets in there and I look like I'm trying to Morse Code him with my blinking. "How's mine?"

Alexei glares for a sec, but when he sees all my lame blinking, he snorts and calls me pathetic. Don't care. I'll be pathetic because Dave is right up behind me now, and Alexei is watching, and his icy blue eyes are even icier.

"Great," Dave says, patting me on the shoulder. "Another few minutes."

I dreamily sigh, and then my head snaps to the other side of the room when Mom and all her forge friends laugh at us. I narrow my eyes at Mom, and she just shrugs like she's proving her point, saying, 'Well, now you get it.' Yeah, I get it! I want to become a master metalsmith just to spend more time around Dave.

"Hey, Dave?" Nick asks from my right, acting way more chill than us. "You think you could help me pour this?" He licks his lips. When Dave walks over to him, putting his hands over Nick's to help him pour, my flirty little brother grins at us, proving that he's got more game than we do.

I'm about to tell Dave that Nick is seventeen, but Alexei smacks me again, and Nick is looking at me like I need reminding that he'll be eighteen in a week. Ugh! Outplayed by my brother. When I look at Alexei, I no longer care. Because he's mine, and no one has shit on the level of attraction I feel for my soulmate.

"Okay, new deal," Alexei says, his lips to my ear. "We can be pathetic on forge nights and have a silly crush, but the rest of the time, we're committed to our soulmateship."

"No deal, complicated. I'm committed to our soulmate-ship even while we're crushing on sexy Dave."

When he bats his lashes at me, I melt from him instead of the forge fire.

After class, Mom goes out with her friends, the twins head to a buddy's place, Owen has a date, and Alexei and I walk uptown to hit a meeting. I told him he didn't have to come, but I'm secretly glad he wants to. Nathan isn't coming tonight because he's on a date I'm not allowed to tell Alexei about, so it's just the two of us. It's late, and Alexei is all about a healthy sleep routine, but he's buzzing after the forge just like Mom does.

"Do you wish I was more manly like him?" he asks me as we approach the community centre.

"Fuck no." I grab his hand, palms together. "You mean masculine?"

"Yeah, that."

"Nah, you're perfect just like this. Still can't read your look, but I like it this way. You don't fit a box. You're grungy and moody and cute and sexy."

"Never will," he declares. "Dave's a bit hairy for my taste."

I bark out a laugh. "Then why were you drooling all over him?"

"Because he looks good in a t-shirt, Gage! But if he took it off and he had a hairy chest, I'd be a little less attracted to him."

"Not a fan of hairy chests?" I lift a brow.

"Some hair is sexy. Never been into the bear type."

Mm, I have. All types. But Alexei's masculine, lean, somewhat scrawny body does it for me best. "What type am I?"

"You don't fit a box either. You defy the boxes because you should be out of shape and unhealthy-looking, but you aren't. Which means your body pisses me off, but it's hard to stay mad at it when it's so... mm."

I smile and lean over, humming against his lips. "Mm," I agree.

When we get to the meeting, we sit together and listen to everyone talk. When it's my turn to share if I want to, I do so willingly. Telling them in a joking way that I'm dating my sponsor's son like it's a bad thing, but it's not a bad thing. It's the best thing. It's just my instincts again, telling me to poke fun at something that makes me feel like I defied the rules. Alexei knows a lot of people here because he's come with his dad before, and when the meeting ends, I end up standing by his side while he chats with Carla. She's telling him about her grandmother passing away and leaving her everything she owns, and Alexei is invested because he loves old things.

"You know, Alexei is awesome at restoring antiques," I tell Carla.

Alexei glares, but an hour later, they're still chatting about it, and Alexei is taking jobs, and she's telling him that she'll spread his new business idea around if anyone needs any work done. Then we walk home, and he's rambling about whether he should set up a new business or not, and I'm just smiling and listening because it makes me happy to see him so excited about something. So much of the focus has been on my recovery that it's finally time to let him have the spotlight as he shifts into a potential new career.

God, it feels good not to be so selfish anymore.

ALEXEI COULDN'T STAND to smell like *fire and brimstone* after the forge, so he rushed into the mansion for a shower while I hung out on the front porch for a cigarette. He's still overly excited about talking with Carla at the meeting, and I smiled the whole walk home, listening to him chat my ear off about the potential of old things.

But now I'm taking a breather, and not the kind of breather I normally need to take. I'm taking a horny breather. Because I'm... really fucking turned on. To see Alexei in his prime, animatedly going on about restoration, having him come to a meeting with me, and feeling his hand in mine on the walk home has my body lit up with need. So, instead of going in there to rush anything, I'm taking a minute to think and assess.

I'm thinking about Natalie. More specifically, something she said to me after a few sessions about my newfound fear of penetration. She doesn't think I'm actually afraid of sex, but she does think I've attached an insane level of pressure to what penetrative sex means. When we got to the root of it, we discovered that I'm afraid of myself. I was an out-of-control sex addict who overindulged and fucked with no purpose other than to come, and I'm afraid of treating Alexei like that. That's my fear. Not trusting myself to treat Alexei the way he deserves to be treated.

So, she told me to try watching myself, holding eye contact with myself during the act, at least as a way to keep tabs on my mind frame. When Alexei had me on my back, all I could see was his face, eyes, and expressions. Not my own. Right now, with my cock as hard as stone and a level of arousal I'm starting to get comfortable with, I feel... ready to try something new, and I'm unafraid if it doesn't go the way I want it to. Alexei will understand.

I stamp out my smoke, walk inside, and climb the creaky stairs to the bathroom Alexei is showering in. He has one in his bedroom bathroom, but ever since he did the dark tile grout in the other one, he prefers to shower in there.

"Alexei?" I call, knocking my knuckles against the door. "Can I brush my teeth?"

"Come in!"

Steam hits me like a wall, the scent of his shampoo making the room smell of him. I grab my toothbrush and look in the mirror while I brush. My eyes are clear and focused, my shoulders are squared and relaxed, and my face isn't etched with anything grotesque. I'm not a filthy sex monster, and it's time I start giving myself some credit.

"Are you thinking about Dave?" he asks from behind the glass wall.

I no longer want this glass wall to separate us like it did before. "No. I'm thinking about you."

"What about me?"

"About how you're—"

"Can't hear you," he shouts. "Might wanna come in here and say it to my naked body."

Yeah, I might. I do. I am.

Pulling my shirt off, I throw it to the floor, a black and blue and orange pile of fabric beside the vanity. Looking through the glass, I watch Alexei's body under the hot spray of the shower as I take my jeans off. Fuck, I want him. Differently than before. I give my cock a rub, letting the arousal build alongside my confidence. We've always run on instinct and the ability to read one another, so now it's my turn to read him. Dropping my boxers, I step into the shower and lick my lips at the sight of his naked body.

Tall and lean, muscled but not overly defined, tattooed with secret codes, and with the fiercest blue eyes I've ever stared into, he's a masterpiece. His eyes dip to my cock, and when they rise, they're as lusty as I feel. Predatorily, I step towards him, letting the water hit my warm skin. Almost matched in height, our eyes stay connected as our bodies brush together, his cock hardening right alongside mine. Without a word, he grabs the back of my neck and pulls me in for a kiss, and I go willingly, pushing against him until his back hits the tile wall.

He groans, tongue brushing against mine in a hot kiss that sends shivers down to my toes. When I swipe my thumb over his nipple, he moans louder, his hips bucking against mine.

"Alexei," I groan against his mouth, my hand moving up to wrap around his throat. "Hold on to my shoulders."

I drop to a crouch, and his fingertips dig into my upper shoulders. I don't hesitate to suck the head of his cock into my mouth, suctioning my cheeks to drag a hissed gasp from between his lips. When his blunt nails bite into my flesh, I suck him down further. I've never been one to focus on my partner, but I've learned to appreciate every reaction I can pull from Alexei. The way he holds his breath when something feels incredible, the sound he makes when he's trying not to moan too loudly, and the sight and feel of all his muscles bunching in restraint and pleasure whenever he's on the precipice of orgasm.

"Fuck, Gage. What are you doing to me?" he rasps, one hand moving to my hair.

I stroke him gently with one hand, looking up at his gorgeous face. "Are we still acting on instinct and the ability to read each other?" I ask.

"Always."

Instead of second-guessing my instinct, I simply ask, "You bottom too, don't you?"

Alexei grins down at me, his cheeks flushed pink and the water turning the rest of him a bit red. He nods, biting his lip.

"Is that a yes?"

"It's a yes," he agrees.

"I fucking want you, Alexei. I want to try something."

He bends down, gripping my jaw tight. "I'm yours. I'm ready to try anything with you." He presses his lips to mine as my arousal surges.

When he straightens, I spin him around and press on his

lower back until he plants his hands on the wall and sticks his ass out. Spreading him open to expose his tight pink hole, I salivate, brimming with the need to please him. I lean forward, tonguing his hole like I've been desperate to since the last time I did. He shakes, and I clamp my hands onto his hips to keep him steady.

Ravenous, I can't stop. When he moans, I lick him harder. When he begs, I fuck my tongue into him and spread him wide open.

"Gage," he moans, and I slick my finger with spit, slowly sliding it inside him. "Oh, fuck."

Yeah, oh fuck is right. Building him up and worshipping him is the most natural thing I've ever done, and it's time I stop holding myself back and remember that during penetrative sex. It's another way to worship him, and that's all I've ever wanted to do.

I add a second finger, easing him open and replacing the stretch with more gentle licks. His cock ruts against the tiles, and his ass presses back against my face. With my fingers in his ass, I say, "I want to fuck you, Alexei. Right now."

He nods, gulping air. "Yes."

"Out there."

He looks backwards at me, seeing my free hand point to the vanity. He nods, not even having to ask me why I want it out there, and shuts off the shower. When I stand, he pulls me against his body, and we trip and tumble our way out of the shower, unable to stop making out. His hands are everywhere, grabbing and groping, unsure where he wants to touch me but unwilling to lose contact, and all it does is build my confidence. Because he wants this as badly as I do, and he's not going to tell me to be careful. He's not going to say we don't have to or that it's okay if I change my mind. He's going to let me lead because he trusts me as much as he trusts himself, and now it's time for me to put the same faith in my control.

"Alexei," I pant against his neck. "I need to watch myself."

"In the mirror?" he asks, lips on my cheek.

"Yes."

"Do it. I want you to see yourself how I see you." With a final kiss, he spins and wipes a towel across the foggy mirror. When the picture of us reflects back, all flushed from the shower and brimming with sexual need, I take a moment to simply admire the way we look together. His blue-blond hair is even darker while wet, but his eyes are brighter, connected with mine. "See? Do you see how amazing we look together, Gage?"

Yes. I do. I see myself as a man in love, not a problem to be solved. I see confidence in myself instead of fear. I see the way he looks at me like he has all the faith in the world in me, and I see the way I look at him like he's the light of my life. I see a beautiful man with a complicated mind and an easy disposition. God, I love him.

There is lube in the drawer from the last time we fooled around in here, and Alexei pulls it out. Pouring some onto his fingers, he bends over and fingers himself right in front of me. My hand lands on my cock, anticipating that lube coating me as I push inside him. I keep my eyes on his fingers, the sound of the lube making me breathe even heavier.

"Fuck, complicated. Look at you." I smooth my hand over his hip and down his ass.

"Look at you," he retorts. "Look at the way you look at me, Gage."

My eyes flash to the mirror, and it's there, in my gaze and the part of my lips, the adoration and attraction I have for Alexei. The trust and comfort that goes with it. The ability to be myself, unsure if I'm going to fuck this up or not, but still go through with it.

"So fucking sexy, Alexei." I take the lube from him, coat my cock, and remove his hand. "You sure my instincts are right?" I smirk at him in the mirror. "You bottom?"

Alexei grins back, wiggling his ass in front of me. "Your instincts haven't failed you yet. Not when it comes to me."

He's right, and that's the confidence boost I need. I grab his wrists and plant his hands on the counter, skimming my fingers all the way up his arms and then down his back until I get to his hips. With my lip between my teeth, I step forward, nudging my cock against his hole.

There is no fear, only want.

He smiles at me, eyes hooded and jaw slack. He bends forward a little more, and I look down, watching the head of my cock disappear inside him. My abs tauten as his rim tightens around me, squeezing my cockhead so hard I pause just to hold myself together.

"Good?"

He pants. "Good. Keep going."

I rock into him slowly until he relaxes, gaining me another easy inch. It's been forever since I've done this, but all my nerve endings are coming alive, my body is turning hot, and my eyes flash to the mirror as I push in deeper.

No strain. No fear. Just want.

"Oh my god," Alexei moans.

I thrust the rest of the way in, and he buckles forward. My hands keep him upright, and when I meet his face in the mirror, he nods at me with pure pleasure on his face. Alexei is a bossy person, but he's not going to boss me around yet. With my eyes on myself, I start to fuck him slowly. My hips move, the glide of my cock in his tight hole and the way my fingers dig into his skin all adding to the build-up of getting here. As I move, getting used to the way he feels and allowing him time to adjust to me, I watch myself. And what I see isn't what I expected.

There's no strain, no greed, no selfish thoughts. My face isn't impatient, my mind isn't fast, and my hips aren't chasing an orgasm I haven't earned yet. I'm not a monster. I'm not a selfish lover.

"I trust you, Gage," Alexei says, making me look at him. "Do you trust yourself?"

I inhale hard and exhale shakily. "Yeah," I admit quietly. "I do."

He folds forward when I thrust into him harder, his breath music to my ears. When he starts rocking back against me, my eyes drift from the mirror to look down at where we're connected.

"Shit," I groan. "I shouldn't have looked."

Alexei laughs. "Keep looking."

I can't. Holy fuck. Because the sight of my cock thrusting in and out of his tight ass is more than my mental state can bear. It's the hottest thing I've seen in so long, his smooth hole, my thick cock, and the way he tightens all around me. God forbid I pull out and see a gape. I'll lose it if I do that.

"I'll come," I warn him, looking at him in the mirror instead.

His hand reaches around to grip his cock. "Then come. I'm right here with you. My god you feel good inside me."

It's been like a minute and a half, but fuck it. With our eyes connected, I fuck him faster until I have to clench every part of my body to hold off until he comes.

"Oh fuck. Oh fuck," he moans. "Gage, oh my god!" His ass clamps down, and I'm a goner.

My balls draw up as his cum hits the vanity, the spasm of his hole milking me and embarrassing me all at once. Because my orgasm hits and there's nothing I can do about it. "I can usually last longer! Fuck, sorry!" I rest my forehead against his shoulders. "Shit, I'm sorry. I can do better." I shake all over, blissful little shivers that make my nape prickle and my mind go drunkenly dumb. But holy hell does this feel good.

The orgasm, yeah, but the pride more than anything.

"I'm a sixty-second man, but at least I didn't get selfish, right?"

Alexei laughs, righting himself and leaning back to kiss

341

my cheek. "If you're a sixty-second man, then so am I." He points to his cum.

Well, he had a build-up. His dick was sucked and his ass was eaten and fingered, but I appreciate him not pointing that out. My pride is full, so let's leave it at that. "That was hot, even though it was also embarrassing for me. I promise I'll get better at this."

He's smiling when he pushes me back, my cock slipping out. He spins and wraps his fingers around the side of my neck. "Save the commentary for the journal and just kiss me right now. I'm so fucking happy."

Smiling because I can't help it, I kiss him. I don't know when or how, but sex will get better. We've got everything else going for us, and I know this will be something we're eventually amazing at, too.

Because I'm starting to trust myself. Fuck, that feels good.

alexei

Drinking soulmate tea out of my sober dope mug, I creep through the mansion in search of my dad. He's been helping me work on one of the spare bedrooms as of late, but a few days ago, I found him creeping around the south wing of the house. We never go there, so I'm not sure what he's doing, but that's where I find him.

Just standing there, hands on his hips in a typical dad pose, looking at the door to the south wing like it's stumping him. Measuring tape is tucked into the back pocket of his jeans, sagging them down.

"How very super dad of you," I say, startling him.

He looks at me, huffing. "I smelled your tea before you even got here. Is that ginger?"

Yes, and it's warming me up on this windy, cool day. "What're you doing? Planning for this section next?"

He hums, walking through the door. "Thinking," he says.

I follow. "About what?"

He leads me through the connecting rooms. "Well, it's like its own house within the house. I got the old blueprints from Town Hall, and apparently, this was a living quarter for a nanny or something many years ago. Has its own bedroom, living room, kitchen, and bathroom. Self-sufficient."

"Yes," is all I say because that's obvious and I don't know why he needs to point it out.

"We could make it into an apartment."

"To rent out?"

He glances at me sort of dubiously, like Gage. "Sure."

"Dad."

He sighs, taking the tape measure out to fiddle with it. "It has everything you'd need to live here. Comfortably. The bedroom is small, but the rest of it is oversized. Big kitchen, but needs some upgrades, massive dining room and sitting room, and the bathroom needs a remodel, but it's fully functional."

Oh. I sip my tea. Sip it again. "For me? You're thinking of fixing this place up for me so I can keep living here?" Flattered, really.

"What? No." He huffs. "For me."

I squint at him.

"Alex, I bought this place for us. At first, I thought we'd fix it up so we could... bond or whatever, and then we'd sell it and split the profits. Then you fell in love with it, and I know you don't like to admit that, but I can see it whenever you work on anything here. I don't want you to have to sell it because it's... you."

"It's us," I tell him. "And you don't have to move into an offshoot apartment. Why can't we just live together like we have been?"

He smiles at me, and it's honestly so heartwarming that it coats me in nerves and fuzzies. He's so terrible at being compassionate that I love it even more whenever he tries. "Because you have a soulmate now."

"I do." I narrow my eyes.

"And someday, you're going to want to live with him. What better place than the one he's also fallen in love with?"

The back of my throat burns, and my eyes do that weird watery thing. "Dad!"

"What?" He laughs. "Don't come at me for trying to plan for your soulship or whatever you call it. I'm invested in it."

"Soulmateship. Soulship sounds cooler, though," I mumble. "But you don't have to move. I don't want you to move. I know it's weird, but I like living with you. Some families do that, so why can't we?"

He snorts. "I'll only move a hundred feet away and will be literally in the same house. Unless you want me out of the house altogether? Totally okay if you—"

"No. I don't want you out. I just said that!" Because I love my dad, and I love the good years, and I don't care that most adults don't live with their parents. I want to! Because this house is big enough for thirty, and three is hardly a crowd, and I know Gage would be fine with it. "We haven't even gotten to the 'I love you' part of our soulmateship yet, so moving and living together isn't on the radar." Even though I bombarded him with an open-door policy in our future house.

"You will," Dad says. "Soon. And this is going to take months, maybe even a year, to fix up and build, so we better start planning, right?"

"Fine," I huff. "We can plan and build it, but we aren't making any moving decisions until... later. Sometime way later in the future because... because I've lived with you my whole life and I don't really wanna stop now."

He turns to hide his emotions, so I turn with him, not letting him hide from me. "You sure?"

"As shit."

Awkwardly, he grabs my shoulder and pulls me and my sober dope mug to his chest for a horrible rendition of the best hug ever. He's here, alive and well, hugging me. It might be one of the happiest ten seconds of my life.

"Plus, I need someone responsible here to make sure I don't burn the place down with my blowtorch."

Dad laughs, and then we plan the apartment.

SINCE GAGE TOOK the advice to measure his progress in projects instead of time, he's been throwing himself into the library. Brian is a fairly handy guy, so he's here, in my house, talking library plans with my soulmate and even my dad.

Becky's little baby bump is not so little anymore. She's farther along than I thought, but she only just started showing because... well, maybe because she was skin and bones and wore baggy clothing, so I didn't notice. I'm detail-oriented, but I don't tend to stare at bellies.

"Here," Dad says, handing Becky a tea in a mug that says, '*I came. I saw. I conquered.*' It fits her.

"Thanks." She smiles at him and sits next to me while we watch our men work. Gage is trying to be a manly man, but he's not the best at it compared to Brian, so it's entertaining. "Are you coming tonight?" Becky asks Dad.

Dad nods, sitting with us. "Yeah, I'll meet you all there."

Because they go to meetings together now. They're like this little band of misfits that all fit together pretty well and support each other. Brian and Becky require the most support, but I'm realizing that maybe they've never really had true friends before, and this is a first for them, so they're clinging to it hard. And Becky really likes my one and only friend, Stefan. She's the only one of us who speaks fluent ASL, so they get along pretty well. I know a few phrases, but I'm a hand talker in general, so my hand motions are usually unclear.

I understand what Gage means now when he says he feels settled. Sitting here, meshing my boyfriend with his former enabler friends turned healthier friends with my dad... and with me, feels rewarding. Like, who knew I'd be chummy with these specific people, feeling so content and excited about a library?

"It's six feet," Gage tells Brian.

"Those are meters, dumbass." Brian takes the tape measure from Gage. "It's just under twenty feet. We can make that work."

Gage blushes, but he looks back at me with a smile on his face. We went to an appointment with Natalie earlier, and she's super pleased with his progress and awareness, and I straight up told her his self-awareness is his sexiest trait. And his abs. And his eyes. And his everything. But yeah, sure, the self-awareness.

"Alex, where'd you put that coffee table?" Brian asks me. "It's done, right?"

I restored the fuck outta that coffee table, so I smile to show my pride and stand up. "I'll get it."

"I'll come with you," Gage says, tripping over the toolbox. "It's big and heavy and handsome."

"Me or the table?"

Gage doesn't answer. He takes my hand, palms together without our fingers linked, because he's an old dog, but I was able to teach him new tricks, and skips down the hallway with me.

"Alexei, oh my god! I can't even with the coffee table! Do you know how awesome it's going to look in there with my ladder?" he asks, beaming at me as we walk down the hall to the basement stairs. "Right? You know it, right?"

Of course I know it because I'm confident in my work and I trust his work, even if Brian is the better handyman.

But what I trust most is how much pride Gage takes in the mansion. Without even being fully aware of it, he's fallen in love with a house that doesn't belong to him. I think it's because I live here, and deep down, his soul knows to love anything that's a part of me, just like mine knows the same.

"And when we get the reading chairs?! God, Alexei! We're going to sit in there and journal for hours. After many, many sexy lessons that hopefully progress into more actual sex, of course." He smirks, leaning over to kiss me on the cheek. He trips and kisses my eyeball instead. "Oop."

I grab his hips to steady him at the bottom of the stairs, absolutely enthralled by the way he looks at me. He's still talking about libraries and tables, and it's the same thing that happened at the diner that night. Sparks are flying, his mouth is moving, and I'm having a moment of pure electricity and rightness right here in the damp basement.

"Gage?"

He stops inside the door to my workshop, sucking in a breath to make up for his rambling. His hands squeeze mine and he smiles. "Alexei?"

I'm complicated, so instead of saying three words, I say, "I've fallen in love with everything about you. Including the fried meats."

His smile falters and his jaw drops. Not only that, but his eyes widen and his body goes entirely still. He stares at me, and I don't feel awkward because it's nice when he takes in the moment. I'm not nervous because I know he loves me too, and when he finishes being shocked and awed, he'll tell me.

"Even the fried... hang on a sec." He drops my hand to reach into his pocket, pulling out his phone. I peek at the screen, seeing him pull up an app that tracks the lunar calendar. "It's a full moon."

I nod. "I know."

"Is it suddenly allowed on a full moon?"

"Yep."

His phone disappears and he slaps his palms on my cheeks. "You love me? Even when I get bacon *and* sausage?"

"I judge you for it, but yeah, I do."

"What about when I get seven coffees and forget to drink my water?"

"Your skin will age so much earlier than mine, but yeah. Even then."

He presses his hands harder against my cheeks, eyes seriously starting to water. "Would you eat a slice of bacon for me?"

"Only if it saved your life."

"Holy fuck, Alexei. That really is love."

"I know." I nod in his grip. "Soulmate-level love. I'm confessing."

"Alexei! Come on!" he shrieks.

"What?"

"I was gonna... and then you... I've been—gah!" He laughs hard, even though he's sort of crying. "I had a whole thing planned and you swooped in here like a heroic rambler and threw me so off course. Never stop, Alexei." He smiles at me. "Look at the bottom of the coffee table."

So dubious, but my chest is tightening with nerves and

good anxiety as I kneel to peer under the coffee table. I pull a sticker off the bottom, holding it up. "This?" It's a 'fried meats are our friends' sticker.

"No. Not that one." He snatches it. "That one was just a joke. Keep looking."

Getting flat on my back to look at the underside of the coffee table, I see something etched into the wood. Like real carved up with a knife style. "You defiled my antique coffee table?! Gage!"

"I did," he admits. "Read it."

A+G= <3

He carved our initials into the wood like it's a romantic tree?! Holy, I love him! I stare at it for so long that my vision gets blurry through watering eyes to match his. They're so blurry and so happy that I almost miss the other sticker. It says, 'look up.' "Up where?" I ask Gage, scanning the whole underside of the table.

"I hadn't really considered you'd be on your back and under the coffee table when you read that, so... here." He takes my hand, hauling me to my feet, big brown eyes full of love. "Up." He motions upward.

I scan all my shelves and the walls in my workshop. I even glance at the ceiling. When I don't see it, Gage rolls his eyes at me and points right at the sign he made me. The piece of wood that says, "Alexei's Old Things' with 'new' angled above the word 'old.' The sign is gorgeous. He finished it a while ago, and he and my dad hung it in my workshop one night. Thinking back on that night, Gage was extra dubious. I study the words, the scrolls, and the border.

He soldered the design and the shop name into the wood, and other than a little shaky line on the first letter, the rest is immaculate.

I drag a stool over to it, climbing on to get a real good look. At eye level, the details are so much more clear. His nerves on the first letter, the detail of the font he used, and the skill that shows he's such an artistic person. I smile at it, and then I gasp. *Gasp!* Hand on my chest, eyes wide, mouth open, gasp!

"Gage Rossum!" The stool shakes and wobbles because I'm shaking and wobbling. "This! You... ohmygod! This has been hanging here for weeks! More than weeks. Over a month!"

"I know," he says, taking my hand to pull me back down.

Because the border, which I thought was just intricate designs, is actually words. *I love you. Soulmate. I love you. Soulmate. Alexei. Gage. Soulmateship. I love you.* All blended together to seamlessly create a dark and even border.

"You told me you love me this long ago and I never noticed?" I ask, an emotional sob making my voice squeak. "Do you know how upset this makes me?"

He nods, smiling because he knows I love a romantic love confession, but he also knows I'm mad for not noticing. Because I'm detail-oriented, and I once told him I don't like people who don't pick up the obvious. This is obvious! Now that I'm looking, it's so obvious, and I missed it because I'm not as detail-oriented as I think.

Meeting his eyes, I just stare at him while I let tears drip down my cheeks. He doesn't get uncomfortable. "This is so romantic."

"I know." He smiles.

"Tell me. Say it out loud." I hiccup.

He smiles, showing me his white teeth. His deep brown eyes bore into mine, and he clears his throat. "Okay, are you listening?"

"I'm listening."

He walks us backward until I'm leaning against the workbench. "Bit of a long-winded confession. Just in case you get tired." He nods at the support behind my back. "Alexei, listen to me, alright?"

"You already said that part."

"Right. Right, okay. Despite having a family who loves me and a healthy environment to grow up in, I lived a life of turmoil because of myself. I never really understood myself, you know? And that led to all the chasing and the numbing. But since I've met you, there isn't a damn thing I want to numb, and there's nothing left to chase because you're... right here. Everything I tried to feel all my life, I've got it now. Because of the way you understand me, see me, and just... get me. For the first time ever, I'm settled and happy and in love."

I smile at him. "You been planning this speech for a bit?"

"Yes." His hands fall to my shoulders, giving me a gentle squeeze. "My point is, as much as it elates me that you're my sober dope, you're so much more than that. You're complicated and intriguing. You're hypocritical and snarky. You're a judgemental dick with the biggest heart and the most intense eye contact. You're weird, I'm weird, and we're weirder together. You're my soulmate, and saying I love you doesn't feel like enough. But I do, Alexei. I just really love ya. I love you." He watches my lips, and I take a moment to let everything sink in.

It's Sunday, our day, in our future house that we both love. It's more romantic than the street because we've put so much of ourselves into this structure. It's where things started and things will grow. Gage loves me. Not some idealized version of what and who he wants me to be, but the real me. Alexei Kopacek, neurotic rambler and social cue ignorer. And I love him, Gage Rossum, addictive personality and artistic-minded genius.

Something more comfortable than warmth fills me, but so do nerves. Because we're gonna live life together! We're gonna make mistakes and fight and have awesome times that lead to even better times. We're going to have to figure out what to eat forever! Every meal! *For-ev-er.* My god, it's going to be horrifying!

And I can't wait.

"So?" I ask him, looking into his eyes. "We're in love from this moment forward?"

"From many moments ago and moving forward." He leans in, pressing his lips to mine. "Think I fell for ya when you asked me what I was addicted to."

I grin against his mouth. "What are you addicted to, Gage?"

"Mm, my sober dope."

gage ②

8 MONTHS LATER

"This isn't even as cool as I thought it'd be," Alexei complains while I look through boxes of cookies. "I thought we'd at least get to see the actual factory."

I grin at a box of sugar cookies and try to link our fingers. Alexei unlinks them. "What? A cookie showroom *in* a cookie factory isn't cool enough for you?"

"Hardly. It's like a non-decorated storefront." His eyes meet mine, and then they brighten. "But I love it because you love it. And this is how you decided to celebrate."

"Celebrate what?" I ask, adding the sugar cookies to my stack on the counter. "My two years of sobriety?"

"The first year of our centuries-long soulmateship, Gage." Timidly, but somehow still with attitude, he adds a box of *Oreo* knockoffs to the growing stack on the counter.

He's gained a sweet tooth, which means he has one cookie every second night, and he calls that overindulging. "And your two years of sobriety. But mostly us because we're ignoring sobriety dates still, right?"

Yes, we are. But I'm also not as scared of time measurements anymore. Because I'm feeling strong and confident. Happy and settled in this new life in Port Baylon. The one where I have friends from all three of my high school friend groups, brothers I get to spend time with, a mom who drinks tea with me and shows me up at the forge. I have a business that's doing so much better now that I'm actually paying attention to it, and a body that's seriously healthier because Alexei has taught me to respect it.

I'm still that guy who used to be an addict. I still get asked if I'm okay whenever my mood dips, and I still make extra sure that my mom knows where I am and what I'm doing because she doesn't deserve any more worrying in her life, and letting her know is no burden to me anymore. Because I'm not ashamed of where I am or what I'm up to. I'm just working my ass off, being in love with Alexei, or trying but failing to quit smoking. I'm a work in progress, but fuck me, progress feels good.

"Centuries long? Do we defy age restrictions?"

"Age is just a number. Our souls will live on forever. Together." He puts another box on the counter and glares at me like I'm judging him for it. "What?! I will freeze them and only take out three a week!"

"And I'll probably finish these four boxes by the time

you get through half of one." I point to the last shelf. "Check for those coconut ones Owen asked for."

He drops my hand and goes over to the shelf to look. I watch him, sticking my hand into my pocket to fiddle with the key. Originally, I was going to give it to him in a velvet box, but I didn't want to accidentally make him say yes to a question I'm not yet asking. Someday, though.

"These ones?" He carries the box over and I peek inside.

"Yep." I set it on the counter and pay an obscene amount of money for four thousand cookies.

We carry everything out to the van. Mom's van with the broken door and the horrible squeal. Alexei's car is in the shop for routine maintenance, and I might be a loser because I haven't bought one yet, but I don't care. It's kinda fun going places with my mom, brothers, or Alexei.

As soon as we close the doors, Alexei looks at me. "You're dubious again."

I smirk and start the van. "Because I was so terrified of turning you into a fried meat heathen that it snuck up on me when you became a cookie monster instead."

"I'm hardly monstrous," he says. "What's in your pocket?"

"How do you know everything?!" I laugh, loving how perceptive he is. "It's a key."

"It better not be to a house."

"Why not?"

He flails his arms, throwing them out wide. "Mansion! Used to be falling down, but now it's only partly falling down. Libraries and tiles and grout. Ringing any bells?"

So many bells. I fucking love that house. "It's not to a house," I assure him, backing out of the cookie factory lot.

"What's it unlock then?" he asks.

"My heart."

He snorts. "Please. I unlocked that forever ago."

"Didn't even need a key." I smile at him.

"Are you gonna tell me what it unlocks?"

"How about you just ramble about something else while I drive us home so the surprise doesn't get ruined?" I look over at him to find him sorta glaring, but mostly just watching me fondly. "Ramble about that prick of a set of old gas station pumps that are keeping you up all hours of the night and ruining your sleep schedule."

"Do not get me started, Gage." But he's already started. He vents about these pumps because they're the first high-paying job he's had that is stumping him. He's trying so hard to restore them to functional use because the owners want to use them to pump water for their gardens, but they're corroded and... yada yada old things shit.

While he talks, I drive us back to Port Baylon. Sundays are our days, and except for the time I messed up by pushing Alexei and walking over him to get to my brothers, I haven't missed a single Sunday with him in our first year together. They've become something special. Something I look forward to. It doesn't matter that I see him every day of the week or that we sleep together most nights. Sundays have a meaning now.

Us. A complicated boyfriend, a recovering addict, a level of communication I've never had before, and a strong hit of the way we make each other feel. And this particular Sunday is special because it's the Sunday I got out of rehab —fifty-two Sundays ago. The second year after the frappuccino Sunday. The Sunday Paul told me I looked good. Healthy. This Sunday, I really do feel good. And I finally feel healthy. Because I did the work, and by doing the work, I earned myself a soulmate. I earned Alexei fucking Kopacek.

When we get back to the mansion and unload all the boxes, Alexei runs down to his workshop because he's had a sudden bout of inspiration for the fuel pumps. We even renovated a lane so customers can pull right up to the basement door to drop off their items for his workshop, and I love how much time he loses to his passion down there, so even though it's our day, I don't mind that he goes to work. He'll snap out of it shortly and come back up, reminding me it's Sunday like I'm the one who forgot.

Stacking cookie boxes in the pantry and setting the others in piles to deliver to my friends and family, I jump when Nathan sneaks up on me.

"Jesus! Warn a guy!"

He's sweaty from moving. Moving out but still within the same house. I don't like that he's moving into the apartment, but we've agreed to have dinner together every night if we're all home. The meal subscription kits are still a thing we do.

"Here." He sets the lockbox I made him guard on the island counter. "You lose the key?"

I touch it in my pocket to make sure it's still there. "Nope."

He pulls his mug from the dishwasher. It's a new one. I drew the mansion on my iPad and Alexei picked the words. *'Sturdy as fuck but still a fixer-upper.'* It fits the house and Nathan, and I know he loves it right along with his *'fucking being there'* mug.

"Where's Alex?" he asks. I look at the basement door. "Ah, well. Don't let him get lost down there for too long. We have a big night and he's gonna fret about it."

We do have a big night. It's our housewarming party. My family, all the neighbours, my quilting night ladies, the friends from forging night, and my three groups of old but new friends are coming. Alexei's friend Stefan is coming with Brian and Becky because he's become really close with Becky, and the older man who taught Alexei to make old things new again will be here, too. I even invited my friends from the coffee shop.

Because I fucking live here now! As of this morning, when I moved in the one and only box of useless shit I own that isn't already here. I accidentally moved into the mansion in slow increments over the last year since I've been with Alexei, and no one thought to warn me that I was doing it! Gah! So embarrassing, but I think Alexei subliminally forced me to, and I'm not mad about it.

"Is Natalie still coming?" Nathan asks.

"Yep!" And I'm done with sex therapy. I'm still close with Natalie because she's a bit of a lifeline if I ever have questions or concerns, but she's shifted to more of an ongoing therapist who helps me with my mental state, fears and worries, and whatever else I happen to need. So Natalies's coming to celebrate with the receptionist from her office, and then they're coming with us to a meeting tonight. A big meeting for me.

"Okay, well, Benedita will be here in a few hours. I'll be back by then." He grabs his keys and heads out to pick up his still new but sorta serious girlfriend, Melody. Alexei thinks she's dubious, but I'm pretty sure that's just because he's skeptical of everyone.

Benedita and my mom are coming to help me cook this massive meal. And Sonya is coming with them, bringing the baby. God, I'm exhausted from this day already. I will need three to five business weeks to recover.

"Gage!" Alexei shouts, not even all the way up the stairs yet. "Do you think I forgot about the key?!"

He totally did because old things sidetracked him, but I won't call him out. "Of course not."

"Show me what it unlocks." He walks right up to me. Literally. Chest to chest, noses touching, foreheads resting. "Distract me from cookies and fuel pumps."

I smile against his lips and kiss him with my whole heart. He's wearing so much blue with his black today, making his eyes stand out and his hair look vibrant. He doesn't paint his nails anymore because his job always ruins them, but I love that they're always a little dirty under the tips. He thinks he's more rugged like Dave now.

"This." I slide the metal box over.

He turns his forehead against mine to look at the box. "A fire-resistant safe?"

"Yes. Can't be too careful." I press the key to his palm. "Unlock it, complicated."

"Did you set up your banking stuff with the rehab centre for the Feel Good Drug line?" he asks, making me laugh.

"Stalling?"

"Yes."

I wrap my arms around him and smile. "Yeah. All the proceeds from that line will be directly deposited into the bank account we set up for it." Because I have a platform now. I shared my website and digital products on social media, which led to me sharing a bit about my addiction and recovery journey, and I tagged the rehab centre to credit them as a big part of my process. Since my website has expanded to include merch and other products, I started a whole line called The Feel Good Drug to raise money for addicts who might not be able to afford rehab. And it took off. Like... majorly. I've never felt cooler.

"Thank you," Alexei says. "For whatever is in the box."

"I hope you never start abiding by social protocols, Alexei. I love you just like this."

"I know," he sighs, pulling away. "Okay. Here we go."

He sits on a stool and pulls the box towards him, looking at it like it will either make his heart explode or ruin his life. Either, or.

Alexei isn't someone who rushes, so I start the kettle to make him tea while he pretends he isn't getting ridiculously emotional over every slip of paper he finds in the box. One for every day since I met him. I quilted him a teapot cozy a while ago, so I pull it out, add it to the teapot, and drop in a few bags of his soulmate tea.

He pulls the slips out one at a time, reading them and then organizing them into neat little piles. The whole time, he stays silent, but I'm not offended. Alexei likes to think, and he's attracted to the reasons behind actions, so he's processing in the best way he knows how. Slowly and with rapt attention.

His eyes are glassy and wet, his mascara smudged a little when he looks at me. "You said this, not me." He holds up a slip of crinkled paper.

It says, '*it's a fried meats kind of Sunday.*'

"No, you said that. When my mom made us fried bologna sandwiches. You whispered it before you forced yourself to eat it just to be polite." I grin at him, watching him remember.

"I didn't think you heard that! Gage! What... what is this?!" He motions to the metal box while his eyes water even more. "All the things I said? All this time?"

"Yep. We had a sex journal going strong, but I had an Alexei memory box going, too. I wrote down my favourite thing you said every single day since I met you. Even the days you just texted me."

A few tears slip down his reddening cheeks. "You know, for someone who only ever chased highs and orgasms, you sure nailed the romance part. How did you even know to do this?"

"Instinct." I step up to him while the kettle shuts off,

boiled. "Probably has something to do with my soul knowing your soul, and even before I helplessly fell in love with you, it knew I needed to remember all the little things. Because I've never remembered the little things before."

He sniffles. "The phrase is 'falling hopelessly in love' not 'helplessly fell in love,' Gage."

"Nah, I like my way better. Because as soon as I met you, I was fucking helpless, Alexei. Thank you for being my soulmate."

"Thank Fate," he says for the second time. "I love you." He cries a bit harder. "I need cookies."

So, we eat cookies and read all the things he's said over the last year. And when our housewarming party is in full swing, I sit back and appreciate the fuck out of how far I've come and all the incredible people we have in our lives. The relationships I've repaired and the new friends I've made. The mingling of Alexei's people with my people, and the pride that comes with knowing we've brought people together.

When we're all complaining about being too full, we have a hunting party for Slash because he's lost somewhere in the mansion. After Owen shouts that he found him in the west-side second floor third bedroom closet, I drag Alexei into the library and kiss him until he can't breathe. And when Alexei holds my hand while we walk to the community centre for a late-night meeting, I smile through my nerves.

Because I'm so fucking nervous.

But he squeezes my hand, kisses my cheek, and pushes

me towards the guy I came here to meet. Glancing back at Nathan for reassurance, I feel my pride swell when he nods at me encouragingly.

"Hey, Dalton, right?" I ask him, holding out my right hand. "I'm Gage. I hear you're looking for a sponsor."

The End.

FATHER SON *bonding*

NATHAN

"Well, well, well."

I pause, the front doorknob still in my hand while my girlfriend, Melody, sneaks down the porch steps to safety. Turning, I find Alex leaning against the railing of the stairs, shrouded in shadows and only wearing black. I'm a grown-ass man, and I don't need to feel guilty about dating, so I lock the door and face my son.

"Problem?"

Alex narrows his eyes at me, arms crossed over his chest, ankles also crossed while he judges me. "Oh, how the tables have turned. You realize I know you have a girlfriend, right? Like, I've met her a whole bunch of times and she joins us for dinner at least three nights a week. You know that, right?"

Yes, I fucking know that, but I'm still weird and awkward about it. I don't know why. Having her over and spending time with her is one thing, but having my son know that she's in my bed, taking it like the good girl I call her, isn't really my cup of tea. I'm still trying to prove my fatherly abilities to him, and sneaking Melody out at dawn is less awkward than having 'the talk' I failed to have with him when he came of age.

"She had to work." I clear my throat and look anywhere but at him.

"She doesn't work on Sundays."

"Overtime shift."

"Sure." His teeth light up when he smiles in the darkness, and then he flicks on a table lamp by the stairs. "Do we need to have a conversation about safe sex? Because I'm too old for siblings."

"Jesus, Alex. Why do you have to make everything weird?" I rub the back of my neck and try to hide how hot my damn face is.

"It's just who I am." He pushes off the railing and walks towards me, which only makes me more nervous because he's going to see all the guilt in my eyes. He's smiling widely when he says, "Do I have to be the parent? Because this is one time I don't mind. Payback for all the times you gave me shit for my dating life."

"What dating life? You never dated. And you sure as hell never snuck anyone out."

"Didn't I?" he asks, smirking.

I grumble, heading into the kitchen. Might as well get this day started now that I've been caught. "I don't want to know. Why are you up?"

He follows me, turning on lights I'd rather he leave off until my face cools down. "Because Gage's sleeping annoys me and I had a hankering for an early breakfast. Maybe that new muesli mix I got."

A hankering? Sometimes I forget the results of him having to grow up so fast, but then again, even people my age barely say hankering. "You know, it's not a crime to eat something that isn't full of fiber."

"I'm aware." He sits at the island while I start coffee. "Tell me why you're sneaking girlfriends out at dawn, Dad."

With my back to him and my neck on fire, I speak to the coffeemaker. "Because. I don't know. I'm supposed to be your dad, not your... roommate."

Alex huffs out a laugh. "Dad's date. That's not a crime either."

"I know."

"Then stop treating her like a vagrant and let her sleep in on her day off! God, Dad. Do you know nothing about relationships? I mean, I'll admit I'm a bit undereducated in vaginas, but—"

"Please stop."

"—but women, and people in general, tend to enjoy waking up together. You don't have to sneak her out like she's some hooker."

I pinch the bridge of my nose. Hankering. Vaginas. Hooker. This morning isn't off to the best start. Sun isn't even up yet. I love my son more than anything in the world, but sometimes, I wish he had a filter. No, I don't. I just wish I wasn't so weird about the things he bluntly voices. It's a strange dynamic to be the father but never know where I stand on authority. I haven't earned the right to give him advice, even if he's trying to make me more comfortable to give it lately, but he sure has the right.

"Dad," he calls. I spin around, not even having started the coffee yet. "I like Melody, and I like how happy you are with her. Please, for the love of all that is holy, let her spend a night. I'm not dumb. I know what happens in bedrooms."

I choke. "You know what? Let's go. We're going out for breakfast."

"We're two towns over and no one knows us here," Alex says to reassure himself. "It's not like he's ever gonna know." He glances around the charming little breakfast restaurant he picked from the internet because, apparently, it has a high cleanliness rating.

"He won't know." I nod at his plate. "You gonna eat it or just gossip about it?"

He huffs, annoyed with himself. I try not to pay too much attention to his internal debate, but it's glaringly obvious he's struggling. Not with the food, but with wanting to eat it no matter how many times he told Gage it was beneath him.

"If you tell Gage about this, I will lock you in my work-shop with the bats."

I laugh, holding up my hands. "Won't say a word."

Eagerly, but with faked reluctance, he stabs a breakfast sausage with a fork and chomps a bite off it. I watch him chew, knowing he'll pretend it's too fatty or greasy, but he'll secretly love it and add it to his list of allowed birthday foods. Maybe sausages will get their own special occasion.

"Shit, that's good," he mumbles, shoving the rest into his mouth. "I hate when he's right."

Gage isn't right about a lot of things, but he's right for my son. "Alright, I won't tell him how much you love breakfast fried meats if you tell me why his sleeping annoys you."

He chews thoughtfully, swallowing before answering. "He sometimes moves around a lot, and you know how lightly I sleep. Tell me why you sneak Melody out at dawn."

Damn him for his rapid pace of conversational switches. "Because I don't want to disrespect you."

"But you're disrespecting her in the process."

I hadn't thought of it that way. "I..."

"Dad."

"Okay," I groan. "Because we're finally good, you and me, and I don't want you to think I'd ever pick someone or something over you ever again. Not drugs. Not a girlfriend. No one. I know you feel like I picked heroin over you, and I guess I did, but that's never going to happen again." Can my face get any hotter? My god.

Alex studies me before picking up a slice of bacon. With it half hanging out of his mouth, he watches me while he chews. His assessments used to fill me with dread, but I've grown fairly comfortable with them over the past few years. He takes his time with things, which is such a contradiction to how fast he flips topics, but it's one of the quirks I love about him.

"I love you," he says.

I look down, my omelette blurring.

"I loved you when I was a kid. I hated you, but I always loved you. I loved you when I was a teen and you barely knew me. I loved you when you went to rehab, and I loved you when you got out. I loved you so much that I chose to move to Port Baylon with you even though I was a legal adult and could have gone out on my own. I've always loved you because you're my dad."

My chest has never been under more pressure. I clear my throat again, unsure what to say because... I did not deserve his love during those times of his life.

"But," he goes on, "I love you more now. Not *because* you're my dad, but because you *are* my dad."

I look up at him, seeing the icy blue eyes he got from his mother. They're wide open and connected to mine because my son does not fear eye contact. At all. "Thank you, Alex, but... I know I gave you fears. Not just me, but your mother. You were neglected for so long that it's understandable that you'd fear it happening again. I never want to make you feel that way. You are loved unconditionally. By me. By Gage. You're our first choice, and you always will be, and I'll do everything I can to prove that to you."

I hate deep conversations in public spaces. Being an addict taught me to hide, but being in recovery taught me to get comfortable being vulnerable. It's been so long since I've had to that it makes me uneasy.

"I know," Alex says, smiling gently. "Because I trust you. Like one hundred percent trust you, which is why you're allowed to love someone else, too."

I narrow my eyes at him in question.

"Melody! Gosh!"

"Oh." More fire to my face. "I don't... she's... I'm not... love her."

"Good grief," Alex sighs, setting down the bacon and pinching his nose like I did over the coffeemaker earlier. "What are you, fifteen?"

Feels like it sometimes. I'm getting all those teenage giddy feelings with Melody, but I know it's not love. Not yet. "No, I'm just being honest. I don't love her like that."

"Yet." Alex puts his second breakfast sausage on my plate and stabs his third one with a fork. "Okay, we're making a pact over fried meats. A father and son pact." He nods at my fork.

This is weird, but it's Alex, so I stick the sausage on my fork and hold it up like it's something special. "What pact?"

"No more skewed relationship dynamics. I'm your son, you're my dad. Gage is my soulmate, and Melody is your girlfriend. Stop fearing me. Yes, I judge people hard, but not you. Not anymore. So, I propose a new dynamic. Where I'm a son in my twenties who never plans to move out of my dad's giant mansion, and you have to date people who agree that they'll eventually have to live with your son and his soulmate. We're two peas in a pod, you and me, and no more hiding, okay?"

I love him beyond measure. How did such a perfect man

373

come from a fuck-up like me? "Okay," I agree, not great with words. "I'll hide a few things I don't think you need to know."

"The house is big, but not that big, Dad. I hear things, and I know Melody is a good girl."

Oh my god. I lower my sausage and cringe so hard I don't even know where to look. The table? My plate? The front door? My feet? The black and blue checkered shoes he's wearing, even though I think they're Gage's?

Alex laughs, not at all uncomfortable in my discomfort. "Cheers your fried meat with mine and make it a pact." When I clink my fork to his with another cringe, he adds, "I trust you, Dad. Wholeheartedly. Please don't be afraid of me anymore."

I'm not afraid of him. I'm afraid of failing him. But I nod, taking a bite of the sausage to appease him. "Deal." With the awkwardness over, I ask, "Now, tell me something about you. Not about Gage. Just you."

Gage's recovery has taken a lot of attention over the past year, and I love Alex for being comfortable to meet his needs, but he's my son, and he'll always be my focal point. He's a content person, healthy in the way he processes and copes with his traumatic childhood, and strong enough to know when he does or doesn't need help. Simply put, he's the most complicated person I know, but he's easy to handle. He's like a bonsai tree: finicky and tedious, but once it's going, it requires very little attention. He just thrives wherever he goes. But that doesn't mean he can't take his time in the light.

With half a strip of bacon hanging out of his mouth again, Alex snugs up his septum piercing and looks at me with wide blue eyes. "Okay, well, first of all, the bacon? I could take it or leave it, but these sausages are greasy goodness that I will never admit to enjoying again outside of this breakfast. It's part of our pact."

I laugh, nodding. "What else?"

While Alex rambles for hours about old things, restoration tips, missing websites a little, ideas he has for the mansion, and his relationship, I admire everything about the human he is. Kind, compassionate, blunt, but the thing I'm most proud of is his ability to put himself first. I trust him with recovered addicts like me and his soulmate because he has such belief in himself that he'll never let someone tear it down.

I know the term is reserved for them, but Alexei is my sober dope, too.

FRIED MEATS
are our friends

THANK YOU

Thank you so much for reading Sober Dope & Sundays!

Gage speaks to me on SUCH a personal level, but Alexei is also half me, so make of that what you will. Addiction and recovery are not easy topics to handle, and with so many different variables to recovery and lifestyle, I thought it would be nice to show a positive take on it. People do recover! They fight and battle and use all the tools in their toolbox, and it's such an epic thing!

We still have 5 days of the week left, so hold on tight because there are more weirdos coming! You might even see some familiar faces from Red Flags & Tuesdays and Sober Dope & Sundays.

THANK YOU FOR BEING HERE!

ALSO BY NORDIKA NIGHT

ALSO IN THE WEEKDAY WEIRDOS SERIES:
- RED FLAGS & TUESDAYS —> click here

Reid and Atticus are battling a slew of Tuesdays and a whole bunch of red flags! Atticus is hard to get, but Reid isn't gonna stop trying. Together, the learn what romance means... to them. It isn't conventional ;)

Garron Park & Lot 62 —> click here

- Meet Maddox and Devon, two rivals. Both in life and motocross. Their trailer park lives aren't easy, but together, they find a way to make things a bit more exciting.

- Not only do they start as rivals, but they stay rivals. This enemies to still enemies but also lovers story is full of tension and aggressive love languages.

Little Demon in the Details —> click here

- Craving a snarky brat that loves button pushing? Come meet Mercer! He's a little demon by nature, but he meets his match in Blake, the lethal man with the patience of a saint. Don't you dare call him daddy, though. Seriously. Don't. Blake doesn't like it.

- Their story is all about empowerment and a rise to the top despite all that is against them. There's spice, brattitude, and a burnt grilled cheese sandwich.

Alter Arlo —> click here

- So, you're craving something dark and twisty, eh? Well, come to this dark dystopian world and meet the boys! This one is psychological, has 2 couples, and comes with a twist that you might see coming. Might not. Go find out! The clues are all there if you look for them.

NORDIKA NIGHT

Nordika Night doesn't know wtf she's doing most of the time, but that's life.

Writer of gritty MM romance in all tropes and hopefully lots of genres, she's still finding her lane.

Canadian.
Coffee lover.
Writing buddy: Waylon, her mastiff!
www.nordikanight.com

I'm looking forward to what's next, grateful to the past, and trying to enjoy the present without letting it overwhelm me!

Nordika Night xo